Yellowstone DNA
A Tale of Wolves, Wildlife, and Humans

Scott Huber

Long Creek Dutch Publishing. P.O. Box 1151, Dubois, Wyoming 82513

First Edition published 2023

Paperback ISBN: 979-8-218-15739-5

Cover image: Christian Jegou/Science Source

Dedicated to my grandson, Levi. May you learn to love the wilderness as I do.

.

PREFACE

There are bloodlines that connect countless generations of birds and mammals within the Greater Yellowstone Ecosystem. Of those, elk, wolves, and humans are the primary focus of this tale. Elk have occupied the North American continent for millions of years, wolves for hundreds of thousands, and humans arrived here tens of thousands of years ago.

Throughout their lineages, the three have crossed paths often. Until the coming of white Europeans, they existed in a state of equilibrium - two predators who hunted in small packs or clans and a prey animal that existed in numerous herds of dozens and hundreds. The predators killed only enough to sustain their small populations. The prey's numbers were kept in balance by their pursuers.

In the eighteenth century, the population of the country grew exponentially. Wild meat, in the form of hooved animals and game birds, was the quickest, easiest way to feed the burgeoning citizenry. By the nineteenth century, market hunting was responsible for the extinction of heath-hens, passenger pigeons, Carolina parakeets, and Labrador ducks. Thanks to the last-minute intervention of conservationists, many of North America's most iconic mammals were just barely saved from the same fate, including the American bison, pronghorn antelope, grizzly bear, elk, prairie dogs, and gray wolves.

Yellowstone DNA is a story of how humans, beginning with indigenous Americans, interacted with Yellowstone's wildlife and each other. From revered to reviled. From honored to annihilated. Finally, to a conflict pitting ranchers and hunters against wildlife watchers and eco-tourists.

Human or animal, they are all threads in the tapestry of Yellowstone. They all possess *Yellowstone DNA*.

Author's Note

My intent in using indigenous words and names throughout the novel is to honor the native peoples and their relationship to the natural world in the regions they lived. Please note that within tribal nations there are often numerous regional variations. For the most part I have attempted to use the form of the word from tribal populations closest to the area that a chapter is set in. Please refer to the Glossary on pages 362-365 for definitions. My apologies for any incorrect forms used herein.

PROLOGUE

A dull red glow illuminated the greasy, soot-covered walls of the cave. Outside, dirty trails in the snow spread in different directions from the cave entrance. Inside it was warm, as three figures draped in furs huddled near the fire pit, watching a crudely carved brisket roasting on the coals.

Shadows appeared at the cave's opening. The beings surrounding the fire barely lifted their heads to acknowledge them, clearly familiar with their visitations. Then, with a nod accompanied by a single-syllable utterance, one dropped to the meat and carved off some gristly tidbits. Rising with a handful of morsels, he walked towards the entrance.

The shadows at the edge of the snow arose, pranced, and licked their lips. Their coats were a mixture of white, gray, tan, and black. Squatting just ten feet away, the man held out a single piece of meat on his flat palm.

A large gray wolf with white highlights crept forward, laying his ears back on his head and curling his tail under his body as signs of submission. With nostrils flaring to drink in the aroma of the meat, the beast stopped just six inches short of the outstretched hand.

The man made a soft chuckling sound through his nose, then a barely audible humming tone. The calming effect of the sound provided encouragement to the hesitant wolf, and he reached forward and took the small chunk between his teeth. With a slight toss of his head, the animal swallowed the morsel.

The two had played this game many times before, but this time was different. After swallowing the bite, the wolf did not back away as he always had before. Instead, he stared into the man's eyes, and the man stared back. After a few seconds, the wolf stepped forward again and licked the still outstretched hand. The man's other hand came up slowly and gently stroked the furry head.

The figures watching from the fire pit uttered excited sounds.

The man rose slowly and tossed the remainder of the pieces to the four other wolves at the entrance. There was a frantic scuffle, a growl, and a yelp, as the treats were quickly devoured. Within minutes, all five animals curled themselves into warming balls at the cave's entrance and went to sleep.

Thus did some *Canis lupus* eventually become the world's first domesticated animals, *Canis familiaris*. Embodied in what was technically one species, was the mammal that would someday be called both "man's greatest enemy" and also "man's best friend".

DUYUPE

"Ayiii!" Duyupe shouted, holding a blood-covered arrow high for his kinsmen to see. In the snow at his feet lay a heavily muscled ram with massive horns like twin corkscrews. To thank the dead ram for his sacrifice, young Duyupe reached into a pouch he had brought for this purpose and pulled out several tobacco leaves. Kneeling at the animal's head, he placed the leaves deep into its mouth. Only after these things had been done did his fellow hunters congratulate him, putting an arm over his shoulder and rubbing their cheeks to his.

Even though by age twelve Duyupe had participated in many game drives in which he helped herd the prey towards the spiral corrals unique to his tribe's method of hunting, today was his first kill with a bow. To the Tukudika, or "Sheep Eater" clan, of the eastern Shoshoni tribe, this was an important symbol of his transformation into manhood. It was also a time when young hunters were expected to demonstrate ritual reverence for the gift of the harvest.

Of all of the tribes that hunted in the Yellowstone region, only the Tukudika stayed year-round. The Kiowa, Coeur d'Alene, Gros Ventre, Nez Perce, Bannock, Crow, and Blackfeet all hunted buffalo and elk in Yellowstone in the summer, but migrated back to their homelands when winter descended. The Sheep Eaters, later known by white explorers as Snake Indians or Mountain Shoshoni, hunted bighorn sheep year-round with bows crafted from the rams' own horns. And where the other tribes used horses for transport and hunting, the Tukudika used domesticated dogs to pack their gear and game.

That night around the communal fire, at their camp near the confluence of Cache Creek and the Lamar River, the clan celebrates Duyupe's great accomplishment. To the pleasure of his peers, he reenacts the details of the hunt. Using hand signs and pantomime to augment his spare use of words, he acts out crawling over a boulder while saying "mattooh" *crawl*. Then holding a hand over his eyes and pointing he whispers excitedly "wasapi, wasapi!" *bighorn*. He ducks back down, fitting an imaginary arrow to his imaginary bowstring, then peeks back over the imaginary boulder. Turning to his audience he holds his arm straight out from his body and points to it with his other hand, indicating a measurement of one yard then says "pahmino" *the number thirty*, meaning thirty yards. Squatting low, he raises himself ever so slowly, his right arm demonstrating the pull of the bowstring. He sucks in a loud breath as his titillated viewers do the same. All of a sudden his fingers open wide and he imitates perfectly the sound of a bowstring snapping and an arrow flying.

Suddenly, he changes characters as he becomes the ram, wincing painfully and bending high in the waist while emitting a loud punctuated gasp. He leaps a great bound in this contorted position, starts a second bound, and then throws himself to the ground. He lays still, twitches his leg once, and then lays unmoving for ten full seconds, his audience breathing hard from the excitement. Finally, he rises on an elbow and says "bihin!" *heart*, putting a finger through a circle made by the thumb and index finger of his other hand. This symbolizes a "heart shot", a clean, honorable, humane shot.

"Bihin, bihin! Bihin!" the assembled group chants while passing the tribe's prized soapstone bowl toward Duyupe. Reaching into the smooth flowerpot-sized bowl, he removes the heart that has been set inside for this ceremony, cuts off a large piece with his knife, and consumes it with exaggerated gusto. By eating the heart, he will inherit the strength and agility of the ram. He then cuts off numerous slivers which he feeds to each member of the clan as they line up to share in the bounty.

The ceremony completed, Duyupe goes to the carcass and slices along the seam of the bulky hind quarter with his obsidian blade, severing the ligaments that hold the ball in the hip socket, easily separating it from the body. Placing it directly on the fire, the clan then signs and chats enthusiastically, anticipating the sweet meat of roast bighorn.

All at once, they fall quiet as a familiar harmony pierces the cool evening. Very near to them, the Isa, the creator gods of Shoshoni mythology, have begun singing their approval. One, two, three, then nearly twenty take up the song. First low and sonorous, then joined by a lilting soprano voice, some notes long and drawn out, some short and abrupt. The Isa, *gray wolves*, are near; it is a sign that Duyupe is no longer a boy.

DOSABI

Dosabi salivated profusely as the tantalizing fragrance of mutton made its way downwind to the spot where the Mount Norris wolf pack loitered near the Sheep Eaters camp. As the meat was laid on the fire, the aroma of the sizzling, dripping fat wafted to the wolves and elicited a song. Dosabi, the pack's alpha male, began in his throaty baritone voice, descanted in a high counter melody moments later by Tsaanti his mate. Soon, the whole pack, the betas, the mid-level members, and finally, even the lowly omega join in the chorus.

The big white alpha was an anomaly this far south, with white wolves being common in the arctic, but something of a rarity in the area that would someday be named Yellowstone. Standing alongside his comely jet-black mate, the pair made a striking impression of size, strength, and conformation. The good genes of the pack's only breeding pair contributed to the uniformly handsome appearance of the large family, the runty gray omega wolf being the lone exception. Not only were they well-built, but they were also robust and healthy, and most importantly, disciplined and smart.

The overall vitality of any wolf pack is largely attributable to its leadership, and Dosabi and Tsaanti led by example. Courageous but not audacious, Dosabi utilized his magnificent power and speed to tackle even the largest elk and moose. Patiently waiting for one of his lieutenants to tear at a shoulder or flank, he would seize upon that distraction to grab the animal by the nose and hang on until his pack-mates helped wrestle the prey to the ground. Tsaanti counterbalanced her mate's physicality by strategically choreographing the hunt. She knew intuitively which way the prey was most likely to run and where to position her support team to haze the animals into a disadvantaged position or location.

In the frequent territorial battles with other packs that crossed into their homeland, the pair was, at once, both terrible and merciful. If the 200-pound male could merely intimidate his rivals, he would selflessly do so. In this way, he would avoid the debilitating and often deadly injuries that would result to his family if tensions escalated into a fight. If, on the other hand, a rival gang insisted on mixing it up, the white giant struck the opposing alpha like lightning, often snapping his spine or severing an artery within moments. Once the invaders acknowledged their defeat, Dosabi and Tsaanti demonstrated mercy, and let the rest of the rivals hobble off without further damage. In this way, the Mount Norris pack not only grew from within, but it often attracted young male and female recruits from other packs, anxious for the security of a strong, stable clan.

The pack's proximity to the Tukudika camp was not unusual. It was a relationship that went back further than the collective memory of either clan. The tribe raised large dogs that they utilized for packing game and gear and pulling their travois. These dogs bore the same cryptic color patterns as their wolf cousins and were in fact descended from them. Their dogs, like their neighbors the wolves, were revered by the Tukudika, often being buried alongside tribe members to accompany them into the afterlife. The wolves themselves were part of the pantheon of gods worshipped by the tribe, considered heroes with admirable qualities to be emulated.

      The mythical, mysterious co-evolution of wolves and man was honored and respected by both the tribe and the Isa. Of all of the region's great predators, grizzly, cougar, and wolf, the wolf alone never killed Tukudika. For their part, the Sheep Eaters considered harming the Isa to be taboo. In this way, the men and their gods lived harmoniously from the time beyond memory. The wolves, for the most part, did not hunt the sheep that the Tukudika depended on. The wolves' favorite quarry was "patuhuya" *elk.*

IICHÍILIKAASHE

The Shoshoni called her kind Patuhuya. To the north, the Blackfoot referred to them as Iinii. The Crow from the east named the animals Iichíilikaashe. In English, they are called elk. In the time before the whites came, her species could be found in all parts of the North American continent, but she lived in Yellowstone's Lamar Valley. "Chili" was a superb example of her kind.

It was early summer and Chili's day began in the late afternoon. It was then that she emerged from the temporary refuge of her willow thicket to begin feeding on the sedges, bromes, and clovers of the valley floor. As dusk began to fall she proceeded, moving up into the aspens on the flanks of the surrounding hills. She would forage throughout the night and into the next morning when she would again seek shelter and shade. Shade, because with her thick hide and insulated coat she greatly preferred coolness to warmth. Shelter, because she was a prey animal, and the continent's top predators - wolves, grizzly bears, and cougars - prized her flesh above all others. Of these, the wolves were her primary nemesis.

The twenty-mile-long Lamar Valley is a classic U-shaped trough, an artifact of the massive sheet glaciers that covered and scoured Yellowstone a mere 150,000 years ago. Now, beaver dams flooded portions of the open valley, which led to dense thickets of willow shrubs and berry patches perfect for hiding out. Chili's elk herd shared their hideaway with many other creatures. Bright yellow warblers and warbling vireos sang in the vegetation all around them, being carefully watched by the hungry sharp-shinned hawks in the adjacent lodgepole pines. In the small brooks and ponds connecting the willow patches, young cutthroat trout dined on flies and nymphs. This consistent food source helped the fish grow big and strong enough to migrate to the Lamar River. The nearby berry patches were a favorite dining spot for both black bears and grizzly bears. The grizzlies would also seek out elk calves among the willows in the late spring.

Towards the end of each day and into the night, Chili, her sisters, and their young would join the wolves in a dance as old as time. The dance began in the late afternoon with Chili's herd leaving the willows and feeding out into the open. As afternoon became dusk, the wolf pack too emerged from their siestas and Chili's band became more vigilant. To even the playing field, nature had provided both elk and wolf with superior night vision.

The wolves began their part of the dance by surrounding the feeding elk and then slowly tightening their circle. Big bull elk and bison, when confronted by a wolf pack, often stand their ground and fight back with their bulk and headgear. This time of year, however, the bulls lived apart from the females and young. The cows' and their calves' only defense was their speed and endurance.

The wolves shivered with anticipation as they closed in. As the breeze swirled, the first cow caught their scent and jolted her head upright. Almost simultaneously, thirty-three other heads snapped into full alert. Within moments, the herd turned on their toes as one and began to run downwind, away from the loathsome smell of wolf. Being young and healthy, and for this year barren of a calf, Chili was not the standard target of the pack. The wolves' attention was fixed on the month-old calves and the infirm elderly.

The wolves' time-worn methodology was to chase the entire herd, watching carefully as they ran, noting the aged or vulnerable. Once the herd's weakest link was identified, the predators became laser-focused, pack members taking turns chasing their intended target. In this way, there was always a fresh replacement if a pursuer tired.

The youngsters are surprisingly fast for their age and their mothers constantly nudge them into the middle of the herd as they run. On this night, an eleven-year-old female was running toward the rear of the group. The pack had earmarked the aging cow as their intended victim. When their target stumbled on a badger mound, a black wolf instantly latched onto her right flank. As the elk listed to her side, a blotchy gray wolf grabbed her by the nose. Within ten seconds, five more wolves helped wrestle her to the ground. As the female struggled valiantly to regain her footing, gnashing teeth tore into the tender skin of her gut, disemboweling her even as she flailed. Eventually, she succumbed, and the pack settled into the process of stripping meat from the carcass.

Sensing that the danger had passed for the time being, Chili and her sisters turned to watch the carnage, the unintended but ritual sacrifice of one of their own. In this way, the size of Chili's herd had neither grown nor had it shrunk significantly in decades.

The year was 1806. It was one year before John Colter became the first white man to set foot in Yellowstone.

HENRY

Camp reeked. The mess tent had been the scene of New Year's Eve debauchery. Bottles of Old Log Cabin whiskey and empty mason jars lay strewn about the muddy floor. Besides the smell of the spirits, the pungent odors of sweat, blood, and vomit combined to overpower the senses.

There had been plenty to celebrate in the final hours of 1899. What to later generations would be viewed as wanton destruction, were to the men in the hunting camp the greatest achievements of the last century, and were to be toasted: the taming of the west, the relocation of the Indians to reservations, and the harvest of millions of buffalo.

With the bison almost completely eradicated, hunters switched to any other wild meat they could find a market for. Like the area's animal predators, humans, too, craved venison.

The men were market hunters and this was an elk camp. For the first couple of years, elk were plentiful here adjacent to the new National Park. Their harvest had been feeding the high-end diners in Bozeman, Montana and the growing town of Cody, Wyoming.

In the corner of the mess tent a wadded blanket quivered. With everyone passed out, no one had stoked the fire in the night and it was well below freezing in the shelter. A head emerged from the jumble, hair in all directions, and a matted beard.

"Hoo-eee!" whistled Henry as he ran his fingers through his greasy hair and got his first semi-sober look around the tent. Upon opening the blanket, he found his clothing was damp and caked with mud, or worse, and his teeth clattered. "Better start a fire," he muttered to himself.

Pulling the blanket tight, he rose and shuffled to the wood pile in the corner of the tent. Filling his arms with logs, he shuffled back to the wood stove made from a 55-gallon metal oil drum. Opening the stove door, he poked around for some coals and blew on them to give them life. Then he threw in some dry grass and twigs from the kindling pile and layered on a few quarter logs. He kneeled there for some time, soaking up the warmth of the blazing fire. Coughs, hacks, and flatulence around him indicated the others were rousing from their stupors.

"Nice fire, now how 'bout some coffee, Henry?" shouted James as he crawled towards the fire.

"Do I look like yer damn wife?" spat Henry back at him playfully.

"No, but you'll do in a pinch!" fired back James, eliciting laughter from four other carcasses strewn about the tent.

Chairs were pulled around the woodstove and soon there were five grizzled figures gathered there. A sixth man, William, put a pot of water on the flat iron mounted to the top of the stove.

"We huntin' today?" asked James to no one in particular.

"How about we kill some of those fuckin' elk-eatin' wolves instead?" hissed a full-bearded hunter named George. "There ain't enough elk for them and us; what good are the sons a' bitches?"

"We still got some strychnine, let's pepper a few carcasses," offered sandy-haired Joseph. "We can start out at Sunlight Basin – they's a pack been doggin' the elk hard over thataway."

"We'll be losin' some good elk-killin' days," William chimed in, "but in the long run, the more wolves we pisun now the better the elk huntin'll git."

"I get it, boys, but it don't hardly seem like they's all that many wolves left in the country as they once was," added Henry. "Seems like they ought to be room in this country for a few of the critters anyway," to which the rest of the men rolled their eyes and cursed under their breath.

"Not that wolf-lovin' shit again, Henry," whined James.

"Why waste the poison when shootin' 'ems more fun? C'mon boys, let's go blast a few dogs!"

BART

"Dammit, Vern, these fuckin' wolves are eatin' up every ounce of my profit," complained rancher Bart Adams. "We had a damned good bunch of calves this spring and we lost a quarter of 'em to those hairy sharks." Bart Adams stood just 5'7" in his boots and hat. With his barrel chest thrust out at anyone he was lecturing, he had a much larger presence than his height would suggest. His face was flushed and his oversized mouth sprayed droplets as he ranted at the beaten-down man on his front porch.

Surrounding them were 19,000 acres of both owned and leased grazing land known as the Draggin' A Ranch. The rolling, lightly wooded grasslands butted up against the eastern border of Yellowstone National Park. Adams' grandfather had homesteaded the property, and his father had expanded upon it. To a Wyoming cattleman, that history bestowed a set of rights over and above all others.

"You better start doin' what you were hired for, Vern, or we'll have yer job!" spat Adams, splattering his victim with spittle as he roared. By "we" he meant the Wyoming Beef Producers Association.

The subject of his wrath, Vernon Bailey, was a government biologist and a darned good one. Bailey had contributed more than 13,000 specimens to his employer, the Bureau of Biological Survey, many of which were species that he himself had discovered, described, and named. But Vernon was not good at standing up to the powerful cattle-ranching industry that controlled the grazing land in northwestern Wyoming. The Bureau had been formed in 1885 for the study of insects and birds, but for years now the ranchers had been pushing the agency hard for the eradication of gray wolves in the west.

The cattlemen saw Vernon and the Bureau of Biological Survey as their mouthpiece.

Wilting under the pressure, Bailey finally relented. "I'll take it to Washington, Bart. We'll get it done."

Not only did Bailey take it to the capitol, he also took it directly to the president. Teddy Roosevelt was developing a confusing legacy regarding conservation; on one hand, he had been instrumental in forming the American Bison Conservation Society, which almost surely brought back the buffalo from the brink of extinction. But Roosevelt was no fan of wolves, and in this case, he sided with the ranchers.

When Bailey returned from Washington, he had good news for the cattlemen - the Biological Survey recommended that the government begin "devising methods for the destruction of the animals [wolves]." By 1915, the Bureau claimed responsibility for killing 3,849 wolves. Bailey would later regret the inhumanity of the barbaric methods used to eradicate the species.

Even without the Bureau's help, Adams and his fellow ranchers had been putting a good dent in the wolf population. Not content with merely hunting down and shooting wolves, the ranchers seemed to derive a sadistic pleasure from finding novel ways of eliminating their sworn enemies. Tracking the parents to their dens and clubbing all the pups, surrounding dead cattle carcasses with steel leg traps, and poisoning meat piles with M44 Cyanide, nothing was off the table in their war against wolves.

Enlisting the government's help just sped up the process and, besides, it was fun bossing them around.

CHEETE

Cheete (Che) was a black male and Aisen (Asa) was a gray and white female. The wolf pair had roamed the fragmented ranges of the Wyoming Rockies together from the Absarokas, to the Wind Rivers, to the Tetons. They were litter mates, part of a pack dominated by another rare white wolf, a female named Chia. Through Chia, they were descended from a long broken line of white wolves, many years before biologists began applying names to Yellowstone's wolf packs.

Asa and Che would not naturally have been together for this long. Ordinarily, both might have dispersed from Chia's pack searching for separate clans. Both were sexually mature and both had strong personalities. These qualities might have led to one or the other, or both eventually becoming the dominant alphas of whichever groups they joined.

But there were gaping holes in their upbringing. Typically, young wolves spend a minimum of three years with their packs. The pair had only been two years with Chia's pack. Often the yearlings and two-year-olds will help raise the pups of subsequent litters. Che and Asa had never seen another wolf pup since the departure of their siblings. Immature wolves learn pack hunting strategy by repetition. The siblings had only participated in a handful of group hunts. Hunting as a pair was not nearly as effective as hunting in a pack, especially with so little training, yet these two had defied the odds and thrived.

One spring morning, they were back in the grasslands of their youth, working their way upwind along

Jasper Creek on the southern slope of the Lamar Valley. Raising their noses to the breeze simultaneously, they quickened their pace and lowered their profiles. A half mile away, a small herd of elk grazed - oblivious to the predators approaching from downwind.

One hundred and twenty winters had passed since Chili's herd had occupied this same vale. The DNA of many of the current herd could be traced directly back to her. During her time, she had become one of the dominant cows in the Lamar. In the current generation, a light-colored descendant called Begapi generally led the herd. Begapi was twenty-four generations removed from Chili. All of which meant nothing to the stalking wolves.

Nearly crawling through the patchy snow, Che and Asa could now make out the butter-colored rumps of the elk as they fed away from them. Without any perceptible sign of communication between the two, Asa turned up a small gully on the right, which would bring her alongside the herd. Che lay down to allow his sister time to get into position.

Like all predators, reading and adapting to the wind direction was critical for hunting success. In the mountains, the breezes followed a highly predictable pattern of downslope winds in the cool of the mornings and upslope winds in the warmer afternoons. The weather on this morning was clear and stable, and the breeze flowed reliably and consistently from above the elk straight down towards where Che lay biding his time. Asa was stealthily taking a position adjacent to Che's location.

Asa was almost where she had intended to begin her assault on the herd. A tiny Uinta ground squirrel nearby stood upright on the rim of its burrow and began chirping its piercing two-note alarm call. A number of the elk raised their heads briefly to look and smell for anything threatening. Asa's disciplined low approach kept her out of sight, and the wind was of no help to them. She lay back down momentarily and collected herself.

Seconds later she burst forward as though shot from a cannon. The elk were caught unaware and turned downhill hoping that the slope would give them an advantage. Watching the single gray wolf peripherally as they fled, they felt confident they could outrun her. Just as they began to check their pace, they saw to their horror the black wolf burst out from immediately ahead of them. Following Begapi's lead, they made a sharp right turn. But Che was now at full speed and made a flying lunge at a yearling cow.

Catching the young female on the left hindquarter, the force of the tackle spun the animal around just as Asa arrived from the side to grab her by the throat. Hanging from the bleating elk like dead weight, their combined 220 pounds pulled her to the ground. Ordinarily, the wolves would assure the elk was dead before starting to feed, to avoid the possibility of injury by way of a kick. In this case, the pair was famished and began ripping into the belly to get at the nutritious organ meat even as the young cow continued trying to get to her feet. Although there were only two of them, they gave each other ample space. Che worked his way up towards the heart and lungs while Asa hungrily gnawed on the stomach and intestines.

They had almost completely sated themselves when a bullet slammed into the elk carcass inches from where Che's head was buried behind the rib cage. A second later they were startled by the delayed bark of a rifle. Without thought, the two vaulted over the carcass and sprinted for the cover of the trees just upslope from them. Two more bullets threw snow and mud into the air on either side of them as they ran. They were now just yards from the scattered lodgepole pines that would shield their escape.

Asa heard the impact of the fourth shot as it shattered ribs and burst lungs. She watched her brother the black wolf, the only wolf she had known for the last two years, somersault to a dead stop in front of her. She bounded over the gore and blood blown across her path. Smart wolf that she was, she never slowed or looked back until she was safely among the pines.

AISEN

When Asa finally stopped running, she turned back in the direction she had come from. With ears erect, panting hard and salivating profusely, she stood and listened. Far away she could hear human voices near where her brother, Che, had fallen. She wailed a long mournful howl, then turned to the south, lowered her head, and padded onward. There was no doubt that she was grieving the loss of her companion. Without a plan or a cohort, she ambled aimlessly, crossing Specimen Ridge, and then wandering down Agate Creek.

When she reached the Yellowstone River she turned north, following it for many days until she was near Livingston, Montana. Subsisting on voles, mice, ground squirrels, and berries along the way, she was hungry but not starving. Each evening at dusk she would find an open area away from the noise of the river. Here she would tilt her head back and howl repeatedly for five minutes or more, listening all the time for a reply that never came.

On the outskirts of Livingston, she was chased by a pack of domestic dogs, which she easily outran. She left the river there and turned west, following train tracks over the Bozeman Pass.

Reaching a broad valley, she again turned north, always watching and sniffing the breeze. She persisted in hoping for any evidence of a pack that she might try to align with, never finding one. At Three Forks, Montana, she chose to follow the Missouri River downstream. After a time, the Lewis and Clark Range rose on her left and she felt a pull towards them. Crossing the river, she made her way up into them, towards the relatively new National Park named Glacier.

Gaining elevation, she sensed that here she would locate a pack to relieve her loneliness. But instead, as she walked through an open valley near West Glacier, bullets began whistling over her and thudding into the ground just short of her. Again she was on the run, this time into the alpine terrain of the Livingston Range.

It was summer in the high meadows of the Livingstons and there were wildflowers in great profusion. As she searched the canyons and ridges she continued to howl and listen, hearing only the alpine winds whistling in reply. Following a long glacier valley, she could see an ice-blue lake to the north and continued towards it.

As she neared the shore, her head reflexively jerked back, thrusting her nose into the breeze - she could smell meat, the scent of a fresh kill. Not only did this mean the possibility of filling her shrunken belly, but it might also indicate the presence of a pack. Running excitedly forward, she nearly stumbled right into a large male grizzly bear sleeping on top of a moose carcass. Grizzlies hate surprises, and this 600-pound male was no different. With a roar, he charged at the bewildered Asa. If the bear hadn't just gorged himself on fifty pounds of moose meat, he might just have caught the startled wolf. Asa regained her wits and was off, following the west shore of South Waterton Lake. After loping for about fifteen minutes, she unknowingly crossed a line. Not a line on the ground, but a line on paper, a line contrived by man.

Upon crossing that line, she had made history, a sad passing in the timeline of North American wildlife. On that day in 1926, she had crossed the border into Canada.

For the first time in thousands of years, not a single gray wolf was left from the massive Greater Yellowstone Ecosystem. Within twenty more years, wolves had been completely eliminated from every state in the Rocky Mountains.

JAMES AND JOHN

It wasn't time yet to celebrate. James waited a good ten minutes, scanning the scattered trees at the top of the meadow. He was watching over the top of his rifle sights for the gray wolf to reappear. It had taken him a couple of shots to get his range just right on the big black male. His fourth shot had hit the wolf in the chest instead of the headshot he was hoping for. He had figured that the gray wolf would stop to sniff her brother for life. Asa, however, had never missed a beat, sprinting for the trees, not even stopping to look back before she entered the cover. James was certain she would reappear somewhere along the tree-line, to scan the plain for her partner. He needed that extra $50 bounty he'd get for bringing back her pelt.

James had continued working as a market hunter ever since his days gunning with Henry at the elk camp in 1900. Under management by the Army and then the National Park Service, all hunting within Yellowstone had become the job of the rangers. All other hunting was forbidden within the park boundary, but James had never cared much for following rules.

Not only were the government employees keeping the elk in check, but they had also been instructed to eliminate all predators in the park. They had been effective, as Asa and Che had been the last remaining wolves in the region. As a result, wolf hunting could no longer be relied upon for income. In fact, this was the first set of wolves James and his son John had gotten a shot at in two years. They'd seen the pair at a distance two or three times during that period, while out poaching elk or while illegally setting the traps they put out for badgers, pine martens, and foxes. A nice addition to their take was the coyotes that had begun to move into the park since the wolf numbers had thinned.

After watching the two wolves stalk and bring down the cow elk, father and son had snuck toward them as near as possible. They then waited until the pair was well engaged in devouring the guts before aiming at the big male. The handsome bounty offered by the government would buy them supplies for a season, and the extra income from the pelt was the icing on the cake.

After five more minutes of sitting and waiting, he was pretty sure the she-wolf wasn't going to show. "That's one smart bitch," he shouted to his 19-year-old son, John.

"Too smart!" John shouted back as he pulled out his knife to begin the skinning. The two went to work, taking care not to cut through the skin. The big hole through both sides of the pelt would greatly reduce its value. A clean headshot would have paid them the maximum return. As it was, the pelt could still be used for collars and hoods.

"Ya' wanna track her, Pa?" asked John, cleaning off his knife blade on his pant leg.

"Nah," huffed James, "the way she was moving she's probably halfway to Jackson Hole by now. Let's go check our trap lines and see what else we got." John gazed south in the direction that Asa had run.

"Sure would like to kill 'er, Pa!" he said into the breeze.

"I know, boy, but they's plenty of other game to kill out there."

Folding then rolling the hide, they carried it back to the horses, stuck it in one of the panniers, and headed east up Soda Butte Creek towards their cabin near Cooke City.

ROBERT

Elk hunting had never been better. Robert and his dad had been hunting together since he was nine years old, eleven years now. Those first years had been full of adventure. His dad, Henry, had loaded up the pack-mules with supplies and led them into the high country. They camped near the headwaters of Sunlight Creek, just east of Yellowstone Park. While the earlier years had been great for adventure, they were not so great for elk hunting. The wolves, the poachers, and the market hunters (which his dad had once been) had put a major dent in the Yellowstone herds that migrated in and out of the park seasonally.

But with the wolves gone and Wyoming getting serious about protecting their remaining wildlife resources by creating specific hunting seasons, elk herds again began to flourish. By clamping down on the take by commercial hunters, implementing temporary moratoriums on certain species, and hiring game wardens, the state had greatly increased the odds of a successful hunt. Within the park, efforts had been even more aggressive, beginning with the U.S. Cavalry being given the task of routing out poachers and market gunners within the park boundaries and eventually leading to park rangers culling the last remaining wolves.

Henry's years as a commercial hunter had taught him a lot about who he wasn't and what he cared about. He had initially become a market hunter for the adventure of living in the high country, and the promise of making big money. As a child growing up in Missouri, he had developed a passion for hunting, starting with squirrels and bobwhites and culminating with white-tailed deer. Henry had spent countless hours afield mastering the art of successful whitetail hunting: patterning the bucks, learning how to read their rubs and scrapes, rattling them in with a pair of last year's shed antlers. Like the indigenous Oto people before him, he always took time to thank his prey after the harvest.

Henry had read accounts in Sports Afield Magazine of dangerous elk hunts in the Rockies surrounded by grizzlies and wolves. He fantasized about hunting outside of the borders of Missouri someday. One day a friend invited him to join him in traveling to Wyoming to shoot elk for money. The young sportsman couldn't think of anything more exciting.

Henry soon found that the reality of market gunning was harsh, nothing like the hunting ethic he had been raised on. There was no sport in it whatsoever, and there was no respect for the animals they slaughtered. Market-hunting was about speed and numbers, the goal was to kill the maximum number of elk in the shortest period of time. Sometimes that meant killing entire herds: bulls, cows, and calves all in one gruesome bloodbath. When the elk numbers dropped precipitously, just as the buffalo had before them, Henry had had enough. He promised himself that he would never kill for money again, that he would only engage in 'fair-chase' hunting and not take more than he needed.

Henry raised his son, Robert, with those same sportsman-like principles. Elk numbers were thin for a decade or so. After years of lean hunts where the game had been scarce and challenging to find, elk numbers rebounded when Robert was in his late teens. The herd sizes had grown significantly. Now he and his father could "pick and choose" the biggest bull or the fattest cow they wanted to pack home for their winter meat supply. When Robert was in his early twenties, the two no longer needed to ride so far into the backcountry to find elk. The herds were often out in open meadows or along the trail in the basin.

Then came the Great Depression. Both Henry and Robert had been working at the lumber mill in Cody. When the mill closed in the early thirties, Henry, now in his mid-fifties, found work doing all kinds of jobs on a cattle ranch. Robert was accepted into President Roosevelt's new Civilian Conservation Corps (CCC's) and was stationed at the Cascade CCC camp in Yellowstone Park. Among the many jobs that corpsmen performed was one that Robert was perfectly suited for – the reduction of Yellowstone's growing elk herds.

The policy and practice of thinning the park's elk herds had only just recently been adopted by the National Park Service (NPS). Since wolves had been eliminated from the park, the elk population had begun to expand beyond what the vegetation could sustain. Citing the park's "carrying capacity", the NPS was paying sharpshooters, including CCC corpsmen, to reduce the herds. The elk were butchered and the meat was sent to the nearby Crow, Northern Cheyenne, Shoshoni, and Bannock Reservations. The CCCs, on the other hand, had thousands of pounds of beef shipped in for their meals.

Robert loved his new role. What could be better than to be paid one dollar a day to hunt elk? It seemed like a dream come true! While his base camp was at Cascade near Yellowstone Falls, his team would often camp remotely in tents near wherever they were currently harvesting elk. Robert's favorite camping spot was the Lamar Valley. He fell in love with the beauty of the place.

But over time, his love of the valley became tainted by the blood of all of the elk that he killed there. Elk hunting, that primal joy that he had grown up with, all of those fulfilling adventures with his father, was becoming ruined for him. Just like his father, Robert had sickened of needless killing. The responsible employee that he was, he continued to fill his quota, but his heart was no longer in it. When the opportunity presented itself, he asked for and was granted a job change. The NPS needed structures removed and new ones built at the park headquarters at Mammoth Hot Springs, and the CCCs were providing much of the labor.

Robert Powell was a diligent, hard worker and he was quickly moved up to assistant leader and then leader, raising his monthly pay to $45. Park Service managers overseeing the CCC's work took note of his craftsmanship. When the regulation two years of employment with the CCCs was up, the Assistant Chief of Engineering at the Mammoth headquarters offered Robert a job in the carpentry shop. Robert jumped at the chance.

In addition to building furniture in the shop, one of Robert's first big projects was also one of his favorites. By 1935, the North East Park Entrance, the "Gateway to the Lamar Valley", needed a permanent entry station. The plans called for a rustic, cabin-like log structure to provide visitors with a "mountain-man" experience. Robert immersed himself in every phase of the project. He felled then peeled the lodgepole pine logs. He set the logs in place, chinking the gaps between them with oakum rope. Once the exterior was completed, Robert was instrumental in building out the interior rooms and even the furnishings and furniture. Park Service management was thrilled with the finished product.

When it came time to construct the new U.S. Post Office at Mammoth in 1938, the plans called for a concrete and travertine building, in keeping with the monumental style of Postal Service structures. Inside the building, wooden walls and counters and rows of post office boxes all needed a carpenter's touch, and Robert was chosen for the job.

Meanwhile, the State of Wyoming had a rich history of promoting gender equality, being the first state in which a woman's right to vote was recognized in 1869. Yellowstone National Park followed the state's example, hiring its first female park ranger in 1916. By the 1930s, there were several female rangers as well as many women who were employed in the park's visitor centers and hotels. One adventurous young woman was Kathy Evers, a recent graduate in Biology at the University of New Jersey, who had longed for the western experience of working in Yellowstone. When her application with the Park Service languished, she jumped on a bus to Wyoming.

From Livingston, Wyoming, she hitched a ride into the park and applied to work at Lyall's Gift Store in Mammoth, just steps from the park's headquarters. Working in a gift shop was not Kathy's dream job, but she was willing to do anything to get her foot in Yellowstone's door. Kathy was an asset to the store, enthusiastically greeting travelers and selling park souvenirs. One day, a young man walked into the store to buy a soda. He looked dashing in his Park Service work uniform. One look at Kathy and he nearly dropped his bottle. Robert was smitten.

Within no time, when their busy work schedules allowed, Robert and Kathy were spending all of their free time together. Kathy had a burning desire to explore the park and Robert had a passion for sharing his love of its secret places. Naturally, he most often took her to explore the Lamar Valley, their favorite hikes being the Lamar River Trail, the Slough Creek Trail, and the Specimen Ridge Trail. Packing picnic lunches, they would spend the day identifying wildflowers and bird species. They would observe the pronghorn, the bison, and the elk go about their natural patterns of eating, sleeping, sparring, and mating. Watching the big mammals copulate, the two would go silent and Robert would blush. As their fondness for each other blossomed, all of this mating activity couldn't help but have a stimulating effect.

Winter always came early to the park and the winter of 1941 was no exception. By mid-November, Kathy and Robert had switched from hiking boots to snowshoes as they continued their weekly treks into the backcountry. Every evening, Robert would stop by the gift shop after getting off work. He would always bring a flower or a poem, and the two would share a meal in the employee dining room. Each had found their soul mates. Robert made plans to propose, purchasing the only ring that he could find and afford in Mammoth – a souvenir ring featuring a picture of Old Faithful. He planned to propose to her on their day off, Monday, December 8,

1941. Neither could have foreseen the tragedy that would strike on Sunday.

Only a few employees were working in the maintenance buildings because most had Sundays off. Robert was finishing a project in the carpentry shop when he was surprised by the door slamming open.

"Holy c-c-crap, Bob, have you heard the news!?" stammered Vinny, a plumber from the shop next door.

"What news?" asked Robert, his head still buried in the arithmetic of designing a staircase.

"The Japs! The dirty stinkin' Japs! They blew up a bunch of our ships in Hawaii, dead American sailors everywhere!!" Vinny was nearly hysterical and had to sit down and put his head in his hands. Robert had barely had time to comprehend the news when Vinny cried "Let's go, Bob! Let's go kill those damned Nips! Are ya' wit' me Bobby? I'm goin' to Bozeman tomorrow or Billings if I got to!"

Robert was in shock, his head spinning. "Yeah," he began. "Yeah, I'm in. But I don't know about tomorrow. I may have to go later in the week," he said confusedly. Somewhere in the blur of all the news and the questions, he knew he had something big planned the next day. "Kathy!" he shouted to himself. "I gotta go see Kathy," he said to Vinny as he left him fretting in the chair.

Forgetting that he was on the clock and leaving his coat behind, Robert ran out into the frigid December air. He galloped through the slushy snow to the gift shop. There he found Kathy and her coworkers huddled around a radio, listening intently to commentary on the National

Mutual Broadcast Network. Two of the girls were quietly sobbing as news of the attack was repeated. Robert went to Kathy's side, held her hand, and listened. A recording of a two-minute live account from KTU in Honolulu was played repeatedly, in which explosions could be heard in the background. Details were few; there was no mention of how many American ships were sunk or any accounting of the dead and wounded. The only thing that was crystal clear was that this had been a sneak attack; there had been no declaration of war as required under the Hague Convention. There had been no warning given to the thousands of Americans stationed on Oahu.

Kathy pulled Robert into a corner of the shop. "Oh, Robert," she said with a hitch in her voice, "what does this mean? How will this affect us?" The emphasis on 'us' was clear. She knew things were about to change and she was afraid of what that meant for their relationship.

Robert held her tight and thought carefully before he spoke. "It doesn't change..." he began haltingly, struggling for each word "...anything about how much I love you, Kathy. It may mean that we will have to be apart for a while. It looks like war for sure and I'll be needed. Oh, Kathy, I love you so much." The two hugged each other tightly, both sobbing now. When they finally separated, Robert went to one knee and pulled the Old Faithful ring from his pocket. "Kathy, will you marry me?"

"Oh, Robert," she smiled and wiped her eyes, "there's no one else on earth for me. Yes, yes, YES!"

As they rejoined the group, Kathy announced to her co-workers, "I'd like to break up this sad gathering with some happy news." Her three co-workers looked at her questioningly. "Robert and I are going to get married!"

The news transformed the gathering instantly, as tears of sorrow turned into tears of elation, hugs, and kisses being shared by all.

"When will the wedding be?" queried Edna, Kathy's boss.

The two looked at each other, and then Robert said, "Tomorrow if possible!" to the astonished joy of all.

The park and indeed the world seemed like a different place on Monday morning. Visitation at the park entrance was at its lowest of the winter season so far. Numerous park staffers took the day off, pulling out of the park in the early morning or catching the Greyhound bus into Bozeman on its daily round trip. Robert and Kathy had decided to travel to Bozeman to get married at the county courthouse there. The love-struck couple waited in line for the bus which was to arrive mid-morning. In line with them were five young men, all headed to Bozeman to enlist. The conversation on the bus was lively and passionate, as everyone on board expressed their sadness, anger, and opinions on the Pearl Harbor attack. The driver had the bulky bus radio tuned to the news and repeatedly shouted out updated casualty numbers. The first accounts indicated a death toll of 104 sailors; by the time they arrived at Bozeman the number had risen to 1,500. The young men aboard were in a frenzy.

Arriving in Bozeman, the men immediately asked for directions to the recruitment office. They were dismayed to find out that the nearest recruiter was in Butte, another three hours away. Robert and Kathy left the frustrated young men and made their way to the county courthouse. Here they found another line. Three other couples were there for the same reason, all wanting to be wed right away as the near certainty of war loomed. As the ceremony required a witness, the four couples took turns witnessing for the others. By 3:00 p.m., Robert and Kathy were Mr. and Mrs. Powell. By 5:00 p.m., President Roosevelt had declared war on Japan.

Another bus back to the park didn't leave until the next day. The two had gotten the blessings of their superiors to take an additional day off of work. They checked into the monolithic brick Hotel Bozeman. In all of their time spent together, there had been plenty of long passionate kisses among the wildflowers of the Lamar Valley, but until this night, the two had never shared a bed. Though they had never discussed sex, it was often on their minds, especially as they had observed nearly every species of animal in the valley court and mate. Both were virgins, but neither was unaware of the mechanics of love-making. All of that watching paid off, as the newlyweds gloriously consummated their union, both claiming it to be the best night of their lives.

The bus to Mammoth left early, designed to get tourists into the park before noon. Robert and Kathy were tired, a little sore, and blissfully happy. They had been avoiding the subject of the impending war, but both knew it had to be discussed. The ride back to the park gave them the time they needed. "I should enlist, shouldn't I?" ventured Robert, effectively turning his announcement into a question.

Tears formed in the corners of Kathy's eyes but she held them back. "Now that I have you to myself, now that you're truly a part of me," she began, "I can't imagine letting go of you. But it's what we must do; it's the right thing to do, no matter how frightening or painful it is."

Robert hugged her tightly to him. "I'll give my notice tomorrow," he answered resolutely. They held each other for the rest of the ride back.

There was a flurry of activity happening at Park Headquarters. Management was in seemingly perpetual meetings, dealing with the sudden loss of employees, diminished visitation, concern over protecting park resources, and planning for predicted impacts. Within 48 hours of the attack, eight employees had already given their notice to enlist; Robert became the ninth.

When the Chief of Engineering returned from hours of meetings to find Robert waiting at his office door, he shook his head. "Not you too, Bob?" he asked rhetorically. "Well, not to worry, old boy…you'll always have a job here when you get back. We'll hold down the park while you're gone. Now go to personnel and settle with them." With that, he shook Robert's hand vigorously, slapped him on the shoulder with the other, and said, "God speed Bobby, come home in one piece will ya'?" and turned to walk away before his emotions betrayed him. Robert stared at the ground momentarily, collected himself, and headed for the business offices.

No one noticed or cared that Kathy stayed with Robert in the Juniper Dorm that evening. The other residents pretended not to hear the sounds of the passionate newlyweds throughout the night. The first thing the next morning, Kathy bid Robert a tearful farewell as he boarded the bus for the long trip to Butte. Later that day, Germany and Italy joined the Japanese by declaring war against the United States.

KATHY

Nothing was normal in Yellowstone in the days and months immediately following FDR's "Reciprocal War Declaration". Visitation, which had never been substantial in winter, dropped by more than sixty percent. With guest numbers so dramatically decreased, the girls that Kathy worked with at the gift shop soon left to work at Red Cross sewing rooms, leaving Kathy as the sole employee of the store. Most troublesome from the standpoint of park management was the danger posed by the possibility of areas being converted for the war effort.

World War I had devastated pristine meadows within Yellowstone, as military stock, horses and mules were allowed to graze the native pastures to bulk up for the war. Other parks were already seeing logging of virgin forests being carried out within their boundaries in the name of the war effort. Yellowstone management quickly developed an "Irreplaceable Treasures" policy to protect the park's wildlife.

While visitation had shrunk, and park staff departed for the South Pacific or Europe, the need for employees to protect Yellowstone's natural resources had only increased. As rationing took effect throughout the country, some living in the remote areas surrounding Yellowstone resorted to poaching to put additional food on the table or a few dollars in their pocket. Others cut down trees from the park to sell the wood. Some even squatted in emptied buildings or campgrounds to save on rent. Balancing the needs of the war machine and caring for the park's irreplaceable treasures was a nearly impossible juggling act. As the number of park rangers fell, there were fewer and fewer eyes on the park's flora and fauna.

Kathy had originally applied for a park ranger job when she graduated from college in 1937. In her five years at the gift shop, she had continued to reapply with the National Park Service for a ranger position every year. In the 1940s, there was no distinction between an interpretive ranger and a law enforcement ranger. Rangers did everything from leading walking tours of the geysers to writing traffic tickets and ferreting out poachers. Edmund Rogers, Yellowstone's superintendent, was well aware of Kathy's desire and determination to work in the field. In the spring of 1942, as the summer tourism season approached, he lost yet another ranger to the war. One afternoon he showed up in the gift store.

"Welcome!" greeted the ever-exuberant Kathy as the door swung open. "Oh, good day, Superintendent Rogers," she added, smiling.

Edmund Rogers had been the park's third superintendent beginning in 1936, just as rumblings of war began in Europe. Now his tenure was being severely impacted by what had become a global conflict. "Why hello, Kathy, still holding down the trading post I see," he replied kindly.

"You bet, sir, probably be here until I can put my biology degree to work for the park, sir," never missing an opportunity to broadcast her desire to work in the field.

Known for being direct, Rogers spoke his mind. "Well, my dear, that's just why I stopped by. Six years ago, I had 30 permanent rangers and 42 seasonals. I just lost another permanent ranger and my budget has been cut for seasonal rangers. However, I do have some discretionary funds stashed away that I could use to pay you for at least the next twelve months. It would be minimum wage but you'd get free room and board. I know you've wanted to work in the field for many years – here is a way to get a toe-hold. We're in a tight spot, Kathy, I need you!"

Kathy's head was spinning with excitement. "Of course, I will!" burst out Kathy. "How soon do you need me?" she inquired.

"Just as soon as Edna can spare you," he said, knowing full well that the gift store manager was hearing every word from the next room.

Edna entered the lobby pointing an accusatory finger at Rogers. "You come into my shop and hire away my only employee right in front of me," the scowl turning to a melancholy smile. Then to Kathy, she said, "My dear child, I don't know what I'll do without you. You've been my rock and the friendly face of this establishment for five years. But you're made for so much more. I know that you've been wanting this for a long time. Robert will be so proud of you. Looks like I'm down to just one now...me!"

Kathy went to her and the two hugged like old friends. "Well?" Edna began again as they separated. "The superintendent said 'as soon as I can spare you.' You'd better just get out of here now before I change my mind," she concluded.

After hugging Edna, then grabbing her coat and purse, Kathy left with Rogers. "It's almost the end of the day," he offered. "Why don't we get you your uniform and gear squared away this afternoon and then we'll get you started training tomorrow? I'll have the assistant chief ranger meet you at the supply room," referring to

Yellowstone's longest-serving and most well-respected ranger, Harry Trischman.

Kathy met Trischman at the supply room, where he helped her pick out a couple of sets of shirts, coats, parkas, pleated skirts, knee socks, and an iconic "lemon squeezer" flat hat. "Better find you a pair of jodhpurs as well," he said, referring to the quirky male ranger's pants that flared at the hips. "They're not regulation for female rangers, but you can't very well do all of the things you need to do in a skirt. You'll be glad to have them this coming winter."

Opening a closet within the room, he began handing Kathy supplies she would need in the field: a belt, flashlight holder and flashlight, and a two-way radio. "When you're in the field, you'll have a rifle with you in the pickup, and I'll have to requisition a sidearm for you. Do you know how to shoot, Kathy?" he queried her.

"You bet, sir," she replied promptly. "Robert showed me how shortly after we met in case we encountered an angry grizzly bear."

"That's good, Kathy," Harry said with relief, "but there's worse than grizzlies out there these days. A ranger was killed by poachers just last year." Kathy was aware of the growing problems along the park's borders.

"Here's your locker," he said as he motioned toward a full-sized gray locker. "You can store your gear here so you don't have to haul all of it back and forth to your dorm. There's no women's changing room yet, so you can change in the ladies' room."

"The superintendent wants me to give you the deluxe tour of the park, Kathy," Trischman said, after Kathy finished trying on her uniform. "It'll take two days just to see the north and south loops. That won't even get us to the west, south, and east entrances. Why don't you pack up an overnight bag and we'll spend tomorrow night at the ranger's quarters at Old Faithful? Can you do that?" Kathy nodded her head emphatically. "Great," concluded Harry, "let's meet at 7 a.m. in the Albright Center, okey-dokey?"

"You bet!" she responded. "Thank you, Harry, I can't think of a better person to educate me on the park," Kathy gushed.

Her thoughts raced as she returned to her dorm. After grabbing a quick dinner which she hardly tasted, she spent the rest of the evening composing a lengthy letter to Robert, describing the exciting events of the day. Kathy wrote Robert daily, though she was unsure of how many of her letters made it to him.

Robert wrote to Kathy daily as well if he had a chance. Based on Robert's carpentry background, he had been assigned to the Navy's "Seabees". The last letter she had received was from Iceland.

Dearest Kathy, I am working with a swell bunch of guys. They are craftsmen like me - carpenters, electricians, plumbers and etc. We are called Seabees – as in C.B. (for Construction Battalion). The difference is that we also fight, which we haven't had to do yet! They send us anywhere that needs a landing strip or an operations center. We have been moved around to many places, in both the Atlantic and the Pacific, as it seems like war is everywhere. We are currently working on a project called Patterson Field Airbase in Iceland. It is beautiful here but chilly.

Will write again soon, Love, Robert

Finishing his letter and working on a reply, she fell asleep with a stack of envelopes clutched to her breast.

TRISCHMAN

Harry Trischman loved being a ranger. Trischman had originally been with the Army during the latter years of their management of the park and protection of its assets. When the National Park Service took over from the Army in 1916 and hired their own rangers, Harry was a natural choice, a personable mountain man who was as comfortable shooting it out with poachers as he was at explaining the biology of the park's fauna, flora and geology. Despite his reluctance to be taken out of the field, Trischman was promoted to assistant chief ranger. The training of new recruits was one of the normal duties of the assistant chief, and at 61 years of age, Harry made a charming and colorful mentor.

Kathy arrived at the Ranger Center at 6:30 a.m., changed into her uniform, and waited for Harry. The sun was already above the eastern horizon on a beautiful midsummer day. Trischman arrived at 6:55 in his Park Service green Ford Model 50 pickup. "Let's go see our park, shall we, Kathy?" he asked cheerily, throwing wide the door for her.

"You know, Kathy," the old ranger began as he idled the truck onto Highway 89 south towards Old Faithful, an hour and a half away, "I see the same spirit and qualities in you that Peg Lindsley had." Trischman was referring to the park's first and best-known female ranger. "Peg, now she was a firecracker for sure," Harry smiled as he recalled her tenure during the 1920s. "Paint Pot Peg we called 'er, always rarin' to go, even after she fell into that boiling mud pot and burned her leg good!" he cackled with laughter.

"Well, I don't plan on falling into any paint pots!" Kathy said, giggling.

Although Kathy had seen many of the park's features with Robert, she was spellbound as Harry Trischman filled her with his nearly forty years of stories about the park. It seemed as though Trischman had a personal anecdote about every site they visited and every animal they saw.

As they passed Swan Lake, Harry handed Kathy his binoculars. "See that white lump way over there?" he asked. "That's one of the last trumpeter swans left in the whole country. Back in about 1914 and '15, we run a whole buncha' poachers outta' here after they shot up just about every swan in the park. Now you're lucky if you see one all season. Eight-foot wing span! Swan Lake's always been one of their favorite haunts."

Coming upon a long marshy valley known as Willow Park, Harry had a similar story but with a different antagonist. "Do you notice that you don't see too many willows here in Willow Park?" he quizzed her. "There used to be lots of moose here that liked to feed on the willow shrubs, and you could always find a beaver pond here blocked by a dam of willow sticks. Not a single, solitary beaver to be found hereabouts these days."

"What happened to them Harry, more poachers?" Kathy asked innocently.

"Elk ate all the doggone willows," he shrugged. "The herds got real big real fast and they love to eat willows. No willows, no moose, no beavers. That's why we been havin' to kill a buncha' elk every year. Makes the tourists mad as hell, so we try to do it in the off-season, away from the highway. Not real sportsman-like, but if we didn't do it there'd be nary a bush left in the park," he said in his homespun way.

"Sounds like trouble in paradise," said Kathy worriedly.

POHOGWE

Coming around a bend, Harry slowed down for a car pulled over by the side of the road with its hood up and a geyser of its own whistling out of the radiator. A man with his back to the road leaned on the fender, peering into the engine compartment, surveying the source.

Stopping alongside, Harry shouted through Kathy's window, "Gonna need some help there?" As the man turned to face them, they were surprised to find a handsome, dark-complected young man with angular facial features wearing a long-sleeved white shirt and a short black tie.

"Busted hose!" he shouted back.

"We're headin' to Old Faithful," shouted Harry. "There's a service station there might have a hose. Wanna lift?"

Looking north towards Mammoth, then south towards Old Faithful, the man thought about distances and amenities for a moment, and then answered, "Why not? Thanks!"

Parking the truck on the shoulder in front of the car, Harry and Kathy stepped out, and after grabbing a couple of belongings from his vehicle, the man began to climb into the back over the tailgate. "There's room in the front!" offered Kathy. "It'll be tight, but it's not all that far."

"Much appreciated," said the man, throwing his things in the back and loosening his tie. "Name's Pohogwe, but call me Po."

"I'm Kathy Powell and this is Ranger Trischman," said Kathy, motioning towards the senior ranger.

"Just call me Harry," said Trischman, thrusting out his hand. After handshakes all around, Trischman got back in and scooted as far towards the driver's door as he could. Kathy modestly turned at a slight angle so as not to have to straddle the stick shifter, and Po slammed the passenger door, and then hugged the right side of the seat. Even with all of the jostling, the three were pressed snugly against each other.

"Well, now we know how a sardine feels!" said Kathy jokingly, causing all three to chuckle.

It was a lovely summer's day and they had the windows down to enjoy the sights and smells of the passing countryside. Never one to beat around the bush, Harry broke the silence. "So what brings you to Yellowstone all by yourself, and with a tie on Po?"

"I had a meeting with your Superintendent Rogers," Po responded. "I had to apply to do some archaeological research in the park. Fortunately, I got permission and I was on my way back home when the hose burst."

"That's so exciting, Po. If you don't mind my asking, what type of research will you be doing?" asked Kathy curiously.

"I don't mind at all, Kathy. I'd bet that as rangers it's something you'd be interested in," he began. "I'll be conducting some digs looking for steatite, or soapstone bowls used by my ancestors – the mountain Shoshoni or Tukudika."

Both Kathy and Harry perked up; the Sheep Eaters were a part of the park's history, a subject that was an integral component of rangers' talks and presentations. "So you are descended from the Tukudika?" asked Harry, wide-eyed.

"Yes, Harry," Po continued, "as you probably know, Chief Wasatchie of the Eastern Shosoni was one of the few Indian chiefs on the continent to avoid warfare with the whites as they expanded across the country. By doing so, he minimized the loss of lives among the Shoshoni people, and in 1868 the tribe took possession of the Wind River Reservation in the Bighorn Valley. My ancestors from this area joined other Shoshoni bands on the reservation. That was where I was headed when my car broke down - home."

Kathy could barely contain her excitement. "So these pre-historic people that we talk about all the time here in the park actually still exist?!"

"Yes Kathy, you're sitting next to one right now," Po chuckled.

Over the next hour, Po went into great detail regarding his work and the history of his people in the region. The archaeological records suggest that the Tukudika had been present in the Greater Yellowstone area for approximately 12,000 years, corresponding to the end of the last major ice age.

The first historical record of the clan's existence came from the 1834 journal of the trapper and writer, Osborne Russell, who described a positive encounter with a mountain band of approximately twenty "Snake Indians" and their thirty pack-dogs. Russell described the clan as "all neatly clothed in dressed deer and sheep skins of the best quality and all seemed to be perfectly contented and happy". Packed among their possessions he observed a "small stone pot". Years later, in an 1881 report, P.W. Norris, then superintendent of Yellowstone National Park, mentioned high country steatite or soapstone bowls found in the park.

It was these stone pots that were the key to Pohogwe's project.

Growing up, Po had been more fortunate than some reservation children. Crime and gang activity on the Wind River Reservation was on par with other Indian reservations in the region, but much higher than for the rest of the state in general, partly due to the staggering 84% unemployment. Fortunately, Po's father had a good job with Merit Energy in nearby Thermopolis, Wyoming. When Po was young, his mother and father decided to send him to school in Riverton, to insulate him from some of the negative conditions on the reservation. Po was an outstanding student, and as a high-school senior, he received a scholarship from the American Indian Education Fund that enabled him to enroll at the University of Wyoming in Laramie. Owing to Wyoming's distinction as the richest source of dinosaur fossils in the country, UW had a robust science department that included a highly regarded anthropology program. Just beginning his Ph.D. research focusing on Paleoindian, plains, and hunter-gatherer archaeology, Po was setting an example for the young people of his tribe to follow in terms of higher education.

Now officially authorized by park management, Po's project entitled *Sheep Corrals, Bighorn Bows, and Soapstone Bowls of Yellowstone* would allow him to conduct archaeological research in some of the park's highest, least visited, and most scenic spots. Kathy was very excited to learn that Po would be working in the ring of peaks surrounding the Lamar Valley, the place where she and Robert had fallen in love.

"I know every inch of the Lamar," claimed Kathy. "My husband Robert and I hiked all the hills and trails around it, but I haven't visited the peaks themselves."

"I could use your expertise, Kathy," replied Po. "I have not been up there yet. Most of my initial work has been checking out the soapstone quarries at the north end of the Tetons."

"I'm your gal!" spouted Kathy.

"You may even be able to work it into your ranger duties, Kathy," offered Harry. "You'll be checking the Lamar from time to time for poachers and the like, walking some of those same trails."

"I'm loving this job more by the minute," Kathy gushed.

Too soon they pulled into the Old Faithful village, having thoroughly enjoyed each other's company. Harry and Kathy waited to see if Po was able to find the hose that he needed.

"No go!" shouted Po, jogging back to the car, "They called their other station in Canyon Village, they have one there – I'm going to see if I can hitch a ride over there before dark."

Before Kathy could object, Harry offered, "Why don't you stay the night here? We're heading to Canyon first thing in the morning. You can ride the rest of the way with us."

"That's a kind offer but..."

Harry, sensing his discomfort, cut him off. "We can get you set up in the ranger station for the night, and we brought plenty of groceries for dinner!"

"Yes," added Kathy, "it's almost dark already. Please stay – we really enjoy your company!"

"Well," answered Po, looking a little relieved, "when you put it that way, how can I say no? Thank you so much!"

The Old Faithful Inn itself was closed down due to the war and the shortage of employees, so the threesome wandered around the perimeter, peering in the windows and marveling at the remarkable log and stonework inside. All three had seen Old Faithful erupt before, but since the moon was nearly full they stuck around to witness it in the moon's glow.

The shooting mist and steam in the moon and starlight were magical, and Po was moved to relate an Indian legend about the geyser. "Buffalo were known for their snorting breaths. Old Woman's Grandchild killed a large buffalo bull near this spot and it turned into a geyser formation that continued to blow out hot steamy snorts."

"We have been telling guests for years that the Indians feared the geysers and wouldn't come near them," stated Harry.

"I'm afraid that is untrue, my friend," Po corrected gently. "It is a mistruth that fits with the casting of indigenous people as ignorant savages. The only shred of truth to it is that the ancestors warned their children to stay away from the thermal areas so as not to fall in."

"Thank you for the education, Po," smiled Kathy. "Now I can provide visitors with a more accurate picture of the relationship between the park and its original human inhabitants!"

"You are quite welcome, Kathy," Po replied solemnly.

The next morning, as the trio drove along Yellowstone Lake towards Canyon Village, Harry and Po took turns tutoring Kathy on park geology and history.

"Believe it or not, Kathy, but Yellowstone Lake is a youngster compared to most of the country's geological features," Harry explained. "It was just 600,000 years ago that the giant Yellowstone Caldera erupted, then collapsed, filled in by what became Yellowstone Lake. Compare that to the Absaroka Mountains just next to it which are 60 million years old!"

To Harry's explanation, Po provided his own interpretation regarding the lake. "Our people were friendly with the Crow tribe, trading obsidian that we gathered nearby. The Crow people told their story of how a Thunderbird asked the Crow to help him fight the giant water beast that lived in Yellowstone Lake and which ate the Thunderbird's young. The Crow built a large fire and heated many rocks and boiled much water. When the beast came out of the lake and climbed up the mountainside, the Indian pitched hot rocks and hot water into its mouth. Steam came out of the monster's mouth and it tumbled down the mountainside and into the lake," Po added, "which explains all of the thermal activity around the lake's perimeter."

"Which do you believe, Po?" asked Kathy innocently.

"That's a great question, Kathy," replied Po, with a grin. "As a scientist, I believe the geologic evidence. As an Indian, I believe that science is nuanced by legends. Science tells a story one way; legends tell the same story another way."

Kathy thought about it a minute, then asked the two men, "Do you think it's okay if I tell people both stories when I teach visitors about the lake?"

Po and Harry looked at each other. "Teaching folks about the native people who lived here is just as important as explaining the processes that shaped the place, Kathy," said Harry.

To this, Po added, "When you attribute creation stories to the ancestors and tell their stories with respect and reverence, our history lives on, and that is a good thing."

Once they passed the lake, the wildlife seemed to become more abundant. The Yellowstone River appeared on their right and elk could be seen among the conifers. Coming around a corner, the landscape opened into a wide grassland, the Hayden Valley. Named for Geologist Ferdinand Hayden who led the first comprehensive mapping expedition of Yellowstone in 1871, it nearly rivaled the Lamar Valley in terms of open spaces and large mammal habitat. Hundreds of buffalo grazed on the west side of the road for as far as they could see.

"All these years we've been calling them buffalo," Harry remarked. "Turns out that true buffalo only live in Africa and Asia, so the park wants us to drop the word buffalo and instead use 'bison', which is what they actually are."

Adding to Harry's explanation, Po contributed, "Neweguchu is our name for the bison – 'guchu' for cow and 'newe' for people, so neweguchu is 'the people's cow'." Kathy just nodded her head and smiled as she immersed herself in the bucolic landscape.

All at once, Harry hit the brakes and the truck skidded momentarily as they narrowly missed hitting a coyote crossing the truck's path. They watched it as it bounded off, looking back over its shoulder at them with what looked like a grin.

"The old trickster," Po said, shaking his head and smiling. "Izhape, we call him, old coyote played a large role in our legends. The best known is the story of how Izhape the trickster himself was tricked by Isa the wolf. Would you like to hear it?" he asked. Kathy nodded her head vigorously.

"Isa, the wolf, was our creator god, the most important animal in our mythology, and as such he was the most revered and important to us. In the old days, Isa could talk like a man and so could Izhape, the coyote, but my people never listened to Izhape because he was always trying to trick us and making trouble. Izhape resented Isa because the Newe loved him, so he decided to play a trick on Isa and get the Newe to dislike the wolf.

"Izhape knew that Isa claimed he could bring dead people back to life by shooting an arrow underneath them. Izhape counseled Isa that people should stay dead or the world would become overrun with people. He knew that if Wolf followed his advice he would fall out of favor with the Newe, and Izhape would look better in their eyes. Wise Isa knew he was being tricked but played along.

"Soon after, Izhape ran to Isa in a panic."

"My pup has been bit by a rattler and will surely die," the coyote cried. "You must shoot an arrow under him and bring him back to life!"

"But you told me that creatures should stay dead," replied Isa. "I took your advice and I can no longer bring back the dead."

"The Newe believe that was the day death came to our people, and Coyote's son was the first to die - to punish Izhape for all of his tricks. And even though Isa never raised anyone from the dead again, the people did not blame the Wolf; instead, they admired him for his cunning and wisdom. It was Izhape who incurred the people's wrath, and he has ever been derided by the Newe for his tricks."

Kathy applauded and Harry said, "That's a good one, Po, thank you for that – I'll never look at a coyote the same again."

Suddenly somber, Po replied, "And unfortunately, it seems that we'll never have a chance to look at wolves here again."

Infected by the mood change, the three sat silently staring out the window for minutes before Kathy said simply, "How sad."

The magic of the morning seemed to have evaporated as they drove the last few miles to Canyon Village. The service station had the hose waiting for him and Po walked back to the truck waving it at them. "I can't thank you enough," Po began. "I got so much more than a ride out of this, it's been great!" he said, shaking hands vigorously with Harry and more gently with Kathy. "You know, my ancestors thought shaking hands was a strange custom that the whites brought with them, but I guess I kind of like it," to which they all laughed.

"Thank you for teaching an old dog some new stories, Po," said Harry. "I'll be sure to add them to my story bag – it's already a big bag but it just got a whole lot bigger," he smiled.

"Oh Po," Kathy began, "do please let me know when you're working around the Lamar. I'll come down and show you the trails," she said sincerely.

"Will do, Kathy, I'll look you up for sure!" answered Po just as genuinely. "Now I'm heading back towards Norris," he said, holding his thumb up to emulate hitch-hiking.

"We're heading north through the Lamar," said Harry. "Good luck, nice knowin' ya," he added warmly.

As they pulled away waving, Harry turned to Kathy and said, "You just got a far better education on the park than I alone coulda' ever given you."

"Yes," replied Kathy wistfully, "I wish Robert had been here to meet him, too."

KENT

In 1939, the Bureau of Biological Survey became the U.S. Fish and Wildlife Service. The stated mission of the USFWS was "Working with others to conserve, protect, and enhance, fish, wildlife, plants, and their habitats for the continuing benefit of the American people." Two years into the war, in 1943, the new service found itself under pressure to assure that there were ample opportunities for Americans to supplement their short war rations. Game meat was a perfect solution, leaving farm-raised meats and produce for the non-hunting populace and the military. As a result, over nine million pounds of elk meat was harvested and consumed as a consequence of the 1942-1943 hunting season.

The Draggin' A Ranch east of Yellowstone under fourth-generation owner, Kent Adams, was having a tough go. The government had capped the price that ranchers could charge for beef to keep inflation in check, while at the same time the price for corn was set artificially high. This combination made feeding corn to cattle prohibitively expensive, putting additional pressure on the ranch's grasslands as the sole source of feed.

Like his father and grandfather before him, Adams had a reputation as a bully and a hothead. Drew Reed stood stiffly and stared straight ahead as Kent Adams gave him a piece of his mind.

"Dammit, Drew, these fuckin' elk are eatin' up every blade of grass on my ranch! With the price of beef capped at sixty goddamn cents per pound, I need to be fattening up as many cows as I can, and instead, I'm fattenin' the mother-fuckin' elk! I thought that the government was encouraging hunters to kill more elk. How come I still got so goddam many of 'em?!" Kent's round face was scarlet red as he gasped for air after his rant.

Drew had the cumbersome title of Assistant Director for Wildlife and Sport Fish Restoration Programs for the United States Fish and Wildlife Service. In 1937, the government created the Pittman-Robertson Act to provide federal aid to the states for the management and restoration of wildlife. As part of the powerful Wyoming Beef Producers Association, Kent Adams had the ear of newly-elected Wyoming State Senator, Frank Barrett. It was Barrett who had arranged for Assistant Director Reed to meet with Adams at the Draggin' A.

Confident that Adams had momentarily worn himself out, Reed began to explain in a monotone voice, "It's the Yellowstone herd, Mr. Adams. We're issuing more licenses in the U.S. this year than ever in our history – 8,500,000, two million more than before the war began. But we're not allowed to issue licenses for the park, sir, and those Yellowstone elk are the ones that migrate onto your ranch. The herd has been growing steadily for the last twenty years. The CCCs were culling them before the war began, but now they're out of control again. They've eaten down a lot of the park vegetation, so now they're coming down to your property to feed. Times like these make you wish we still had a few wolves around to…"

Before he could finish, Adams exploded again. "Wolves!? Are you fuckin' kidding me?! You think wolves are the answer?" He took out a red handkerchief and mopped his forehead. "Turn one problem into two much bigger problems?! That's not a god-dammed solution! What do we pay you people for?"

"The answer is easy," Adams barked. "Allow hunting in the park and issue me a bunch of depredation permits. While you're at it, go up to Canada and Alaska and wipe every fuckin' wolf off the face of the earth – those are solutions." Clearly spent, the rancher fell into a chair to avoid falling over.

The assistant director knew that there was nothing that he could do in the short term that would appease the cattleman, so he deflected. "I'll make sure that we communicate the situation to the Park Service," he said matter-of-factly. "Perhaps they'll make an exception regarding sport-hunting within the park."

"Shit!" snarled Adams.

Reed then added, "In the meantime, I'll make sure that your ranch receives a bunch of special exemptions. I'll arrange special permission for hazing, the use of repellants, temporary or permanent stackyard fencing, and a specified number of kill permits. We'll even allow a damage hunt and some supplemental game damage licenses for the ranch."

"It's about damned time," whined Adams.

JOHN

Although he hadn't hunted it much in many years, John still remembered the Lamar Valley as though it had been just yesterday. He could remember vividly the last wolf he and his dad, James, had taken there nearly twenty years earlier, and the one that got away. In the years that followed, Yellowstone had become crowded and it had become increasingly harder to keep their illegal trap sets from being discovered. For a while, they had switched to checking and setting their traps at night. After a short time, they removed all of their sets from around the Lamar and moved further east into the mountains around Pilot Peak.

John's father, James, had been a heavy drinker and had died of liver failure in the late 1930s. When the war broke out in 1941, John had neglected to enlist and never registered for the draft. He married an Irish girl named Rosie, with bright red hair and green eyes. Their two boys, twelve-year-old Albert and ten-year-old Jake, both shared Rose's coloration. The four of them occupied a handmade cabin off of Emma Mine Road near Cooke City, Montana, just feet from the Wyoming border. They poached all of their own meat, foraged much of their other food, or traded game meat to their neighbors for necessities. Once or twice a year, John would take all of his pelts to Bozeman to sell, that being the only source of income the family existed on. No one questioned the reclusive family about James' draft status.

The war had quickly changed the illegal trapping and hunting business for the better. Yellowstone Park had grown rich in numerous fur-bearing species in recent years.

Pine martens, coyotes, and foxes were John's stock-in-trade, though foxes were becoming more scarce while coyotes were becoming more common. Prices for all furs were on the rise, and depressed park visitation and staffing meant that he could again poach around the Lamar Valley without getting caught. It was too good for John to resist.

Day length is the most important factor affecting the quality of furs in the Rockies, and the shorter days on either side of the winter solstice were primetime for trapping. John had been bringing his twelve-year-old son, Albert, along with him regularly since late October, both for the help he provided and to teach him the tricks of the trade.

Albert was big for his age and, having worked in the outdoors since early childhood, was strong and capable, offsetting his poor verbal and communicative skills. The dates also coincided nicely with the denning period of both black and grizzly bears. The blacks they considered a nuisance, while the grizzlies were definitely a threat. By late January, Albert had become quite adept at setting the different types of snares needed for the animals they were trapping. For foxes, coyotes, and bobcats he had a productive routine. He would chop out a shallow trough in the snow, put some moss in the bottom, put a little crumpled-up wax paper over the trap, put another 1/2 inch or so of dry moss over the top, sprinkle loose snow over that and then bait them with a scent lure. Fish scent worked best for the foxes and coyotes; catnip oil was effective for bobcats. For pine martens, he learned to build small boxes that he would affix at chest height to the pine trees, outfitted with bait and a body-gripper trap.

Their camp was hidden at the far eastern end of the valley along Cache Creek. Their trap line followed the perimeter of the Lamar, dipping up into the various creek canyons surrounding it: Soda Butte Creek, Rose Creek, and Slough Creek on the north side, Crystal Creek and Amethyst Creek on the south side. Every time that they checked their trap line without seeing another human, they grew more confident. Eventually, they abandoned night and evening work for the light and relative warmth of daytime. By late winter of early 1944, they had stopped taking any precautions.

While not as numerous in winter, a small herd of bison was toughing out the snowy conditions in the Lamar Valley that year. Seeing a young bison cow trailing behind a big shaggy bull plowing through the thick snow near their camp one morning, John impulsively decided that he and the boy had endured enough marten and fox meat. With seemingly no one around to care, he decided it was time to enjoy some real food. He aimed and fired his rifle at close range, unconcerned that there was no sport to the killing, only the anticipation of sweet buffalo meat roasted over a fire.

The big bull glanced back over his shoulder at the fallen cow, then lowered his massive head and continued pushing through the snow. John and Albert immediately descended upon the downed female to gut and cape her.

A half mile away in opposite directions, two potentially dangerous mammals snapped to attention at the crack of the rifle's single shot. The less lethal of the two was Park Ranger Kathy Powell; the other was Wid-dah' – the Shoshoni name for grizzly bear.

WID-DAH'

Old Wid-dah' was in a bad mood. A large tree had fallen directly onto his comfortable den located under a pile of rotting, snow-covered logs. When the tree landed on them, the logs had collapsed into the den, filling it with snow. Wid-dah' was forced to claw his way out of the blocked entryway. He was disoriented, his tooth hurt and he was immediately hungry. Nothing made an aged grizzly madder than being rousted from a deep sleep in mid-winter.

Standing there outside of his ruined den, shaking his head trying to rid himself of the pain in his mouth, he stopped suddenly and looked to the east. He had heard a familiar popping sound, hundreds of yards away, up Cache Creek. Wid-dah' had lived outside of the park for much of his life, and he knew very well what that sound meant. It meant food. It was the sound that the skinny, upright creatures made when they killed their food with the sticks that belched fire. Sometimes it meant deer meat, sometimes antelope meat, often it meant elk meat. In any case, to Wid-dah' it meant filling his stomach so he could go back to sleep for a couple more months. He forgot about his tooth for the moment and took off at a jog towards the noise.

Like wolves, grizzly bears had nearly been completely eradicated from the lower 48 states, with Yellowstone and Glacier National Park holding the remaining few dozen individuals. Wid-dah' was about average in weight for a male grizzly bear, about five-hundred pounds, but at twenty-six years old he was having a hard time putting enough fat on to get him comfortably through winter dormancy.

Few male grizzlies live beyond age twenty-five in the wild and his body was beginning to give out on him. Last spring, during the breeding season, he lacked the ability to copulate with the one sow that he was able to locate. It didn't help that he had cracked a tooth last fall. He hadn't been able to eat on that side of his mouth when he should have been bulking up in preparation for winter, and now the tooth was infected.

As he continued to lope toward where the noise had come from, the pain returned and it infuriated him. Wid-dah' stopped abruptly and put his nose in the air. A grizzly's nose is one hundred times more sensitive than a human's. The bear was coming from downwind and the scent hit him like a slap in the face. It was buffalo! He was going to eat buffalo. He never gave a thought to whom or what might have killed the animal. The big male cared not whether something or someone might be defending its kill. He knew quite assuredly that he would be the one consuming the meat he was smelling. His pace increased to a bounding run.

Coming out of the trees into a small open flat, he could now see his prey, lying there between two of the skinny beings. Rather than slowing him down, the sight of others at his carcass further enraged him and he snarled as he galloped towards his prize.

John and Albert were caught wholly off-guard. Before John could even raise the rifle to shoot, the bear was on him, grabbing John's head in his mouth. As Wid-dah's cracked tooth glanced off of John's hard skull, the old grizzly roared in pain, spitting John away from him. At the last moment before John lost consciousness, he shouted to Albert, "Go!" The sound enraged Wid-dah' and he again seized John by the head, this time with only the good side of his mouth. Albert, frozen in place just feet away, heard the terrible crack as the beast split open his father's skull. No sooner had Wid-dah' pierced the man's cranium, than he dropped John's body to the bloody snow and looked up, first at the quivering boy, then at the enticing meal lying nearby. Making his decision, he leapt…onto the bison carcass. The boy held no interest or threat to him. Shaking and sobbing, the anguished boy finally began to back away, as the preoccupied beast tore off a great chunk of hump meat.

Just as it seemed that the bear had forgotten him, Albert watched Wid-dah' refocus his attention in the boy's direction. It appeared as though the big animal was staring right through him, and he could see the bear's back slowly arch. A blood-chilling snarl again froze the boy in place. His worst fear realized, the beast leaped towards him. Albert's eyes closed shut in anticipation of the end he knew was coming.

At that moment, a shot rang out from over Albert's shoulder, deafening him. Albert's eyes snapped open wide in surprise. The bear was charging now, seemingly right at him. Another shot thundered close to Albert's head. Wid-dah' was just inches away, but bounding past him, not onto him.

Shots were now roaring in quick succession. Albert turned to watch the bear make a long last leap as a final shot boomed. Then it was deathly silent.

The only sound that Albert could hear was a painful high-pitched ringing in his ears. The great bear was lying nearby in the snow, completely still. Albert's head was spinning from the intensity of the last sixty seconds. It was all he could do to stare dumbfounded at the massive brown form lying just feet away.

He was shaken out of his trance by the curious up-and-down bobbing of the grizzly's enormous head. Albert took a terrified step back as he thought, *"Oh no, he's getting back up!"* Scanning his surroundings for a place to escape, the movement became more and more animated. Suddenly, an even more terrifying sight made the boy blanch in fright. Two flailing appendages appeared to grow out of either side of the creature's head.

Spent and incapable of defending himself, he gazed blankly as the two projections seized the bear's head and pushed it to one side. After much struggling and thrashing, a dark green form finally emerged from underneath the front of the hulking body.

Ranger Kathy Powell had just extricated herself from under a quarter-ton of dead grizzly bear.

DISUA

There was vivid red blood everywhere on the
gleaming white snow. A ragged circle of it surrounded the
bodies of John and the bison. An erratic trail of it led from
the corpses thirty or so yards past Albert. A lopsided oval
of it encircled the mound that was the bear. And Kathy
was covered in it. Her forest green uniform was now
mostly brown from it, and the whites of her eyes were the
only part of her face that was not crimson.

Albert, in shock from the trauma of the scene,
stared blankly as Kathy took inventory of her parts. First,
she shook her legs, stomping up and down – *check*. She ran
each hand up and down the opposite arm and rolled her
shoulders in a circle – *check*. She patted her chest and ribs
and sucked in exaggerated breaths – *ouch!* Saving her face
for last and fearing the worst, she ran her fingers over
every inch of it. She probed a vertical gash running from
her left eyebrow for an inch-and-a-half up her forehead –
not life-threatening! She cleared the blood flowing from it into
her left eye with her sleeve. With the fingers of both
hands, she tested her nose; halfway along the bridge there
was a change of direction not there before – *broken!* She
picked bits of tissue and bone from her scalp – *not hers!*
Her checklist complete, she sighed with a hint of relief. It
wasn't until then that she remembered the boy.

It was clear to Kathy that the boy was in shock.
His already pale skin was ghostly white, and he was
shivering and dazed. The ranger was wearing a wool jacket
under her NPS-issued parka. She was perspiring profusely
from her run through the snow and the adrenaline was still

surging through her system. She stripped off the parka and wrapped it around the boy, then looked in all directions, trying to orient herself to familiar landmarks and develop a plan.

Her first priority was to try to stabilize the child, and then she would check on the man that she presumed was deceased, and decide how to get them all out of there. She was a couple of miles from the road and it was doubtful that the two-way radio on her belt would reach anyone at headquarters. Whatever needed to be done, she alone was the one that would have to do it.

Kneeling down to the 12-year-old's level, she began gently, "My name is Kathy, Ranger Kathy. I'm going to take care of you." This seemingly innocuous declaration was meant to reassure the boy, but to Albert, the word "Ranger" triggered fear. His dad had warned him about rangers and what they would do if they caught the pair poaching in the park. The boy's shaking became spasmodic. Kathy had no way of knowing that it was her words that had had this effect on the lad. All she knew was that she needed to get him into a warm vehicle and then get medical help as soon as possible. Leaving him briefly to check on the father, Kathy put two fingers to the man's neck but found no indication of a heartbeat.

Returning to Albert she said, "I will come back for your dad, but for now, I'm going to get you to safety," in a soft, level voice, reaching for his hand. The moment she touched him he collapsed to the ground, writhing in a fit of delirium. "Oh God," Kathy whispered to herself. For lack of a better solution, she lay down on the snow next to him, put her arms around him as he flailed, and held him snugly. After a few minutes, the fit began to subside. In five minutes he had passed out. "This is my chance," she thought, rising to her feet. She hesitated for a minute, evaluating the various ways she might get his limp body back the two miles to the truck, settling on dragging him by the arms across the snow. Snow conditions were in her favor, crusted hard on top. On the other hand, the boy was surprisingly heavy despite his obviously young face. Turning towards the truck, she leaned down and reached behind her for his hands, then began the long slog back to the road.

It was late afternoon before Kathy was close enough for the radio to work. The windshield was steamed up from her labored breathing and she had to wipe it off continuously with the side of her hand to see the road. She had been trying to raise a response on the two-way since she got Albert into the truck. "Ranger in need of assistance, ranger in need of assistance," she called out repeatedly, even now maintaining an admirable level of calm. "Does anyone copy?"

Finally, the radio crackled a reply. "This is Trischman, Kathy," came the steady voice "What's the 10-33?"

Only then did she break down. "Oh God, Harry, I'm so glad it's you!" she cried. "I've got an unconscious boy in my truck, a deceased adult male a mile up Cache Creek from where it meets the Lamar River, a dead bison, and a dead grizzly at the same spot. I'm about 15 minutes from HQ, rolling your way," she sobbed as she finished.

Understanding the gravity of what she was reporting, Harry did his best to model calmness. "10-4, copy that, Kathy, I got every word. I'll have medical help waiting when you get here, and I'll grab another ranger and some emergency supplies and head out to the Lamar to take care of the rest," he stated methodically as his mind raced, for what else he needed to do. "I'll let the superintendent know too. Kathy?" he paused to make sure she was still with him. "How about you dear girl? Are you OK?"

There was a long pause as Kathy collected herself. "I'm a mess, Harry," came the reply, "and I think I peed my pants," she said, with a tearful giggle.

After informing Superintendent Rogers of the situation and arranging for the staff doctor to meet Kathy when she arrived, Harry rushed to prepare for whatever conditions awaited him on Cache Creek.

With the help of Ranger Mike Ryan, Harry quickly loaded his truck with all of the additional gear he thought he might need based on Kathy's description of the scene. In addition to the standard emergency gear that they always packed with them, they loaded a full-size stretcher and two pairs of Nordic skis into the truck bed and double-checked all of their flashlights and cold weather gear. Finally, they both checked the clips on their pistols and packed two rifles and a shotgun in the cab.

Just as Harry and Mike were about to pull out, Kathy turned into the parking lot. The moment she parked the truck, the doctor pushed a gurney to the passenger side ready to take the boy. Looking past the boy at Kathy with alarm, he said, "Good lord, woman! I wasn't informed I'd have two patients...you need to be looked at. Can you walk?"

"Yessir," Kathy said crisply, "I just dragged this boy two miles through the snow, so I think I can make it across the parking lot."

Not satisfied with her answer, the doctor waved to Harry who was walking over to check on things. "You, Trischman," he shouted, "help this young lady to the infirmary, please!"

"With pleasure, sir," saluted the senior ranger.

While Mike Ryan helped the doctor load Albert's limp form onto the gurney, Harry carefully put one hand on Kathy's shoulder. The other hand gently cupped her chin and slowly turned her head from side to side as he assessed the damage.

"Well," he said warmly, "looks like you topped ol' Paint Pot Peg! Matter of fact, I can't remember a male ranger this bloody!" he chuckled under his breath. "What the hell happened, darlin'?"

"Oh Harry!" she sighed as she leaned on him for the walk to the infirmary. "It all seems like a dream, a bad one! I was checking out the Lamar for winter kills when I heard a gunshot up Cache Creek. Suspecting a poacher, I hiked toward the shot. Just as I came out of the trees into a small meadow, I saw two men butchering a buffalo, then a second later I watched as a griz came out of the opposite side, running straight at them. It all happened so fast! The griz had the man's head in his mouth and the other man, the boy, just stood there frozen."

"I came up right behind the boy and pulled my service pistol; the bear saw me and charged. I emptied the gun into him as he came. I guess the last shot did him in, but not until he'd tackled me, knocking the gun into my face and, I think, breaking a rib or two."

Harry whistled, saying, "Damn girl, you're one cool cucumber and a tough one at that! I bet there's not another ranger on the payroll that coulda' held it together like you did. Now get in there and get that pretty face patched up...and take a few days off - that's an order! I'll look in on the boy and mop up the mess on Cache Creek. Darned poachers, I guess it wouldn't be Christian to say 'it served him right'?"

"Don't worry, Harry, I'm guessing there's not a lot of good Christians out poaching buffalo in National Parks." They shared a knowing smile and Harry hurried back to the truck.

As the doctor stitched Kathy's wound, she inquired about the boy.

"We've got him wrapped in blankets and have him on a warm IV drip," replied the doctor. "He's still unconscious but all of his vital signs look normal. This is an extreme response to emotional trauma, but not unprecedented, Kathy," he said as he carefully pulled the gash together with another stitch.

"Is it okay if I look in on him for a bit?" she asked, unconcerned about her own injuries.

"That's fine, my dear, but then you need to get some rest. I stitched your forehead up as prettily as my limited talent will allow. There's not much we can do about the nose, but frankly, I don't think it's that bad. We'll know better once the swelling subsides - you're going to have a couple of nice shiners for a few days," he said in a fatherly tone. "Those ribs are going to make it tough to sleep or cough or laugh or, well just about everything's going to make them hurt. I'm going to give you some pills for the pain; they should help you sleep." Going to a cabinet, he shook out a couple of long white tablets and handed them to Kathy with a cup of water. That's a good girl," he said, as Kathy downed the pills.

In a hurry to check on the boy, she winced as she stood. "Want to take a look at those stitches now, Kathy?" the doctor asked, offering her a mirror.

"No thanks, doc, I've had enough trauma for one day!" she replied with a dubious grin.

Albert was still on a gurney in an adjacent room but was now bundled in blue blankets with an infusion bag attached by a clear plastic tube to his right arm. He was a handsome boy with an abundance of freckles, and hair the color of carrots. He was well-built but his face still had the soft edges of a pre-teen. His red hair was long and Kathy instinctively brushed a lock that hung over his eyes back onto his forehead.

She wondered just what it was that had led him to the Lamar. She assumed that he was the son of the man he had been with and that they had poached the bison cow they had been butchering. But where had they come from, and why were they there in mid-winter?

As she began to stretch her arms in preparation for a yawn, she winced in pain. "Ouch," she squeaked, reflexively hunching her shoulders to stop the ache. As the pain medication began to take effect, she realized that she was tired, bone-tired. Slumping in a padded chair, her chin dipped to her chest and she fell into a hard sleep.

It was hours later when she eventually roused, grimacing as she straightened up. Glancing around, she was confused. Was it just the fog of waking or had the room changed since she fell asleep? The gurney was still there, as was the stand holding the IV solution, but the blankets were in a pile on the floor and the boy was gone. "Doctor?" she called loudly. "Doctor?!!" she called again in a louder voice.

The doctor opened the door, looked at the gurney, looked at Kathy, looked back at the gurney, and said, "I'll be damned!" then turned and strode down the hallway. Kathy could hear him opening and closing doors as he checked the restroom, supply room, and finally all the closets. She heard him walk to the exit door, then after a minute she heard him re-enter and his footsteps returned towards her. He entered the room scratching his head. "He's not here, anywhere!" he said to Kathy perplexedly.

"Dang Harry!" said Ranger Mike Ryan, "I'da shit my drawers for sure," he commented, as the two surveyed the hole that Kathy had dug out from beneath the bear.

"I told you, Mike, she's one in a million," Harry replied with a broad grin.

"What was this old boar doin' out of his den at this time of year, I wonder?" Mike mused.

"First let's figure out what the dolgurn poacher was doing, then we'll come back tomorrow to figure out what Mr. Griz was thinkin'," answered Harry.

They had already checked the man's body for life, surprised to find him relatively intact but clearly deceased. Aside from the large holes in his skull, and the empty eye sockets where the magpies had feasted soon after Kathy departed, his clothing was undisturbed but there was no I.D. in any of his pockets. "John Doe for now," Mike shrugged.

Following the tracks of the two towards the trees, they came upon the well-camouflaged tent. Upon entering, the rangers pinched their noses. A pile of small animal skins had a strong, disagreeable stench. "Damned trappers!" Harry spat. "Those are the public's animals there. Why'd they have to do this in my park?" he asked rhetorically.

"Wow, that's quite a haul," said Ranger Mike. "They've obviously been at this for a while."

"Can't wait to get the boy's story," said Trischman sternly.

After taking a quick inventory of the evidence, Harry warned, "It's gonna get dark and real cold here shortly; we'd better haul the body outta here now and come back for everything else tomorrow. I'd sure like to figure out the extent of this operation."

"Yeah," added Mike, "and how the bear got mixed up in it."

Rolling the body onto the stretcher, Harry took the front and Mike the rear. Carrying a stretcher on cross-country skis was an awkward project, and the pair had to stop often to readjust their grips. It was dark by the time they loaded the body into the back of the Ford.

"At least we don't have to worry about keeping him warm," Mike quipped and Harry chuckled at the dark humor. After an uneventful drive back to Mammoth, Harry left Mike to hand off the body to the Sheriff's Department while he went to check on Kathy.

"Well, if that don't beat all!" was Trischman's response to finding that the boy was missing. "He can't have gone far on foot. I guess I'll be putting in some O.T.

tonight looking for him. I'll see if I can get some assistance from the Sheriff."

"Can I help?" asked Kathy with concern.

"Not a chance, ranger, you're officially restricted to quarters until further notice!"

Neither had any way of knowing that Albert was already miles away, stowed away in the back of a tourist's station wagon headed to somewhere in Montana.

PÜHÜPPÜH

Months had passed since Kathy's encounter with the bear and the boy. Rangers Trischman and Ryan had found and removed all of John's traps, many of which held dead or injured animals. They speculated that the poachers had come from the Cooke City area but couldn't be sure at first. The mystery of the bear was solved when they retraced its tracks back to the collapsed den.

It had taken them three days to pack out all of the furs, traps, and personal effects of the law-breakers. They did a field autopsy on the bear and retrieved six bullets, three from the bear's head. "Never missed a single shot!" Harry chuckled, blood up to his elbows.

"Amazing! The legend grows!" said Ryan, shaking his head.

During her recuperation, Kathy was visited by many well-wishers: Edna from the gift shop, Superintendent Rogers, all of her fellow rangers, and a surprise visitor.

"Look who the cat dragged in!" announced Harry one afternoon, followed closely by a familiar face.

"Po!" Kathy beamed when she saw him.

"I was here to do some research when I heard about the legendary grizzly slayer!" Po laughed. "So I thought I'd better get some of that warrior energy from you. If you were an Indian in the old days, we'd have held a big feast to honor your bravery."

"There's nothing courageous about just trying to save your own skin," Kathy giggled, minimizing the accomplishment. The three of them sat and chatted for a long time, rekindling their friendship, until Po had to leave.

In the days that followed, Kathy had penned and mailed several long letters to Robert. Robert's Seabee unit had been moved onto the European continent in 1943, and many of his friends had been killed in the heavy bombardment of the cargo handling facilities that Robert's unit had built and defended in Anzio, Italy. From there Robert's team had been sent to Londonderry in Northern Ireland to work on the construction of a Naval Air Station. Although the news indicated that the war in Europe was going well, she was becoming concerned that she hadn't heard from him for a while. She made light of the grizzly story in her letter, not wanting to worry him, although she did mention breaking her nose so that he wouldn't be shocked when he saw her next. She wrote mostly about the beauty of the park and how she wished she could experience it with him.

It was now early February and Kathy was itching to get back to work. The doctor had in fact done a nice job on the stitches on her forehead, and in time one would have to look closely to detect the scar. The bruising around her eyes had faded in a week and with it the swelling of her nose, which now had an almost undetectable small bump at the top of the bridge. "Doc says the ribs are just bruised, not broken," she explained to Trischman proudly. "Can I at least help with the investigation?"

Harry soon relented, saying, "Okay, but no patrolling for now - phone calls and door knocking only."

Kathy took the investigation seriously. Her two objectives were to find out who the adult poacher had been and where the boy had gone. Her inquiries eventually led her to a fur buyer in Bozeman. With Trischman's permission, Kathy drove the Park Service pickup to a rural neighborhood on the outskirts of the handsome Montana community.

A sign next to the driveway advertising "We Buy Furs!" told Kathy she had found the place. After first knocking on the front door twice with no response, she could hear sounds coming from a barn behind the home. Walking back along the driveway to the barn, she said loudly, "Hello, anyone home? Hello!"

The tinkering in the barn stopped and the door swung open. A man in overalls and a heavy canvas jacket looked curiously at Kathy in her green uniform and asked cordially, "Help ya' ma'am?"

"Thank you, yessir," Kathy said in her most non-threatening voice. "I have some furs here. I wondered if you could look at them for me?"

Focusing on her badge, his eyebrows raised in surprise, then lowered as though perplexed. "Name's Chet Andrews, ma'am," he began. "Pardon my surprise, but I don't normally get Yellowstone employees tryin' to sell me furs!"

"Oh no, I'm sorry to confuse you, Mr. Andrews, I'm not selling, I'm conducting an investigation," she explained. "My name's Kathy, ummm, Ranger Powell. I'm investigating the death of a man who was illegally trapping in the park."

A look of concern came over the man's face. "I don't want any trouble, Ranger Powell. I run an honest business. I don't know anything about poaching in the park."

"I'm sure you don't, sir, and I wouldn't expect you to," Kathy replied quickly, not wanting to worry the man. "After all, you have no way of knowing where a fur comes from, right? I mean, you're not required to ask people where they got their furs, are you?"

"That's correct ma'am, there's nothing that indicates where a fur mighta' come from, not a thing," he said, as though convincing himself that he was not culpable in any way.

"Good! Then would you mind having a look at these furs and telling me if you see anything unusual or distinctive about them?" Kathy asked sweetly.

Pondering it for another second, Andrews finally said, "Be happy to, ma'am. Bring 'em on in. Do you need some help?"

Using a wheelbarrow, the fur buyer helped Kathy get a large pile of mixed furs from the truck into the barn. The majority of the pelts were pine martens and coyotes, with a dozen or so lovely red foxes mixed in. As he laid the pelts out on two long tables in the center, he instinctively separated them first by species and then by quality, giving Kathy an education in fur-grading as he did so.

"Using the fox pelts as an example, you first separate by color type – he's got all three here: red, silver, and cross, the majority of them being red foxes." Clearly enjoying being the teacher he went on, "Then I separate by length, then by shade, you see how this one red fox is a dark red and this one is pale?" Kathy nodded. "The dark red is worth a lot more money. Then there's density; unless they're trapped in the warmer months almost all of our Montana foxes have a dense underwool because of the cold winters. We call that a heavy coat, worth more," he said as he had Kathy run her fingers through the fur. "Finally there's quality," he said grabbing two of the pelts. "See how this one is finely haired throughout? This would be judged 'First' quality. And now look at the areas where the hair is very sparse on this one," he said, pointing to nearly hairless patches of skin. "This would be graded as 'second' or even 'slightly damaged'."

"Wow, I had no idea it was so complex," smiled Kathy, preparing to ask the big question. "Sooo, from what you see here, Mr. Andrews, does it tell you anything about the man who trapped or prepared them?"

"Hmmm," pondered Andrews. As he rolled over the pelts and examined each one closely, she watched as his eyebrows arched with a hint of recognition. "Hmm," he said again, this time followed by, "I do see something here that's a little unusual, but I see it once in a while." He stopped again as though searching his memory. "All of these have two things in common, neither is all that unusual - but the combination of the two is."

At that, he picked up both a fox pelt and a pine marten pelt and held them out for Kathy to examine. "The first is the legs or the lack of them. Most of my sellers are diligent about cutting right down to the footpad, so you get all of the hair. But this trapper cuts way up high on the leg," showing Kathy the stubby cuts on both species. "It's just a shortcut that doesn't affect the value all that much, but I don't think it looks as nice." Kathy nodded her head in agreement.

"Now here's the other thing," he started back up, getting excited. "See this ragged loop hanging off the heads?" he asked, flopping a loose piece of skin back and forth on the two pelts. "That's the animal's lower jaw, useless to a furrier. Very few of my guys leave that on, skinning it out is extra work!"

"So here we have a trapper who's in a hurry to cut the legs off, but at the same time, takes time to skin out the lower jaw." He stopped, took off his cap and scratched his scalp, then put his cap back on and said, "I can only think of one guy who brought in his pelts this way."

"Do you remember his name?" Kathy asked anxiously.

Now combing out his short beard with his fingers, he took a minute and finally said, "Nope. And no idea where he's from. He came in here once, sometimes twice a year for a number of years. I paid him in cash. Quiet guy, always had his family with him. Wife and two boys, all of them except the father had flaming red hair."

He could see Kathy's eyes go wide upon hearing about the family. "Does that help, ma'am?" Andrews asked sincerely.

"Yes, it helps very much, Mr. Andrews. It sounds just like our dead trapper," confided Powell. "One of his red-headed sons was with him when he was killed. The boy was traumatized. We were treating him at the infirmary and then – poof, he disappeared. I'd like to wrap up the investigation and see if there is any other evidence, but more than that, I'd like to know that the boy is okay."

"Well, I'm no detective, Ranger Powell," Andrews offered, "but seeing the way those folks was dressed, and the condition of the truck he drove, I'd say they can't be very far away from either the park or Bozeman, somewhere between would be my guess. And they didn't seem like town folks either. I think they'd be livin' off in the sticks."

"Great information, Mr. Andrews," Kathy replied earnestly. "Perhaps you should be a detective!"

"I'll stick to grading pelts, ma'am," the fur buyer laughed. "They're much easier to figure out than people!"

Kathy thanked him for his time, and he helped her cart the furs back to the truck. "If, after your investigation, you want to sell those furs," he suggested, "you know where to find me."

"Thank you sir, but I'm guessing the Park Service won't go for that," she answered. "Good luck to you and thanks again."

Soon afterward, she was back to her regular ranger duties and patrol, though Harry allowed Kathy one day a week to continue her search for the boy. Over the next three months, she inquired about the red-haired family in every town, and at every ranch and business between Bozeman and Gardiner. A few people recalled seeing them but no one knew who they were or where they lived.

One afternoon in early June, upon returning to headquarters, she found many of her fellow rangers gathered around the large radio console. "What is it?" Kathy asked apprehensively.

"It's D-Day, Kathy!" answered Mike Ryan. "It's an all-out assault by the allies, it's 'do-or-die.'" They listened with rapt attention as BBC announcer John Snagge provided a comprehensive accounting of all known facts: Eisenhower was in command of naval forces landing allied armies on the coast of France near Normandy, saying "we will expect nothing less than a full victory".

While the news was thrilling and promising, all Kathy could think about was Robert.

She would not learn until months later that Robert had served heroically during the invasion of Normandy. Robert's battalion had been among the first to arrive on Omaha beach in the predawn darkness of June 6, 1944. Their assignment was to demolish the hazardous steel landing craft obstructions known as "Czech Hedgehogs" that had been erected by the Germans to deter an invasion. As night became day, the Seabees came under heavy German attack. Robert had survived the initial onslaught and surged up the beach to work on dismantling or detonating the landmines hidden beneath the sands. His efforts and those of his fellow C.B.s paved the way for thousands of troops and vehicles to land, and ultimately wrest Europe back from the Nazis.

Regrettably, it was not from Robert that she learned of his heroism.

On June 10, a telegram arrived addressed to "Mrs. Kathy Powell, Yellowstone National Park, WY". Sensing the worst, her fellow rangers excused themselves or feigned distraction as Kathy read the first few words, "The Navy Department deeply regrets to inform you..." Shaking back her strawberry blonde curls and cocking her chin, she strode to the back door and stepped outside, where she spent the next ten minutes crying quietly.

OMAHKAPI'SI

Life in the Canadian Rockies near Jasper, Alberta was no easier for Omah than it had been for Asa, her grandmother from five generations earlier, in Yellowstone.

Asa herself had never traveled as far as the mountains surrounding Jasper National Park. After fleeing north into Canada, she had finally found a pair of young male wolves near Mt. Assiniboine on the Alberta and British Columbia border. The brothers had struck out from their pack near Banff to the north. They were looking to either join a new pack with more upward mobility or start one of their own. The brothers were both black. The smaller of the two, Inak, had a white blaze on his chest, and the larger, Sspii, sported brownish patches on his shoulders and hips. Though smaller than his sibling, Inak was clearly the leader of the two – the brains of the operation.

It had proven to be the best possible result for Asa after her long, harrowing journey. The brothers were immediately receptive to the company of the female, and it saved Asa from the inherent danger of attempting to join an established pack. When February rolled around and Asa came into heat, there was already a strong pair bond with Inak, the result of which was the birth of five handsome pups in early May.

Asa and Inak became the alpha pair of a successful pack that grew to include fifteen wolves including the offspring of two litters of their own and three other wolves which had joined from other packs. Three years after the birth of their first set of pups, a strong-willed black female from that litter named Sikimi broke away from the pack. With her was one of the three wolves who had recently joined the group, a light gray and brown male named Apoyi.

Sikimi and Apoyi traveled together to the distant Kootenay River, where in the early spring of 1931 they bred and began their own family. The Kootenay Valley was lush, game-rich, and sparsely populated by humans. Other packs also occupied the long curving valley but were spread out enough that conflicts over boundaries rarely surfaced. Their pups thrived until their first winter when an epidemic of mange weakened them and three of the four froze to death from the loss of their winter coats. The remaining pup, a mostly brown male named Sikotahko, was only slightly affected by the mange and remained healthy and robust. The following spring, the alphas produced another litter, this time of six pups. The mange that had doomed their first litter had been cyclical. These pups had a successful first winter of watching their parents and older brother hunt elk and bighorn sheep.

In their third spring together, Sikimi again became pregnant. On the day she gave birth to the year's pups, Sikotahko struck out on his own, the pack beginning to be too large for him. Heading northeast, he crossed the continental divide and wandered into the valley of the Bow River in western Alberta. After trying to join one group near Johnston Canyon and sustaining a nasty bite in the process, he turned north towards Lake Louise. Here he encountered a more receptive pack that had recently lost its alpha male after his jaw was broken by a bull moose. There was much posturing and jostling among the males of the floundering clan, but the females were anxious for new genetic material. The widowed alpha bitch immediately began siding with the handsome brown male against all comers. Soon it was clear that the tundra-colored head female named Niimiapii had chosen Sikotahko as her future partner.

The Bow River Valley presented several challenges to the pack and its new alpha pair. The Trans-Canada highway bisected the valley and while the tourist traffic during the summer was dangerous, the winter traffic was an even greater interruption to their hunting activities. To remedy this, Sikotahko led his family farther north, away from the human crowds, and established a new territory near Hector Lake. The alphas finally consummated their union with Niimiapii's estrus in the spring of 1936, adding four new hunters to the pack.

Game was abundant and people were few around Hector Lake. It was fortunate that no other packs currently hunted the area. Sikotahko and their progeny flourished and the family swelled. After four years of a trouble-free existence, another pack discovered the area. Led by an aggressive gray and white male named Oksina, the rival family attacked the entrenched Hector Lake pack without warning. Sikotahko, at eight years old, was not as strong as he had been in his youth and had not had to fight for years. Oksina went straight for Sikotahko and mercilessly clenched down on his throat until he was dead. The vanquished clan was confused and many immediately rolled on their backs as a show of submission to their new leader. The remainder of the pack headed north in a panic, unwilling to join the hostile victors.

The four defectors, two male and two female siblings, roamed the Bow River north, crossed Bow Pass, and generally followed the path of Hwy. 93 to the Northern Saskatchewan River. Here they encountered a massive white wolf with rusty highlights named Apisoyiinat. Api, a strong and smart two-year-old, had left his family to the north near Jasper, anxious to form a pack of his own. In his first encounter with the four wandering Hector Lake wolves, he quickly established his dominance over the two males and impressed the two females.

Of the two bitches, coal-black Matsi was the obvious ascendant. It was the beginning of another winter and the five wolves immediately began hunting as a cohesive team, killing many moose and staying strong throughout the cold months. As expected, when the she-wolf's estrus season began in February, Api and Matsi bred and produced a large litter of six pups, five blacks, and one white.

Thus began the long reign of Api and Matsi. Traveling east along the Northern Saskatchewan River to Abraham Lake, they had settled into miles of unoccupied wolf habitat and hunted far and wide both up and downstream. Api was unusually healthy at eight years of age when the pack's troubles began.

To the east, the mountains gave way to the plains, and in the plains not only was there abundant big game but there were also sheep and cattle. At nearly thirty wolves, the pack had grown so large that it was hunting farther and farther afield. They soon discovered that taking a Suffolk ewe or a Hereford calf presented a far lower risk of injury than trying to take down a moose or elk. When the Abraham Lake pack began taking calves and lambs near the west-central Alberta town of Rocky Mountain House, both ranchers and hunters began a concerted campaign to eliminate wolves from the region.

Hunting over bait gave shooters the odious satisfaction of watching the animal die, but it was an ineffective way to kill a large number of wolves. In 1948, a rabies outbreak in Canada was blamed on wolves, and the government encouraged full-scale eradication, issuing 39,960 cyanide guns, 106,000 cyanide cartridges, and 628,000 strychnine pellets.

Api, now nearly ten years old, had finally relinquished leadership of the pack to his four-year-old son, Siikapi, in a peaceful transfer of power. Siikapi, a dark gray wolf, was a brash commander who led by example. One day, while leading a large hunting party near the small town of Horburg, the wolves came upon three dead steers in close proximity. Sensing danger, the young alpha hung back but was having a hard time convincing the lesser pack members to follow his example. As a measure of his leadership, he alone circled all three carcasses, sniffing cautiously. Convinced that there was no threatening scent, he tentatively pulled at a bit of intestine bulging out of a gash along a steer's belly. There was a snapping sound and a cloud of mist enveloped the gray leader's head as he yipped and put his muzzle between his feet to try to wipe off the offending spray.

Advertised as "Humane Coyote Getters", M-44s or "cyanide bombs" were, in fact, cruel and indiscriminate devices designed to spray cyanide gas into the mouth of any animal who took the bait: hawk, badger, fox, or in this case, wolf. The cyanide shuts down the body's ability to utilize oxygen, leading to a frantic, agonizing suffocation.

The pack, frightened by the triggering of the device and the uncharacteristic contortions of their leader, had backed off and watched as Siikapi struggled for air. When he flopped to the ground in a seizure, they realized their danger and turned to the west at a run. Their path took them right past where the members of the local "sportsmen" club lay in hiding behind a blind of hay bales. All at once, the shooters opened fire on the now leaderless pack. Confused about where the shots were coming from, individuals ran back and forth, providing their assassins with numerous opportunities. When the shooting finally stopped, seven more wolves lay dead not far from where Siikapi had died. Six had somehow escaped death though two of them were injured.

Returning to where the pack had been staging for their hunts near the village of Nordegg, the group was in mournful chaos. For days after the attack they were listless and forlorn, reluctant to even go hunt. It was here, gathered together in grief, that the government hunters found them. The "war-on-wolves' had ramped up, and the large and effective Abraham Lake pack had gotten the government's attention. A group of ten 'deputized' Dominion Wildlife Service agents had been recruited to rout out the entrenched wolf band. Setting up around the last known den used by the family, the hunters waited for the clan to assemble. The mustered gunners had multiple family members in their scopes, and at a signal from their commander, they fired as a unit, instantly killing another eight wolves. Those who had survived the first volley disappeared into the woods. Among the dead were Api and Matsi, and in an instant, the Abraham Lake pack was no more.

The panicked survivors headed out in various directions, in singles, doubles, and a few larger groups. They were of mixed ages, genders, and social statuses. All they knew was fright and flight. Many never saw each other again, and some did not stop fleeing for days.

A group of three, year-and-a-half old youngsters, led by a long and lithe white and brown female named Omah ran continuously to the north. Inexperienced hunters, they made up for their lack of skill with determined enthusiasm, surviving on hares, rodents, and even a beaver that they caught out in the open. Under Omah's leadership, the group covered the nearly two hundred miles to the Athabasca River in present-day Jasper National Park.

Here, in the center of a large knot of mountains and valleys, far from the temptations of human settlements on the eastern prairie, the three grew to become accomplished hunters through trial and error and good luck. After surviving a mild early winter together in the park, a shining black male wolf named Nuni wandered into their territory in early February. The three immediately tested him; when they ran at him, he ran away, but only as far as needed to check their resolve. Then Nuni ran at the three, and the three gave ground. Finally, all four strode slowly towards each other with heads and tails held high. The black wanderer tolerated the invasive sniffing of the resident wolves, and they tolerated his. There was no fear, nor submission from either side. Without warning, Omah jumped onto Nuni's back – playfully. Not only was there acceptance of the handsome northerner, there was a definite pre-estrus attraction. In a matter of weeks, Nuni and Omah would conceive. A new generation of wolves whose lineage could be traced back to the Lamar Valley became the dominant wolf pack of Jasper National Park.

POTUHUCH

The intricacies of lineage and bloodlines among herd ungulates such as elk are complex. One bull inseminates many cows and fathers many calves. A single dominant bull will breed 15-20 cows annually, producing roughly the same number of offspring. In sixteen months, the female offspring will be ready to be bred for the first time, as will the original cows. The males, on the other hand, cannot breed until their third year, and then only if they can out-compete more mature bulls for breeding rights. Each female can produce one, occasionally twin, calves each year, while each male can father 15-20 calves annually. These herd dynamics can lead to exponential growth in a short time. In a documented study, a herd of thirty-two wild elk living under natural conditions grew to five hundred in twenty years. Domestically raised elk under optimal conditions, without hunting, disease, or predation can double their herd size roughly every four years.

So it was that most, if not all, of the elk in the Northern Yellowstone herd of the Lamar Valley shared a common ancestry which included Ishii and Chili before her. Much more surprising was that eventually elk in North Carolina, Pennsylvania, California's Channel Islands, Argentina, and even New Zealand shared Yellowstone DNA.

In 1933, NPS biologists were called into Yellowstone to check on the condition of the park's rangeland habitat. The resultant report was bleak; the biologists found that in the span of just a few decades, the condition of the range was "deplorable". The culprits:

large, prolific herd animals living virtually predator-free and protected from recreational hunting. Once again, Yellowstone National Park rangers were put in the unenviable position of both protecting and killing wildlife. For the next thirty-four years, Yellowstone's elk management plan incorporated three major elements.

First, allowing recreational hunting along the park's northern border with Montana – where most of the Northern Yellowstone herd spent their winters.

A second element was for park rangers to become the de facto hunters inside the park boundaries.

A third component would be for park personnel to trap them in elaborately constructed "corral traps". The animals would then be packed in padded cages, crates, or stock trailers and shipped to other parks, zoos, farms, hunting reserves, and even foreign countries near and far.

It was this third element that led to the surprisingly distant distribution of *Cervus canadensis nelsoni*, or Rocky Mountain Elk.

HAYANGENAA

It was mid-winter and Hayangenaa, the patriarch of a herd of eighteen cow and calf elk, was becoming uncomfortably thin from a large snowpack that made it difficult to reach good forage. In the parlance of trophy hunters, the majestic bull was what is called an "imperial", meaning that he sported seven points on each antler, larger than a six-point "royal" but not as massive as an eight-point "monarch".

It was early January and there were still two months left until the male would naturally shed this year's antlers in preparation for growing even larger ones next year. As challenging as winter conditions were for the elk, they were ideal for the Park Service biologists who were charged with trapping them. The temporary double corral they had erected had been baited with sweet alfalfa hay to lure the hungry elk inside. To overcome the natural suspicion that the animals had of the manmade structures, the sides were made of woven wire so that they could still see outside of the enclosure. A quarter of a mile of cable had been strung from the entry gate to a copse of trees, where three seasoned biologists waited to spring a trap.

As is typical of mature bull elk, Hayangenaa waited for the cows to enter the enclosure before he risked stepping inside. As soon as he did his suspicions were confirmed, when the rangers pulled the cable that tripped the latch that allowed the gate to snap shut. The bull and his cows panicked, running in a circle around the perimeter of the enclosure. The experienced biologists knew that they must act quickly, but move calmly to avoid terrorizing the herd. After raising the gate to the second round corral, they walked slowly back to the main entry gate. Here they silently waved their arms to alarm the elk just enough to move them through the gate to the fully fenced second corral.

Waiting for the group in the secondary corral was more hay to take their minds off of the biologists. Left alone for the time being, the herd eventually calmed down again and began feeding peacefully on the alfalfa. Their captors left them unmolested overnight in preparation for the following day's stress of loading and shipping them.

Early the next morning, the biologists backed the large livestock trailer, or "bull-hauler", up to the ramp that was attached by a chute to the corral where the elk were being held. The gate to the chute was opened while one of the men climbed atop the opposite side of the corral and the elk naturally fled through the chute and up the ramp into the 53-foot trailer. As expected and hoped for, the last animal left in the pen was Hayangenaa.

From atop the fence, one of the biologists took aim with a compressed gas dart gun, loaded with a 50mm ballistic syringe filled with an appropriate dose of Etorphine hydrochloride.

Squeezing the trigger, there was only a 'whoosh' as the compression expelled the dart into the bull. The momentum of a steel ball at the rear of the dart pushed the syringe plunger and injected the dose of barbiturate into the animal.

In a short time the magnificent animal was humbled, and sank first to his knees and then rolled slowly onto his side. As soon as he was laying down all three men climbed cautiously into the enclosure and went to work on him. Cognizant of the potentially lethal effect that the stress of the incident could have on a wild creature, they worked efficiently and silently. While one immobilized the animal's head and covered his eyes, another produced a large bone saw and began methodically sawing through the thick bases of the antlers. Although the bull would naturally shed the antlers in another two months, the four-foot-wide growths were a dangerous liability inside the crowded livestock trailer. Removing them just inches above their base would not harm the animal. Once the removal was completed, the bases were coated with an antiseptic paste as a precaution against any infection. After checking the otherwise healthy animal for general soundness, an antidote to the tranquilizer was administered and the biologists left the pen. Within minutes the bull raised his head, wide-eyed with apprehension. After a couple of tries, he regained his feet and stood wobbling in place. The men stayed out of sight while he reoriented himself spatially. Once he appeared fully recovered they mounted the fence opposite the gate, as the bull sought the refuge of the chute and the ramp into the trailer and a calming reunion with his cows.

With the entire herd now secure in the trailer, the truck was started and the diesel idled for a few minutes as the men made their final preparations. Finally, the truck pulled out for its long non-stop journey. The elk needed to be transported as quickly as possible to their destination, as the longer they were in the truck, the greater the chances of physical injury or emotional trauma. To assure this, the two men in the cab would take turns driving the 30 hours to their destination, stopping only when needed for gas and coffee.

The last eastern elk, a subspecies of elk that were abundant along the Atlantic Coast of the United States before European colonization, was killed in Pennsylvania in 1877. For more than 35 years, the iconic mammals were essentially extinct east of the Mississippi. By 1912, the boom and bust cycle of abundance and starvation among the elk of the Rocky Mountain west was a well-known phenomenon. The government was already appealing to other regions to take some of the pesky ungulates off of their hands. Seeing an opportunity to restore their lost biological diversity, and by no means blind to the potential revenue possibilities of reintroducing a large game animal into their wildlands, the state of Pennsylvania jumped at the opportunity. The state readily paid thirty dollars per head for their first shipment of Yellowstone elk in 1913 and supplemented that supply for many years to come.

When Hayangenaa and his band stampeded away from the stock trailer that had been their home for 1,900 grueling miles, they were completely disoriented. The Allegheny National Forest near Johnsonburg, Pennsylvania was as different from the plains and woods of the Lamar Valley as it could be. Even though it was the middle of winter, there was no snow on the ground. At an elevation of 1,325 feet, the air was thick compared to the thin oxygen of their 6,500-foot-high home range. Making directly for the shelter of the woods, they found that the trees were all foreign to them – gone were the lodgepole and whitebark pines, Engleman and white spruce of the forested hillsides. Here were all deciduous trees: beeches, oaks, maples, cherry, and ash, and between the trees grew dense tangles of rhododendrons. In the open spaces where they would ordinarily graze on wheatgrass, brome, bunchgrass, and fescue, they found instead Indian grass, switchgrass, and bluestem, or non-native introduced rough bluegrass and hardy pampas grass.

Fortunately for the transplants, they possessed a higher level of adaptability than many animals. Their prehistoric predecessors had crossed the Bering Land Bridge from their ancestral homeland in Eurasia. Eons later they moved south from what is now Canada, as ice-age glaciers began to retreat from the North American continent. This hardiness provided Yellowstone elk the resilience they needed to quickly adapt to their Pennsylvania home. Within months of their release, only three of the clan had died due to their lack of knowledge of the local flora, having foraged on the highly lethal poison hemlock plant abundant in the area. The remaining sixteen animals had made the switch from montane rangeland to the temperate deciduous forest with surprising ease.

It should not have surprised anyone that the same pattern of events that led to the government thinning of the Yellowstone herds would replay in the farmlands of Pennsylvania. Keystone State hunters were thrilled, of course, to have an oversized alternative to the diminutive white-tailed deer that had been their only option for many years. Farmers, on the other hand, were immediately outraged at the depredations inflicted upon their crops by the growing herds of reintroduced grazers. In the once-productive cornfields adjacent to the elk woodlands, farmers complained of elk eating just two inches off of the ends of every ear of corn in their field to get at the silk, thereby completely destroying the crop.

But unlike in Yellowstone, recreational hunting was allowed throughout Pennsylvania's National Forests. After much trial and error, a sustainable harvest number was achieved that kept both hunters and farmers generally satisfied, while eliminating the need for further imports from the Rockies.

Hayangeneaa had unknowingly done his part to continue to disperse the Lamar Valley bloodline in the east, where elk had long since disappeared. At the same time, on the opposite side of the country, another of Yellowstone lineage was expanding the reach of the Rocky Mountain elk.

WAHATEHWE

"The ones on the right are threes and fours, Bing. The one you want is on the far left. He's a big, thick-horned six-by-six," whispered guide, Eddy Vail, who also happened to be the manager of the sprawling 51,000 acre Vail & Vickers Ranch on California's Santa Rosa Island. By "threes and fours" he meant smaller three-point and four-point bull elk, sometimes referred to as 'raghorns' or 'satellite bulls' as opposed to the big six-point 'herd bull'.

Like other well-to-do hunters of the time, Bing had made the short twenty-seven-mile flight from Ventura to the island to hunt the exotic species there. At fifteen miles long by ten miles wide, Santa Rosa is the second largest of the eight Channel Islands off of California's southern coast. The islands were originally inhabited by the Chumash people, who were eventually removed to the mainland by the Spanish. In missions and on farms they were assimilated or perished from the white man's diseases. The island chain also served as a regular stopping-off point for the explorers and traders who plied the coast beginning in the eighteenth and nineteenth centuries. The sailors couldn't know and likely wouldn't have cared that the goats, pigs, sheep, dogs, cats, and rats that they introduced to these pristine islands would eventually wreak an ecological catastrophe. Twentieth century inhabitants of the islands continued the dubious tradition of introducing non-native species: ranching cattle and sheep on several islands, importing bison to Santa Catalina to film a western, and stocking Kaibab Plateau mule deer and three subspecies of elk. Rocky Mountain elk, Roosevelt elk and Tule elk had been planted on Santa Rosa Island for hunting. It was the elk that Bing had come to hunt.

The first mention of elk on Santa Rosa appeared in the Santa Barbara News Press in 1879, referring to a lone cow elk, failing to mention where it had originated from. By 1905 the number of elk on the island stood at seventeen. Over the next half century, the Santa Rosa herd was supplemented by shipments of all three subspecies of North American elk: tule elk came from California's central valley, Roosevelt elk were barged in from Washington's Olympic Peninsula, and Rocky Mountain elk were transported by rail from Yellowstone National Park.

One of the Yellowstone transplants was a handsome bull by the name of Wahatehwe. When he first arrived by boat on the island as a three-point raghorn, he was sickly and gaunt from the trip – first by train from Montana to Ventura, then by boat for three hours to the pier on Santa Rosa, where he was lifted awkwardly in a net by a crane and deposited onto the pier. The Vail and Vickers cowboys doctored him and the other eleven elk that had suffered the trip with him. After holding the new additions in a cattle pen for a few days to allow them to acclimate and recuperate, the wranglers drove them east, towards the grassy mesas above Belcher's Bay.

Of the three bulls in the group, Wahatehwe was the youngest. Most of the year, his youth and smaller size were of little consequence, as the three males lived somewhat detached from the females and got along just fine together. It wasn't until the rut, or breeding season, that his younger frame and lighter antlers were a disadvantage. As much as his instincts drove him to want to mate with the ovulating females, the larger bulls easily overpowered him and kept him away from the cows. After two years of playing third string in his original herd, he struck out to the west into the heart of the island.

Now sporting a handsome five-by-five rack, the athletic young adult encountered a small herd being led by a more mature but smaller framed bull of the tule subspecies. Tule elk were less stout in stature and had generally smaller antlers than bulls originating in Yellowstone. Even though the group's leader was a six-by-six bull, his antlers lacked the girth of Wahatehwe's. The now more confident Rockies elk challenged the herd bull for the right to breed the females. The fight was long and tiring as fives locked with sixes and drove them backward repeatedly. In the end, the tule male was vanquished and the Yellowstone elk prevailed. A new generation of mixed California and Wyoming genes was conceived that fall.

The tables turned the following fall when now 'royal' Wahatehwe was challenged by a gnarly Roosevelt bull. The challenger came from a line of big, beefy elk from the rainforests of the Pacific Northwest, and had a hundred-pound advantage over the now-established herd bull. The battle was impressive as the two adrenaline-charged titans pirouetted across the arroyo-pocked mesa. It was not until Wahatehwe drove the heavyweight over the lip of a ditch, rolling uninjured to the bottom, that the would-be usurper had had enough and ran off to the west, chased for a quarter mile by the now twice-proven leader.

At seven years of age, Wahatehwe had earned the respect of not only his own harem of cows, but had a following of younger three and four-point satellite bulls, both under his protection and also waiting to take his place. The rut was over for the season and it was a time of year when bulls associated with the cows and were no longer fighting with the other bulls. It was a peaceful, clear morning, the ocean breeze blowing across the ridge both cooled his perpetually warm body and kept the mosquitos and flies away. He lay slightly apart from his satellite bulls, surveying the territory that he had successfully defended and the cows that he had rightfully earned.

From just yards away his entourage jerked to attention as their herd bull lurched to one side and his head collapsed to the ground. His lungs had suddenly popped and his heart had burst then stopped. A split second later came the delayed explosion of gunpowder, and in an instant, all excepting Wahatehwe were bounding towards cover.

On January 27, 1950, the Los Angeles Times reported:

Santa Barbara. Bing Crosby party has good hunting. Three elk and one deer were bagged by Bing Crosby and his hunting party on Santa Rosa Island, it was learned here today after the party arrived at Stearn's Wharf.

TIA

Considering the alternatives, Tia's life on Maybury Farm was about as good as it gets for an elk in captivity. The weather at the southern tip of New Zealand's South Island rarely got above 66 degrees or below 32. He had plenty of open space, was fed nutritious grains, received regular health checks, and each fall he was provided dozens of cows in estrus to service. He was coddled and cared for like a thoroughbred, which, in fact, he was. The eight-by-eight "Monarch" was the finest that Maybury Farms had to offer their customers, and one of the leading bull elk in the country. Back in Yellowstone, he would have been just another tourist attraction.

The path to excellence had been a circuitous journey and had taken many generations to achieve. It began in 1907, when Theodore Roosevelt, out to show the world America's military prowess, dispatched a fleet of sixteen U.S. warships on a global tour. After visiting Australia, the fleet made a six-day stop in New Zealand, where they were celebrated by the entire Parliament. Roosevelt was so impressed by the respect shown to the fleet by the New Zealanders that the following year he shipped them a gift: a herd of twenty Yellowstone elk. Unsure of just what exactly they should do with this present, they settled on releasing them in the extremely rugged Fiordlands of the large and sparsely populated South Island.

For a while, the herd grew and prospered, the lack of predators and the abundance of food and water contributing to exceptional antler growth in the males.

When word got around that New Zealand was growing 'record-book elk', hunters from around the world began traveling down under to get in on the action. Seeing the opportunity to become an international hunting destination, some of the wild elk were captured to become the breeding stock for private hunting ranches. Not only were more North American elk imported from Yellowstone to diversify the gene pool, but European elk known as 'red stags' were brought in as well. Red stags were genetically very similar to American elk, close enough to interbreed. Superficially the European elk were near duplicates of their New World cousins, though a keen observer would note minor variations in size, color, antler shape, and voice. It didn't take long for the big American bulls to dominate their smaller red cousins and soon hybrid elk were mixed in with the wild purebred elk.

Fearing a loss of size and quality, the game ranchers and breeders guarded against hybridization on their properties, while the wild population continued to become more and more mixed. Soon a new use for the elk emerged as elk venison became popular, first as an exotic delicacy and later as a low-fat, low-cholesterol alternative to beef. The early elk meat farmers were not quite as picky about the mixed blood hybrids and their initial breeding stock came from trapped wild elk and elk crosses. As the demand for elk venison grew, the farmers began importing more of the large-bodied North American elk to introduce into their bloodlines and increase their yields.

Maybury Farm was among the first New Zealand sheep farms to be converted to elk production. Their success was built on diversifying their offerings. Not only did they sell live Safari Club International record book bulls to game ranches to satisfy international trophy hunters, but they also sold elk semen for $1,000 per dose, elk velvet for over $100 per pound, and elk meat for $1.00 per ounce. There was even a market for elk by-products including hides, tails, leg sinews, antler buttons, and ivories or eye teeth.

But of all of the farm's assets and income streams, Tia was the most valuable. Appraised at a quarter million dollars based on the voracity of his genetic material, he had spread the Yellowstone DNA to generations of elk that graced both the tables of fine restaurants and the walls of grand hunting lodges.

PO AND KATHY

Even though it was mid-July, it was cold atop "The Thunderer", a 10,558 foot peak looming above Soda Butte Canyon at the northeast end of Yellowstone's Lamar Valley. A lone dark cloud hovered over the summit and the wind blowing across the ridge dropped the perceived temperature into the forties, a common occurrence for a peak that was named for its propensity to attract thunderstorms by members of the Hague Geological Survey of 1885.

The intense weather had not discouraged the Tukudika people, however, when centuries earlier they camped at the wooded base of a rocky cirque on the western slope of the mountain.

The first clue that the ridge had been used by the Sheep Eaters was the faint outline of a crescent-shaped rock wall near the summit – a textbook example of a primitive sheep corral that the Tukudika specialized in. Once the sheep trap had been located, the search began to find a village site associated with it.

This was the third time Pohogwe had visited the ridge. The hike was an arduous one, starting just opposite the Pebble Creek Campground on Soda Butte Creek. Po might never have found the access if not for the help of Ranger Kathy Powell, now a seasoned veteran with six years of service under her belt. Not only had Kathy led him up the first time, but she had also accompanied him on the second and now the third trip up the mountain.

It took four full hours to hike the steep seven-plus miles, so the pair began before sunrise to allow them as much time searching and excavating as possible. In addition to finding the sheep trap, they had been rewarded with looks at bighorn sheep and mountain goats on both of the previous trips.

Although he had never met Robert, Po had made another trip over from the Wind River Reservation in 1944 to attend the funeral services held in the Mammoth Chapel in Yellowstone. Kathy was grateful that he had come, and he had joined her and Harry and the other rangers for a meal in the hotel dining room in Robert's honor.

After the funeral, Kathy had not seen Po for over a year, when one day she bumped into him as he was coming into the Visitor Center looking for maps. "Hey stranger," she called to him.

"How!" Po replied with his hand up, mocking the popular stereotypical greeting attributed to Indians.

Skipping up to him she almost hugged him, but thinking better of it put out her hand instead. Looking at the maps she asked, "Finally going to get started on your research?"

"Yes, it's taken me longer than I thought to get funding and equipment, but I'm finally ready," he answered. "I just rented a little place in Gardiner so I can be close to the project."

"That's terrific!" she gushed. "Let me know when you want some expert guiding."

"Thanks, Kathy, I definitely will," Po replied.

"Well, gotta go entertain some visitors," Kathy said as she waved and backed towards the door. "See ya' around, neighbor!"

It wasn't long afterward that Po stopped by the ranger station early one morning asking for Kathy, who was in the back preparing for her shift.

Hearing Po's voice, she came to the desk. "Got yer hiking boots on, Po?" she asked jovially.

"I do, Kathy," Po replied. "I was hoping you could point me to the Specimen Ridge Trail, on the south side of Lamar Valley?"

"Point you to it?!" she laughed. "Throw your stuff in my pickup. I'm going to give you the deluxe tour!"

"That's okay, Kathy, I'm sure you got work to…"

"Are you questioning my work ethic, sir?" she cut him off mid-sentence. "It just so happens that I need to check the condition of that trail and assist any out-of-breath visitors," she said with a wink.

"Great! I'll get my stuff," he said as he headed towards the door.

Rather than starting near Junction Butte where most of the tourists began the hike, Kathy took Po to the far end of the trail near Soda Butte Creek. "Fewer people, shorter distance, but steep!" she warned. "This will get us up to Amethyst Peak," she explained.

"That's just where I was hoping to go," said Po excitedly.

Kathy was in great shape and had to stop several times for Po, who although fit, was not acclimated to steep hikes at 9,000 feet. To allow him to rest without making it obvious, Kathy took the opportunity to educate Po on the history of Specimen Ridge at every stop.

"When the Geological Survey explored this ridge in 1872," she began, "they found all this beautiful purple quartz scattered around the peak of Amethyst Mountain, thus its name. Did you know that the ancient Greeks used mugs made of amethyst because they believed that it kept you from getting drunk?" she asked playfully.

"Well, at least they weren't drinking out of lead goblets like the Romans," puffed Po, catching his breath.

At the next stop Kathy pointed to what looked like a stone chimney. "Know what that is?" she inquired.

"Giant termite mound?" joked Po.

"Hah! Nice guess," quipped Kathy, "but the answer I was looking for was 'petrified tree'."

On closer inspection, they could make out the trapezoidal shape of a tree base, the craggy exterior that was once bark, and in a broken chunk adjacent to it they could see the tree rings preserved in stone. "That's amazing," said Po reverently.

"This is Yellowstone's 'Petrified Forest'," Kathy explained. "When the Absaroka volcanos were active 50 million years ago, they created a mud-flow of ash that covered the trees, which included redwoods, magnolia, and maples, none of which are found anywhere near here now. The trees absorbed silica and calcite in the ash and it clogged the xylem, and...umm – think of xylem as a plant's veins, and the trees eventually just became solid rock."

"Wow – great description, Kathy. The visitors must love you," Po said, impressed with her knowledge.

Kathy blushed and added, "Jim Bridger, the old mountain man from the 1800s, claimed that you could hear 'petrified birds singing petrified songs' here in the Petrified Forest," to which both Kathy and Po burst out laughing.

Upon reaching the highest point at Amethyst Mountain, the archaeologist dropped his pack with relief. "This is where the project starts," he said excitedly. "First I'm going to lay out a survey grid. Next, I'll follow the grid lines, looking carefully for any evidence of past human activity. Typical evidence could include walls or foundations, artifacts, or color changes in the soil that may indicate features."

"Sounds like fun, Po, can I help?" asked Kathy.

"I was hoping that you would, Kathy. Two of us can cover a lot more ground, and there's a lot to cover up here," Po replied. "How about we eat a little breakfast before we get started? That hike made me hungry!"

The two broke out canteens, fruit, and biscuits they had brought and surveyed the Lamar Valley below as they ate. "This was one of Robert's favorite spots," said Kathy quietly.

"I'm honored that you are sharing it with me," replied Po sincerely.

After breakfast, Po educated Kathy on how he would be setting up the survey. "First we'll lay out a line of stones, each about 5 yards apart, then we'll move about a hundred yards across and perpendicular to the slope and set up a similar line. The rocks will provide us our grid lines, this will keep us relatively straight," he started, "then we will each slowly walk adjacent lines, very slowly, looking for anything on the surface that looks unusual…anything that indicates the presence of humans." Gazing down the line he continued, "If you do see something that stands out, it can even just be a change in the color of the soil, let me know and I'll check it out. If we locate something significant, we'll mark it and come back to it once we've completed this first quadrant."

After setting out all of the marker rocks, the two reassembled at the starting point. "This is so exciting!" exclaimed Kathy. "Do you think we'll find anything here, Po?" she asked.

"Looking around I actually think the elevation is a little low, but I'd bet we'll find something of interest," Po answered pragmatically.

The search began. Kathy found herself moving much faster than Po, so she watched his movements and tried to imitate them. Po shuffled at a snail's pace, intentionally dislodging stones with his feet as he moved and occasionally bending over to feel something or to pick it up and examine it. Kathy began doing the same, focusing on irregularly shaped or colored stones, unusual humps, and abrupt changes in soil type or hue. In this way, they maintained roughly the same pace.

After a couple of hours of this, they were about two-thirds of their way through the grid, when Po called to Kathy. "Kathy, mark your spot then come over and take a look at this." Kathy placed one stone atop another as a placeholder and came over to where he was turning something over in his hands. "Hold out your hands," he said reverently. She cupped her hands as he gently placed what, at first glance, appeared to be a broken piece of dark glass. She brought it closer to her face to better see the details. It definitely seemed to be a piece of dark glass, but the edges had been chipped away from the flattish, roughly spade-shaped object, creating a sort of feathered look to its perimeter. Where the tip of the spade should have been it was flat, appearing to have been broken. Along the edges at the opposite end were two indentations, deftly chiseled from the object.

It looked to Kathy like an oversized, broken arrowhead. "Obsidian?" she asked.

"Yes, Kathy, and can you guess where that is from?" Po quizzed her.

"Obsidian Cliff, here in the park?"

"Bingo! You know your park!" he congratulated her. "Obsidian Cliff was the largest source of obsidian for hunter-gatherers in the United States. Volcanic glass from the site was traded widely, and many stone tools and points made from it have been found in the Ohio Valley, 1,500 miles from here." Kathy's eyes widened as Po continued. "I'm guessing that this is an 'atlatl point', a two-piece spear thrower. This would have been attached to the spear."

"Oh my gosh, Po, does this help with your research?" Kathy asked.

"Just in a very general way, Kathy," Po explained. "It tells us that indigenous people hunted here, so that's promising. We know that the Tukudika quarried obsidian at the Obsidian Cliff site. We also know that my ancestors fashioned obsidian arrowheads that they used for sheep hunting. What we don't know is…" he stopped in thought for a moment. "We don't know that the tribe used atlatls; spear points have not been found at any of their known sites to date, so from that angle we may be able to add something to our knowledge of their weapon use," ending the statement with a hint of excitement.

"How will we know for sure?" Kathy asked.

"Great question. I can test the point for any evidence of sheep protein. That would help support the possibility that it was used by Tukudika," he stopped and then said, "but to answer your original question, no, this isn't exactly what I'm looking for, but it may be all that we find here…and it's pretty darned neat!" He smiled as he held out his hands and Kathy returned the stone tool to him. Placing it in a pouch he had on his belt he said, "Why don't we finish up on the grid and that will be enough for one day? When we get back I'll work on an analysis of the point. I'll definitely come back up here and continue searching – we haven't even scratched the surface," he concluded.

"Can I come back with you next time?" asked Kathy hopefully.

"Of course, Kathy, it is a huge help to me to have your assistance!" Po said genuinely.

For the next two years, Kathy assisted Po, one or sometimes two days a week from spring to fall. Winters were the season that Po conducted much of his lab work, library research, and writing. Kathy did not see Po nearly as much from November through May, though he did accompany her on a couple of winter mammal surveys. The snow on the high summits where Po conducted his searches did not melt off until late May, and by then both of them were itching to get back to the peaks.

Over three seasons they had completed a semicircle of surveys around the Lamar Valley. Beginning with Specimen Ridge, they went on to survey the Mirror Plateau, Saddle Mountain and Little Saddle Mountain, the Needle, Cache Mountain, and Mount Norris. Some were multi-day trips, so Kathy would combine days off to coordinate with Po's plans, packing in with full backpacks and each with their own small tent. They had made some exciting finds during those trips: numerous obsidian weapon points, scraping tools, and more atlatl points, and near the rocky crest of the peak named "the Needle," they found the ruins of a classic stone corral of the type built by the Tukudika. But the artifact that eluded them was the one that Po most hoped to find, a soapstone bowl.

The soapstone bowls crafted from steatite deposits quarried in the Tetons, Absarokas, and Wind River Mountains were a trademark of the Tukudika. Many had been found in the Jackson Hole area south of Yellowstone. The bowls were an anomaly among the cooking and storage vessels made and used by other tribes throughout the country. The Comanche Indians, relatives of the Shoshoni, would hang a buffalo stomach from a stand made of sticks and drop hot stones inside to boil their simmering meal. The ancestral Puebloans and Mogollon cultures in the southwestern United States made beautiful clay pottery. The Penobscot Indians in the eastern U.S. boiled water in a birch-bark container. The Tukudika alone carved stone bowls. The metamorphic steatite used by the Tukudika was composed of consolidated talc, and soft enough to be carved by an elk antler, but then would be hardened once exposed to fire. The bowls were most commonly about a foot tall by eight to ten inches wide, shaped like a flowerpot, and devoid of any markings. Po wanted to prove that the Tukudika had used the mountains surrounding the Lamar Valley; so far the pair had not even located a shard.

On their third survey of The Thunderer, as Kathy was kicking through some pine needle duff among a small group of pinyon pines along her survey line, her boot bounced off of something solid. Assuming that it was just another rock she mindlessly brushed the debris away to have a quick look at it before moving on. As she did so, she did a double-take. What she thought she was seeing looked like the rounded lip of a vessel. Bending over again she hurriedly brushed more needles and soil away with her fingers. "Po! Poooo! Get over here!" she screamed. Never having heard quite this type of excitement in Kathy's voice, Po dropped everything and ran to her side. She was staring at the ground, laughing nervously and pointing in front of her foot.

"Holy mackerel!" was all that Po could come up with. Going slowly to one knee, he removed a small paint brush from his belt, and ever-so-gently brushed away more detritus, eventually encountering hard-packed soil encasing the object. Nearly a third of the article was now exposed; it was the edge of a bowl. Po turned his head to look at Kathy and whispered, "You did it Kathy! You really and truly did it." It almost looked as though there was a tear in his eye.

She dropped to his side. "We did it, Po. We're a team!" she said, and then suddenly embarrassed, she flushed red and turned away.

Sensing the awkwardness of the moment, Po said, "Let me get some tools out of the pack and we'll see if we can safely excavate it." Just as they stood to get his implements, a blinding bolt of lightning struck a tree fifty yards away, followed a split second later by a deafening crack of thunder. "Let's get off of this exposed ridge!" he yelled and they ran for cover.

It was the monsoon season far away in the desert southwest and sometimes the pattern of daily thunderstorms crept as far north as the Wyoming Rockies. Large hailstones and a howling wind followed on the heels of the lightning; The Thunderer was living up to its name. Kathy and Po found a low cluster of pinion pines surrounded by taller trees and sat huddled together for protection from the hail and warmth. Po held his jacket over Kathy's head as extra protection, resting his arm on her shoulder. Kathy burrowed in closer, wrapping her arms around him. They began laughing, softly at first, and their laughter made them laugh more until they nearly wore themselves out. After the last chuckle, Kathy raised her head from where it rested against Po's chest. Her eyes were glazed and her lips were moist, her face just inches from his. "You can kiss me, Po," she stated, reading his mind. Po leaned down and tenderly put his lips to hers.

Both Po and Kathy had been denying their attraction to each other for years now, and the kiss instantly awakened the longing they had for each other. Aside from some teenage experimentation on the reservation and a handful of short-lived liaisons during his college years, Po had been so immersed in his work that he had not been intimate with a woman in years.

Robert had been the first and last man that Kathy had ever given herself to, and four years after his death she was more than ready to be held and loved again. The thick layer of pine duff made a fragrant mattress as Kathy melted into it and Po obligingly continued the kiss. Po was surprised when Kathy rolled him over onto his back, but his surprise turned to wonder as she removed her clothing, laid them over the pine needles, and lay back down on

them, gazing at him all the while. Wordlessly, the
Shoshonian archaeologist stood to disrobe, his eyes locked
on hers. Joining her again on the ground the kissing was
renewed, evolving naturally into sexual intimacy. Their
love for each other, which had begun with respect and
friendship, had been steadily growing and finally, they were
able to manifest it physically. Their lovemaking was both
tender and intense, and afterward, they fell asleep in a tight
embrace.

When they awoke next, it was becoming late
afternoon. They kissed and Po said, "I don't want to rush
the excavation of the pot. It's safe where it is for now. I'll
come back up here tomorrow so I can take my time
getting it out."

"Not without me you're not," Kathy said giving
him a quick kiss. "You're going to have an even harder
time getting rid of me now," she quipped.

"I don't want to get rid of you, Kathy," Po
answered earnestly. "Not ever."

ALBERT

The years since the grizzly attack on his father had been rough ones.

When Albert snuck out of the Mammoth Ranger Station, he had stowed away in the back of a station wagon, which didn't stop until it got to Missoula, Montana, 280 miles in the wrong direction. Waiting until the owners got out to use the restroom at a gas station, Albert climbed out of the car, still dressed in the soiled clothing he had been hunting in. He hadn't eaten in twenty-four hours so his first objective was to find food. Hiding behind the station, he watched as an employee took out the trash. Once the coast was clear he climbed into the dumpster where he found a half-eaten donut, pieces of potato chips at the bottom of an unfinished bag, and the remnants of some Coca-Cola in a discarded bottle, all of which did little to assuage his hunger. Wandering down the alley behind the station he could smell bacon being fried. Up ahead was a diner and that dumpster held a treasure trove of toast crust, bacon fat, pancake bits, and soggy cereal, all mixed together in large bags. Sated for the time being, he embarked on his next goal, a ride back home.

Missoula was farther away from home than he had ever been in his twelve years. He lacked knowledge of basic geography, knowing only the name of the town nearest the family's cabin, the small town of Gardiner, and the "big cities" of Livingston and Bozeman. He figured that the gas station, located at the crossroads of two highways was his surest bet for a ride back to Cooke City.

He decided that his best option was to make it back to "Yellerstone", where he could hop out before the North Entrance, sneak into the park then get another ride east back to Cooke City.

Since the war had ended three years earlier, park visitation had sky-rocketed, and even now in mid-winter, carloads of tourists were flocking to see Old Faithful and feed the famous black bears. Albert's parents had not spent any time teaching him politeness or graciousness, so his communication skills were lacking. Approaching cars stopped for gas, he would ask the first person he saw if they were "Goin' to Yellerstone?"

The occupants would take one look at his dirty clothes and wild hair and shake their heads "No!"

Albert had no idea why he was having such bad luck. Switching tactics he decided to ask everyone, every car, truck, and bus the same question. Approaching the driver of a big rig who was just getting back into his truck, he was surprised to get a "No, not to Yellowstone, kid, but I can get you as close as Livingston." As Livingston was on his short list of known places, he jumped at the chance.

From Livingston, it was much easier to get a ride, as the driver had conscientiously dropped him right at Highway 89, the road into the park. This time, approaching a mixed group of college-aged boys, they looked at each other and the driver said, "Hop in red, and make yourself at home."

As soon as he sat down in the now-crowded back seat of the big Ford sedan, the black-haired boy next to him handed him a bottle of beer. "Cheers mate," he said, clicking his bottle to the one Albert was holding. Now hungry and thirsty again, Albert took a big swig, and choked on the bitter dryness, blowing foam out his nose. "Woah there, pardner!" said the boy next to him, scooting away from him to avoid getting sprayed, then to the driver shouted, "Hey dickhead, next time you pick up a hitcher can you make it a girl, and preferably one who knows how to drink beer!" All six occupants laughed hysterically, even Albert.

Albert didn't have much to say in response to the boys' questions, so eventually, they forgot about him and went back to talking about girls, cars, and what they expected to see in Yellowstone. As the tall Roosevelt Arch just north of the entrance came into view Albert simply said, "Stop."

"Here?" asked the driver quizzically.

"Yeah, right here, I gotta get out here." Confused, the driver stopped and Albert leaped out the door without a word.

As they pulled away he heard one of them say, "That was one weird-ass kid," to which they laughed uproariously.

At last, he was back in relatively familiar surroundings. Heading east on foot he dropped into the trough of the Gardiner River, followed it south for about two miles, bypassed the check station, then hiked back up to the road and waved his arms to cars as they passed by.

The third car to pass stopped, the passenger side window rolled down and the driver leaned out and said, "You need help, son?"

Albert replied, "Yep, my pa got killed by a bear and I'm tryin' to git home."

"Oh my God," gasped Katie, the woman in the passenger seat. "Bruce, give this boy a ride!" she ordered.

"Come on, son, we'll help you out," Bruce said as he hopped out of the car to get the door for the boy. Once inside Bruce asked, "Where are you trying to get to, son?"

"Back home, near Cooke City," replied Albert.

Bruce looked at Katie and said, "Katie, look at the map and see where Cooke City is."

Taking the map from the dashboard, she unfolded it across her lap, first locating the north entrance, then tracing the route with her finger to Mammoth Hot Springs then east on their intended route along the Grand Loop Road when she finally said, "Oh there it is! It's not far from where we were planning on going anyway, Bruce. We need to get this boy home."

The couple from Iowa plied the boy with questions about the incident, but Albert would say only, "We was campin' in the woods and a grizzly bear got 'im." Then, to avoid any more probing questions he put his face in his hands and pretended to cry.

"There, there poor boy, we'll have you home soon enough," Katie said to comfort him. The rest of the drive was spent in silence as Albert managed to fall asleep in the rear seat.

As they slowed down upon entering Cooke City, Albert jolted upright and said, "Here! I can walk the rest."

"Are you sure?" asked Katie kindly. "We can take you right to the house, it's no problem."

"No, here's good," said Albert, anxious about having them know too much about where the cabin was.

The moment the car stopped Albert leaped out the door without a word and trotted away. "Strange boy," muttered Bruce.

"He must be in shock over his dad," Katie answered, shaking her head sympathetically as she watched him bound away.

It took him a good forty-five minutes to reach the cabin from where he had gotten out of the car. Opening the door he found the place in its normal state of chaos, the few pieces of furniture strewn around the room, grimy dishes in stacks and his ten-year-old brother carving a piece of wood next to the wood stove.

"Pa's dead," announced Albert cryptically.

Jake looked up confusedly. "What!?"

"Pa's dead, grizzly killed him. Where's Ma?"

"Shiiit!" wailed Jake. "Pa's dead?! What're we gonna do for food and shit?"

"Guess yer gonna have to get off yer ass and start huntin'…where's Ma?" Albert asked again, obviously irritated.

"In there. Drunk again as usual," answered Jake pointing to the bedroom door, then picking up his wood to start carving again.

"Great, fuckin' great," spat Albert.

It had been thirteen years since the grizzly incident, and Albert's life had seen its share of tragedy. His mother Rose, already a serious alcoholic, had literally drunk herself to death within three years of John's passing. Brother Jake had turned to crime, first breaking into neighboring cabins, then into the few shops in Cooke City before getting caught by the local sheriff and put in juvenile detention in Livingston. Released to abusive foster parents, he soon ran away to the 'big city' of Butte,

Montana, where he lived on the streets. By seventeen he was dead of a drug overdose.

Albert stayed at the family cabin, continuing the only way of life he knew, hunting, trapping, and fishing for food and trading his bounty for everything else he needed. It was a lonely existence and for all of his toil, it was insufficient to keep him nourished and provisioned. At seventeen he went to work for the Parkmont Mining Company based in Cooke City.

He worked long hours at the remote Homestead Mine in the mountains north of Cooke City. His schedule was typically twelve-hour shifts, working twenty days in a row and then getting ten days off. On his breaks, he did his shopping and laundry and he hunted, whether it was hunting season or not. The job not only provided him with the means to acquire necessities like food and clothing, it finally gave him the resources to upgrade from the ancient hunting gear he had been left with. The cussed rangers had kept his father's best rifle and pistol. Since then he had been shooting the only rifle left in the cabin, a .30-30 Model 1894 Winchester with iron sights. His only sidearm was a forty-year-old .22 Colt Woodsman revolver. As hunting was his sole interest and means of extra food and income, he decided it was time to invest in his future.

Among the options in the rifle rack at the Cooke City store was one that he couldn't stop thinking about. Because the store not only catered to local hunters but also occasionally to visiting hunters from around the globe, the owner had picked up a big-bore, lever action Marlin model 336 in the .450 Marlin caliber, with a pre-mounted Weaver K 10-60 riflescope. More of a novelty domestically, this weapon was better known as an African "elephant gun".

After Albert's childhood experience with the grizzly, this magnum-sized firearm would help assure that he would never fall victim to another bear, and he was big enough to wield it. It would also leave a fist-sized exit hole in his favorite game species: elk. It was a big gun and he was becoming a big man. After weeks of staring at the gun, he finally bought it. "Rhino hunting, Albert?" asked the store owner jokingly as he handed over the weapon.

"Or whatever gets in the way..." replied Albert eerily. For a backup gun to wear on his belt, Albert again went big, choosing a Smith and Wesson Model 29 in .44 magnum.

A number of the other miners were hunters as well. In their scant free time, or anytime they congregated in Hoosier's Saloon on days off when they weren't talking about women, they talked about hunting: Who was hunting in which zone this year? What was the biggest bull or buck they had ever taken? Or what were their 'guaranteed' tricks for killing an elk? Although Albert had never owned a hunting license and knew nothing about zones, he readily joined in the conversation. A couple of them brought up the hunting organizations they belonged to. The Boone and Crockett Club and the National Gun Owners Association (NGOA) were two that were mentioned. Albert had no idea that there were hunting 'groups', and with his growing social skills and shared passion, he thought them a good idea to join. He even bought himself a hunting license.

The local chapter of the NGOA, the Park County Hook and Bullet Club, met the first Thursday of each month in Livingston, two hours away, and had an annual picnic once each summer. Albert had bought a ten-year-old Chevy pickup truck, and when his days off coincided with a meeting date he would attend, sometimes giving a ride to one of his work-mates or a fellow hunter from town. In the coming years, he would become more and more involved.

Albert was amazed to find so many men who shared his preoccupation with killing. At these meetings, he learned for the first time about the fight to protect gun rights and, of particular interest to Albert, the outrage over the National Park Service's plan to cull a record 5,000 elk from the Yellowstone herd in the coming months.

The reality of the situation was that Yellowstone had officially adopted a policy termed 'direct reduction', a euphemism for 'ranger-killed-elk'. The program had been initiated to save the park's overgrazed vegetation, thereby keeping the elk and other park mammals from starving. Critics mocked the practice as 'killing elk to save elk'. Although it had just surfaced as a news item, rangers had been killing Yellowstone elk for more than a quarter of a century. During that time, park employees had shot 13,753 elk, and live-shipped another 6,700 to zoos, game parks, and other national and state parks. This number paled however in comparison to the 41,000 elk killed by hunters over the same period just outside Yellowstone's boundary.

The size of the planned 1961 reduction though had made the headlines around the country, and hunters were fuming. Groups like Albert's besieged their game departments and government officials. The Wyoming Game and Fish Department, the International Game and Fish Association, the Wyoming Legislature, and Montana Governor Donald Nutter all insisted that hunters, not park rangers, be the ones to harvest Yellowstone's overpopulated elk.

Next door in majestic Grand Teton National Park, the Park Service caved, in a deal that allowed elk hunting in that park. The result: eleven dead moose, mistaken either accidentally or intentionally for elk by hunters who had been heralded as the experts who should be the ones to manage elk herd overgrazing. The Park Service learned from this fiasco that they wanted no part of recreational hunting on National Park property, especially not in the crown jewel of the park system.

Supported by an independent panel that found Yellowstone's direct reduction program ecologically sound, rangers culled more than 4,300 elk in that winter of 1961-62. It was an ugly bloody affair, not only out in the killing fields, but politically and personally, as park employees suffered harassment and even death threats.

That season marked the beginning of a change in the way that Yellowstone and its elk were viewed by many people, not the least of which was the strapping twenty-five-year-old redhead from Cooke City.

HAIWI

Kathy had been thirty-four and Po thirty-five when Haiwi was born, her lovely soft cooing leading to her being bestowed with the Shoshoni name, Haiwi, meaning "mourning dove". For a surname, the family adopted the last name of Poe.

As the daughter of a Shoshoni anthropologist father and a National Park Service ranger mother, Haiwi could not help but grow up with a love of nature and history. From early childhood, she accompanied her parents on everything from ranger-led campfire talks to archaeological digs. Attending elementary school and high school in Gardiner, Montana, her enthusiasm for wildlife advocacy was not dampened by the harassment she endured at the hands of the more strident pro-hunting and ranching students, choosing instead to associate with the handful of "park brats", as the children of Yellowstone National Park employees were pejoratively referred to.

The post-war years had been good for Po's career. After locating the first soapstone bowl from around the Lamar Valley, Po subsequently found two more. These together with the high altitude stone sheep corrals provided him the evidence he needed to complete his doctoral thesis at the University of Wyoming where he received his Ph.D. The Bureau of Indian Affairs (BIA) of the Rocky Mountain Region was thrilled to hire Pohogwe as an archeologist where his job was to help keep the Region in compliance with the National Historic Preservation Act, Native American Graves Protection and Repatriation Act, and the Archaeological Resources

Protection Act. While the position required that he travel extensively around the Rockies, Yellowstone was in the geographical center of the region.

Kathy worked until Haiwi was born, about the same time as Po started working for the BIA. Living on a single salary was challenging, but the rewards of being able to spend so much time with their young daughter were well worth the sacrifices. Kathy and Haiwi spent countless days together in the fields and forests of Yellowstone, just as Kathy and Robert, and then Kathy and Po once had. Once Haiwi started school, Kathy began working part-time again in the park. By eight years of age, Haiwi knew the names of every plant, tree, insect, bird, and animal in Yellowstone. Kathy never tried to shield her daughter from the realities of nature, providing her instead with the biological explanation for everything they witnessed: from courtship and mating to birth, the contrasting gender imperatives of males and females, the symbiotic roles of predator and prey, and finally the necessity of killing and death.

Thanks to this honest detailing of the facts of life, Haiwi had never been inclined towards overly sympathetic responses to death. The exception to this was the culling of the elk herds. She had been eleven when Kathy took her on an icy winter day to check on the herd reduction taking place in the Lamar Valley. The winter of 1961-1962 featured one of the largest government-run elk killing programs in the park's history, as more than 4,300 elk were shot by Park Service employees. Kathy explained to Haiwi that the Park Service had a responsibility to not only the elk but to the habitat that they occupied and the plants and animals that survived on the same vegetation. With no wolves and few grizzlies to keep the population in check, humans had to artificially control the herd size. Haiwi understood the science behind the need to keep the elk population under control, but the cold, calculated solution of a mass shooting was starkly different than the natural drama of predator taking prey.

"Aren't there still wolves in Alaska, Mom? Why don't we catch some and let them go here? That way we wouldn't have to do all this shooting."

Kathy smiled sadly and replied, "You know how the boys at school talk about wolves? The ranchers and hunters will never allow wolves to roam free here again."

The boys at Gardiner High School never missed an opportunity to torment Haiwi on the topic of the elk killing. They heard from their fathers and other adults in the community that the Park Service would selfishly rather "shoot fish in a barrel" than let sport hunters enjoy "the thrill of the hunt". Everyone in school knew which were 'park brats'; they talked differently, they acted differently, and their parents weren't native to the Rockies but were from places like New York City and Los Angeles. Many of the local kids were the children of ranchers, farmers, and hunters, whose families had lived in the region for many generations, and now the park was depriving them of their birthright. They knew that Haiwi's mother had been a park ranger and her father did research in the park. They taunted her with, "Your mom shoot any big bulls today?" or "How's it smell over in Lamar with all those dead bodies?" and "Keeping the Indians well fed?" But Haiwi was unflappable, avoiding arguments with her unreasonable classmates, choosing instead to discuss the issue with the few students who had an open mind to the topic. In this way Haiwi became something of a leader, founding the school's first-ever Ecology Club. All five members voted unanimously for Haiwi to serve as the club's first president.

Having grown up how and where she did, Haiwi's stand on many environmental issues differed from those students demonstrating against pollution and pesticides in places like San Francisco and Washington D.C. Contrary to what many of her classmates believed about her, she was not anti-hunting. She understood the role that hunting played in wildlife management and how most conservation programs in the country were funded by the sale of hunting licenses. She did believe, however, that national parks were sacrosanct, and must be forever preserved as places where wild animals could live in a relatively pristine setting free of human predation. This belief not only put her at odds with the majority of Montana and Wyoming hunters who were clamoring for Yellowstone to be opened to them, but it also put her squarely against what had long been the park's policy of direct reduction.

From 1962 until 1967, the park mostly refrained from their herd reduction practices, in part because of the enormous outcry over the '61-'62 debacle. But then in the winter of 1967-1968, the culling began again, this time with approximately 1,000 animals being harvested. Again there was outrage, not only from local hunting groups like the Skyline Sportsmen of Butte, Montana, and groups from as far away as the San Diego Rod and Gun Club, but from new and newly empowered environmental groups like the Defenders of Wildlife and the Environmental Defense Fund. There were even protests held in Gardiner,

Montana, led by Haiwi Poe of the Gardiner High Ecology Club.

By September of 1968, the Park Service relented, and although they still reserved the right, they never again employed direct reduction. The service had determined that given the choice of allowing the public to hunt in the park or discontinuing all sanctioned culling of elk, they would do whatever it took to never open the park to sport hunting.

For Haiwi's eighteenth birthday, there could have been no greater gift than the announcement that Yellowstone was ending its program of direct reduction of elk, initiating an experiment that Resource Management Specialist, Edmund J. Bucknall, called the "Total Ecosystem Approach" to the management of wildlife.

The Total Ecosystem Approach was a novel form of herd management that would allow natural "controls" such as food availability and disease, reduced reproduction, natural winter loss, and hunting just outside the park boundary to naturally regulate the elk population. "Predation" was also on the list of natural controls, but with few grizzlies and no wolves, predators were only a hypothetical component of the plan.

The science was sketchy at best, relying on a new interpretation of Yellowstone's historical data and anecdotal reports on elk numbers and range conditions. But for the time being, it got the National Park Service out of hot water: sportsman's groups were satisfied that no one else would be having the pleasure of shooting "their elk" and new regulations would allow for greater flexibility and availability of hunting opportunities just beyond "the firing line" where elk crossed onto public land from the park. Wildlife rights groups were satisfied that the seemingly wanton destruction of large mammals would cease. The general public was relieved to hear that recreational hunting would not be allowed in "their park". And the Ecology Club at Gardiner High School celebrated their victory by reelecting eighteen-year-old Haiwi Poe to her second term as president of that prestigious organization.

TOYATUKKUPITTSI

Toyatukkupittsi (Toya) was amazed by the abundance of game he had stumbled upon. Having traveled east from the rugged mountains of Idaho, he was completely alone, which was not unusual for a mature tom mountain lion, or cougar as they were sometimes called.

Dropping into the Lamar Valley by the light of a full moon, boxes were being checked off on a subconscious checklist: Food – *elk and pronghorn*. Water – *Lamar River and numerous tributaries*. Shelter – *various rock outcroppings and caves*. Lack of competition – *no wolves or grizzlies present*. Absence of humans – he had crossed a road and the human stench was everywhere, he couldn't check this box. Nevertheless, his instincts told him that he could work with four out of five, and the overwhelming number of elk mitigated the human presence.

As his low shadow crept across the valley in the moonlight, the elk herd parted as he passed, catching his scent without seeing him. He was not hunting yet, this was not how he hunted, this was a reconnaissance mission. He could not outrun the elk in a race, not a long race anyway. He would get to know the paths that the elk frequented in and out of the surrounding woods and below the rocky points and he would wait there for them.

His natural counterparts and enemies, grizzly and wolf, had very different hunting styles. Grizzly hunted by brute force, running down elk calves or stealing elk carcasses from wolf and lion. Wolf hunted pack style, analyzing and strategizing then chasing, often long distances. But they were absent here now, not that he had ever felt their presence within his own life, but his kind had a deep memory of their kinds.

His hunting style relied on patience and stealth. Like a phantom he moved silently through the woods, always keeping the wind in his favor. He would come to know the location of every tree with a suitable limb overhanging a game trail and every rock fall with a boulder that he could perch upon adjacent to an elk path. If elk were nearby he would prepare his ruse, settling into his hiding place in their path and waiting, waiting. Often, his plans were derailed as the elk unpredictably chose another path, or the wind direction changed and they scented the smell of a predator. But enough of the time, about once a week, he was successful, dropping onto the back of a calf, young cow, or spike bull. Then he would feed on the kill for three or four days before starting over again.

The elk were confused that night he had first entered their valley. While his scent was unmistakably predatory, an odor as offensive to them as a skunk might be to a human, it was foreign to them, existing only in the part of their brain containing primal instinct. Even though Toya was the first mountain lion to enter their valley since the 1930s, their kind remembered his kind, and they instinctively realized that his returned presence meant death.

Like the wolf and the grizzly, mountain lions had been hunted, poisoned, and trapped out of existence in the Yellowstone area, and for nearly fifty years there were no detections of the big cats within the park. Fortunately, lions still existed throughout the arid high-desert as far north as Idaho, their cryptic coloring and solitary lifestyle making it difficult for men to eradicate them in the more inhospitable parts of their range. With territories as large as 400 square miles, it was inevitable that the cats would eventually find their way back to Yellowstone, where nature was so out of balance that, for the time being, they would have the elk all to themselves. Being opportunistic eaters, mountain lions predated many different types of prey animals throughout their range, from javelina in the southern deserts to bighorn sheep in the mountains of Idaho, but given a choice, elk was their preferred food. In fact, in areas where they had a choice of prey species, elk made up 50 to 75 percent of their diets.

Despite having the valley pretty much to himself, Toya did not flaunt his hunting prowess. The rangers and biologists were soon aware of him, occasionally stumbling upon his cached, half-eaten carcasses covered with leaves and sticks, a cougar trademark. The magpies, ravens, turkey vultures, and both bald and golden eagles were delighted to once again have a predator in the valley capable of providing large mammal carcasses for them to scavenge. The foxes, too, were sometimes able to sneak in for a bite once the cat had filled himself for the day. The coyotes, however, were a problem. They dogged the cougar whenever they saw him, and often attempted to get in on his kills while he was still feeding. Occasionally, if a pack was out together, they could harass the cat until he left the kill, but usually not without the big cat killing or at least injuring one or more of the coyotes in the process.

The following year, as Toya was patrolling his territory, he came upon a familiar scent. After putting his nose to the ground and inhaling repeatedly, he lay down and rolled in the damp spot among the pine needles, then crouched and urinated on the spot, hoping that the female he had detected would return. He spent the next few days in the area, waiting for her to reappear. On the third day the female, Dukubichi (Duku), could be heard caterwauling from the ridge above him, the raspy scream of a cougar in heat. Unlike wolves, which only ovulate in late winter, female mountain lions can mate throughout the year. Finding her was simple; every animal for a mile could hear her lusty screams, and after a playful courtship that lasted for three or four days, Toya inseminated her repeatedly. And then it was over as quickly as it had begun, both going their own ways, he back to his solitary life, she to raise the kittens that would arrive in about 91 days.

Duku had followed much the same route that Toya had, but she had spent two seasons in the Lemhi Pass area on the Idaho-Montana border before making her way into Yellowstone. Although Duku was not immediately aware that she was impregnated, her subconscious directed her to begin looking for suitable caves to have her kittens. Making her way north, she found the pocked crags all along the ridge above Amphitheater Creek to her liking, allowing her to hunt the slope of Cache Creek as well. While five kittens were developing inside of her, she was learning the paths and hiding places of the territory that would become their first home.

It was mid-August when the kittens came into the world, in a cave on the northern flank of The Thunderer, near a saddle that would allow Duku easy access to either drainage. For a week and a half she neither hunted nor left the lair; her sole activity was purring and nursing the kits. When she emerged from the den she was parched and famished, and headed straight downhill to slake her thirst, finding a small pool of water in a tributary of

Amphitheater Creek. Rehydrated, she hunted around the outcroppings nearest the lair, where she found a fat yellow-bellied marmot that she consumed in its entirety. It would be 60 to 90 days before the kittens could be weaned, so for the time being she would hunt just enough to keep her milk production and herself healthy.

By three months of age, the five kittens were following their mother between hunting areas. Most often she would stash them in a rock crevice or under a stack of deadfall timber while she sought out prey nearby, and then would bring the prey, or parts of it, back to the kittens to eat. Sometimes, if the area seemed very safe, she would lead the bouncing spotted babies to the kill, allowing them to feed directly on it.

The kittens were only eight months old and weighed close to fifty pounds each when they first encountered Izhape - the coyotes. Duku had been patiently leading them farther into the open and had taken them to the body of a young elk she had killed near the confluence of the forks of Cache Creek. The youngsters were excited to be out in the wide-open bottomland and pounced on the carcass before Duku had cleared it of the debris she had hidden it with. While the kittens feasted on the meat, Duku kept an eye out for trouble. The first that the kittens knew of the presence of coyotes was Duku's low growl as she saw them approaching from downwind. She had trained the kittens well, and they immediately slunk off through the deepest grass they could find, making their way to the creek where they bounded upstream. Duku however stayed with the carcass, both to distract the coyotes from following the kittens and because she hated giving up her hard-earned meat to the ever-annoying canines.

Coyotes only rarely hunt as a pack, preferring to hunt in ones and twos, but today there were six traveling together and they had smelled the dead elk as well as the cats. As they approached, four of them headed for the elk and Duku, while the other two took off after the irresistible scent of kittens running upstream. This provided an unpleasant but automatic choice for Duku, as she left the meat to chase the coyotes racing toward her offspring.

Few animal mothers are as fierce and unforgiving as a mountain lion protecting her young. The slower of the two coyotes had no idea what was approaching from behind, his last conscious thought was of a heavy weight dropping onto him as a three-inch-long tooth pierced his spinal column. Releasing the limp canine instantaneously Duku made a series of twenty-foot bounds towards the leading coyote, who, having turned to see his pack-mate slain, had veered from trailing the kittens to running for his life. The race was no contest, and this time Duku made the most of the situation, after easily severing the windpipe and jugular the eighty-pound lion drug the thirty-pound coyote carcass to the base of a tree and covered it with sticks for later consumption. Surveying her surroundings she could see no more coyotes coming her way. The remaining four were preoccupied with the elk carcass. Angered by the loss of the elk, she nevertheless had secured meat for the kittens in the form of fresh coyote. She found the kittens hiding in a rock jumble about a half mile up the slope. They would return for the meat once the coyote pack had finished and departed.

Three months later they were not so lucky. As the entire family fed on a pronghorn doe who had wandered too close to the trees, a female grizzly with cubs to feed wandered over a small rise twenty yards behind them and immediately charged at the oblivious group. Duku turned to face the bear, snarling with her back arched. The kittens were startled and confused, not knowing whether to run or help. The bear was on them in a moment, but instead of attacking Duku, she veered to her right, swinging her front paw and catching one of the young lions on the hip just as it was turning to flee. The force of the slap sent the kitten flying, rolling as it hit the ground, then struggling to stand. In the meantime Duku had leaped onto the back of the 350-pound sow, sinking her teeth into the bear's back. The sound was terrifying as the bear bellowed and the lion screamed. The four kittens had collected themselves and ran up the hillside into the protection of the trees. The sow had only meant to scare the cats off of the kill and had not anticipated the female lion's reaction. In a panic from the intensity of her wrath, the she-bear turned and began running back in the direction she had come from, with Duku still attached. Seeing that the bear had surrendered the fight, Duku leaped off and ran to her injured kitten.

At just sixty pounds the young cat was not built to withstand such brute strength. The kitten had dragged itself away from the scene, attempting to join its siblings. Pulling itself forward with its front legs, its rear legs trailed along the ground uselessly. Duku licked the kitten all over, nudging it to stand up, but to no avail. Grizzlies had a reputation for breaking the spines of thousand-pound bison with one slap of their powerful limbs.

Duku lay down next to the kitten and purred. Eventually, the four other kittens joined them, the five of them lying together throughout the night. By morning the injured kitten had died from the injury.

Duku was an exemplary mother, but by the fifteenth month she had taught her offspring everything she could, and feeding four full-grown lions and herself had become too much. One day after taking a good-sized young spike elk all by herself, she went back to where she had left her brood and led them to the kill. As the four of them pounced on the carcass and began to eat ravenously, Duku turned and headed into the hills, her job complete. Duku would live alone until either Toya or another male, came along, starting the whole process over again.

For the mountain lion at least, Yellowstone would again become an island of refuge.

IZHAPE AND WAAHNI'

When Kathy had brought the furs from John and Albert's tent to the fur buyer in Bozeman for analysis, there had been a noticeable dearth of fox pelts and a surprising abundance of coyote furs. In the nearly twenty-five years since, the ratio of coyotes to foxes had become even more pronounced. None were more alarmed by this phenomenon than Oha. Oha was a Waahni, Shoshoni for fox.

Oha was pale, almost blonde in color, a dead giveaway that she was one of Yellowstone's high-elevation foxes who were uniquely light in color. The fact that she lived most of her life above 7,000 feet in elevation was both a curse and a blessing for her: a curse in that life was inherently harder during northern Wyoming's frigid winters as one gained elevation, a blessing in that she encountered fewer of her nemesis, Izhape, the coyote.

It was the middle of a particularly stormy winter, and the snow where she normally hunted was so deep and fluffy that she had trouble finding the montane voles that she depended on for food. The voles built and maintained tunnels under the snow in winter, but the storms had been so persistent at the higher elevation meadows that the voles had not kept up in their tunnel building. Oha was forced by hunger to descend onto the Lamar Valley floor where the depth and firmness of the snow was more conducive to foraging. It was also home to more than one large pack of coyotes. In the Soda Butte Creek arm of the valley lived an Izhape family called the Küttaa pack, their leader a smart and capable male named Nasuyekwi.

Many generations earlier, Oha's forebearers rarely encountered Izhape in the land now called Yellowstone. At that time, Izhape's packs were small, just two parents and their pups. But in recent years the packs had grown to include nearly a dozen adults plus pups.

As Oha hunted, she concentrated intently, listening for the subtle scuffling indicating voles moving beneath the snow, while at the same time regularly cocking one ear to her rear, listening for the possible approach of Izhape.

As the coyote packs had grown they had become more territorially aggressive, routing out and killing foxes in the area that might compete with them for food, and occasionally even eating them. Oha and her kind had moved farther up the mountains in part to avoid conflicts with the larger and stronger coyotes. Oha's ancestors had a better relationship with the larger and stronger gray wolves that used to inhabit the valley. The wolves were much more interested in pursuing large game: bison, moose, elk, deer, and pronghorn, and they considered the coyotes, not the fox, a competitor. Just as the coyotes killed foxes when they could, so did the wolves kill the coyotes when the opportunity presented itself.

The barely audible scuffling of tiny feet, many inches below the surface of the snow suddenly caught Oha's attention. Both ears now stood straight up as her head cocked towards the sound. Leaning back on her haunches she collected her energy like coiling a spring, shook her tail slightly, then leaped. Like a springboard diver, she first went straight up. Once her head had reached its highest point, her body arced, her head came down, then her hips and tail followed the arc. She then descended straight down, pointed nose piercing deeply into the snow. For a moment her back feet pedaled air as her nose sought out the warm scent of the vole just inches away. Twisting and turning, her head carved a void a foot below the surface of the snow. Within that space, the vole fell from its tunnel into the void, where Oha's lightning-fast reflexes caught it and clamped down. Using her hind legs to extricate herself from the hole, she came up triumphantly dangling the tiny rodent from her mouth.

She stared for a split second at the scene directly in front of her. There, just yards away, were Nasuyekwi and his mate Gita, the coyote packs alphas, coming for her at a full gallop. Without dropping her prize she turned in an instant and bounded towards the nearby trees. The coyotes were right on her tail, snarling in anticipation of the kill when Oha spied a dead tree leaning against a snow-covered spruce. Her long full tail helped to keep her from toppling as she turned abruptly at a dead run for the tree. The coyote pair did not lose an inch as they banked the same turn at the same speed.

One final long leap put slender Oha onto the leaning tree, her semi-retractable claws digging into dead wood as she scampered all the way up to where the log met the live, snow-laden spruce. Unable to climb the narrow pole as the cat-like fox could, the two coyotes slid into the base of the log, then stood staring and growling. Oha turned at the top of the log and shot them a mocking glance then burrowed into the protection of the densely limbed spruce.

Proud Nasuyekwi was not accustomed to failure in such situations, and though Gita tried to console him by licking his muzzle, Nasuyekwi was having none of it. He was in the mood to kill something and hardly cared what it was. Unfortunately, his choices were limited by both the winter weather and the loss of diversity in the valley. While there was a seemingly never-ending supply of elk, they were too large for him and the pack. Generally, the only time elk were on the coyote's menu was during the birthing season in May and June, and then it was often scavenged placenta. Other than the elk there seemed to be a growing shortage of everything else he liked to eat, fewer hares, grouse, and even berries. His best odds were searching out winter-killed elk and bison or resorting to loitering near the highway, hoping for some fresh roadkill.

There had been a time when coyotes could find carcasses to scavenge by watching the sky. The carrion birds: Golden eagle and bald eagle, black-billed magpies, and the ubiquitous common raven, with their keen eyes and a commanding view of the valley, were a reliable indicator of where a winter-killed mammal might be hidden. But because few large terrestrial predators were bringing down large animals these days, leaving fewer sources of leftovers, the eagles were less common than they had been. With the once large aspen stands chewed down to nubs, there were few places for the raven and magpies to perch. Grizzlies, never adept at chasing down full-grown mammals themselves, had always made their living stealing the kills of the pack hunters, the wolves. These days only the secretive cougar was bringing down large mammals, mostly mule deer farther up the mountain. The coyote alphas had many mouths to feed; perhaps they would have to migrate out of the park to find food this winter.

Arguably the most adaptable mammal in the park, coyotes were once considered an animal of the plains and deserts, though they had always existed here in small numbers. Within the last century, the coyote population had suddenly blossomed, moving east as far as New England and north well into the Alaskan interior. Their proliferation and range expansion seemed to mirror the reduction and elimination of their larger cousins the wolves. But 'the trickster', as the Shoshoni had once called him, was better at hiding and avoiding extirpation.

The U.S. Department of Agriculture claimed to have killed 3.6 million coyotes between 1945 and 1972, and it has been estimated that another 3 million died of poisoning and were never found. Despite this mass destruction, coyotes not only survived, they thrived. Despite an annual kill rate sometimes as high as 70% of their population, coyotes were masterful at expanding their range. Among the species' incredible adaptations were having larger litters, allowing beta females to takeover breeding when alpha females were killed, and an adaptation that biologists referred to as "fission-fusion" whereby packs would break up regularly to colonize new areas.

Given the diminishing prospects of food in the valley, the time had come for the oversized Küttaa pack to split up and locate new more productive hunting areas, leaving behind Nasuyekwi and Gita to dominate the Lamar. If any animal in Yellowstone was going to survive and thrive, it was going to be the trickster.

JAKE

The Draggin' A Ranch had always been big by Wyoming standards, but after buying out several neighboring ranches, they had become big by any standard. More surprisingly, after nearly a century and a half, the ranch was still owned and operated by an Adams - three of them.

The three Adams boys were built like all of the Adams men before them, short and stout with dark hair and ruddy complexions, but their size had no bearing on either their ruggedness or their business acumen.

The youngest, Cory, was a senior at the University of Wyoming where he was majoring in Agricultural Business Operations. Laramie was a long way from the ranch, but he made the six-plus hour drive home in his diesel flatbed for every holiday, vacation, and at least once each month. In addition to his studies, Cory was on the school's wrestling team and was among the country's best wrestlers in the 165-pound weight class. While not the best roper of the three brothers, Cory was considered the strongest, able to flip a steer with ease when needed or carry an injured calf out of a canyon on his shoulders. Cory was also the most likely to lose his temper, a family tradition passed down from many generations of Adams.

Hank, the middle brother, was the thinker of the trio. When his older and younger brother would rail against some new tax or government overreach, Hank was the one who tried to understand the other side, and occasionally convince his brothers to do the same. Other times his brothers shook their heads and called him a

"Frisco hippie". In many ways Hank was the best cowboy of the three; he seemed to better understand the horses and cattle and had a way of calming them. He was also the brother who everyone looked to when a heifer was missing or when a predator trail needed to be followed.

As the firstborn, management of the ranch was Jake's responsibility. Matt, the boy's father, had been grooming Jake for many years and Jake had proved to be a capable manager. Jake's abilities allowed Matt to focus on needs like procuring bulls for breeding stock, negotiating purchases of equipment and services, and getting the most possible for each year's crop of calves. Jake was relatively cool-headed for an Adams. At 5'10" he was the tallest of the bunch and had been a damned good team roper in local and regional rodeos.

Of the three, Jake was the only one who was married. Jake had met Angie at a rodeo in Jackson Hole where she won a gold buckle for her speed in the barrel race. Angie fit in perfectly on the Draggin' A, performing all of the same tasks as the brothers. Even though Jake was considered the manager, it was the two of them together that made the decisions, with Matt's blessings.

The eastern slope of the Absaroka Mountains was God's country when it came to raising cattle. Stretching from the border with Yellowstone to the tiny farming town of Clark, there was everything a cow needed to raise quality calves: good water, natural forage, and hay fields to provide winter feed when the weather got cold and the snow deep. As a traditional "cow-calf operation", their most important asset was their breeding females, a line of cows that they had been cultivating and improving upon since the ranch began. Early each summer the cows would be lured into fenced pastures in the valley of the Clark's Fork River with sweet alfalfa hay, where the bulls would be put with them for two months. Turned back out to forage on wild grasses for the remainder of summer and fall, the cows would again return for winter feeding and would begin calving in March.

The Adams boys weren't old enough to remember when wolves would occasionally take a calf or a yearling, but they knew what it was to have a grizzly bear take a cow. There were less than a 150 of the big bears left in the 34,000 square miles of what biologists defined as the Greater Yellowstone Ecosystem. A number of those bears called the range that ran through the ranch their home. Over the last thirty years, they had lost a handful of cattle to grizzlies, and in two instances they shot the beasts when they were found feeding on the carcasses. One of those two bears charged Hank on his horse even after having been shot three times and was only stopped when all three brothers unloaded their revolvers on him at once.

So when then President Richard Nixon signed into law the Endangered Species Act in 1973, they became concerned over what that meant for the ranch.

"Looks like ol' tricky Dick's tryin' to take everbody's mind off of that trial," said Hank cynically, referring to the Watergate hearings.

"The feds have been talkin' about the bears for years now," spouted Cory. "I'd bet dollars to donuts they're gonna make it impossible to shoot one, even when you catch 'em with one of yer cows in their mouth!"

"Slow down, you two," interjected Jake. "We gotta be smart about this. We got a lot of cards to call in at the state level. Pa will get hold of Governor Hathaway and I know Jim White at Fish and Wildlife. In the meantime we need to shoot every bear we can find before they get listed."

"Woah, hold on there, Jake," said Hank abruptly. "I'm not shooting any bears that ain't killin' cows, especially not with them under the microscope right now because of this new law. We get caught killin' bears now, we're gonna get our asses thrown in jail."

"Hmmm, you may be right, Hank. I'm gonna call Hathaway myself and get him to derail this thing."

Cattle predation on the Draggin' A aside, the grizzly bear was in real danger of going the way of the passenger pigeon. Once occupying the western half of the country from the great plains to the California coast, and from central Mexico to the Arctic, they were now found only in northwestern Wyoming and northern Montana in the lower 48. Fewer than a thousand of our largest mammalian predators survived in the United States excluding Alaska, from an estimated 50,000 at the beginning of the nineteenth century. And now they were on the short-list of some of the most iconic North American mammals slated for endangered species listing.

The brothers had seen it coming for a while. In 1966, "those Frisco hippies" pressured Congress to pass the Endangered Species Preservation Act, which officially set aside federal lands to protect certain species of wildlife and fish. Grizzly bears had been on that list alongside the American alligator, bald eagle, and gray whale. But that set-aside hadn't directly impacted operations at the Draggin' A.

After a huge oil spill blanketed wildlife-rich areas of the California coast in 1969, it seemed that the whole country began 'hugging trees'. Zoos began a program called the *Wild Animal Propagation Trust* to breed endangered animals. Radicals were driving spikes into trees or chaining themselves to them to protect spotted owls. Fanatics were putting their rubber boats between whales and whaling ships. It was amidst this backdrop that one of the least likely champions of the environment emerged, President Richard Nixon. Nixon enacted some of the most impactful programs in the history of conservation, creating the Environmental Protection Agency in 1970, signing the Marine Mammal Protection Act in 1972, followed by the Endangered Species Act in 1973.

"That's what we get for electin' a president from California!" said Cory wryly on the subject.

Matt Adams and his sons, along with the Wyoming Beef Producer's Association (WBPA), packed a political punch when dealing with Governor Stan Hathaway. As owners of one of Wyoming's larger ranches, the Adams were major players in the WBPA, once considered "the de facto territorial government" of early Wyoming. The Association had the power to make or break political careers in the Cowboy State.

Matt's meeting with the governor was casual and congenial, the two sharing brandy and cigars before Matt even brought up grizzlies. With a wave of his hand over his shoulder, Hathaway brushed away any thought that he might support the listing of the bear. "This is cattle country, Matt, not bear country."

"Exactly what I thought you'd say, Stan," beamed Matt, feeling the brandy. "Let's put the kibosh on this bear crap."

Jake's meeting with the head of Wyoming Fish and Wildlife was a little more heavy-handed. "Now Jim," Jake began over coffee in the Game and Fish office in Cody, "Angie and I have had you out to the ranch for a big steak feed. Did you enjoy it?"

"Yes, Jake, it was great," replied James White, aware of where the conversation was going. "Thanks again for having me over."

"Well, Jim," Jake began again as though he had rehearsed it, "those steaks don't grow on trees. You know as well as we do what protecting grizzly bears is gonna mean, right? It's gonna mean fewer steaks for you and me!" His voice rose and his face flushed as he finished his pitch. "You've seen yerself what those grizzlies will do to a cow. They start doing that to our herd that we've worked for generations to build and steak is off the table!" Stopping to replenish his air, he added, "Do you understand what I mean?"

"Of course I do, Jake," White blurted, having been ready with his answer since before the lecture. "I'm on your side, Jake. If Game and Fish has our way we'll still have a limited grizzly quota outside of the park, for as long as I'm director."

"That's great, Jim, we want you to keep being the director for a long time," said Jake, his threat barely veiled.

When the Department of the Interior was debating which animals were to be protected under the E.S.A., both Hathaway and Wyoming Game and Fish Director, Jim White, submitted a petition vigorously opposing the classification of the grizzly bear as endangered.

Matt and Jake both publicly spoke against listing at a crowded meeting in Cody hosted by Wyoming Senator, Gale McGee, as did many Wyoming ranchers and sportsman's groups. But the tide was flowing in favor of the grizzly for the time being, and despite vociferous objection, the great bear was finally added to the protected list. At least one of Yellowstone's two keystone predators would soon be restored to its proper place in the natural fabric of the Rockies. The other only existed north of the Canadian border.

REINITA

The coffee cherries were nearly ripe and the leaf miner moths were numerous as Reinita flitted furiously from bush to bush. By night the dense assortment of orchids, mosses, ferns, lichens, and bromeliads along the perimeter of the plantation provided comforting shelter from rain and the ravages of foraging coatis and peccaries. Costa Rica's rainforests and coffee plantations made an excellent winter alternative to the willow bogs of northern Yellowstone where she was fledged and where she would soon be returning for her fourth consecutive summer.

Months of gorging on insects had fattened her up to more than a quarter of an ounce, about as much weight as she could reasonably carry on her tiny three-and-a-half-inch frame. Her feathers had just molted, purging last year's worn primary flight feathers for glossy new ones. She was in fine color with a bold yellow breast and throat, fading to an olive-colored body, with a greenish gray crown, and shining black eyes. As the vernal equinox approached, Reinita instinctively began testing the weather for signs of the strong south winds she would rely on for transportation.

This year, the wind she needed arose in the middle of a moonlit night and knowing that the time was right, she ascended. A weather radar station nearby recorded a pattern of dots so dense that they resembled a storm cloud over the Nicaraguan border as more than a million warblers, vireos, tanagers, and other small birds began their migration all on the same March night.

Her trip north was halted for two days in the mountains of central Mexico, as the winds shifted to northerly. Landing among a grove of Apache pines, she found nearly every branch packed with other grounded warblers. Emitting the flat "chuff" call note specific to her species, she was reassured to hear many other Wilson's warblers in the surrounding trees. The stalled birds fed ravenously, anxious to assure no loss of stored energy while they waited for the wind to turn favorable.

At the end of the second day the winds calmed enough for her to resume her journey, though they were not strong enough that she could merely float. She had to actively pump her wings towards the north. This expenditure of energy came at a cost, and for the next several days she was forced to spend daylight hours foraging in the Chihuahuan desert so she could return to the sky each evening.

Though it was of no concern to her, on the fifth night she passed over the U.S. border near Ciudad Juarez. The Rio Grande River provided miles and miles of quality riparian vegetation, and her trip had been biologically programmed to correspond with mosquito and caterpillar hatches all along her route. Lacking a strong south wind, she fed her way somewhat leisurely in the river corridor, all the while continuing north.

Making it to the southern point of the Rocky Mountains near Taos, she again was buoyed by a strong wind from the south. For three nights she virtually sailed above the Colorado Rockies, dropping down by day to feed. On April tenth, just west of Boulder, a breeze out of the southeast carried her toward the Wyoming border near Flaming Gorge Reservoir. From there she followed the

Green River into the Wind River Range until it petered out near Togwotee Pass. While the damp meadows on the west side of the pass were richly endowed with willows, Reinita was intent on one particular spot, the specific tree that at the base of which she had now raised three clutches of chicks, still a hundred more miles to the north. Humans often marvel at the story of how the salmon return from the ocean to the same streams they were born in, but few know that migratory birds often return to the same bush or tree each year. So it had been with Reinita for three consecutive seasons.

Reinita's willow was along Crystal Creek in the Lamar Valley. In her first year as an adult, she found the willow thicket to be completely adequate for her needs. There had been plenty of nearby grasses and mosses to build the cup nest that she would line with feathers. In the surrounding shrubs lived a plethora of caterpillars and aphids for feeding her nestlings. The dense leaves of the thicket were perfect for hiding the nest from weasels and merlins. Perhaps most importantly, there were eligible males to father her young.

The second year that she raised her brood in the thicket the experience was not quite as comfortable. The normally dense foliage she relied on for camouflage was not nearly as lush, but the grass at the base of the bush was tall enough that she successfully fledged four of her five chicks.

In year three, the same bush was nearly bare, and the grasses beneath it had been grazed down to ground level, so Reinita moved to another, taller willow about 50 yards away. The less robust cover allowed the nest to be discovered by a female brown-headed cowbird, a bird known as a 'brood parasite' for its unsavory practice of laying its eggs in the nests of other bird species. When the cowbird eggs hatched earlier than the warbler eggs, the baby cowbirds tricked Reinita into feeding them. By the time her own chicks hatched, the cowbird chicks were big and aggressive, out-competing them for the morsels that Reinita brought back to the nest. That year all three cowbird chicks successfully fledged, joining others of their kind as they followed bison around the park. Only one of Reinita's own chicks was strong enough to fledge.

In a rocky spire nearby, a merlin falcon had nested for years, as had many generations of her predecessors. For a bird-eating raptor like the merlin, the Crystal Creek willow patch had been a smorgasbord of Wilson's and yellow warblers, as well as warbling vireos and others. With the willows nearly gone, and so few perching birds left in them, the merlin nest was vacant for the first time in decades.

In her fourth and likely final year, Reinita arrived in the Lamar Valley on April sixteenth. A creature of habit and instinct, she headed straight to her preferred willow patch, where she fluttered about, perplexed. Only the tallest willows now had leaves, and then only at the very top. Medium-sized willows were devoid of leaves and smaller willows were nowhere to be found. Gone, too, were the grasses and mosses she would use for nest building, the ground was hard and brown, and the small vein of the creek flowing nearby was full of dry silt. There were no males nearby to father her chicks, not even a familiar chuff note of another female. There were no birds of prey or short-tailed weasels to hide from.

Expending precious energy, Reinita took to the sky, this time heading south. In a small inlet along the east side of Yellowstone Lake, she found an intact patch of willows growing at the waterline. A handsome yellow and black warbler, sporting the distinctive black beanie of a male Wilson's warbler, sang a sputtering trill, and Reinita, now anxious to breed, went to him. Though she did most of the work, together they gathered the traditional nest-building materials, and she plucked downy breast feathers to line the cup. In early fall her brood would migrate south with her and millions of others, some stopping in Mexico, others in El Salvador, Belize, Nicaragua, and Panama. It would be Reinita's last round trip, but now her offspring were imprinted with the location of their birth. Reinita's line would no longer be returning to Crystal Creek; that destination did not exist in their internal navigation systems.

MAHIHKAM AND ATISOW

When Nuni and Omah began what would later become known as the Brazeau Pack in Jasper National Park, wolves already had a long history in Alberta. In 1754, the first European explorer to reach Alberta noted that gray wolves were nearly as numerous as the bison herds that they followed. By the late 1850s, trappers with the Hudson Bay Company in the Jasper area were aggressively poisoning wolves that were killing their horses. Wolves were nearly completely wiped out in the region until after 1920 when 88 elk from Yellowstone were reintroduced in an attempt to mitigate the scarcity of game due to human overhunting and unusually severe winters. By the 1940s, the elk population in the park had grown to approximately 3,000 head, which led to a rebound in the wolf population. It was at this time of relative abundance that Nuni and Omah settled near the Brazeau River at the south end of the park.

Responding to over-grazing by the growing elk herds and following the same ill-advised methodology that had been employed in Yellowstone, the Province of Alberta embarked on cyclical culling of elk as well as the poisoning of wolves. By 1957, wolves were again nearly absent from the landscape. The Brazeau Pack, now led by descendants of its founders, had endured in part because of the relative remoteness of Brazeau Lake and partly because of the pack's leadership. As elk numbers peaked again in 1970, wolves made a corresponding comeback, and denning sites were noted in numerous valleys throughout the park. The Athabasca Valley, which had not held wolves since the 1950s eradication campaigns, was again home to a growing pack. By 1974, the wolf population in Jasper National Park was estimated to be at 80-100.

The current Brazeau Pack alpha pair was Mahihkam (Mahi) and Atisow (Ati), a large dark gray male and a small but fierce tan bitch. Mahi and Ati had developed a unique hunting technique along with the rest of their pack of eleven wolves. The elk in Jasper National Park had learned that their best defense against wolves was to take to the water, and they tended to give birth to their calves on river islands surrounded by swift currents. When pursued by a wolf pack, the elk headed for the safety of the river. They knew the stretches where the near-shore current was too rapid and the bottom too deep for the wolves to withstand. The elk, however, could stand chest deep for as long as needed to elude their assailants.

The Brazeau pack was known for hunting strategically, and they systematically approached the problem of elk using the swift water for safe harbor. Whether by accident or astute planning, the pack had entered the river at a bend well upstream of a small group of elk standing belly-deep in the water. The bend and the distance had put them perfectly on a course that swept them directly at the confused elk. The elk nevertheless had an easy time scrambling back to shore, running off into the safety of the woods before the pack could make a landing and pursue them.

The next time that the elk were driven into the water, Mahi seemed to deliberately lead the pack upstream for the group swim, but the results were precisely the same. After a couple more failed repeats of the 'upstream-bend-strategy,' the wolves tried something new, this time leaving the majority of the pack directly ashore of the elk, while the alpha pair and the beta male, Pawamiw (Paw), floated down as before. The elk, knowing the pack was waiting just alongside them, merely swam downstream as the three floating wolves approached, hitting the shore at a run a quarter mile below the pack.

When yet another opportunity presented itself, Mahi first led his subordinates into hiding, then the three leaders embarked on their well-rehearsed float. This time as the trio approached, the elk made for shore and then straight for the trees where the pack had secreted themselves. Just as Mahi, Api, and Paw made it to shore, their pack-mates were toppling a cow elk just inside the tree line. The alphas took the place of the others at the carcass, and once they were sated, the remainder of the pack dined in a specified order. From that day on, no elk was safe in the Brazeau River.

AASHI

Except for the very few cougars in the park, it was the first time in the collective memories of the Northern Yellowstone elk herd they were virtually unmolested: no sport hunting, no sanctioned culling, no trapping and shipping, no wolves, and few grizzlies. Once again their existence had been manipulated by man, but this time instead of artificially controlling them by hunting, they were artificially free of all predators.

No one knows how many elk lived in Yellowstone before John Colter's first visit in 1807, much less how many existed before the First People arrived in the Yellowstone region ten to twenty thousand years prior. Accurate counts began being kept in the 1920s. At that time the population was at a robust 13,000 animals. In 1934, the government began implementing its controversial "Direct Reduction" program, and elk numbers began a long bumpy slide to a low of approximately 4,000 by 1967. It was the following year that the National Park Service switched gears and began their "Total Ecosystem Approach" of allowing the natural controls of food availability, weather, predation, and hunting of elk that migrated beyond the park border to control herd size.

Aashi was a relatively new elk to the Lamar Valley. His bloodline came from northeast of the park, in an area long the homeland of the Crow Indians. His name, Aashi, was a Crow word meaning "antler". Aashi's defining feature was not the spread of his antlers, which was quite average for a mature bull, it was the thickness of the antler's main beams that was so impressive, as big around as a man's forearm. And he seemed to love to show them off. The girthy antlers matched an equally stout frame and wide chest. At over 700 pounds, he was the epitome of a strong and capable bull elk.

It had taken a few years but eventually, Aashi understood that his kind had become untouchable as long as they remained inside the park boundaries. Some of Yellowstone's biggest bull elk had become anthropomorphized as "show-offs" based on their tendency to hang out right alongside the park road. Because most animals avoided the road, these bulls were taking advantage of the ungrazed shoulders to satisfy their twenty-pound-a-day diets. These days, satisfying that need had become difficult.

Moose and deer are considered "browsers" in that their year-round preference is to browse on twigs and leaves. Elk on the other hand are considered to be primarily "grazers" preferring grass to shrubs and trees when the grass is available. In winter, however, elk could not afford to be choosy, as the grass was often beneath many feet of snow, while the tender tips of willow, aspen, and cottonwood were still accessible. With the elk herd at 20,000-30,000 in the summer, the grasslands of both the Lamar Valley and the Hayden Valley had been eaten down to bare dirt, so the elk turned to browsing, first the green leaves of the willow, aspen, and cottonwood, then the tender twigs, then the woody parts of the trees. Young trees didn't have a chance as they were gnawed down to ground level. Thirty years of aerial photos showed huge groves of aspen eliminated from the environment. Where expansive willow patches had once grown in marshy places, there were now patches of dead grass on parched and cracked soil.

Aashi didn't linger near the decimated grasslands; he had found the ungrazed roadsides, much to the pleasure of park visitors. But after repeated seasons of resorting to the road edges, even those spots were beginning to look haggard, and devoid of their usual vegetation. Suddenly not even the highway corridors seemed to hold enough food for the ravenous elk.

For the past few years, this shortage of feed had manifested itself most dramatically in winter, when the elk were the most vulnerable, and a couple of hard winters had resulted in hundreds of dead elk strewn about the park. Up until now, Aashi had always been able to build up enough reserves to make it through the coldest months, not comfortably, but adequately. But as the winter of 1975 approached, Aashi was fifty pounds lighter than in previous winters.

Then came the rut.

In a normal September, the elk mating season, known as "the rut", was a raucous, noisy, testosterone-packed battle of the bulls for breeding rights to "harems" of cows. With the unprecedented size of the Yellowstone herd and the varied condition of the undernourished bulls, the rut promised to be a dangerous energy drain on the cusp of the cold season. As it turned out, some of the fighting was more subdued than normal. Some of the big bulls expended far more energy and fat stores than they should have, and some of the lesser bulls just decided to sit this year's contest out.

As one of the park's most dominant bulls, Aashi had been one of those who had overdrawn their energy savings. By the end of three weeks of fighting and copulating, he was spent. Intent on recuperating before winter arrived, he moved up onto Mt. Norris, where he ate as much as he could and rested frequently. When the first snow of the season fell in mid-October, he was reluctant to leave. He was relatively comfortable but very tired. When a major storm in early November brought blizzard-like conditions and five feet of snow, Aashi attempted to get back to the valley. But it was too late.

Not only bulls, but cows and many six-month-old calves perished that winter, their emaciated bodies buried under the snow. The following spring when the meadows thawed, rangers and biologists were shocked at what they found. So many bodies and so few predators to take advantage of them. Clearly, the Total Ecosystem Approach was not as total as it aspired to be.

HA'NII'

The year was 1985, and Ha'nii' and his mate
Iishíile were on the move again, leaving the beaver pond
that they had created just two years earlier. It seemed that
every time they found a stream with a promising stand of
aspens, the only trees left were the oldest, largest
individuals. Beavers preferred young aspen to all other
types of trees; the inner bark was thinner and easier to
digest than that of other trees. Lacking younger trees, the
pair was happy to drop full-sized aspens, to get at the
slender outer branches that were every bit as tender and
palatable as the immature trees. The problem came once
they had felled all of the big trees around the pond. They
had used the larger branches for dam and lodge
construction and stored the smaller, more edible branches
within the lodge. Now there was a lack of new, young trees
to replace them.

The nearby elk herd also loved this bucolic spot.
The mature aspen trees had provided cooling shade in
summer and the elk shared the beaver's preference for
tender baby aspen. At some time far beyond the memory
of this generation of elk, the herd would stop here only
fleetingly, foraging as they moved, ever on the lookout for
the lions, bears, and wolves that seemed to shadow them
wherever they went. Now, however, they were
comfortable feeding among the trees for hours on end,
oftentimes napping in the breezy grove. In time, all of the
new aspen trees had been grazed down to ground level. To
compensate for the loss of young aspen, the elk began

feeding on the coyote willows growing in small clusters around the pond.

In the first year or two of their construction project, this lack of young trees had not been a problem for Ha'nii' and Iishíile. They were able to sustain themselves and their litter of kits on the branches of big aspen and the remaining willows. Soon though, the once stately grove of mixed-age trees not only had no aspen seedlings or clones to thrive and grow, it had no medium-aged trees and few remaining large trees. As the shade gradually decreased with the felling of each mature tree, the native fescues and bluegrasses gave way to the non-native cheatgrass.

With the banks denuded, each thunderstorm began washing sediment into the impoundment, decreasing the depth of the water. The now unshaded pond warmed in the sun, and the cutthroat fingerlings moved to deeper, cooler water upstream. The belted kingfishers and river otters that snacked on young cutthroat stopped visiting, preferring less disturbed pools. Eventually, the elk that, lacking their traditional antagonists, had been responsible for the decay of the beaver-pond habitat, moved on to greener groves to decimate.

Finally, the normally dauntless beavers decided to abandon the pond and look for a waterway that featured a healthy aspen nursery. Letting the flow of the waterway below the dam propel them downstream, they eventually came to a culvert that passed under a highway. Because the diminished upstream vegetation no longer held as much moisture in the soil, the creek held more water than the culvert was designed for. Rather than swim through the culvert, the beavers decided to cross the road instead.

Beavers have poor vision, and their cryptic coloration can make them look like brush on the road. Ha'nii' was already across and waited for Iishíile to catch up to him before he reentered the water below the road. He heard the screech of what was rubber skidding on asphalt, and the double thump of tires passing over a solid object. When Iishíile failed to join him at the stream, he climbed back onto the shoulder of the road, where he could smell the odor of castoreum and other bodily fluids. Waddling out to inspect, he circled the misshapen remains of his mate, and sensing that she was no longer vital, he turned and continued his downstream journey.

Ha'nii' had no way of knowing that he was among the last of his kind in Yellowstone, and now the only beaver left in the park's northern reaches. For the next year, he lived at a subsistence level, chewing up any woody plants that he could find. His search for aspens and willows often led him far from the waterways that protected him.

When eventually a coyote pair found him out in the open, he put up a valiant defense, but he was no match for the determined attack of the duo. Beavers had become the latest casualty of the unraveling of Yellowstone's wild tapestry.

THOMAS

1988 was a watershed year in the lives of most any creature connected to Yellowstone National Park.

Kathy had retired from the National Park Service seven years earlier, and Po had retired from the Bureau of Indian Affairs two years before that. The two had settled in Bozeman, Montana, a relatively more progressive community than many in the region. Kathy remained involved in issues related to the park, attending public meetings of the Montana Department of Fish, Wildlife and Parks, especially those dealing with questions of elk or grizzly bears. When Po wasn't leading archaeological field methods trips for the University of Montana, he was writing on the subject he liked the best, Shoshoni pre-history.

After high-school, Haiwi had left too-small Gardiner to go away to college. Given her passion for ecology and conservation, California State University at Humboldt, in rural Northern California, had been a logical choice. There she associated with others who shared her activist leanings. Soon she was involved in numerous environmental causes, traveling to Santa Barbara, California to help clean up marine mammals and birds after the massive oil spill there, and demonstrating in favor of the Clean Air Act of 1970, the Clean Water Act of 1972 and the Endangered Species Act of 1973. At the beginning of her senior year, at a meeting of the Humboldt State Forestry Club, she met Thomas. With lovely mahogany skin and intensely black hair tied in a long ponytail,

Thomas was a member of the Yurok tribe, original inhabitants of the land occupied by Humboldt State, as well as a member of A.I.M., the American Indian Movement.

While not one of the famous occupiers of Alcatraz Island in 1969 and 1970, Thomas had been part of an A.I.M. delegation sent to observe the methods of civil disobedience being employed. In January of 1973 when A.I.M. was preparing to occupy the town of Wounded Knee, South Dakota, Thomas was ready, and Haiwi was going with him.

While he hadn't been looking for a mate, Haiwi was almost everything that Thomas would have looked for. She was part native-American with an indigenous name no less, which was very important to him; she was environmentally aware, intelligent, and dedicated. It did not hurt that she had a chiseled jawline, copper-colored skin, and large almond-shaped eyes.

The pair loaded up Thomas' Econoline van and headed out on a long three-day drive. They would spend the next two and half months on the Pine Ridge Oglala Sioux Reservation. Thomas holed up in the town's high-steepled white chapel with other occupiers, while Haiwi lent what support she could from a campground of sympathizers just outside of the occupied zone. After 71 days that included federal negotiators, lethal gun battles, and a media circus, Thomas Oketo walked out of Wounded Knee unharmed, armed with renewed pride in his native heritage.

Haiwi had missed the last semester of her senior year, so intending to return to Humboldt to make up the credits needed to graduate, the two began a roundabout journey back to California. Thomas was interested in learning more about the tribes of the Rockies and eastern plains, and Haiwi wanted to introduce Thomas to her parents. They took a northerly route home through Wyoming and Southern Montana, visiting the Shoshoni/Arapaho Wind River Reservation, and the Northern Cheyenne and Crow Reservations. The couple was depressed, but not surprised, by what they saw on the reservations – widespread poverty and clear evidence of alcohol and drug abuse. It was a scenario common to almost all reservations throughout the country, cultures broken by genocide and indigenous people turning to substances to cope.

"My tribe, the Yuroks, was one of the most fortunate in the nation as we were never forced off our ancestral lands," said Thomas sympathetically. "It's hard to imagine having everything taken from you as these people have; it's no wonder that they use chemicals to help them forget."

"My dad grew up on the Res at Wind River. He can tell you a lot about the experience," offered Haiwi.

"I would like that," replied Thomas.

Haiwi's homecoming had been a joyous one, the first time she had returned to her home state in nearly four years. Kathy and Po were excited to get to know Thomas, who had obviously become an important part of their daughter's life. The young couple stayed for nearly a month, Haiwi helping her mom with projects around the home as well as providing an educated perspective on environmental issues going on in the park. Po invited Thomas along on a series of archaeological digs, giving the two of them numerous opportunities to discuss Po's experiences growing up on the Shoshoni reservation and Thomas' thoughts on Indian rights.

The month flew by and when it was time to leave, Thomas surprised them all by announcing, "Once Haiwi graduates, I'd be interested in moving out here. The ratio of indigenous people to whites is high and there are many opportunities to try to improve their lives." Kathy and Po were thrilled at the thought of Haiwi moving closer.

Haiwi looked blind-sided. "What!?" she asked Thomas incredulously. "You never said anything about this to me!"

"That's because I just thought of it!" he answered, to which the whole group laughed.

"Looks like we've got a lot of talking to do," explained Haiwi to her parents, with one arched eyebrow aimed toward Thomas.

"Luckily we have a long drive ahead of us," Thomas countered.

The drive back to Arcata was long and productive.

Shortly after arriving back home, the two traveled north to the village of Klamath, the administrative center for the Yuroks. There they were joined in marriage by a judge of the Yurok tribe. Thomas had explained to Haiwi that it was traditional in Yurok marriages for the couple to live with either the groom's parents or the bride's parents. Because Thomas' parents were deceased, he hoped that she would agree that they should move to Montana, to be nearer Po and Kathy. Haiwi couldn't be happier; she had realized during their visit how much she missed her folks and also thought that a degree in Environmental Science would be marketable in the area north of the park.

When Haiwi called home to inform her folks, Kathy and Po were ecstatic at the news of both the marriage and the move. "Can we throw you some kind of reception here?" her mom asked excitedly.

"No thanks, Mom," replied Haiwi pragmatically. "I haven't kept in touch with any of my high school friends and most of them have left town anyways."

"Well, then we'll just have a little celebration with the four of us as soon as you get back?" Kathy asked hopefully.

"That sounds wonderful, Mother," answered Haiwi, settling it.

Her final semester at CSU Humboldt crept by slowly as the two were anxious to move on. Haiwi graduated at the top of her class with a B.S. Degree in Environmental Science. As graduation ceremonies would not be held until May, Haiwi informed her graduate advisors that she wouldn't be back for the ceremonies and instructed them to mail her diploma and transcripts as soon as possible.

The newlyweds had moved in temporarily with Po and Kathy, and Haiwi had just started a job for an environmental consulting firm in Livingston, about an hour's drive from Gardiner, when she found out that she was pregnant.

"Change of plans!" she announced cryptically that night over dinner with Thomas, Po, and Kathy. Everyone looked at her inquisitively, and when she didn't elaborate immediately, they began asking questions.

"Not liking the job?" asked Thomas curiously.

"You're not moving out already, I hope?" queried Po.

Kathy was watching her daughter's face carefully and thought she could read the sly smile on her face. "I think I know," Kathy said smugly.

"What do you know?" asked Haiwi, enjoying the game.

"Are you pregnant?" asked Kathy excitedly.

"What! How in the world did you guess?!"

With that, Thomas jumped up, pulled her from her chair, and hugged her, while her parents beamed and grasped each other's hands across the table.

"How did that happen?!" asked Thomas without thinking, to which the whole group erupted into happy laughter.

Toni, short for Tekwoni, came into the world in 1975. Her name was the Yurok word for the black-eyed northern spotted owl that lived in the forests of the coastal mountains where Thomas had spent his childhood. Like Haiwi and Kathy before her, Toni was intelligent and full of wonder, but unlike her mother and grandmother, she was full of rebelliousness. That was clear even at thirteen, in 1988.

LUCILLE

More than thirty years of working in the mines had been hard on Albert's body, but several good things had happened to him along the way, the first had been Lucille. When she began waitressing at the Miner's Saloon, every single male for miles around cleaned up their act, brushing their teeth, combing their hair, even checking their breath. One of the few who didn't was Albert, and that was the first thing that attracted her to him.

Lucille had been around; she'd waitressed at resort bars all over Colorado, Wyoming, and Montana. She had bartended at fishing lodges in Canada and even worked briefly as a stripper in Anchorage, Alaska. She'd heard every pickup line that a man could cast, and she'd slapped a few so hard they nearly fell over, and if that didn't work, she'd kicked a couple where it hurt. She was a hell of a pool player and could shoot a .308 rifle without flinching. Everything about Lucille was big, from her hair, eyes, and lips to her breasts straining against a one-size-too-small t-shirt and a bottom that left every man hoping to watch her walk away. Hoosier's Bar down the street was empty when Lucille was waitressing at Miner's.

Lucille didn't give a damn about all the cleaned and polished miners and cowboys who came in to watch her while they drank. She was intent on the mountain of a man that she called "Red" who stood at the end of the bar telling hunting stories, never saying a word to her other than "one more" as he pointed to his beer mug.

She had never seen a man less interested in her. He wasn't wearing a ring so that wasn't it, although she usually got hit on more by the married ones than anyone else. It wasn't that he was shy; he exuded abundant confidence among the circle of men that crowded around to hear his latest elk, moose, or deer killing stories. Nothing about him suggested that he was a queer, his masculinity was overflowing. So what the hell was wrong with him? The absence of even a spark of interest in her intrigued and annoyed her. Even bending over in front of him in her low-cut blouse got no reaction. She had to have him!

Albert, for his part, wasn't playing hard to get, he was just obsessive about hunting and guns. In the years since he started working at the mine, he spent nearly all of his take-home pay on weaponry. First, it was limited to just the tools he needed for hunting: rifles for big game, shotguns for grouse and ducks, handguns for protection in grizzly country and pistol hunting. Once his hunting arsenal was complete, he began collecting what he called "protection weaponry", including assault rifles with detachable high-capacity magazines. Eventually, he began acquiring military-grade tactical weapons, such as grenade launchers, mortars, and bazookas. The cabin began to look more like a military museum or arsenal, although he never allowed anyone inside.

This weapons fixation eventually led to his becoming the president of the Park County Hook and Bullet Club in nearby Livingston, as well as the American Patriot Movement. It also made him the local Cooke City authority on everything hunting and shooting. At nights in the Miner's Saloon, Albert presided over a group of followers at the end of the bar, discussing everything from ballistics and bullet drop to the "Loch Ness Monster of

Flathead Lake" to the white nationalist "Northwest Territorial Imperative". Nothing seemed too far out for the group to tackle and Albert always had the final word.

Lucille was not used to being ignored. Her self-image was based on the belief that no man could resist her, so one night she had finally had enough. Following Albert into the men's restroom without his knowing, she locked the door behind them as he was using the urinal. When Albert turned around Lucille had her back against the door blocking him from leaving. "Uhhhhh, Hi Lucille, think yer' in the wrong bathroom," stammered Albert cluelessly.

"No, I'm not," declared Lucille. "You don't know yet how much you want me. I'm here to help you figure that out." She reached out and closed her fingers tight around the front of his t-shirt, pulling him towards her, thrusting her sizeable breasts into his chest, and bringing his lips right to hers. Albert had kissed women before, but this was unlike any kiss he had ever experienced, long and very wet. Pulling away from him she searched his eyes and finally found them filled with the desire she had been hoping for.

"If you want more you're gonna need to ask me out, Red," Lucille declared, then turned, unlocked the door, and went back to work as though nothing had happened. The boys at the end of the bar had never before seen Albert speechless, but now that she had made him take notice, he couldn't stop thinking about her.

For a while in fact, Albert stopped thinking about anything but Lucille. He definitely wanted more, but he had never been on a date and didn't know exactly what was involved in asking a woman out. Approaching her at closing time the same night he took a stab at it. "Wanna come over?" he blurted out, still under the influence of numerous pitchers of beer.

"Nope, that's not the way it's gonna go, Red," she replied, loving the desire she had finally created. "Tomorrow night, before you start drinking, come over and ask me to go have dinner with you on my night off," she instructed.

"Okay, see ya," was all that Albert could muster.

Lucille was working the next evening and Albert, for the first time that anyone could remember, hurried home from the mine, took a shower, trimmed his beard, and showed up at Miner's smelling like soap. Before taking his standard place at the end of the bar, Albert approached Lucille, took a deep breath, and asked, "Like to have dinner with me?"

Lucille turned, looked him up and down, raised her eyebrows, and said, "Damn, you clean up nice, Red! I'm off tomorrow night, where did you have in mind?"

Albert's eyes widened as he struggled to come up with an answer to a question he hadn't anticipated. "Uh, they's a restaurant down at the Antler's lodge?" he finally said, sounding more like a question than a statement.

"Ok, good job cowboy, you passed the first test," she said with a mischievous smile. "Pick me up at six, I'm in the trailer park on West Broadway."

"I'll be there!" replied Albert, looking a little like a dog groveling for a bite of meat, the first time anyone could ever remember seeing Albert look this way.

Despite her strong original come-on, Lucille was not about to put out any more than she needed to keep Albert wanting more. Over the next month, they went on six dates, each time ending up back at Lucille's trailer, and each time Albert was allowed to explore just a little more of her. Lucille was making sure that the bait was swallowed deep before she set the hook, and the feverish pitch of their petting was setting Albert up to be gut-hooked.

At twenty-seven, Lucille's biological alarm clock had suddenly gone off, and Albert looked to be the right man at the right time. Lucille saw in Albert a man who could be molded into a reliable provider, a man strong enough to protect her when needed, and a man who could provide her with the thing she wanted most: a baby.

On their eighth date, Louise was ready to make her play. Back at her trailer after dinner, most clothing was shed and the foreplay had almost reached the point of fulfillment of Albert's ultimate goal when suddenly, Lucille crossed her legs tightly and sat upright. Abruptly cut off from where he believed the evening was leading, Albert looked up at her questioningly. It was then that she asked the dreaded question, "So Red, this is all so much fun, but where's it all going?"

Broadsided by the question and sensing that there would be no further activity until it was answered, Albert offered, "What do ya' mean 'where's it goin'? Lucille, it's going just fine, right?!"

"Well, Red, it actually doesn't seem to be going anywhere right now," Lucille began her stratagem with a pouty look. "Every date we go a little further, and I get sooo excited," her eyes widening for effect, "and I want sooo much more, Red. Don't you want so much more?" she asked coquettishly.

"Of course, I want more, Lucille!" Albert replied quickly, a strained pitch to his voice.

"As much as I want what you want, Red, I need to know that you're serious."

"I'm super serious, Lucille!" panted Albert, now at a fever pitch from all of the talk about 'so much more'.

Running her slender fingers through her hair and uncrossing her legs seductively she dangled the hook. "Serious, Albert? To me 'serious' means a commitment." Tracing a circle on his hairy chest she began again, "You know what this shape is, Albert? It's a ring. A ring is a commitment. Rings are what men give when they're serious. Are you serious, Red?" Clear on where Albert's attention was focused, she symbolically re-crossed her legs. Albert could take no more; he was ready to do whatever it took to advance their physical relationship.

"A ring?" said Albert, his voice now shrill. "Of course a ring, Lucille. If that's what it takes for you to know I'm serious, then a ring it is!"

Confirming his offer she again uncrossed her legs, lifting her hips a little as she did so. "So this Saturday, we'll head to Livingston and get a ring. Is that what you're proposing, Red?"

"Yes!" Albert's response almost came out like a shout "Yes, yes, yes, it's a deal, this Saturday we get a ring!"

"Well okay, sweetheart, if that's what you really want. Guess we're going to have to put this off until Saturday then." Seeing the pain on his face from the unexpected delay, she added, "But I'm sure I can do something to help you make it through until then…"

Albert and Lucille were married in the Mt. Republic Chapel of Peace in Cooke City. The first act of the new Mrs. Stewart was to clean up Albert's cabin. "You're going to have to find a place for all of these guns, Red." Albert had a 72-gun safe delivered to the cabin, filled it with his favorites, and sold the rest.

The two of them worked quite well together as Lucille came up with ideas to remodel and expand the cabin and Albert provided the labor. One day Albert came home from the mine and Lucille had elk spaghetti ready for him. "Red," Lucille began as Albert slurped down his noodles, "I need ya' to add another room."

Albert looked up from his plate curiously. "Another room? What's this one gonna be for? Ya' don't sew, so I know it ain't gonna be a sewing room!" he laughed.

"Gimme' yer' hand," she ordered, grabbing his free hand, putting it under her shirt, and rubbing it back and forth.

"Right now!? Can I finish my dinner first?" asked Albert, clueless.

"Not that, ya' dummy! A baby! I'm pregnant, can you feel my bump?"

Albert literally dropped his fork to his plate. "A baby!? Who's the father?!" he asked in a rare attempt at humor.

"Fuck you!" Lucille laughed, flipping him off, pretending to be hurt.

"Yep, that's what did it alright!" he countered, then they were both laughing hysterically.

Albert wiped the spaghetti from his beard, stood, then scooped Lucille up into his arms and carried her to the bedroom. "Now show me how this works?!" he said and she giggled as they fell to the bed.

Even though Albert's relationship with his own dad, John, had been tainted by the austere conditions that they had lived under and the secrecy of the illegal trapping they had done, Albert looked forward to having a child and being a father. Boy or girl, it didn't matter to him, he was going to raise them to love hunting as he did. Lucille for her part wanted a boy. She'd seen how mean teenage girls could be, and she preferred the relative simplicity of a male child. She'd take stitches and broken bones over drama and trauma anytime. As luck would have it, Lucille got what she was hoping for and Albert was thrilled as well when the doctor at Livingston Health Care laid the nine-pound red-headed boy on Lucille's stomach.

"Shall we call him Rusty?" she asked.

"I like it better than Ginger," chuckled Albert, with happy tears in his eyes.

As Lucille had foreseen, Rusty got a lot of stitches and broke a few bones growing up. He was like Albert in many ways, including his coloration and size, and his preference for being out of doors whenever possible. He developed a passion for hunting, but it manifested differently in Rusty. For Rusty it was never about the killing, it was all about the stalking, the strategizing, reading the sign, and an intimate knowledge of the animal's behavior.

And it wasn't about the firearms. Rusty could care less about the guns, caliber, bullet drop, velocity, dismantling them, cleaning them - he had no interest in any of it. Rusty would be happier hunting deer with a rock or a club than with one of Albert's expensive hunting rifles. By the time Rusty was a teenager, his hunting tools of choice were bow and arrow. And not a complex compound bow with cams and wheels, not even a recurve bow with its fancy shape, but a long bow, just like the American Indians had used.

Albert didn't mind at all that Rusty had rejected his style of hunting. Albert decided that if their different styles meant that they couldn't hunt together, he would just change his style. By the summer of 1988 when Rusty was seventeen, Albert and Rusty had already been archery hunting together for a few years. In the off-season they practiced on the shooting range Albert had built in the woods behind the cabin. Here they had several life-size foam replicas of elk, deer, pronghorn, and bear. In this way, they were preparing themselves for the Fall '88 archery hunting season, the season that never came to be.

TYLER

The eight Adams cousins played well when they were together, which was often. Jake and Angie's four, Cory and Melissa's three, and Hank's one. It was easy to do. Jake and Angie had moved into the main house on the Draggin' A after Matt Adams had passed away in 1976. Cory and Melissa had moved into the roomy guest house, and Hank and his son lived in the renovated linesman's cabin near the base of the mountains. They were good kids. The younger cousins attended Clark Elementary School, and the older ones rode the bus to middle school in Powell. If there was a loner among them it was Hank's boy, Tyler, who, like his father before him, always seemed to have a contrary opinion, and like as not was out catching bugs and butterflies while his cousins were playing tag.

Hank had always been the odd man out among the three brothers who shared control of the ranch. While Jake and Cory had protested the listing of grizzly bears, Hank had remained quiet on the topic, choosing to not get involved. As it turned out, grizzly bear predation did not become an issue for the cattlemen. It grew into a bigger issue for hunters who were getting bluff-charged and occasionally mauled more often than they once had been. Where his brothers had bought big Dodge diesel pickups, Hank had bought a Toyota Hilux. While his brothers were steak and potatoes eaters, Hank preferred fish. Jake and Cory had married red-blooded, all-American girls, and Hank met and married a dark-skinned Mexican girl who was working in Cody, who left him with the baby just a year after Tyler was born.

Tyler had inherited his mother's rich brown skin, which hadn't been a problem at Clark Elementary School where the Adams kids made up two-thirds of the school's fourteen-student enrollment. But once he began middle school in Powell, his skin color became an issue, with kids calling him "beaner" and "wetback" and referring to his mother as a "putah". Tyler had never been exposed to this sort of bigotry before and didn't understand it.

When the school bully, a kid named Rod, pushed Ty to the ground, taunting "Pick up yer' beans, beaner!" Tyler just lay there, confused, but Tyler's cousins had had enough. Two of the cousins, Jason and David, both a year older than Tyler, rushed the bully. Jason got him in a headlock while David punched him in the face. Jennifer, Tyler's oldest girl cousin came up behind and kicked Rod repeatedly in the ass.

Someone yelled "teacher". Jason released his grip on Rod and by the time the teacher arrived there was not a single Adams cousin to be found, just Rod bloodied and crying. Familiar with the boy's bullying, the male teacher never even bothered to find out who the offenders had been, secretly glad to see Rod get his comeuppance.

It was clear that Ty was not a fighter, another quality that set him apart from the tough rancher kids in rural Wyoming. But he was durable, never crying out like the other kids did when they tore their knees or got stung by a wasp. And he never fought back - hit him as hard as you could and he would take the punch, turn and walk away.

While these qualities made Tyler an anomaly as well as a frequent target, they also made him a strong, reliable worker. While the other cousins often looked for ways to get out of chores, Ty was looking for a way to take on more. By the time he was thirteen, he could buck three-wire hay bales from dawn until dusk. By age fourteen, he was mending miles of fences with Hank. At fifteen, as the cousins were comparing what they wanted to be at the holiday dinner table, Ty surprised everyone when he spoke up, "I'm going to be a firefighter." Compared to the high ideals of those aspiring to become veterinarians, attorneys, and pilots, this announcement seemed to set a low bar. Nevertheless, the cousins were supportive, congratulating Ty on what seemed "the perfect job" for a kid who thrived on hard physical work.

Little did any of them realize how soon Ty would get to put his interest to the test.

GOTOOPE (FIRE)

Storm Creek Fire

It was June 14, 1988. School had been out for two weeks and already thirteen-year-old Tekwoni and her friends were bored. Toni's friends, Ashlee and Shondra from Sleeping Giant Middle School in Livingston, were with her, driven by Ashlee's older brother, Lucas. Toni's mother, Haiwi, was working on an environmental impact report for a subdivision being planned in Bozeman. Her father, Thomas, was in Nicaragua with a group from the American Indian Movement, working with the Miskito Indians on their opposition to the Sandinista regime. Toni had been expressly forbidden to go anywhere with Lucas, whom she had a crush on, virtually guaranteeing that she would do the opposite of what she had been told.

The wildflowers were blooming up on Daisy Pass, halfway between Livingston and Cooke City, just north of the park boundary. The road was more of a trail, steep and rutted, which made it all the more exciting in Lucas' Jeep. In addition to the wildflowers, there were the ruins of the New World Mine, perfect for teenagers looking to relieve their boredom for a while.

Parking at the pass, they hiked along the hillside towards the 9,700' summit. After taking photos of some of the most stunning wildflowers - bluebells, Indian paintbrush, and Toni's favorite, blue columbines - they sat among the carpet of flowers and cracked beers that sixteen-year-old Lucas had appropriated from the fridge in his dad's trophy room. As they gazed to the south, they suddenly noticed what looked like a thunderhead, not unexpected over the Beartooth Mountains during summer;

192

but this cloud was different, it was brown. "Holy crap!" shouted Lucas, pointing, "That's not a storm cloud, that's smoke from a forest fire!"

The fire was still many miles away, and they spent the afternoon mesmerized by the smoke while picking out landmarks to help determine just what area was burning. It appeared that the fire was to the east of them, north of Cooke City. Occasionally they could see the orange of the flames as the fire crested a small ridge or torched one of the millions of beetle-killed pines. As the afternoon wore on they ran out of beer and interest in the fire, and had just begun hiking back to the Jeep when Ashlee called out, "Wait! What's that?" gesturing down towards a grassy drainage a mile away.

The rest of the group put their hands above their eyes as sun shields and searched for the object that Ashlee was motioning towards. "I see it!" shrieked Toni, followed by "I see it now," and "I'm on it," from the others.

"It's a human, I'm pretty sure, and it looks like they have a dog with them," relayed Ashlee, having analyzed them the longest.

"That's a crazy place for a person, there's no trail down there or anything," said Lucas.

"I wonder if they're lost?" thought Toni aloud. At that the four teens began shouting, whistling, and waving their arms. After ten seconds or so they watched the figure stop, as though they were looking around for the source of the sound. The group resumed their noise-making, increasing their volume, and added jumping up and down to the hand waving. They could all detect a change in the figure's body language as it and the dog began climbing the hillside toward the teens. They watched the figure's progress in silence as the pair was obscured by rocks and passed through small groups of trees.

As the shapes got nearer they could see that it was a man, his clothing stained with dirt and who knows what else, and the dog, a border collie, didn't look much better. When he finally climbed over the lip of the hill next to them, he sat down, covered his face with his hat, and began to cry. The dog sniffed everyone tiredly then lay down next to the man.

Some of what looked like dirt on his clothing was indeed brown soil; the black spots looked as though he had rubbed charcoal on his pants and shirt. The dog's black and white coat was similarly filthy and parts of its wavy hair looked singed and matted.

"Are you okay, mister?" Toni asked.

"We were camping near Mystic Lake," the man began haltingly, referring to himself and the dog. "We had back-packed in. Everything had been fine, beautiful. We were fishing along west Rosebud Creek when, poof! a fire blew up not far from us. I said to Rocky, my dog, 'let's get outta' here!'" He stopped and wiped his dirty face with his filthy bandana. "We turned towards camp figuring we would pack up our gear and make our way out. Before we knew it the fire was gaining on us, we began running," he choked on his words. "Then the fire was all around us, I was sure we were gonna die. Rocky's coat actually started smoking! Just then we came to the end of the lake and dove in. The fire burned everything around us as we lay there in the freezing cold water. I actually had to keep dunking my head because my face was so hot," he stopped while choking back more tears. "I had to hold Rocky under the water, which he didn't like at all."

"By nightfall last night it had burned down enough that we could get out and walk to where our camp had been. All of my gear was burned up, or melted; all I had was the clothes I was wearing. We spent the night huddled together near smoldering logs for warmth. The fire was burning in the direction of the Mystic Lake trailhead, so that way was blocked. We started wandering this way looking for a trail but never really found one." He coughed a few times, took a few deep breaths, and asked, "You kids wouldn't happen to have any food would ya? I haven't eaten since yesterday."

The foursome went into action. Fortunately, Lucas was something of a slob so there were many snack-food packages strewn about the floor of the Jeep. The sum of the contents almost made enough for a meal: nuts, Doritos, Oreos, and a half-eaten Sausage McBiscuit. The man, whose name was Alan, wolfed down two-thirds of the food and gave the rest to Rocky, who perked up considerably.

"You're gonna need a ride outta here, right?" asked Lucas.

"I guess I am," said Alan, as though he hadn't yet considered it.

"We're heading back to Livingston right now and the girls and the dog can cram into the back seat," offered Lucas, to which the girls all responded enthusiastically.

"Oh God, thank you!" said Alan as he choked up again. "If I can just get to Livingston, I can call my wife in Billings to pick us up there. Thank you!"

"You bet, we'd better get going. It's gonna be a chilly ride back in the Jeep," said Lucas as the girls helped Alan to his feet. Rocky, sensing that the worst was now over, was suddenly invigorated, prancing from person to person and squirming happily as he was lifted into the Jeep.

As they began descending the rocky road back out of the mountains, Lucas could see an ominous orange glow in his rearview mirror. It was as though the entire eastern horizon was smoldering.

Had all mining not ceased in the New World Mining District where Albert had been employed for more than 20 years, he would have surely been chased off the mountain by what was now being called the Storm Creek Fire, the same fire that Toni and her friends had just witnessed. As luck would have it, President Bill Clinton had come to Cooke City just a year before to sign a deal that effectively killed the mine's future. Too many years had the mine been discharging an acidic orange plume, that eventually flowed into Yellowstone's legendary Lamar River and beyond into the storied Yellowstone River. Years of fighting over the mine's expansion plans came to a halt with that momentous signing, and just like that Albert was out of a job.

Lucille was still working at the Miner's Saloon and was still turning heads at forty-four. Rusty was working at the Cooke City Store and guiding fly-fishing trips on the Clark's Fork of the Yellowstone River during the summer months. Albert began cutting firewood to make money, a fairly lucrative pursuit for a strong, hard-working fifty-two-year-old. Anytime that Rusty and Albert shared a day off, they were shooting their bows and planning their next hunts.

They were practicing at their target range when Rusty first noticed that something was wrong. "There's a weird color to everything today, kinda yellowish," he remarked to his dad as they were removing the arrows from a foam mule deer.

"Yeah, I kinda noticed that too," replied Albert.

Then tilting his head back slightly Rusty drew in three short breaths through his nose. "Smells smoky," he offered.

Albert did the same, turning in a complete circle as he did so, determining which way the slight scent was coming from. "Breeze is coming from the north. Somebody must be burning trash down near the highway," he guessed.

"Guess so," answered Rusty as they strode back to the forty-yard mark they had been shooting from.

Later that afternoon, it was clear that it was something much bigger than a trash fire, as a brown cloud the shape of a morel mushroom cloaked the northern horizon.

"Shit!" croaked Albert. "That's a real gol-durned fire!"

"Looks like it's between us and Red Lodge," replied Rusty.

"Sure docs," said Albert "I hope it's headed north."

For a month and a half, the fire languished deep in the Beartooth Mountains, stalled out, barely growing. On that June day, Cooke City seemed safe. A week later, two more fires, the Shoshone Fire and the Fan Fire, broke out in Yellowstone Park to the south. Montana's "big sky" would still be big that summer, but it would be big and brown, not blue.

Clover Mist Fire

It was early July and far to the southeast of the Beartooths and Cooke City, the Draggin' A Ranch crew had just trailed their herd into the high country. In the Absaroka Mountains west of the ranch, they could take advantage of summer grazing on the Forest Service land they leased for that purpose. Far to the north of them, they had seen the dull brown scrim of smoke from the Storm Creek Fire. The brothers and their children were enjoying the annual tradition of the cattle drive to the mountains, and the campfires, guitar playing, and cookouts that went along with them.

As usual, Hank and Tyler spent much of the time apart from the rest of the group, helping with the cows when needed, exploring mountain meadows in their downtime, and joining the family in the evening for dinner and a fire. As they were wandering along the upper reaches of Sunlight Creek, Tyler was the first to notice a change in the weather.

"Breeze comin' out of the park, Pa," observed Tyler to his dad on the bay horse behind him. "Smells a little smoky!"

"It shore ain't that Storm Creek Fire, that's too far north of us," Hank shouted from the rear. "Might be another fire. We should let the others know!" Turning their horses back down the canyon they headed back to camp.

The family had just met back in camp to grab some lunch after checking the cows.

"Back so soon?" shouted Cory as he saw the pair approaching. "Thought you two mountain men would be gone all day!"

"Smells like fire up the canyon, comin' outta the park probably," Hank said loudly for all to hear. "No idea how far away it might be but it's somethin' to be aware of, in case we gotta get these cows outta here!"

The cousins gathered around to hear more. Jake spoke up. "There's no reason to get too excited yet. Angie, can you and Meredith ride back down to the ranch and check the news, see if there's anything about a fire? No need to run, take yer' time and be safe."

"Sure will," Angie replied crisply. "C'mon, Mer', let's saddle back up."

It was about a two-hour ride back to the ranch complex, and as soon as they got there the two went in and Angie turned on the radio while Meredith started making phone calls. There was nothing on the radio news, which was tentatively relieving. Meredith first called two friends, neither of whom knew anything about a fire; her third call was to the Forest Service Ranger Station in Cody.

"Yes ma'am, there are actually three new fires, all burning inside of the park," reported the ranger. "Did you say your ranch is over near Clark?"

"That's right," replied Meredith, "between Clark and Yellowstone."

"Well then it looks like the fire is due west of your property." Then the ranger added, "I wouldn't be too concerned, Miss Adams. We see these kinda' fires almost every summer and they rarely turn into anything."

"Thank you, sir, that's reassuring. Goodbye."

Angie had wandered into the kitchen to listen in on Meredith's conversation, and when she hung up the phone, Angie said, "Reassuring, yes, but it still makes me nervous. Let's go up and tell the rest and see what Jake thinks we should do." Taking the opportunity to pick up a few things at the house, the two were on the trail in ten minutes and made it to cow camp just as the sun was dipping behind the peaks to the west. The sunset was spectacular, the few clouds turning crimson and purple with gilded edges. The older family members had seen enough fires in their lives to know that vivid sunsets often accompanied wildfires, the additional particles in the air from the smoke refracting more of the red and orange colors.

Angie had Meredith recite what the ranger had said. When she finished, everyone began speaking at once, each sharing their thoughts on this development. The cousins were nervously excited; this would be their first experience with fire near the ranch. There was nothing resembling excitement on the faces of the adults. Fires were scary, more frightening than a grizzly bear. The brothers pow-wowed for a few minutes as the others continued speculating, then Jake banged a pot with a spoon to get everyone's attention.

"Here's what we're gonna do, guys and gals," Jake began. "The first thing is, all the cousins except the three oldest boys are going back home," to which there was a uniform moan of displeasure from all of the others. "Shhh, now I know you want to stay but this is deadly serious stuff, and we're not going to take any more risks than we need to," to which the group quieted back down. "Jason, David, and Ty are going to stay up here with Cory, Hank, and me to watch the herd and get 'em movin' if needed. The rest of you can take turns bringing us news, two at a time." This perked the cousins back up a little; at least they could be of some assistance and still get to camp occasionally

"We're probably over-reacting," Jake was concluding his talk. "We'll look back at this later and laugh about what a big deal we made over a little smoke," to which they all chuckled and blew off a little bit of anxiety. In reality, they were not overreacting at all, and they would never look back and laugh about the events that had just begun to unfold.

That night as they were settling into their bedrolls, Ty propped himself up on an elbow and said to Hank, "You know I got my Firefighter certification, right?"

"Yeah, buddy, I'm proud of you!"

"If there were a fire, I'll be expected to help with the District 4 Station in Clark."

"I understand, son," said Hank thoughtfully, "but as of right now we don't even have a fire here. Yellowstone's got one, and Yellowstone will have federal firefighters workin' on that one. We'll worry about where you're fightin' a fire if, God forbid, it crosses outta the park, alright?"

"Right, Pa, goodnight."

"Goodnight, Ty."

Once the bulk of the family returned to the flatlands, the uncles and three nephews were kept busy keeping an eye on the cows, and the other eye on the sky. On July 14th, the sky provided quite a show, as what looked like a military helicopter raced by about a mile south of them and then an hour later raced back, looking to be headed towards Cody. When Haley and cousin Heather arrived the next morning to provide the men with news and treats, they informed them that then Vice-President, George H. Bush, had been fishing with an outfitter in the wilderness nearby, and had been rushed out by helicopter for fear that the fire was getting dangerously close to his camp. They also learned that rangers working at the Calfee Creek Backcountry Ranger Station had been forced to take cover in their emergency fire shelters as flames overtook them near the confluence of the Lamar River and Miller Creek, less than twenty miles away.

"This fire's startin' to get on my nerves," understated Jake.

When Justin and Kevin took their turn bringing news to the cowboys, the update angered the men. "The park announced yesterday that they are now officially starting to fight the fires," recited twelve-year-old Justin.

"What?!" the uncles shouted in unison.

"What the hell have they been doin' until now?!" groused Jake.

"Lettin' their goddam fire burn towards our ranch," replied Cory.

"Wow, well that sure makes me feel better," continued Jake. "Now that the fires have grown into big, out-of-control beasts, now they're gonna start doing something about them?! Pardon my French boys but fuck the feds! Fuck Yellowstone!"

For the next few weeks, the fire, originally called the Clover Fire, spread mostly to the north and south within the park, joining with two other fires: the Mist Fire and the Raven Fire, officially being renamed the Clover-

Mist Fire. Then on July 30th, it breached the park boundary, but only slightly and to the south of the ranch. Two and a half more nerve-wracking weeks passed with the fire repeatedly testing the park's perimeter. Finally on August 22nd, it began making a serious run into the ranch's leaseholds.

Even though it was Heather and Haley's turn, Angie had instead sent the two boys, Justin and Kevin, to bring the concerning news. After hearing what the boys had to report, the three uncles were in agreement as Jake made it official.

"That's it, boys, the fun's over. Let's start moving these dogs downhill, not too fast, don't spook 'em, but let 'em know we're serious." The assembled men and boys hurriedly gathered their remaining belongings, stuffing what they could onto the panniers of the few mules they had with them.

"David, you think you can handle these mules?" questioned Jake of his oldest son.

"Yes, sir," replied David seriously.

"Justin and Kevin, you stay with David and the mules. Get straight back to the barn and get unloaded. Hank and Cory, you look for strays, while me and Jason and Ty start drivin' the bulk of the herd down the mountain."

"Got it," said Cory and Hank simultaneously.

"Good luck, boys, and be careful, it's gonna be a dangerous coupla' days."

Fan Fire

It was now late August 1988 and there were eleven separate, named fires burning in Yellowstone. To the west of the park headquarters in Mammoth Hot Springs, the Fan Fire was the only one that was virtually under control. Toni began volunteering at the Big Sky Bird Rehabilitation Center just north of the park, and while no small birds had been brought in for rehab (many had been sitting on eggs), a few raptors and corvids had been found singed and disoriented. A great gray owl had been brought in for rehabilitation as had a large common raven. Toni had been volunteering at the new Rodford Animal Shelter in Livingston, but she had decided she wanted to help with burned animals during the fires. The Bird Rehab Center was not far away, so Haiwi would drop her off three days a week to assist with feeding and other chores.

Small roadkill - badgers, squirrels, and coyotes - were salvaged for the feeding of the raven that volunteers had named "Vader". Toni's favorite task was feeding the owl, which preferred its food live. Toni would place a living pet-store mouse on the floor of the owl's large enclosure and watch the great gray turn its head back and forth, eyeing the prey before pouncing upon it and consuming it whole.

North Fork Fire

Just as the Fan Fire was petering out, the North Fork Fire to the west of Old Faithful was gathering strength. The aggressive fire was heading to the northeast and consuming the wildlands around Madison, then Norris, then Canyon. Every hotel, motel, and city park around Livingston was full of fire engines and firefighters, resting up between long shifts on the fire lines. No place within or even near Yellowstone seemed safe from fire, so the crews drove the hour north to Livingston for respite.

There were even crews camped at Sleeping Giant Middle School, so Toni and her friends began bringing treats to the firefighters: cookies, punch, and sandwiches. The firemen were thrilled to get the homemade items, a wonderful alternative to the military-style MREs common at fire camps.

When the Northfork Fire suddenly turned and ran straight at the Old Faithful Inn on September 7th, every available firefighter rushed to defend the iconic 105-year-old architectural wonder. Wind gusts were blowing embers the size of softballs toward the structure at 75 miles an hour and saving the all-wooden building seemed like a long shot. Firefighters climbed onto the 92-foot-high roof to drape hoses over the building, to be able to soak as much of the exterior as possible. Helicopters made water drops on the approaching fire all day long. Most fortuitously, the century-old sprinkler system had been completely renovated just one year earlier and included an "exterior deluge" function which poured a continuous cascade of water onto all parts of the roof. As evening approached, it was clear that the flames had surrounded, and then passed the building, continuing eastward but sparing the Inn. Park staff on hand applauded the heroic efforts of the firemen.

Storm Creek Fire

Outside of the park in the Beartooth Mountains, the sluggish Storm Creek Fire had been biding its time. By August 18th, two full months after it had first begun, it had barely moved from its original charred footprint. On August 19th, a strong north wind began to blow through the canyons, and by the end of the next day, it had covered nearly twenty miles in the direction of Cooke City. For the next two weeks, Cooke City residents held their breath as the fire turned west, away from town. Then on September 4th, the "shit hit the fan", as the fire began racing back towards the town with a vengeance. Sheriff cars, fire engines, and diesel trucks hauling bulldozers on lowboy trailers were suddenly everywhere as helicopters flew back and forth over Main Street. The sheriffs were driving through the town with their loudspeakers on, or going door-to-door asking residents to leave. One of the last roads they traveled down was Emma Mine Road, where Albert, Lucille, and Rusty were busy cutting down small trees and limbing up larger ones around the cabin.

Albert's long disdain for law enforcement was obvious as he refused to even acknowledge the Sheriff's presence, even after being hailed on the loudspeaker. Lucille and Rusty had no such problem with authority and trotted over to the cruiser.

"I see Albert hasn't changed in fifty years," the Sheriff began. Then remembering his haste, said, "Everybody needs to get out now. Fire's makin' a run on the town! I know Albert won't leave but Lucille, you and the boy should get out, now!"

"Thanks, Vern, how much time would you guess we have?" asked Lucille, clearly spooked.

"Fire Captain is talking about lightin' some backfires. No telling how that might go, could save the town but could burn it down quicker. If it were me, I'd throw my most valuable things in the truck and start drivin'. Good luck!" Then shouting towards Albert as he was pulling away, "Get out while you can you stubborn son-of-a-bitch!" Albert just went on cutting brush.

Once the Sheriff was out of sight, Albert came over to where Lucille and Rusty were standing in a daze. "He's right, you know," one of the only times Albert had ever agreed with an officer. "You two need to get outta here. I'll stay and keep clearing brush then keep the cabin doused if the fire makes it here."

Never one to directly contradict his father, Rusty took a stand. "No way, Pa!" he said forcefully. "I'm staying here to help save the cabin while Mom drives to someplace safe."

Lucille was the only one who was ready to comply. "Okay boys, I'm not gonna' lie, I'm damned scared," she admitted "Promise me that if it gets too hot you'll go lay in the deep hole in the creek," referring to Republic Creek just a hundred feet away.

"That's the plan," Albert and Rusty said in agreement.

Over the next two days, there was a flurry of activity around the cabin. Three large tractor-trailers parked along Emma Mine Road, each unloading fire-engine red D8 bulldozers. The dozers began chewing up a massive seventy-foot-wide fire line from the end of the road, west along the northern flank of Republic Mountain all the way to Silver Gate, the even tinier community between Cooke City and the park's northeast entrance station that Robert had constructed fifty years earlier. Then came the decision that would be questioned long afterward among fire scientists; the crews were instructed to start lighting backfires.

"Like hell you are!" shouted Albert, charging the battalion chief who was giving orders just beyond the cabin. Three firemen, as well as Rusty, had to restrain Albert.

"Dad, stop! Dad, let 'em do their jobs!"

"I'm gonna call the sheriff if you don't back off, sir," shouted the surprised chief. "Put a couple of men on that guy. We got a fire to fight!"

Albert was already allowing Rusty to pull him back towards the cabin as two firemen took a position between them and the chief. "They're gonna burn the whole damned town down Rusty, just you watch," Albert said, shaking his head in resignation. At the same time, sixty miles away as the crow flies, firefighters at the Old Faithful Inn were scaling the roof to save that building.

Clover Mist Fire

At the same moment that Rusty Stewart was pulling Albert away from the battalion chief battling the Storm Creek Fire, Tyler Adams was following orders of the Park County Department Four fire chief. The all-volunteer crew was assisting in the offensive against the Clover Mist Fire as it roared eastward across the Draggin' A's leaseholds around Sugarloaf Mountain. The fire had been burning into the park for the past two weeks and the Adams had begun to feel a little less anxious. The uncles and cousins had successfully driven the herd back into the valley flatlands with very few incidents, those being mostly cuts and bruises from riding through vegetation-choked draws, and the loss of a single calf that was never located.

But then the same weather system that had whipped the Storm Creek Fire south towards Cooke City began breathing new life into long-smoldering logs along Yellowstone's border. The gusts invigorated embers, sending them to the east towards the Draggin' A. It was then that the Department Four volunteers were called to action, the call that junior firefighter, Ty Adams, had been anxiously waiting for.

Department Four's job was to help defend a handful of vacation homes and cabins in the path of the fire. As in Cooke City, numerous fire apparatus had been brought in and parked adjacent to the threatened structures. Tyler was stationed with two senior volunteers at a cabin along Crandall Road. As the flames neared, there was an eerie orange glow to the smoke-clogged air, and Tyler and his partners repeatedly hosed down the wooden structure.

The valley of the Clark's Fork of the Yellowstone River was normally cool in early September but the winds coming out of the west were superheated. The men were pushing themselves, removing as much vegetation as they could in a wide circle around the cabin, throwing shovels full of soil on any ember that blew into their space. Tyler saw 64-year-old Jesse bend over and then crumple to the ground. Running to him, he dragged the much heavier man to the truck where he administered oxygen from an emergency bottle he had there, and then got on the truck's two-way radio.

"Fireman down, assistance needed! Fireman down on Black Rock Lane in Crandall, does anyone copy?!" The radio was full of static and the roar of the approaching fire made it hard to hear. "Fireman down, need assistance on Black Rock Lane, anyone copy?!" Ty screamed into the handset. Nothing except garbled chatter could be heard, so Tyler made a life or death decision. "Tim!" he shouted to the third man in the group who was busy chasing down embers. "Tim!!" Ty shouted again then began running to the man. Grabbing Tim by the sleeve, he pulled him towards the truck as he shouted, "Jesse went down, I got him in the truck on oxygen. We need to get him outta here, c'mon!" Tim ran to the driver's side of the already-running truck as Ty jumped back into the back seat of the crew cab with Jesse, and they were rolling before the door was even closed. "Go down to Painter Outpost, that's where command is set up," Ty instructed.

Painter Outpost was the center of the loose-knit community of Crandall: bar, eatery, gift shop, and gathering place. The huge gravel parking area provided a great staging area for fire crews that had flooded in during the last 24 hours. Ty had been right to come. Not only had Jesse been put in an ambulance headed for Cody, but the Chief had demanded that Tyler get checked up as well just to be safe. Tyler was livid but kept it in check as he pleaded not to be taken off of the fire. He was allowed to ride in the back with Jesse, who was now alert and breathing easier.

By the time the ambulance arrived at the hospital, it was dark out, and Tyler was no longer feeling so well. As he stepped out of the ambulance he discreetly vomited, hoping that no one would see. Fortunately, one of the EMTs had caught him in the act and took him by the arm into the hospital, where he was admitted with symptoms of smoke inhalation.

Although he argued that he should be allowed back on the fire with his fellow volunteers, there was no way that Tyler would return to the Clover Mist fire. He would spend that night in the hospital. By the time he had arrived at the hospital in Cody, the fire had destroyed four dwellings, fourteen trailers, numerous outbuildings, and a store in the Crandall area.

RUSTY AND TYLER

As luck would have it, Rusty Stewart and Tyler Adams had been brought into the Cody Regional Health Center at about the same time. Shortly after the backfires were lit outside of Cooke City, Rusty and Albert had resumed falling conifers around the cabin. Stepping between two downed trees laying parallel, he heard his dad yell, "Heads up!" as another lodgepole began to sway. Although the tree was not headed his way, he instinctively tried to jump out of the way, catching his foot between the logs and falling, fracturing his tibia. The roads were closed in both directions out of Cooke City, so despite his loud protestations, he was placed on a helicopter that was transporting fire personnel back and forth from Cody, while Albert stayed at the cabin.

Once in Cody, he was taken to the Health Center for x-rays and to have his lower leg put in a cast. While waiting for his x-ray, he was seated in a room with a brown-skinned boy about the same age. "Fire get ya'?" Rusty asked to break the silence.

"Yeah, I was fighting the fire near Crandall and I guess I inhaled a little too much smoke," replied Ty in a hoarse voice.

"That sucks!" said Rusty supportively.

"How about you?" Ty reciprocated once he'd stopped coughing. "What'd you do to your leg?"

"I was on the other fire – Storm Creek. I fractured my tibia while my dad and I were falling trees near our cabin."

"Oh man, did the cabin make it?" asked Rusty sincerely.

"It was still standing when I left. I'm pretty sure it's okay. We had a shitpile of firefighters along our road."

The two laughed, then Ty said, "I'm pretty sure the cabin I was trying to save didn't make it. The fire was headed right for it when we bugged out."

"You were protecting somebody else's cabin?" Rusty asked, confused,

"I'm on the Clark Volunteer Fire Crew. Three of us were supposed to save this cabin; I think we failed," Ty said with a hint of self-blame.

"Oh man, that's awesome that you were in there helping. It's not your fault man, you're a hero!" to which Ty just blushed and shook his head.

Tyler was taken in first to have his chest x-rayed. While Rusty sat alone in the lobby, a group of people filed in, filling the waiting room. A pretty teenage girl turned to Rusty and asked, "Was there just a dark-haired boy in here?" and then, remembering her manners asked, "Oh, are you okay?"

Rusty replied, "Yeah, he just went in for an x-ray, and yeah I'm okay – thanks."

"That's good, about the leg I mean! And that boy is my cousin; we came by to cheer him up!"

Rusty looked around the room, and although he couldn't see much family resemblance, he was nevertheless intrigued by balloons and signs. "What's with all the decorations and stuff?" asked Rusty curiously.

"Didn't he tell you? Ty's a hero!" Ty's cousin Meredith gushed. "He dragged another firefighter that passed out to safety, and he's only sixteen."

"Wow!" exclaimed Rusty earnestly. "I told him he was a hero just for fightin' the fire, but he's a real by-God hero!"

The whole group was now listening to the exchange, and an older man in the group asked, "What's yer' name son, and what happened to ya'?"

"Name's Rusty, sir, Rusty Stewart. Broke my leg falling logs around my family's cabin over near Cooke City."

"Where's yer family now, son?" asked the man - Tyler's father, Hank.

"My dad's still over there fightin' the fire far as I know," answered Rusty. "We sent my mom off before it got too bad, I think she's probably in Livingston."

"Well don't you worry about anything, Rusty Stewart. We're gonna be your family while yer' in Cody!" stated Hank as the rest of the group nodded in agreement.

Just then the door opened and Tyler stepped back into the room accompanied by a nurse, as the whole family applauded and everyone took turns hugging him, shaking his hand, and patting him on the back.

"What's the verdict?" asked Ty's Uncle Jake.

"I'm gonna be okay," Ty replied in a raspy voice.

"He needs to get plenty of rest and we're going to send him home with some inhalers to open up his airway, which is a little swollen," said the nurse authoritatively.

"Can we take him out for a celebration dinner?" asked Jake.

"Yes, but don't overdo it. He needs to heal, no hot liquids, soft food," the nurse answered.

"Great," smiled Jake, "and can we take this boy, Rusty, with us too?" he asked.

"He needs to get that leg in a cast. It's going to be a while," she proclaimed.

"We'll be waitin' for him when he gets out," said Hank.

"What about the fire?" asked Ty. "Shouldn't we get back to the ranch?"

"Have you looked outside lately, Ty?" his Uncle Cory asked. "Come over and check this out," he said, motioning him over to the window where he had been standing.

Looking over the top of the town to the Absarokas, Tyler beheld a beautiful sight. "It's snowing!" he cried, and the whole group laughed with joy and relief. "Started this morning, Ty. It's snowing all over the fires." It was September 11th, the beginning of the end of the most nightmarish fire season anyone could recall.

Although the various fires would continue to smolder until November, the rains and snows of September effectively eliminated the dry conditions they needed to expand. By the numbers: there had been a total of fifty-one fires, eleven of which had become named fires. Forty-two of the fires were started by lightning; the remaining nine were human-caused.

Inside the park, 793,880 acres were burned, a little more than one-third of the park's total acreage. Outside of the park on National Forest and private lands, hundreds of thousands more were scorched. More than $120 million was spent on suppressing the fires, primarily to save lives and structures. Over five months, more than 25,000 personnel were involved in the effort, which included creating over 792 miles of fire line. Over 100 fire engines and 120 aircraft were employed to combat the various fires.

Elk numbers had been at their peak in the 1987-1988 season, at about 19,000 year-round resident elk and as many as 10,000–20,000 more that migrated into the park seasonally. Due to the loss of habitat and forage in the years immediately following the fire, elk numbers dipped to 12,000 resident animals in 1990, but then herds rebounded to their pre-fire peak again in 1994. Of the large mammals known to have perished as a result of the fires, there were 345 elk, 36 mule deer, 12 moose, 9 bison, 6 black bears, and 1 grizzly bear. Losses of small mammals and birds were impossible to assess.

It was the birds that were the primary focus of Tekwoni's volunteer efforts. A few additional birds of prey had been brought into the rehabilitation center in August, including a Cooper's hawk and a Swainson's hawk, both of which were fed mice in the same way as the great gray owl had been. In September, just as the Storm Creek and Clover Mist fires were reaching their apex, a bird that made all of the others before it seem small was found pacing alongside a burned-out section of highway - a golden eagle. Bald eagles were traditionally more conspicuous in the ecosystem than golden eagles. One of the reasons was that bald eagles typically hunted near waterways, as fish and waterfowl made up the largest part of their diet, and people and roads are usually close to rivers, streams, and lakes. Golden eagles were denizens of hillsides and mountain peaks, small mammals making up the bulk of their diets, and because they preferred these high places, they were not observed as frequently as their white-headed kin. What the two eagles had in common was their preference for carrion; both would readily scavenge road-killed and winter-killed large animal remains. A century earlier when all three of the park's large predators were still common in the region, the eagles were at their peak of abundance, feeding on weather-killed animals in the early spring and predator-killed carcasses year-round.

"This is a two-year-old," explained one of the veteran volunteers named Grace to Toni, who was fascinated by the majesty of the bird.

"How do you know how old it is?" Toni asked in response, eager to learn anything she could about the creature.

"Do you see the white band on its tail?" pointed out Grace, to which Toni nodded affirmatively. "In its first year it is pure white and arcs with the tail. By three years of age, the tail band develops long dark central tail feathers, called rectrices. But in year two, that band has lost its arc and brightness but still hasn't developed the dark central rectrices."

"Amazing!" replied Toni, smitten with the animal.

The big bird was surprisingly calm for a wild eagle, and to assess its health and any injuries, Toni was shown how to hold it by the legs while wrapping her leather-gloved arms around its wings to keep it from flapping them. A specially made hood was placed over its head, further calming the bird.

"It's not the bill that will get you, it's those talons!" Grace warned. Measurements were then taken and feathers were inspected, after which Grace concluded, "Although determining the sex of eagles is difficult, this appears to be a female based on measurements of the culmen and Hallex claw," eliciting a big smile from Toni. "The feathers aren't singed, so I don't believe that the bird has been injured by fire." Grace continued, "But it does seem as though there has been some damage to her right wing. The radius bone appears dislocated. I think she must have run into a vehicle and came away pretty lucky!"

"What will we do with her?" asked Toni, concern written all over her face.

"We're not going to do anything with her," interjected Julie, the staff biologist who had been over-seeing the exam. "I think we need to send her over to either the Teton Raptor Center in Wilson, down by Jackson Hole, or the one in Cody. They're better equipped to rehab eagles."

Considering that the shortest route to Wilson was through the still-burning park, Phoenix Bird Rescue in Cody was the safer choice. The organization had only been in operation for a year but already had a reputation for rehabilitating injured hawks and eagles.

Julie, the biologist, would drive the young golden eagle, which Toni had dubbed "Band-she", the four hours to Cody, but she needed someone to monitor the bird during the trip.

"Me, me, pleeeease me?" Toni pleaded.

As no one else was available, Julie had Toni arrange permission from her mom for the overnight trip the following day. "I'll pick you up at your house early tomorrow," offered Julie. "Bring a change of clothes and something to sleep in; we're going out to dinner with the owner of the rescue facility."

Toni had never been to Cody so she was thrilled with the whole plan. "Great, I'll be ready first thing!" she said enthusiastically as she headed out the door at the end of her shift.

The ride to Cody was lovely as it had begun to rain, and the smoke from the fires had been diminished. Their arcing route took them along the northern slope, and then the eastern face of the Beartooth Mountains, and snow could be seen on the peaks. The bird was hooded and seemed to sleep the entire way. Toni marveled as they pulled into Cody, noting how much drier the surrounding hills seemed than the forested areas surrounding her home in Montana.

The bird rescue facility in the flatlands east of town was fascinating, with hundreds of birds in various stages of rehabilitation and separate barns for raptors and owls. Susan, the director, listened to Julie's concerns about the eagle's wing and then had a look herself, determining that the problem was over-stretched ligaments of the carpal joint.

"This is a relatively common injury, often the result of contact with a windshield," announced Susan optimistically. "We'll apply a small metal clamp and immobilize the wing for one to two months. Metal works best because they just tear off anything softer. I think she's got a really good chance at a full recovery. Both Julie and especially Toni were thrilled with the prognosis. "Toni, if you'd like to help me feed the animals today, I can be done with chores in time to go dinner," Susan offered. "It's not often that I get to go out for a meal, but one of our donors gave me a gift certificate for the Irma Hotel, one of Cody's most iconic landmarks."

Toni was sold on helping before the dinner was even offered. "I'd love to help," she replied energetically.

After confirming the fracture in Rusty's shin, the doctor immediately began applying a plaster cast, the entire procedure taking a little more than an hour. Much to Rusty's surprise, most of the Adams clan was still in the waiting room when he was wheeled out.

"We'll take him from here," ordered Hank, commandeering the wheelchair from the nurse.

"You can't do that, sir!" said the flustered nurse. "We have to follow protocol."

"Call the Sheriff!" Hank joked as he continued pushing Rusty toward the lobby.

"He's going to have to check out and take care of any billing!" the nurse went on, following the entourage out the door.

"Just bill it to the Draggin' A Ranch," Hank said over his shoulder as he helped Rusty climb into the back seat of the big one-ton Dodge. "Let's go get some dinner, shall we Rusty?" Hank asked, firing up the truck. "The rest of the gang's already there. You ever been to ol' Buffalo Bill's place?" he asked.

"Buffalo Bill's got a place?" puzzled Rusty.

"Yup. We're doin' our 'hero's dinner' at the hotel that Bill Cody built – the Irma!"

It was Monday night and they had the restaurant nearly all to themselves, except for the three women occupying a table near where the family had hung balloons and streamers, and a sign that said "WELCOME HEROES". The women made an interesting group: one fiftyish and serious, one who looked to be in her mid-twenties and intense, and a stunning dark-haired teenager who did not look related to the other two. The Adams clan was in a festive mood, joking and laughing, and when Hank showed up with Rusty they all stood and cheered and began a round of "For He's a Jolly Good Fellow". Tyler was at one end of the table wearing a toy fireman's helmet and Rusty was given the seat next to him.

Jake, noticing the three women staring and whispering, called out to them. "Sorry for all the noise, ladies. We're celebrating a couple of heroes here. Would you care to join us?"

The partiers quieted down as Susan replied, "Well, what a coincidence. I've got a couple of heroes here as well; we'd love to join you!" Everyone was pleasantly surprised at Susan's acceptance of the offer, no one more than Toni who had been watching the activity at the next table with envy. Chairs were moved and more were added as the three ladies found seats among the family - Susan next to Jake's wife Angie, Julie next to Cory's wife Keri, and Toni next to Tyler's cousins Meredith and Haley.

As soon as Susan was seated, she inquired, "Okay, we'd love to hear the story of your two heroes," to which Hank told the story of how Tyler had dragged his unconscious partner to safety.

When it came to the telling of Rusty's story, Rusty began "I'm no hero ma'am, not like Tyler…"

"That's B.S.!" Hank spouted. "He broke his leg while trying to save his family's cabin. That's a hero in our book," to which everyone cheered their support. "Now tell us about your heroes, ma'am?" Hank asked.

"Well first of all, my name's Susan. I own the bird rescue facility east of town," to which most of the group nodded in acknowledgment of the location. "These two ladies, Julie and Toni, drove an injured golden eagle almost five hours so that we can try to repair its damaged wing." The wound-up group all cheered.

"What are the odds? Four heroes at one table!" announced Hank. The table was abuzz with questions and stories.

While Meredith and Haley plied Toni with questions about the eagle, Toni repeatedly caught the eyes of the boys at the ends of the table.

"Okay, now who's related to who?" Toni asked, trying to conceal her interest in the two boys.

"Well, Tyler is our cousin, my Uncle Hank's boy."

"Uh-huh, is he part Indian? He looks a little different from the rest of the family."

"Uncle Hank was married to a Mexican woman, but she left when Tyler was a baby," answered Meredith.

"Ohhh, and how about the other boy, Rusty?" Toni asked.

"He's not family. We met him in the hospital. He's here in Cody all by himself. He is sooo handsome!" said Haley dreamily. Toni didn't say a thing to give away her interest but continued to lock eyes from time to time with the two heroes.

After dinner, people moved around, talking to different family members and guests. Not surprisingly, Rusty and Tyler both came and sat on either side of Toni. "So you like working with eagles, huh?" asked Rusty.

Before Toni could answer, Tyler chimed in, "We've got a big golden eagle nest on the ranch, way up high in a rock formation on Sugarloaf. Next time you visit, I could show it to you."

Not to be outdone, Rusty added, "You said you were from Livingston right? There are goldens all over Republic Mountain right behind our cabin near Cooke City. You must get down there once in a while, right?" Toni's head was spinning from all of the attention, which she was soaking up like a sponge.

All too soon, Julie called to Toni, "Grab your coat Toni, we need to get going."

"Ok, right there," replied Toni, searching for a reason to extend her visit with these two handsome and engaging boys.

Tyler gave her the opportunity she was looking for. "Where are you staying?" he asked in a hushed tone.

"We're staying at the Big Bear Motel," whispered Toni, picking up on the secrecy in his voice. "I don't even know where that is from here."

"I do," said Tyler. "A few of my cousins and me, and Rusty of course, will probably go do some more celebrating tonight. What if we pick you up behind the Big Bear in an hour or two?"

Toni, who could never resist the idea of breaking a few rules, giggled and nervously said, "Okay, it'll probably have to be after Julie falls asleep."

"Great, we'll wait for you out back!" said Tyler. The deal was sealed.

When Julie and Toni got back to their room, Toni grabbed the bed closest to the door and immediately began the "I'm so tired routine" hoping to lull Julie into an early slumber. Leaving her shoes next to the door side of the bed, she went to the restroom to change, rolling up her pant legs and putting on her nightgown over her clothes.

Crawling quickly into bed, she gave a dramatic yawn and stretch along with a "Goodnight Julie", and then watched her roommate through slitted eyes as she feigned sleep.

Toni heard the deep growl of a diesel pickup pull into the motel lot, and thought she could make out the opening and closing of doors and the occasional buzz of voices or laughter. Julie did not seem to notice the sounds and read for about half an hour before turning out the light next to her bed. Toni was a master of sneaking out at night and patiently listened for the telltale slowing of Julie's breathing indicating she was securely asleep. Crawling out of the covers, she slid the nightgown over her head, silently picked up her shoes, and as carefully as possible slipped out the door. Freedom!

Spotting a four-door pickup loaded with teens, she made her way over towards them, holding her hands above her head to shield her from the light rain. As soon as they saw her they began to call out, but she put her finger to her lips for silence while Tyler and Rusty did the same.

"Hop in, we saved you the seat of honor," Tyler whispered as he stepped aside and motioned to the spot in the middle of the front seat.

Rusty sat grinning at the far end of the seat. "Glad you could make it," he said enthusiastically. Toni was in heaven!

"Beer?" offered Rusty, holding out a Coors Light to Toni.

"Thought you'd never ask!" answered Toni confidently. Tyler fired up the Cummins diesel in the brand-new Dodge.

"Nice truck," said Toni.

"Thanks" replied Tyler, adding "this is my Uncle Jake's truck; he let me drive it tonight!"

"Well let's see if we can get 'er stuck," challenged Rusty.

"Hah! My uncle would stinkin' kill me!" laughed Tyler. "Let's go up to the lookout on Cedar Mountain, you can see all of Cody from there. Tyler informed the cousins in the rear seat, "Were goin' to the lookout!" to which there was an assortment of whistles and yeehaws.

Crowded into the backseat of the crew cab pickup were Meredith, Haley, Heather, and Justin, each with a beer in their hand, busy talking about other girls and boys, paying no attention to the small talk in the front seat. Tyler acted as tour guide, pointing out the landmarks on the way to the popular overlook. "There's the new Walmart," Ty pointed out sarcastically. "Those bright lights over there, that's the Yellowstone Airport." A few miles later, "There's Old Trail Town," pointed Ty, referring to the open-air museum. "We sneak in there at night sometimes and hang out in the old wagons! Cedar Mountain's just up there ahead of us."

Enjoying their beer buzz, the whole group began singing country songs as they wound their way up the steep switchbacks heading to the summit.

Toni could sense the boys' interest in her by the way they repeatedly tried to one-up each other as they regaled her with stories. Whatever one mentioned they had done, it seemed as though the other had done it better. Toni laughed at every story.

Arriving at the summit, the whole gang piled out. There were patches of snow scattered about, but the rain had stopped and the clouds had lifted, creating a glow as the lights of Cody reflected off of them to the east. Looking to the left, the Buffalo Bill Reservoir appeared as a dark hole at the base of the mountains and the entrance to Yellowstone beyond. The summit was a jumble of large boulders and the group soon spread out and found their own favorite rocks where two or three would assemble for a while, and then they would shift and hang out with others. Tyler found a flat-topped boulder just big enough for the three of them, brushed off the inch of snow, laid down a towel, then both Rusty and Toni helped him negotiate getting his cast leg up.

Toni was interested to hear their thoughts on the topic that she was the most interested in: animal welfare and conservation. "Okay, so one of you is a rancher and one is a hunter. I'm not sure that I should be hanging out with either one of you," she began, only half-jokingly. "I'm super into saving injured animals," she explained, "like the kinds that are wounded by hunters or mistreated by farmers and ranchers, and that's what you guys do!"

"Woah, wait a minute!" snapped Rusty before Tyler could get the words out. "You said that you were three-fourths native-American, right?"

"Yeah, but…" Toni began before being cut off.

"So are you denying your heritage?" Rusty continued, mockingly agitated. "Because Indians were the original hunters in this area – the Sioux, Crow, Shoshoni, Blackfoot, and others hunted here for centuries. I'm just continuing the tradition!"

While Rusty took a breath to continue his explanation, Toni jumped back in. "Yeah, but now you're using high-powered rifles with long-distance scopes, and wounding animals a mile away with them!" she said, beginning to rouse herself.

"Except I don't!" replied Rusty loudly. "I've never hunted with a rifle. I'm an archery hunter, just like your ancestors. I never shoot at an animal over thirty yards away to make sure I don't just injure them. Getting that close I feel very much a part of the animal that I'm hunting. To be able to do that I need to totally understand the thinking of the animal I'm pursuing. I'm pretty sure I know way more about these animals than you do!"

Rusty was red in the face from his heated defense, and Toni was just about to reply when Tyler took over. "And ranchers are some of the best protectors of the rangelands you'll find," he countered.

"Oh man," Toni said rolling her eyes. "I've heard that a thousand times! You use pesticides on your crops that kill birds, your cattle ruin spring streams where the young trout grow, and you want to kill off any animal that threatens your sacred cows. You guys fought against listing grizzly bears!"

Tyler was ready. "It's true that some ranchers care only about their crops or cattle, and don't care about the land or the animals on it." He stopped, glancing over at his cousins on the next rock. "But we're not that kind of ranch family, at least not anymore. Sure, my grandpa and even my uncles were against listing grizzlies, but my dad wasn't, neither am I, and neither are some of my cousins. We get that we need to coexist with nature, not eliminate it."

Rusty was ready to start back up, but Toni beat him to it. "Wow, okay guys, you're not the ignorant rednecks that I thought you might be. Maybe we can be friends after all."

"Hmmm, not so sure about that," Rusty said tauntingly. "How do we know you're not one of those radical activist types that want to put an end to all hunting and force us to all eat tofu?"

To this Tyler laughed and added, "Yeah, you're not going to be chaining yourself to any trees are ya?!'"

"Just because I love animals doesn't mean I don't recognize my place in the food chain," replied Toni, now on the defense. "You're right, Rusty, my people were the original environmentalists. They hunted yeah, but it was always a fair chase, and when they took a life they honored the animal's spirit and didn't waste a single part of the creatures they killed. I don't hunt personally but I accept that when done responsibly, and when the number of animals to be harvested is managed by science, human predators can be one part of a functional ecosystem."

"And how do cattle fit into that system?" asked Tyler, anxious for an answer.

"Cows allowed to live their life in a free range setting rather than a feedlot, but not being allowed to over-graze meadows and forests, and not being subjected to inhumane conditions like veal pens and the like, can also co-exist next to natural systems," Toni concluded, sounding much older than her almost fourteen years of age.

After a few moments of processing all that had been said, Rusty offered, "Well, I guess yer okay." Then turning to Tyler said, "What do ya' say, Ty, should we be friends with her or not?"

"I guess she'll do" replied Tyler, smirking. "I've had friends worse than her before!" which got them all laughing.

"Gotta put some of this beer back in the environment!" Ty joked as he climbed down from the boulder to take a leak. As soon as Tyler was out of sight, Toni took the beer from Rusty's hand just as he was about to take a sip, leaned over, and kissed him. The kiss caught him off guard but he adapted quickly and began kissing back. The whole incident lasted just five seconds, as Toni pulled away upon hearing Tyler approaching again.

"Did I miss anything?" Ty asked as he climbed back onto the rock.

"Not a thing," said Toni convincingly while shooting a sly wink at Rusty.

"Okay, my turn," announced Rusty. "I'll be right back." The moment he was out of sight, Toni grabbed Tyler by both hands, pulling him towards her, and planted her second kiss of the night. Like Rusty, it only took Tyler a moment to get into the spirit. Just as before, it was over quickly as Rusty began pulling his immobilized leg onto the rock.

"What'd you guys see?" Rusty asked.

"Just the lights of Cody," Toni responded without missing a beat.

"Shit!" said Toni suddenly. "What time is it?!"

Both boys looked at their wristwatches and Tyler said, "Wow! How did it get to be 4 a.m.!?"

"You're kidding, right?" asked Toni anxiously.

"No, he's dead on," answered Rusty. "4:02 to be exact."

"Holy crap!" said Toni in a panic. "You guys better get me back! If Julie gets up and finds me gone, this may be the last time I get to go anywhere!"

"No problem," said Tyler, then yelling to his cousins, "come on guys, we gotta' get this filly home." Everyone crawled down off of their rocky perches and jogged to the pickup. "We'll have you back before five," promised Tyler as all four wheels flung mud.

Neither boy knew it, but Toni was discretely holding hands with both as they headed for the motel. Pulling into the parking lot as quietly as possible, Rusty got out and Toni shimmied off the seat. Tyler had come around from the driver's side to say goodbye. Toni leaned in the rear window and bid all of the cousins farewell then stood between the two boys. Throwing her arms wide, she invited them each for a hug, first Tyler, then Rusty.

"Guess I'll be seeing ya," she said, trying to sound casual.

"You bet," said Rusty.

"Hope so," added Tyler. With that, she headed for the door, where they watched her take off her shoes before cautiously opening the door and disappearing behind it.

"Some gal," understated Tyler.

"She's something," replied Rusty just as nonchalantly.

It would be five years before the three would be reunited.

BAHAITEE'

The landmark passage of the Endangered Species Act (ESA) in 1973 had an immediate impact on many animal populations in decline. The cessation of public and commercial hunting of game animals that had been included on the list provided the most immediate results, while others strategies that included preserving critical habitat resulted in a long-term recovery rate of over ninety percent. Not surprisingly, even though gray wolves had been included in the 1973 list, no real action had been taken to restore their numbers, with only about 700 left in the entire lower 48 states. Most of those were in northern Michigan and Wisconsin.

The administration of Yellowstone National Park began toying with the idea of reintroduction as far back as the 1930s, but with their addition to the ESA, there was now a compelling reason to do so. In 1987, the Park Service surveyed visitors to determine their interest in the possibility of wolf reintroduction. They were surprised to find that nine out of ten visitors were in favor of wolves in the park. The same survey conducted throughout Idaho, Montana, and Wyoming revealed that a majority of participants favored wolf restoration. Numerous surveys conducted by various pollsters since 1972 yielded similar results.

Finally, in November of 1991, the United States Congress instructed their three agencies charged with public land - U.S. Fish and Wildlife Service, the U.S. Forest Service, and the National Park Service to prepare a draft statement on the anticipated impacts of wolf reintroduction in both Yellowstone and central Idaho. A big part of that process would include public input at numerous formal meetings and open houses on the topic.

In July 1993, the draft Environmental Impact Statement (EIS) was released and public meetings were scheduled. Toni, now 18 years of age, had become active in several conservation groups, including the National Audubon Society. Audubon, while fully in support of wolf reintroduction, was protesting wording within the EIS that defined the soon-to-be restored wolf population as "experimental" as opposed to "endangered". What appeared to be an innocuous word change would later give the anti-wolf contingent ammunition for terminating the plan. They argued that because it called for Canadian wolves to be released in the U.S., they were not the same endangered animal. When one of the first meetings was scheduled in Cody, Toni leaped at the opportunity to attend, recalling the wonderful night she had spent there five years earlier.

The meeting room at the Holiday Inn was overflowing with cowboy hats and camouflage jackets as Toni and Julie took their seats. Julie still had the same bookish appearance as when she had visited in 1988. Toni, however, had changed considerably. The chubby cheeks of the 13-year-old had sculpted into the same graceful jawline of her mother, and the black sweater and blue jeans she wore showed off the classic feminine form of an eighteen-year-old in the bloom of life. Excusing herself as she shimmied past the ranchers and hunters on the way to her seat, the young men couldn't help but stare and the older men had to discipline themselves not to.

The presentation began with introductions of the speakers: all representatives of the U.S. Fish and Wildlife Service. Other VIPs in attendance were recognized: Craig Thomas, Wyoming's lone congressman, various department heads of the Wyoming Fish and Game Department, and the president of the Wyoming Beef Producers Association. The crowd was polite and well-disciplined throughout the opening statements. When the lights went down and a video was shown touting the environmental benefits of wolf reintroduction, hecklers could be heard making negative comments about the claims being made.

Once the presentation was complete, it was time for what most of the audience had really come there for, an opportunity to give their opinions on the concept. Two microphones were set up at the end of each walkway leading to the stage and lines formed at each. It seemed as though many of the intended speakers had donned costumes intended to illustrate the "team" they represented. One faction consistently exhibited National Gun Owners Association caps and bulky Mossy Oak camo jackets; another wore western hats, leather vests, jeans and had spectacular mustaches. A minority of speakers wore down jackets and glasses, some in designer jeans or khakis. Most were fair-skinned or tanned, but one young woman stood out for her darker skin tone and exotic features.

"Holy-crap, dude!" whispered Rusty excitedly to the Hispanic-looking young man to his right. "Is that who I think it is?!" referring to the statuesque young woman who had just taken her place in line.

"No way, man," replied Tyler, though not confidently. "No way could she have grown into that!"

They looked at each other and chuckled discreetly at the thought of 13-year-old Toni blossoming into the woman in line at the front of the auditorium. Rusty and Tyler had remained fast friends in the five years since the fires and their shared injuries, Rusty driving the Beartooth Pass regularly to hang out with Tyler on the ranch, and Tyler driving up to Cooke City to archery hunt in the fall, or to check out the park's wildlife in nearby Yellowstone the rest of the year. They spoke often of that night that Toni had so brazenly flirted with both of them, and how her thoughts on the way that hunting and ranching could coexist with wildlife restoration had resonated with them.

As might have been expected based on the history of the century-old debate over Yellowstone wildlife, most speakers reiterated positions that had been established decades earlier.

The first speaker, a middle-aged man wearing a collared khaki shirt with a camouflage patch over one shoulder, identified himself as the president of a local sportsmen's organization. "Wolves will absolutely destroy the quality elk hunting that local hunters have enjoyed for decades and that non-resident hunters spend millions of dollars locally to pursue."

A heavy-set man in stiff new Wranglers and a western cut shirt was an officer of the Wyoming Beef Producer's Association. "Cattle ranching is not much more than a break-even business to begin with. We've seen the wanton destruction of sheep and cattle by wolves in northern Montana and Canada and we cannot afford it! We've already got the damned grizzlies eatin' our calves. We got rid of wolves seventy years ago with good reason; let's not make the mistake of reintroducing them."

A tall, slim man wearing a high-crowned cowboy hat stepped forward, spurs jingling for all to hear. "I run one of the most successful guide businesses in the state. Wolves will make it impossible to find the elk that my clients pay thousands to hunt. They'll also put my clients, my wranglers, and my stock in danger. If y'all bring back wolves, we'll shoot ever' last one of 'em!" to which some in the audience gasped while others laughed and clapped.

Rusty and Tyler leaned forward as the young woman in the black sweater stepped to the microphone.

"My name is Tekwoni Poe. I'm here representing several organizations, including the Protectors of Wildlife, the Indigenous Justice Coalition, and the Audubon Society." The two young men fell back in their chairs, slapping their hands on their knees as those sitting around them wondered about their excitement.

"I told you, I told you! Look at her will ya'?" giggled Rusty.

"Her looks have sure changed but sounds like her politics haven't," Tyler exclaimed.

"Shhh!" shushed a woman sitting behind them.

"We understand," Toni began again confidently, "that both ranching and hunting are important to Wyoming's economy, culture, and heritage." The assembled groups sat forward in their chairs, intrigued by her opening. "Cody sits on the edge of what scientists refer to as the Greater Yellowstone Ecosystem, the largest nearly intact temperate zone ecosystem on Earth, extending from Cody on the east almost to Idaho Falls on the west, and Bozeman and Pinedale on the north and south." Some in the audience seemed surprised by the width and breadth she suggested. "It's the words 'nearly intact' that keep our region from being fully functioning," she added.

"Of equal importance to ranching and hunting are wilderness, biological diversity, and eco-tourism. Seventy years ago we completely eliminated a primary component of our system, an integral component in the management of our rangelands, grasslands, and wild animals."

"As most of you know, park rangers were forced to destroy thousands of elk and bison for over thirty years to keep them from denuding the park's meadows and hillsides." To this many in the hall nodded and grumbled. "Since the late sixties, that program has been suspended, the results of which are areas of the park now completely devoid of young trees, shrubs, wildflowers, and grasses."

"We agree with many of you that rangers should never hunt in the park."

This statement met with nods and comments of "Yes!"

"We also agree with the Park Service, that no one should hunt in the park." The agreement turned to scowls and head shaking.

"The solution that will restore our rangeland, and bring wildlife populations into proper balance is the restoration of gray wolves to their natural home." The majority of the audience muttered their disapproval of this statement.

Tekwoni continued undaunted. "To our ranching neighbors, the truth is, yes, there will be a small amount of depredation of beef calves by wolves, but our research shows that wolves prefer wild game – deer, elk, even bison – to beef cattle." Exasperated sighs and grumbling could be heard around the room.

"To mitigate the loss of the small percentage of calves and lambs which may be taken by the wolves, our organizations have created a fund to compensate ranchers for each and every loss." A surprised murmur among the crowd was evident. "Furthermore, we support the use of range riders, livestock guarding dogs, and trail cameras in areas of concern to help monitor nearby predators so ranchers can better protect their livestock. We also condone tools like noisemakers, spotlights, fladry lines, and temporary electrified corrals to dissuade predators." A few heads nodded in support of these allowances.

"To our hunting neighbors, yes, game populations will evolve to a more sustainable level. Studies have proven that in areas where wolves coexist with elk, the elk become healthier in general, as the wolves tend to take the old, the weak, and the sick in much higher percentages." Doubters rolled their eyes and shook their heads. "As populations adapt, the range will become more robust, providing more fodder to keep the elk herds healthier and better prepared for cold winters." A few in the crowd understood the long-term benefits and listened attentively.

"Numerous polls conducted of Yellowstone tourists show overwhelming support for wolf restoration in the park. Tourists from all over the globe and businesses surrounding the park on all sides will benefit from the addition of this charismatic species and the positive benefits wolves will have on the Greater Yellowstone Ecosystem." A few scoffed at the description of wolves as 'charismatic'.

"Last year, visitors spent over 2.5 million dollars in businesses surrounding the park." The few park boundary business owners in attendance gave a subdued cheer.

"That spending supported over 3,500 jobs and had a cumulative benefit to the local economy of $3.75 million. We anticipate that the opportunity to see wolves in the park will significantly increase those amounts." Though the hunters and ranchers were mostly unmoved by this information, the remainder of the audience was clearly impressed.

"Wyoming has long been a leader in thoughtful, intelligent solutions," she began her conclusion. "We were the first state to recognize women's right to vote." Applause came from the few women in the room and a number of the men. "The chief of my people's tribe, Chief Washakie of the eastern Shoshoni here in Wyoming, was one of the few chiefs in North America who chose cooperation with the U.S. Government over warfare." The previously silent group of native Americans in the hall now applauded or whooped. "Returning wolves to their historic home, patching the torn fabric of a 'nearly' intact ecosystem, creating more sustainable rangelands inside and around the perimeter of the park, mitigating the challenges created by that restoration, and reaping the fringe benefits of increased tourism are the thoughtful and intelligent choices to make. The sort of choices that Wyomingites have been making throughout history." To this, those without a strong anti-wolf bias stood and applauded.

As Tekwoni walked from the microphone, Rusty and Tyler rose to go and meet her. Instead of returning to her seat, she headed for the lobby to cool down from her impassioned presentation and get a drink of water.

As the young men caught up to her in the deserted lobby, she took one look at them and exclaimed, "Oh my God – it's my Cody cowboys!" Forgetting everything else for the moment, she flung herself at each of them, hugging each in turn. Then pulling away she got a sheepish look on her face and asked, "Were you in there? Did I sound like a nut-case?"

The two young men answered in near unison, "Hell no, you sounded like an honest-to-God scientist!"

Toni blushed slightly, and then asked, "Do you think I changed any minds?"

Rusty replied, "If they were on the fence about wolves, you may have talked them into giving the plan a chance."

Tyler added, "Yeah, all two or three of them!" to which even Toni laughed.

The three caught up for a few minutes, and then Toni indicated that she wanted to return to the hall to assess the direction of the conversation. Nothing much seemed to have changed in the tone of the speakers at the microphones, but as she shuffled towards her seat a number of those she passed whispered to her.

"Great job!"

"Compelling argument."

"I agree."

She knew in her heart and soul that the plan was ecologically and ethically correct. Perhaps, she now thought, there is a chance that the plan will actually be accepted by the majority.

As the meeting concluded, the Wildlife Service reiterated its intent to hold similar meetings throughout the region, present the science behind the plan, listen to concerns, and answer questions. Rusty and Tyler stood with Toni as attendees made their way out, and even a few of those opposed to reintroduction gave Toni a polite nod or tip of the hat.

Most surprisingly, Tyler's father, Hank, had been among the audience, and now put out his hand to Toni saying, "You're a brave woman. I hope that you're right about all this."

"Thank you, sir," replied Toni. "If we all just give a little bit, I know that in the long run, it is the best thing for all."

Cocking his head he gave a half-smile, pulled on the bill of his hat, and said softly, "Yes 'm," as he backed away.

Only the three of them were now left in the hall, other than the officials gathering up their papers and packing up their electronics on stage.

"Well boys, is somebody gonna offer to buy me a beer or do I have to find a man for that?" Toni said with a flirtatious smirk.

Tyler and Rusty looked at each other, and then Tyler replied, "Considering that you're not even legal drinking age we'd be contributing to the delinquency of a minor!"

Rusty added, "Yeah but all she'd have to do is start talking and they'd think she's fifty!" to which they all laughed. "Come on then, girl, we been waiting to take you back out on the town for a long time!" And with that, they headed for downtown Cody.

The Silver Saddle Saloon was spendier than the boy's regular haunt – the Bull Sitter Bar – but it was the place where locals took out-of-town guests, and Toni qualified as that. After an hour or so, and two or three beers apiece, a couple of men at the bar next to them began raising their voices.

"Yeah, that cute little squaw got everybody feeling sorry for the poor wolves," said one in a brown Carhartt jacket.

"Little bitch needs to go back to the reservation and stay out of our business," said the other in a camo baseball cap.

Tyler and Rusty rose immediately from their stools. "Excuse me?" asked Rusty rhetorically.

"Holy shit!" exclaimed Tyler, "I think you boys got some apologizing to do to our friend here!"

"Fuck you, squaw man!" spat the first man, and before the words were completely out of his mouth Rusty broke his nose with a lightning-quick left jab. The man in the cap grabbed his beer mug and tossed the contents at Rusty as Tyler tackled him, knocking him into the bar and following him onto the floor, where he pummeled him with a series of rights and lefts to the face.

Holding his bloody nose, the first man grabbed a beer bottle with his free hand and was just about to break it on the bar to use as a weapon when the bartender leveled a double-barreled shotgun at him and yelled, "Cops are on the way, better get your asses outta my bar!" Tyler got up off of the bruised and bloodied man on the floor and together the two men made for the door.

"You guys better go out the back door," the bartender said to Rusty, Tyler, and Toni. "I heard what those assholes said. I'm glad you busted them!"

"Thanks, man," said Rusty as the three hustled out the back door, then ran for their pickup laughing. "Damn girl, you could get a guy killed!"

"I wasn't the one breaking noses," Toni said giggling.

The trio stopped by a bottle store for a twelve-pack of beer and started driving west. This time Tyler didn't stop at the Cedar Mountain Lookout but instead kept driving west on Hwy 14 to Yellowstone Park. The hour-long drive gave the trio plenty of time for getting reacquainted.

"Where'd ya' learn all that stuff?" questioned Tyler.

"Both my mom and my grandmother are biologists," replied Toni, "so I've been learning it since I was old enough to understand. School came easy to me – I graduated high school at 15 and began taking college courses right away. I should graduate with a Bachelor of Science degree next year. In my spare time, I began working for Protectors of Wildlife on ways to try to make wolf reintroduction a success."

"Although they weren't openly hostile in the meeting, you definitely made a few enemies tonight," chimed in Rusty. "I saw some old friends of my dad's from the hunting club in there and their faces were as red as tomatoes when you brought up the elk."

"Hey, I'm three-quarters Indian, I'm used to old white guys wanting to kill me!" Toni said sardonically, to which the two young men grimaced.

The entry station was unmanned but open, so they continued to the Lake Butte parking area. Tyler parked at the edge of Yellowstone Lake and the three continued talking.

"Soooo, how did you guys feel about the information I presented and the feds' reintroduction plan?"

Rusty jumped in. "Well, I think you're probably right about the elk population adjusting but then stabilizing," he began, having thought a lot about it on his own. "I mean, the Park Service was culling thousands of elk a year for decades and yet they rebounded every year; wouldn't be any different with the wolves I imagine. Some hunters only care about making the kill. Those guys are going to be mad if those kills aren't as easy as they have been. Guys like me – I'm just as excited to see a wolf in the wild, or watch a pack hunting, as I am to get an elk. The truth is, guys that are good hunters will continue to harvest elk even if the numbers are down. It's the lousy hunters that are going to come up short."

Then it was Tyler's turn. "That idea about having a fund to pay ranchers for their wolf-killed livestock was genius – I heard a bunch of cattlemen in the room snort at that one. You know how us ranchers are – we complain about everything and anything that affects our stock. The reality is, we won't know how our livelihoods are affected until we're a couple of years into it."

"I'm not living on the ranch; I'm living at the firehouse, so I'm a little removed from ranch life. With a couple of exceptions, I'm sure most of the rest of my family is pretty nervous about the plan."

"What's with this 'experimental population' crap that Fish and Wildlife was talking about?" asked Rusty.

"Oh yeah, the anti-wolf crowd is claiming that the original wolf population in the region were so-called 'prairie wolves'," Toni began her explanation. "There is no actual subspecies of wolf named 'prairie-wolf' and scientists believe that what settlers once called prairie wolves were in fact coyotes. There is a subspecies named Great Plains Wolves, medium-sized wolves that ranged from Texas to Manitoba, but the Fish and Wildlife Service biologists identified the wolves that were extirpated from Yellowstone in 1926 as Northern Rocky Mountain Wolves, medium to large-sized wolves."

"The anti-wolfers cite that the wolves that are being considered for reintroduction are bigger, more ferocious wolves from Canada. It's true that, because Northern Rocky Mountain Wolves were virtually eliminated from the continent, a subspecies called the Mackenzie River Wolf is being considered for the reintroduction – but they are essentially the same wolf, similar in size and habits."

"So in other words, it's just a red herring to try to derail the plan," noted Tyler.

"Precisely," quipped Toni.

As the beer ran out the conversation turned from wolves to more personal questions. Toni led off, "So, you two handsome buckaroos must have some pretty top-shelf girlfriends by now, huh?"

Tyler answered first, "Actually, I'm too busy at the firehouse and Cody's short on my type of women."

"Your type of women?!" Toni snorted. "And what type would that be?"

"Oh you know, smart, sweet, and good-looking!" Tyler laughed at his own response.

"Uh-huh…and how about you, Rusty?" Toni redirected her question. "Are you as picky as your pal here?"

"Well, there's been a few, but I'm waitin' to find one that doesn't mind getting some mud on her boots, or goin' without makeup for a few days."

"I seee," hissed Toni doubtfully. "Sounds like you've both set unrealistic standards so that you can avoid any kind of committed relationship."

The two men looked at each other, shrugged, and agreed. "You're probably right," which got all of them laughing hysterically.

The three were sitting on the tailgate, looking out over Yellowstone Lake as the Milky Way lit up the night sky and shimmered on the lake's surface. Without warning, Toni leaned over and gave Tyler a long deep, probing kiss, reluctantly breaking it off with an "ohhh-kay, yup, yup, nothin' wrong with that, nothin' at all!"

She then leaned in the opposite direction and planted a duplicate kiss on Rusty, culminating in, "Holy hell boys, the gals in Cody don't know what they're missin' – you guys definitely know how to kiss!"

Tyler and Rusty, both flabbergasted by what had just happened, were shaking their heads.

"Damn girl," Rusty finally said, "you haven't changed a bit!"

"Yeah," chimed in Tyler, "you absolutely know how to shake up an evening!"

"Now don't get the wrong idea you guys," Toni said, putting up her hand like a stop sign. "I was just making sure you boys had what it takes. I mean, it's a little weird that two guys as attractive as you two don't have girlfriends. I just wanted to make sure you possessed some of the necessary skills!"

"And so, in your eminently experienced and professional opinion we passed the kiss test?" asked Tyler sarcastically.

"Ohhh yeah!" replied Toni, pretending to fan her face.

"Okay then, miss expert," added Rusty, "then which one was the best of the two?" he asked with arms crossed and a furrowed brow.

"Oh shit!" Toni gulped under her breath. "Isn't that just like a guy? Every dang thing's gotta be a competition!" She had expected them to laugh but instead, they just stared at her, awaiting an answer.

Toni was in a predicament and knew it. "I couldn't poss..." she stuttered but was cut off by Rusty.

"I got the solution," he offered. "You close your eyes, and we'll each kiss you, then without seeing who's who, you gotta' pick the better kiss!"

What had started as a flirtatious game had suddenly gotten more serious, and Toni was nervous about taking it much farther. On the other hand, the kisses had been exciting and she was loving being the object of their attention. "Well okay, but don't think that I'm enjoying this! I'm just doing it in the interest of science and to try to help you two improve your lousy social lives," she giggled.

Tyler took off his red bandana and tied it around her eyes, although the starlit night was dark enough that it would be hard to identify them even with the bandana off. The two men walked about ten feet away, whispered strategy to each other, then Rusty called out, "hands behind your back – no touching to try to figure out who we are!" They took off their hats and, just in case she could smell the difference between them, exchanged shirts.

"What the hell are you guys doing over there – you're supposed to be kissing me, not each other!" she laughed nervously.

"Just hold your horses, gal, we gotta make sure this is done right!" They each took a swig of beer so their breath smelled the same, and then did a quick round of rock-paper-scissors to decide who was to go first – Rusty got the honor.

Shuffling his feet over to her through the gravel to disguise his footfalls, Rusty planted his lips on Toni's waiting mouth. Toni, who was now extremely turned on with anticipation, brazenly parted her lips, inviting Rusty to explore her mouth with his tongue. This was by no means Rusty's first rodeo and he didn't hesitate to accept the open invitation. Tyler began watching with a huge smile, but after ten seconds was getting tired of being the spectator. After twenty seconds Rusty slowly pulled away, creating a slight smacking sound as their lips parted. Toni gave a big, sensuous sigh but Rusty kept his cool and did not make a sound.

"S-h-i-i-i-i-t! I don't know if this is such a good idea," Toni sighed, breathing heavily. "How cold is that lake? I may need to cool off!"

The boys, standing together ten feet away laughed nervously, looked at each other and Rusty said, "We're not done yet; you still have one more to go!"

"Phewww, well let's get it over with, huh? I'm not sure this girl can take much more of this." After a few seconds of silence, Tyler shuffled over, duplicating Rusty's approach. Toni's lips were moist and her breath was hot as

Tyler put his lips to hers. Without meaning to, Toni began nibbling on Tyler's lips, to which Tyler responded in kind. The nibbling went from lips to tongues, to a deep, delving kiss when suddenly Toni pushed Tyler away with both hands, turned away from them and screamed, "Enough! Holy shit – I can't do this! I need to cool off!"

Without looking back she threw off the bandana and ran for the water. Stripping off her sweater and jeans at the lake's edge she ran into the frigid water in her bra and panties. Meanwhile, the two men ran after her laughing, tugged off their jeans and shirts, and swam out to her.

"Get away from me you animals!" she laughed, splashing at them as they approached.

"But, we gotta' know!" they shouted in unison "Which kiss was better? Rules are rules!"

"To hell with rules," she spat at them while side-stroking away. "Those kisses did not comply with any rules! You guys get outta here and let me cool down for a minute!"

Not knowing if she was serious or not, the men thought it best to obey her request and swam back to shore, shivering as they got out of their wet underwear and back into their jeans and shirts.

"You sure you're okay out there?!" yelled Rusty.

"I'm coming back in," Toni replied. "Find me a towel or something then wait for me at the truck while I get dressed."

Tyler grabbed a spare sweatshirt he had in the backseat of the crew cab, brought it to the shore, and said, "This is the best I could find."

"That'll do, thanks. Now get outta there while I get out."

Tyler started the truck and got the heater working. As they waited for Toni, the two were ribbing each other about the kisses and laughing about Toni's response. When she got to the truck she ordered Rusty out and slid into the center of the seat between them.

"All right girl, you owe us an answer, right now!" Tyler said with a big grin.

"I don't want to talk about it!" said Toni resolutely. "Think of some other subject to talk about on the way back because I can't even think about it for a while!" The two men looked at each other, shrugged their shoulders, and cracked up laughing. Slugging them each, Toni objected, "You assholes! You don't know what that does to a girl! Let's talk about football or rodeo or anything, just not about those damned kisses!"

Sensing that she meant what she said, the two turned the conversation to hunting and ranching, while Toni sat nearly silent the whole way back to Cody.

BIA

There was still a wolf pack living in the Brazeau River drainage in Jasper National Park, Alberta, Canada in 1994. The cast and composition had all changed in the twenty years since Mahi and Ati had presided. They were still masterful hunters, but like most wolves they were nomadic, and their ramblings eventually found them migrating east onto the prairie.

It was here on the flats that the trappers found them. The wolves were used to being shot at, poisoned, gassed, and trapped, but never before had they been pursued by helicopters to be captured alive. In Phase I of the Fish and Wildlife Service plan, the trappers, some of the orneriest old backwoodsmen in Canada, had to be convinced to assist with the live-trapping of the animals. This was only barely achieved by offering them three times the $500 they ordinarily got for wolf pelts. The trappers were remarkably successful at securing live wolves in their snares, which were then outfitted with tracking collars and released. This strategy would eventually lead the biologists with air rifles and tranquilizer darts to whole family groups traveling with the collared individuals. Pursuing the packs by helicopter, the U.S. Fish and Wildlife shooters would attempt to dart multiple family members at once, helping to assure compatibility between individuals once the wolves were transferred to congregate acclimation pens. The trappers, enlisted under the reintroduction project, had received special take permits from the Alberta Department of Fish and Wildlife, which was easy as Alberta was always happy to get rid of some wolves. Six wolves - four males and two females from the Brazeau pack, were darted that morning before the rest of the pack disappeared into the trees.

Over several days the trappers and the attendant biologist would chase various packs in the Smoky, Moosehorn, Snake Indian, and Miette River drainages of Jasper National Park. The result was a total of fourteen wolves from three different packs.

The wolves were vet-checked and vaccinated at a holding facility near Hinton, Alberta. After nearly a week at the holding facility, eight of the animals were loaded into aluminum crates and arranged inside a gooseneck livestock trailer. A stout Ford F750 flatbed roared to life and the first load of Canadian wolves pulled out of Hinton.

The journey was long and the weather was cold but the wolves, curled up in their individual cages, seemed impervious to the temperature, and resigned to whatever destiny awaited them. After two long days of driving, the truck and trailer were unexpectedly greeted by throngs of spectators waiting by the Roosevelt Arch at the north entrance to the park. As nature enthusiasts waved and shouted with excitement, it was clear to the crew of biologists, veterinarians, and assistants that the news of their arrival had been leaked. There was some concern that well-meaning fans or project opponents might interfere with the very specific plans for acclimation and release. For that reason, the road to the release site was closed to the public and the area around the holding pens and release sites had been cleared of visitors.

Anxious to get the wolves situated in the meticulously designed enclosures, the project crew was angry and frustrated to find that during their drive, a last-second lawsuit had been filed. The Farm Bureau was contesting the legality of the move, and instead of being able to transfer the animals as planned, the wolves were forced to spend yet another night in their crates. Thankfully, the case was deemed to be without merit the next day and so finally, on January 12, 1995, the first eight travel kennels were pushed, pulled, carried, and carted by horse teams to three secret locations in the woods ringing the Lamar Valley. One week later a second group of six more wolves joined the original eight.

The team had tried to foresee every way that the wolves might attempt to escape the large one-acre pens. The chain link panels had been built to ten feet in height with a folded inward mantle at the top to inhibit climbing out. At the base of the panels, a four-foot wide skirt prevented digging out under the wire. Nevertheless, one persistent wolf managed to leap the ten feet to the top mantle, hang on with his teeth and eventually claw his way over, damaging his teeth in the process. The wolves were to spend ten weeks in the stockades, a period of time determined to be needed to assure that their internal compasses were recalibrated to Yellowstone rather than their previous locations in Canada.

Although unintended, the various lawsuits and legal wrangling that had delayed the release until after the wolves' traditional breeding season, had helped assure the success of the project's first year. Because the wolves had been forced into artificially close proximity, it had virtually assured that some breeding would take place in the enclosures. Releasing the wolves towards the end of winter, rather than at the beginning of it, had an unanticipated benefit. A large elk herd living nearby had endured a long, difficult winter and was uniquely vulnerable. Thanks in part to these factors, the new Yellowstone wolves were able to score successful kills of large prey immediately upon being released.

From this dubious beginning arose a number of standout individual wolves upon whom the foundation was laid for the future of the species in the Rocky Mountains. The methodology utilized by the project biologists dictated that numbers, not names, be assigned to the repatriated animals, but as the matriarch of so many who came after her, an appropriate name for one special wolf is Bia.

Under natural conditions in the wilderness, Bia might never have become an Alpha female. Shy, unassuming, and timid, she might easily have become the handmaiden to a more dominant female, perhaps even been a so-called "omega" wolf, the lowest-ranking member of a pack. Whether willing or not, thanks to the contrived grouping of both related and unrelated wolves in the Rose Creek acclimation pen, Bia became the mate of Hoawoppih (Hoa), a big, rugged, and independent male. By the time the pen gates were opened and the wolves were free to roam, Bia was pregnant with Hoa's progeny.

Aside from impregnating Bia, Hoa's only other contribution to Bia's life story was encouraging her to run far from the pen, forty miles to the northeast to Mount Maurice, well outside of the park in Montana. It was near there that Hoa's part of the story ended. His radio collar gave off the mortality tone, indicating that there had been no movement for days, and his body was found where he had been shot. With his death, he became the first of many of the new generations of Yellowstone's wolves to fall victim to man's unfounded hatred, less than a month after his liberation.

After nearly two agonizing weeks for the biologists with no clear indication of where Bia was, her signal was detected. She was moving only a little, a short distance from where Hoa's body had been found. Not knowing that she had been pregnant upon release from the pen, researchers thought that she might be injured. Upon searching for her on the ground, they discovered to their surprise and guarded delight that she had given birth to a litter of pups. It was debated, then decided, that the team would intervene for the good of the project. They knew that defending and feeding eight newborns without the help of a mate was an insurmountable task. But while the biologists were preparing to capture them, Bia gave them the slip and moved all of the pups to a new, hidden location. Again, her radio collar showed that she had an affinity for a different point on the mountain, and the rescuers were able to locate and extricate all of the pups from a cave formed beneath a pile of rocks. Luring Bia into a trap, they were then able to fly the whole family back to the acclimation pen for their protection and eventually another attempt at release.

It was nearing Autumn when Bia and her brood were again released into Yellowstone. In addition to the handicap of being the sole parent to provide for eight rapidly growing pups, Fall was the time when the wolf's prey had the advantage of being in peak condition. Serendipitously, immediately following their release, a lone male wolf from the Crystal Creek group showed up like a knight in armor. Tekai became Bia's new mate and acted as a co-parent for her pups. Not only did Bia's first set of offspring survive the coming winter, Bia and Tekai together produced litters for each of the next four years.

Several of Bia's progeny themselves were highly successful at expanding Yellowstone's burgeoning wolf population. One daughter gave birth to thirty-two pups throughout her life, while a son fathered litters of pups for seven consecutive years between 1998 and 2004. In four short years between 1996 to 1999, seventy-nine percent of all wolves born among the Yellowstone packs shared DNA from Bia, a reserved and timid female that became the progenitor of many.

JASON

"This was just what we told ya' was gonna happen," fumed Jason Adams, Jake's son, and at 34, the foreman of the Draggin' A. It was 2003, and over the last eight years the ranch had lost more calves to wolves than any other operation in the region. "Eleven! Eleven friggin' calves, Rob. Just look at this shit!" Jason said nudging the scant remains of what had been a fifty-pound Angus calf with the toe of his boot.

Rob, who worked for Wyoming Game and Fish, not the U.S. Fish and Wildlife Service, replied, "Yer' preachin' to the choir here, Jason. You know as well as anyone that Game and Fish has been against the wolves from day one. It's the feds, pardner, the feds that are forcing the wolves down our throats, and enviros hoping they can shut ya' up by paying ya' for yer losses."

"It's not the money, Rob, it's the killin'! Those damned wolves waltz onto my ranch like someone rang the dinner bell. I'm sick of it and I'm not gonna take it. I'm going to the governor."

"The Department's with you, Jason," sympathized Rob. "We've been asking the governor to intervene as well. If we get enough ranchers to scream bloody murder, maybe we'll get some action."

"We sure as hell better, or we'll get a new governor!" exclaimed Jason.

Concern over the wolf kills had led to some contentious fights among siblings and cousins at the holiday dinner table. Family members that still worked on the ranch were uniformly opposed to the wolves, as were most of those who had moved off the ranch and into Cody or other nearby towns. Among those that had moved farther away, to college towns or to where their spouses and young families were, there was a schism between those who believed as their parents had and those who had developed more enlightened feelings about the wolves and their place in the ecosystem. Of those still living nearby, only Tyler and to a lesser extent his dad, Hank, expressed any tolerance for the project or the wolves themselves.

No one on the ranch was more hostile on the subject than the patriarch, Jake, still just as active as ever at nearly sixty years of age. "According to the Beef Producer's Association, there have been 41 cattle slaughtered since the devil's spawn returned," Jake complained while the Thanksgiving dishes made the rounds. "And the sheep guys got hit much worse – 256 lambs and sheep murdered by the bastards…pardon my French!" Kids and grandkids snickered at the expression.

Jake's wife, Angie, was even less hospitable. "Montana and Idaho are demanding that wolf control be returned to their states. That will allow them to poison them again. Why isn't Wyoming involved in that proposal?"

Cory, ever the hothead, muttered, "We oughta start by poisoning the dad-gum tree-huggers over in Disneyl… I mean Jackson Hole!" to which most of the table laughed.

Tyler and Hank smiled politely and said nothing until Cory confronted them directly. "Well, as the two 'greenies' at the table, what do you guys have to say for the wolves?"

Dad and son looked at each other, then Hank spoke up. "Well first, I wouldn't call myself a 'greenie', I just happen to believe that we don't have to kill off all the world's predators to raise cattle," to which some of the younger family members giggled while the adults just stared. "Secondly, we've been compensated pretty damned well for those calves. We've been paid nearly $15,000 for those eleven calves, probably more than we could have made on them alive!"

At this, the whole table erupted, the gist of which was, "It isn't about the money, it's about the principle!"

Once the table settled down, Tyler spoke up. "As Wyomingites, we always talk about how proud we are of our state and the beautiful mountains and incredible wildlife. But it's a farce really. We actually only care about the things that don't interfere with our way of doing things. If some of Wyoming's natural beauty, like a wolf or a grizzly, happen to affect our profits, well we don't care so much about that part of our natural beauty. I care about our family and this ranch, but I think it's possible to coexist with the predators we share the land with."

This was too much for a couple of Tyler's cousins who were barking insults at him, which he disregarded until his younger cousin Justin made a remark about his "Indian girlfriend" to which Tyler threw his napkin on the table and challenged him.

"You watch your mouth, Justin!" said Tyler as he pushed his chair back and stood, silencing the table. Tyler had always been the quiet one and his standing up to his cousin was unlike him.

"Or what?" said a cocky Justin, four years his junior.

"Or I'm gonna have to shut it for you," said Tyler quietly but resolutely. You could have heard a pin drop in the room as Justin and the rest of the table suddenly looked at Tyler in a new light. Fifteen years as a firefighter had turned this once unassuming, quiet boy into a hardened athlete, with the arms of a pro-football player. As the group looked from Tyler back to Justin, it seemed as though the younger man visibly gulped, and it was clear that he had lost his nerve.

"Woah there, guys!" shouted Cory's wife, Keri, standing up and slapping the table-top. "We are not going to do this, not at Thanksgiving and not in this house," to which the group seemed suddenly in agreement. "We may not all agree on every issue, but we're a family, dammit, and we're going to act respectfully to each other regardless of those differences. Justin, Tyler, you two shake hands and shake it off."

Tense shoulders dropped, scowls softened nearly to smiles and the young men approached each other and shook hands. For the third time in one night, Tyler surprised everyone and spoke up again. "Although I love her to death, Toni is not my girlfriend. Her and Rusty are getting married."

TONI

Certain years stand out in the lives of most people as benchmarks for memorable events that happened: births, deaths, marriages, vacations, and others. For Toni, 2005 would be remembered for both difficult lows and incredible highs.

After many years of contributing numerous scholarly research papers and prehistoric artifacts related to the eastern Shoshoni and specifically the Tukudika, Toni's grandfather Pohogwe passed away peacefully at 91 years of age. Po had led a life of giving, having been a selfless volunteer, assisting tribe members with BIA claims and curating the Shoshoni Cultural Center Museum in Fort Washakie, Wyoming.

A traditional Shoshoni funeral was held, whereby a small tipi was erected and Po's body lay inside for several days with a campfire kept burning outside. Family, friends, and associates visited the site and told stories about Po's life and accomplishments, which were many. Family members worried most about Kathy, but at 89 years of age, she took Po's passing in stride and seemed happy at the tributes and respect shown for her beloved partner.

A more pleasant development occurred with Toni's mother, Haiwi, who had been a partner in an environmental consulting firm in Livingston for nearly twenty-five years. Upon his death, Po had left Haiwi a small inheritance, and she could think of no more honorable use for it than to start her own non-profit, the Lamar Regional Land Trust, with a mission of assisting landowners and public agencies in the voluntary protection and conservation of open space, wildlife habitat, agricultural land, and other natural resources in the area surrounding northern Yellowstone. One of Haiwi's most impactful early successes was the formation of the Yellowstone-to-the-Artic Initiative (Y2A). Y2A had a lofty goal of creating a natural corridor for wildlife and indigenous people from the Greater Yellowstone Ecosystem north to the Beaufort Sea. The swath included parts of five American states, two Canadian provinces, two Canadian territories, and the homelands of at least 75 indigenous groups.

The high point of Toni's year was undoubtedly her marriage to Rusty. Although she had enjoyed the attention and affection of both Tyler and Rusty, as time went on she could feel in her heart a stronger pull toward the unconventional hunter who loved the wilderness. For many years after the "kissing contest", the three had been nearly inseparable. Toni had taken a job with the Yellowstone Regional Alliance and worked out of their office in Cody, renting a small cottage there. Rusty worked as a fly-fishing guide on the Shoshone River from June through August, a bow-hunting guide from September through October, and built fly-rods and repaired hunting bows the rest of the year. Tyler continued working as a firefighter but had moved to the Park County Fire District Two Fire Station in Cody. Rusty and Tyler shared an apartment in Cody.

The three were tight friends, and Toni was careful not to endanger that friendship by pitting the two against each other just to feed her ego. Despite her best efforts, Tyler and Rusty were constantly trying to outdo each other in her presence, but to her credit she ignored it. While the two men were both attracted to Toni, they and she dated other people on and off. Toni was a hard judge of the men's dates and found herself curiously jealous when Rusty took out a new girl. In reality, they all worked long, hard hours and had only a limited amount of time for romance, so none of the encounters lasted more than a couple of dates.

In 2002, after nearly a decade of close companionship, Rusty had shown up one Friday afternoon at their usual end-of-the-week happy hour spot, the Proud Cut Saloon, not looking himself.

"What's up Rust, lose a big fish?" asked Tyler jovially. The absence of a sarcastic comeback immediately raised a red flag for Toni and Tyler. "Somethin' bad happen, Rusty?" questioned Toni with concern.

"It's my mom; she and my dad were in a head-on up on the Beartooth pass." Rusty took a deep breath and continued. "My mom was killed instantly; they took my dad to the emergency clinic in Red Lodge. Sounds like he's going to be all right."

"Oh my God!" gasped Toni inadvertently, bringing her hand to her mouth.

"Shit buddy, that's terrible about your mom," sympathized Tyler, putting a hand on Rusty's shoulder. "What can we do to help you with your dad?"

"I'm gonna head up there right now if either of you wants to ride up with me?" replied Rusty.

"I'll go for sure," volunteered Toni before Tyler could speak.

"Why don't you two go," said Tyler. "Call me from up there and let me know if there's anything I can do down here. I may be able to mobilize an ambulance from

Cody Regional Health if your dad needs to be transferred down here."

"Thanks, buddy, I'll definitely keep you in the loop," said Rusty, appearing a little relieved.

Rusty was worked-up, and the two talked continually on the hour drive up to Red Lodge. As they spoke, Toni heard a side of Rusty she hadn't known. Rusty had never talked at length about his dad and mom, but now she could clearly hear the love and admiration of a son for his parents. Lucille had been a doting mom, and she and Rusty had been quite close. For all of their differences, Rusty and his dad shared a craving for the outdoors, and Rusty attributed his wood lore to time spent with his father in the mountains. Like a switch being toggled, Toni was unexpectedly struck by a deeper level of feeling for this man she had now known for fifteen years. But now was not the time to evaluate those feelings; now she needed to be available to help with his emotions.

"I guess I may need to deal with my mom's...body?" said Rusty haltingly as they approached the clinic.

"How about you go check in on your dad and I'll find out about your mom?" answered Toni.

"Thanks, Toni, that would be great," Rusty said, squeezing her hand in gratitude before exiting the car. Toni's heart jumped at the touch in a way that it never had before.

As Rusty hurried in to find his father, Toni went to the reception desk and asked where she would find Lucille's body.

"You'll want to contact the Carbon County Coroner here in Red Lodge, dear," said the caring older woman at the desk. "You can use this phone if you like, dear, in fact I can dial the number for you." Dialing the phone she handed the handset to Toni and turned to organize things on the desk to give Toni some privacy. A recorded message indicated that it was past normal business hours but provided an emergency number. Toni hung up and dialed the number provided.

"Coroner," a male voice said simply.

"Hello, my name is Toni Poe. I'm at the clinic with my friend, Rusty Stewart, and I am helping him locate his mother's…remains. I'm not sure how to proceed. What should we do next?"

"Ah yes, thank you, Toni, it would be good to get a positive I.D. if he's up for it…I'm afraid it's not pretty," said the coroner respectfully. "Why don't you bring him over once you're done there. I'm just now finishing up paperwork here in the office."

"Thank you, sir; we'll be over in a while," replied Toni, pleased to have found such a calming and accommodating person in the coroner.

Heading back to the clinic, a nurse led Toni to a curtained-off cubicle where Rusty was talking with his dad. The nurse asked Rusty if it was okay for Toni to enter and then parted the curtain for her. Toni's eyes met Albert's, which were red and drooping, but they lit up slightly upon recognition of the young woman. Toni was suddenly at a loss at what she would say to a man who was injured and had just lost his wife, so instead, she gently took hold of his fingers and stroked his hand.

Albert struggled to form a word but Rusty intervened. "No need to talk, Dad, just lay still." To Toni,

Rusty whispered, "He's on some heavy pain meds; I'll tell you more in a minute."

Turning back to Albert, Rusty enunciated slowly, "We're going to let you sleep for a while, Dad. We'll be back tomorrow," to which Albert gave a slight nod of his head and closed his eyes.

As they exited the clinic, Toni and Rusty found each other's hands and held them as they walked to the car. "Is he going to be okay?" Toni inquired.

"Yes, he is," replied Rusty. "I'll tell you all about it later, but first - what were you able to find out about my mom?"

Although Toni had dreaded this part of the evening, she knew it had to be done. "The coroner is waiting for us to stop by so you can confirm it's your mom," Toni said softly. "He said it's not pretty."

"Shit," muttered Rusty. "Well, I guess I better go do it," he said resignedly. As Rusty stretched his neck to relieve some tension, Toni reached over and rubbed the back of it for him. While they had always been close, there was a different sensation in this touch.

Reaching the coroner's office, Toni asked, "Would you like me to come in with you? I want to if you want me to."

Thinking about it for a couple of seconds, Rusty finally replied, "Are you sure?" he asked.

"Absolutely," she answered.

"Thank you," he said genuinely, and they entered the building hand-in-hand.

The coroner was a personable older gentleman, the perfect person for an unpleasant task. They were taken to another room, very clean and sterile, where the coroner kindly turned down the harsh white lighting and turned on a hanging light directly over a body covered in a clean blue sheet. "I've attempted to make her look as good as I could for you. She was obviously an attractive woman. I'm sorry for this. Will you have a look and just let me know if she's your mother?"

Rusty nodded, released Toni's hand, and walked to the end of the sheet where the coroner was standing. The man held the corner of the sheet and looked for a sign from Rusty that he was ready. Rusty gave a small nod and the sheet was pulled back just enough that Rusty could see his mother's whole face, but the view was shielded from Toni. Rusty stared, his face at first showing little emotion, then he moved his head slightly back and forth to get different perspectives on what he was seeing. After perhaps twenty long seconds of gazing, Rusty turned his moist eyes up to the coroner, blinked, and nodded three times.

Putting the blanket carefully back down, the coroner said quietly, "Thank you, I'll just have you sign a statement on the way out. Follow me." Rusty signed the postmortem identification form and made arrangements for her remains to be conveyed to the Cooke City Cemetery. Then, thanking the coroner, Rusty and Toni headed back to Rusty's pickup.

After a few minutes of sitting silently in the vehicle, Toni asked, "Can you eat, Rusty? You haven't had any dinner," oblivious to the fact that she had not had anything since lunchtime either.

"Yeah, I can eat. In fact, I'm starving," answered Rusty honestly. The only place open to eat was the casino on the edge of town, so they found a quiet booth and ordered meals. Rusty relayed to Toni what the doctor had to say about Albert's condition, and the few details he was able to glean about the accident, as Toni stared at him and stroked his forearm. "The doctor said he's going to be fine," Rusty began. "My mom always made him wear his seatbelt...that and the airbag saved him. His foot was crushed, they think he had a minor concussion; he's got some whiplash and probably some broken ribs, so he's in a fair amount of pain. They're sending him to Cody Regional tomorrow morning to get the foot worked on. I let Tyler know and he'll have everything arranged at that end. I'd like to be here for him in the morning, so I'm thinking about getting a room for the night. You can just leave me here and I'll figure out how to get back in the morning," he said.

"I'm staying too," Toni said matter-of-factly. "I'll just get a room wherever you're staying; there will probably be some logistics to work out and I can help."

"You're an angel, Toni," Rusty said looking intently into her eyes. For the second time this evening, he leaned over and kissed her gently.

Just as Toni had earlier, Rusty was suddenly struck by the acknowledgment that his feelings for Toni were much deeper than he had realized. As he pulled away from the kiss, he felt a flush of emotion overcome him and again leaned into her, this time the kiss was long and passionate. It wasn't until the waitress cleared her throat that the two parted abruptly, cheeks red with a combination of embarrassment and something else.

"Sorry folks, here's your food," said the waitress, hurriedly setting down the plates and leaving them alone.

Toni and Rusty looked at the food, then at each other, and again locked in a fevered embrace.

Coming up for air, Toni finally said, "We'd better eat, it's getting late."

Looking a little sheepish, Rusty said, "Yeah, I guess…but I'd rather keep doing that!"

"Eat your dinner and let's go," replied Toni with a twinkle in her eye.

Neither knew quite how to handle how they were feeling or what they both wanted next. Although their ardor was nearing a fever pitch, there was a feeling of guilt at being so excited amid a devastating loss. But it was precisely that loss that had laid bare their feelings about each other and had created a need for the healing power of physical closeness and affection.

After rushing through their late dinner, they drove to the nearby Super 8 to check in. "Are we still getting two rooms? Or will one do?" Rusty asked Toni unsurely before they entered the office, the implications of which were clear.

Toni looked intently into his eyes, bit the corner of her lip, and answered, "If one room feels right for you, then I would like that." After paying for a single room with a king-sized bed, Rusty led Toni by the hand to the room, opened the door, stepped inside, closed the door, and the two locked in a tight embrace and long soulful kiss. When they finally pulled apart it was just like a scene from a movie – shirts were yanked off, pants were wriggled out of and underthings were tossed in all directions. This time Toni grabbed Rusty's hand and pulled him to the bed, threw off the blanket, and they fell together to the mattress. That night, the nature of the long friendship between the three friends was forever altered, and a new relationship bloomed.

There was no embarrassment in the morning, no regrets, only more love-making in the early glow of dawn.

It was immediately as though the two had been a couple forever, knowing each other so well from their many years as friends. After coffee in the motel room and continental breakfast in the lobby, they went back to the clinic to check on Albert and finalize any arrangements for his transport.

Albert, for his part, was obviously feeling better, as evidenced by his orneriness as he vociferously objected to the notion of being transported by ambulance. "There's no stinkin' way I'm gettin' in an ambulance. For a broken foot and some sore ribs?! No way!"

"It's not your foot that we're worried about, sir," said a young doctor that had been summoned to deal with Albert's objection. "We think that you had a concussion, and we can't be liable for you traveling in anything other than an ambulance."

"That's B.S.! I know my rights and you cannot make me ride in an ambulance if I don't want to!" The doctor looked to Rusty who had his arms folded and was wearing a knowing smirk.

"Yeah," said Rusty to the doctor. "I don't think you're gonna win this one, doc – you have no idea who you're dealing with here," nodding his head toward his dad who was now smirking himself. "We have room in the pickup and we'll get him into Cody Regional," offered Rusty.

The doctor huffed and instructed a nurse to have the patient and the driver sign a Release of Liability form, and then he stormed off.

"Anger issues!" said Albert grinning, gesturing towards the departing doctor. Nobody else laughed.

SENKAPIN

"Wes, are you coming up with the same results I am?" shouted Master's student, Paul Muslin, to his partner.

Fellow botanist, Wes Dunphy, raised his head from the sapling he was evaluating. "If you mean 'are these things suddenly growing like weeds?', the answer is yes," he yelled back from the opposite side of the small thicket.

Wes and Paul were in their sixth year at the University of Montana in Missoula and were on their first visit to a study plot, part of an ongoing project that they had inherited from previous researchers in northern Yellowstone. Research in the park was not novel; Yellowstone had served as a 'petri dish' of sorts for scientific evaluation for decades, with the highest number of annual research permits issued in the National Park system – up to 200 per year.

Paul made his way towards Wes, making note of any animal scat piles along the way. "This project has recorded nothing but declines every year since it began. Are you sure we're in the right plot? I don't want to look like an idiot showing the only increase in all these years."

"I know, right?" responded Wes. "Let's go over the protocol again and make sure we're not screwing something up."

"First of all, our sample plot is supposed to be a two-meter by thirty-meter slice of the grove, commencing from the center outward, right?" recited Paul.

"That's a 10-4," stated Wes.

"Ok, within the random plot we're evaluating saplings that are less than six centimeters DBH, little guys, not trees yet," continued Paul.

"DBH - Diameter at Breast Height, check," replied Wes.

"And the last time this stand was measured, none of the little guys were taller than one meter in height," enumerated Paul.

"Correct," replied Wes.

"We're also supposed to be examining the growth nodes on the five tallest youngsters within the entire stand to ascertain the number of years elapsed since they had been less than one meter in height, correct?"

"You got that all right, buddy!" confirmed his partner.

Muslin removed his glasses, rubbed his eyes, and put his glasses back on while thinking. "Under ideal climate conditions and lacking exceptional browsing pressure, these saplings should be growing up to 24 inches per year..." he began.

"And the last time this plot was sampled," interjected Dunphy, "was two years ago. That means if you're getting the same results I am from the other end of the plot, than a lot of these two-plus meter saplings were less than a meter tall at the last visit? Is that what you're coming up with?"

"Yeah," replied Muslin thoughtfully. "What the fuck happened here?" he said breaking into a puzzled smile, causing Dunphy to crack up.

Muslin and Dunphy were not alone. Beginning in about 2004, researchers in various disciplines began scratching their heads at some subtle changes that seemed to be taking place within the park. Paul and Wes were part of a long-term project investigating the decline of aspen stands in Yellowstone. Despite the trees' ability to root sprout into large groves of clones, young aspens within the park had, for the most part, failed to grow to more than a meter in height in recent times.

In the coming weeks and months, upon checking study plots in the numerous aspen stands that had been regularly monitored for decades, the grad students were repeatedly excited to note what appeared to be a widespread reversal in the decline of viable sprouts. Although they themselves had only been involved in the project for months, the data and photos collected by their predecessors clearly demonstrated that the groves were inexplicably increasing in size and were experiencing greater success in the recruitment of saplings.

Similar increases in sapling height and recruitment were found in willow, cottonwood, alder, and berry-producing shrubs throughout the park.

IDAHO

"It's a fuckin' train wreck out here!" yelled rancher, Glen Deming, into the mouthpiece, so loud that Idaho Fish and Game warden, Tony Yerthurn, had to hold his phone a foot away from his ear. "Sheep and dogs and blood and guts everywhere. Monsters! That's what they are, fuckin' monsters!"

"I'll be right out, Glen," responded Yerthurn sympathetically. "Don't move or touch anything until I get there."

Yerthurn was shocked and saddened. He had been one of the few in his department to secretly support the concept of returning wolves to the Frank Church – River of No Return Wilderness in 1995. But that was more than twenty years ago now and his opinion had changed; none of the projections about wolf reproduction had been correct. The long-term goal of ten breeding pairs maintaining a population of 100 wolves had been reached in just three short years. In year four, the population had grown to 140 wolves, and the depredation figures for that one year were 19 dead cattle and 64 dead sheep. By 2003 there were 38 packs containing 375 wolves. Recently, a new pack had moved into the Sawtooth National Recreation area, just a few short miles from Ketchum, Idaho, and Deming's sheep operation.

What Yerthurn found at Deming's ranch was worse than a train wreck; it was a macabre scene worthy of a graphic horror movie. Even more grisly than the long strings of intestines and blood-soaked wool strewn over multiple acres were the eviscerated bodies of what had been magnificent Great Pyrenees dogs that had been guarding the flock. If Idahoans didn't already have enough reasons to hate federal intervention in their state, they now had a gruesome image to rally to.

Unfortunately, this wasn't the first time that the mostly unwelcomed Idaho wolves had been responsible for large numbers of livestock deaths. Among those packs implicated in the incidents - the Whitehawk Pack, Champion Creek Pack, Buffalo Ridge Pack, and Pine Creek Pack - had all made the news in the past few years. In fairness to the wolves, many of the sheep had died of suffocation when they ran into ravines and piled up on one another, while only a small number of these were consumed by the predators. The wolves on the other hand had paid dearly for their sins; one pack near the Wyoming border having four adults and eight pups euthanized in revenge for their transgressions.

If there was a silver lining to this dark cloud, it was that ranchers and biologists, both bound by the protected status then afforded to gray wolves, were galvanized into cooperation on how best to prevent wildlife losses. Indeed, it was Deming's loss that led to the formation of an alliance that came to be known as the Forest Creek Wolf Project.

Both sides could agree on the primary goal, which was to reduce the predation of livestock by wolves. The secondary goal was agreed upon grudgingly, to practice ranching protocols that included non-deadly wolf deterrents.

Rick Bilson, a wolf specialist for the Idaho Wildlife Service, led the search for effective, non-lethal deterrents. Among the methods tested were handheld spotlights, air horns, whistles, boom boxes, guitars, and starter pistols. Searching far and wide for methods used in other parts of the globe, as well as brainstorming creative solutions, Bilson came up with two very effective devices. The first, he found being used in Australia, where sheep-rancher, Ian Whalen, had designed solar-powered lights that replicated the motion of a flashlight being carried across the landscape, which had proven to be remarkably effective at frightening off foxes that had been killing his lambs. Controlled by a simple program, this system that later came to be marketed as "Fox-Lights" had similar results when employed against wolves. Based on the success of the lights against foxes and wolves, Fox-Lights were eventually used on every continent except Antarctica, to control everything from African elephants to Asian snow leopards.

Where Fox-Lights proved effective against nighttime wolf incursions, an even simpler solution proved surprisingly effective during daylight hours. A visual deterrent called fladry had been utilized in Europe for centuries to keep wolves from crossing boundaries; it is even mentioned in a famous Russian song, *Wolf Hunt,* from 1968. In its most rudimentary form, fladry is nothing more than bright strips of cloth, hung from trees, fences, or poles in such a way that it can be waved by any breeze. Finding immediately that it was effective at preventing wolves from entering areas where livestock were grazing, a concerted effort was made to produce and deliver long strings of fladry to vulnerable ranchers all over the state. To enhance the effectiveness of the benign flagging, Bilson eventually created what was called "Turbo Fladry", incorporating an electrified wire connecting the flags. If a wolf was bold enough to brave the frightening pennants, the electrical shock would convince him to respect them.

The newly formed clan that had attacked Deming's flock had been named the "Phantom Hill Pack". The group had been subsisting well on the ample wild game in the Sawtooth Mountains since moving into the area just months earlier. Not knowing that wolves had recently made a home nearby, Deming had unwittingly moved his entire sheep herd to fields adjacent to the new pack's hunting grounds. Nuki, Phantom Hill's durable matriarch, had followed her nose to the overpowering smell of mutton. Intoxicated by the frenzied actions of the terrified sheep, a blood-lust overcame the pack, and the powerful Great Pyrenees sheep dogs were no match for the feverish wolves.

As though anticipating the backlash that would follow, Nuki afterwards moved the pack far into the wilderness. It was a year before they again ventured into the farmlands at the edge of the Sawtooths. As before, the sweet smell from the lanolin in the sheep's wool drew them towards a large flock congregated in a small valley at the base of the foothills. It was just after dusk, and Nuki was comfortable with the protection afforded by the darkness. Despite her confidence, the wolves slunk toward the flock low to the ground from the downwind side.

All at once, every wolf's ear was cocked and noses thrust skyward. Someone was coming. It wasn't a vehicle, which was less scary for them; the single, bobbing light was too small. Every head in the pack turned as if connected, as a second, and then a third light began moving to either side of the first. No, this had to be a human, or a group of them, out patrolling the fence line, protecting the flock. While the wolves had no qualms about taking on a 150-pound sheepdog, they were terror-stricken by the thought of humans. The wary leader that she was, Nuki knew when the odds were stacked against her, and looking over her shoulder as she ran, she led the pack back into the wilderness. This flock was not worth the destruction of her pack; they would not return to this spot.

The Fox-Lights had worked, and proven that human ingenuity could effectively change wolf behavior. Within months, both Fox-Lights and fladry were being used on almost every livestock operation surrounding Yellowstone.

KWI'NA

Even from 900 feet, Kwi'na could make out the human forms below. He was heading north on the prevailing wind and had just enjoyed a buoying updraft as he crossed Commissary Ridge a little north of the town of Kemmerer in southwestern Wyoming. The humans saw him too, through their binoculars, as that's precisely what they were there for, to identify and count raptor species. They were volunteers with Hawkwatch International, a conservation organization that monitored migrating hawks, falcons, and eagles as indicators of ecosystem health.

"I've got an accipiter coming in hot from due south!" shouted Suzi to her partner, Bill.

"Sharpie or Coop?" shouted back Bill, his pen against his clipboard ready to check one of two boxes, either a sharp-shinned hawk or a Cooper's hawk.

"Can't tell yet, once he's directly overhead I'll have a better view of his tail," replied Suzi.

Bill set his clipboard down on his stool, raised his field glasses and found the bird now almost directly above them. "I'm getting what looks like a pretty short tail," he offered.

"Yes, and it looks quite squared off to me – if it were a Cooper's it would be longer and more rounded," confirmed Suzi.

"Check," said Bill as he raised the clipboard and assigned a hash mark to the line titled SSHA, the ornithologist's code for sharp-shinned hawk. "We're at 623 sharpies for the season so far; lookin' like a good year!" he added happily.

As the watchers went back to searching the sky, Kwi'na continued soaring northward, scanning the landscape for a patch of habitat that contained all of the ingredients for a successful summer of hunting and nesting. Later that same day, Kwi'na found exactly what he was looking for. He located a large patch of mixed willow shrubs growing along a small stream, with nearby conifers. This habitat would support the nest that he would build with the mate that he hadn't met yet. The stream was Slough Creek in northern Yellowstone.

It had been a couple of decades since any of Kwi'na's predecessors had nested in the northern end of the park, as the habitat had not matched their search criteria in many years. Like the other two North American accipiter species, Cooper's hawk and northern goshawk, sharp-shinned hawks are bird-eaters, preferring to pursue and catch their prey in flight. Because of their strong dietary preference, they tended to choose territories with ample populations of small birds such as sparrows, warblers, and finches. This was the first year in recent memories that there had been a profusion of these petite birds in the Lamar River drainage that Slough Creek was a tributary of.

Rather than dropping immediately down into the shrubs and trees, he began systematically coursing back and forth about fifty feet above the vegetation. What minutes before had been filled with the songs and calls of numerous birds now went completely silent, as every tiny head was cocked skyward to mark the passing predator.

A lesser goldfinch that had been perched atop a coyote willow lost its nerve and took off in fright. This was just what Kwi'na had hoped for, and pumping his short, powerful wings, he rocketed towards the hapless goldfinch. In just seconds, there was an explosion of downy feathers as the hawk hit the tiny bird at full speed, locking onto it with his talons and then flying to a low limb in a nearby lodgepole to carefully pick apart the edible bits. Somewhere within his psyche, a choice was made; this willow patch would be his summer hunting grounds.

Within a week, a female of his species arrived, keying in on the same habitat attributes that Kwi'na had been attracted to. The male began performing ritualistic courtship dives from high above the female, and soon the pair was circling together, calling to each other as they did so and showing off the white patches at the base of their tails.

Not long afterward, the two constructed a well-hidden nest, tucked just below the tree canopy. The high-pitched "kiw-kiw-kiw-kiw-kiw" call they made any time they detected a threat, either from the ground or overhead, was the only clue to the nest's general location. After incubating her five eggs for a little over a month, all hatched successfully and thanks to a steady supply of small bird morsels, they all fledged at three weeks of age.

These five followed their parents in and among the willows, having plenty of opportunities to watch, practice and hone their hunting skills. In mid-September, four short months after Kwi'na arrived in Wyoming, seven sharpies winged back towards the Mexico border on their way to Honduras. The following spring, six of the seven would return to the increasingly bountiful riparian corridors of northwestern Wyoming.

Yellowstone was reawakening.

PAIKKAH

In the three years since the accident, and considering his age, Albert had recovered remarkably well. The fourteen pins in his foot had eventually enabled him to do many of the same things he'd been doing most of his life – cutting firewood, working on the cabin, fishing, drinking beer with the old guys at the Miner's Saloon, and attending his gun meetings. The only activity he had scaled back on was hunting, and not so much because of his foot, but because he was now 72 years of age, and even with Rusty's help, his mobility was not what it had once been.

Although Albert had taken up bow-hunting so that he could spend time afield with Rusty, he had never lost his passion for guns, which were still his favorite way to hunt. Dropping a big animal at 200, 300, 400 yards or more with a long gun was satisfying to him in a way that only the most accurate bow shots could be. The knock-down power of a high-caliber rifle could literally topple 700 pounds of bull elk on the spot, whereas even a perfectly placed arrow at thirty yards almost always led to a short run at best and minutes to hours of blood-trailing or even loss of an animal at worst. Albert was not in it for the excitement of the stalk; he was in it for the thrill of the kill.

Rusty accepted that his dad favored gun hunting, and although he had declined to join him on rifle hunts in his teenage years, he had compromised now that Albert was less able to pursue game very far on foot. The first hunting season after the crash, with Albert's foot still recovering, Rusty offered to drive his father down miles of dirt roads within his hunt zone, a practice known as road-hunting and looked down upon by hunting purists. After not seeing any elk and only a few small deer, they finally spotted a respectable four-by-four mule deer buck just 150 yards off the road in some sparse trees. Idling forward so as not to spook the buck by slamming on the brakes, Rusty slowly rolled to a stop as Albert quietly eased open the truck door, walked to the front end, and laid the heavy .450 Marlin across the hood. The big-bore rifle, better suited for 1200-pound moose than 200-pound deer, slammed into the buck with a wallop that virtually threw it to the ground.

Albert let out a victory whoop as Rusty gritted his teeth and rolled his eyes. "Nice shot, pop," Rusty said flatly. Together they walked to where the deer had dropped, and just as they had dozens of times since Rusty was old enough to accompany his dad hunting, field-dressed the buck and dragged him to the truck.

As they drove back towards the family cabin, Albert brought up the one topic that he and Rusty most strongly disagreed on. "Take yer time, Rust, keep an eye out for wolves. I'd love to blast one of the fuckers on the way!"

Rusty, already slightly disgusted that he had taken part in the unsportsmanlike shooting of the deer, took exception. "Dad! I'm not gonna stop for you to illegally shoot a wolf," Rusty said in exasperation. "I know that I come from a long line of wolf-hunters, but the line stops here! I've watched the packs, watched them at their dens playing with their pups. Sure they're predators, just like us, but they have just as much right to the prey as we do."

Albert looked startled, his brow furrowed as Rusty continued. "Do you know that I've harvested an elk every year since the wolves were restored? I hear guys whinin' all the time about how the wolves have killed off all the elk, that there's nothin' left for hunters. That's bullshit! There's plenty of elk left out there for guys that are true hunters. It's the dad-gum weekend warriors and the road hunters that aren't seeing elk. Those guys aren't hunters, they're nothin' but shooters. Fuck those guys."

"Well shit, Buddy, it sounds like you're calling me one of those guys," Albert started. "Hunters have bought and paid for every elk and deer alive today. A hundred years ago every game animal you see here was nearly played out, the trappers and the market hunters like my dad and grandpa had killed just about everything that moved." Rusty cocked his head quizzically as Albert continued. "Yep, it wasn't until ol' Teddy Roosevelt came along that we come up with some rules that started bringing back the buffalo and the antelope and the elk. States wrote game laws, sold hundreds of thousands of hunting licenses, and all of sudden there was money to hire game wardens and the critters began makin' a comeback." Rusty had never heard his father sound so supportive of game laws or so knowledgeable of history.

"But you know," Albert sucked in a breath for effect, "even ol' Roosevelt knew those wolves were no good. He called 'em 'beasts of waste and desolation'. All they do is kill, maim, and ravage – ain't good for a single thing, like a mosquito, a big, hairy, toothy mosquito."

"Creatures don't have to prove their worth to exist," sighed Rusty. "Someone or something put every living thing on this planet for reasons that we may never understand. But actually, it's not that hard to see why wolves were meant to be here. Just look at the fifty years or so that elk overpopulated Yellowstone. Park rangers had to shoot them because they were eating every blade of grass in the park."

"Exactly," shot back Albert. "Those were elk that hunters should have had the right to shoot. Those elk were public property. Our taxes paid for those god-damned elk!" Albert was now agitated and his face was flushed.

"Look, Dad," Rusty said earnestly, "I don't want to fight with you. Can we just agree to disagree on the subject of wolves? I won't bring up how much I admire them if you won't talk about how much you want to kill them."

Cooling down with a big exhaled puff of air, Albert conceded. "That'll work, son."

Albert discontinued his complaints about wolves in Rusty's presence, but in the meeting of the Hook and Bullet Club the following week, Albert became even more vociferous.

"The eco-freaks have done it again!" he announced at the beginning of his monthly wolf update to the assembled members. The response was as he had anticipated - angry and laced with profanity.

"Even though the wolf population is now up to 497 wolves in 34 packs. And despite the fact that we were promised the goal of the plan was only ten breeding pairs. And despite the court siding with delisting and opening up a hunting and trapping season on wolves. Despite all of these things, no fewer than twelve, yep count 'em twelve cco-terrorist groups filed a lawsuit against delisting, including…" Here Albert fumbled to put on his reading glasses. "Defenders of Wildlife, Natural Resources

Defense Council, Sierra Club, Center for Biological Diversity, The Humane Society of the United States, Jackson Hole Conservation Alliance, Friends of the Clearwater, Alliance for the Wild Rockies, Oregon Wild, Cascadia Wildlands Project, Western Watersheds Project, and Wildlands Project."

By the time he had finished the exhaustive list, the members were livid, angrily chatting among themselves and generally working themselves into a lather.

"Fellow members," Albert started again, "fellow members!" he repeated more loudly to try to quiet those still ranting. "As you can see, the greenies don't fight fair! We present sound scientific evidence and get a judgment to allow us to kill some wolves and before hunting season comes around they sue us because they don't like the science."

"We must go on fighting!" Here he paused for the group to applaud, as he would after each dramatic directive. "Fighting to protect wildlife. Fighting against outside interventionists. Fighting the ultraliberal, anti-hunting enviro-whackos." He paused again for his most impactful plea. "Fighting to protect our Second Amendment rights!" This, the rallying cry of such organizations everywhere, provided a crescendo finish to his impassioned appeal.

The game was on; the enemies were clearly identified. The 2008 wolf-hunting season was off the table, but the 2009 season was in their sights.

BAINGWI

It was a fall afternoon and the male mayflies were swarming over a recently dammed portion of Amethyst Creek in the Lamar Valley. By nature's design, a female was attracted to the swarm, and flying near she was coupled in midair with one of the males. Their brief union completed, the female fluttered to the creek below and immediately laid her fertilized eggs on the water's surface. Her egg release came not a moment too soon, as Baingwi had been lying in wait for just such an opportunity. With an audible slurp he sucked her off the top of the water.

At three years of age, Baingwi was now sixteen inches long and displayed the distinguishing red lower jaw of a cutthroat trout and the kype, or slight hooking of the jaw, that identified him as a male.

Baingwi had been born in the Yellowstone River and had eventually found his way to its confluence with the Lamar River. The wandering trout's "smell memory bank" did not recognize the route he was taking, as the tributaries of the Lamar River had not been producing many young trout over the previous few decades. Feeder creeks like Amethyst Creek lacked the necessary ingredients needed for a trout nursery. In the absence of adequate shade along its banks, exacerbated by the footfalls of countless hooves, the shore had eroded over time, choking the waterway with sediment and warming it to undesirable temperatures. A dearth of willows and cottonwoods made it unattractive for beavers. The scarcity of beavers meant that there would be no structure to slow the water or create a pond.

But of late, something had happened to the lower portion of Amethyst Creek near its meeting with the Lamar River. After years of relative sterility, young willows had again begun to crowd the banks. The shrubs were a magnet for all manner of insects, which in turn brought in songbirds to feed and nest. The roots of the young bushes helped stabilize the banks. A beaver that had been released by biologists in the Lamar River as part of a reintroduction plan had made its way to Amethyst Creek and found willows enough to build a small dam.

As water pooled behind the barrier, the willows grew faster and other riparian plants recolonized the marshy edges. The expanding footprint of the impoundment led the beaver to add-on to the dam. As the flow of the water was slowed in the shade of the surrounding vegetation, pondweed began to grow along the bottom and the water temperature dropped. A moose discovered the pondweed and became an occasional visitor. The habitat had grown to become ideal for sheltering young trout known as fry, or parr, and larger trout, too, sought out the rich insect life it attracted.

Only years before, elk would linger for hours on end, unconcernedly browsing the creek-side vegetation down to ground level and napping in the warm barren spots along the bank. Now small bands foraged only fleetingly, nipping off a few leaves and moving on. They were furtive, nervously jolting their heads erect and scanning the horizon as they chewed. Thanks to their new foraging style, the growing trees and shrubs remained viable and grew dense.

Baingwi, oblivious to the process that had created the pond, was nevertheless the beneficiary of it. He grew large and healthy on a steady diet of aquatic nymphs and flying adult caddisflies, stoneflies, and mayflies. When it came time to mate, he swam downstream and into the Lamar River. Finding a female cutthroat excavating a nest, or redd, of pebbles in the stream bed, he fought with other males for the right to father her young. After the female had laid her eggs in the redd, Baingwi passed over them repeatedly, covering them with his milt.

The fertilized eggs would become alevin, tiny trout with large yolk sacs still attached. Hiding among the stones in the shallow water, they would grow to become fingerlings. The fingerlings eventually found their way to the mouth of Amethyst Creek and headed up-current towards the pond. In the shady coolness of the beaver pond, some would grow to become spawners, as a whole new population of cutthroat trout would enhance the fishery of Northern Yellowstone. It was a fishery that had been in peril for decades.

KIMMY

Rusty had been adamant. "I want her to have a Shoshoni name, to honor your heritage."

Toni was initially opposed to the idea. "She," Toni started, gesturing to her distended belly, "may not look indigenous. If she ends up being a redhead like you, a Shoshoni name will be more of a liability."

Rusty had prepared an answer. "Look at you. You can go by Tekwoni when you want to identify as tribal, or just Toni when you don't, although your features make it kind of obvious," he said with a smile. "Why not a name like yours, that can go either way?" he pitched, and then laid out his idea. "I've always liked the name, Kim or Kimmy… I read that Kimana is a Shoshoni word meaning butterfly. It's a beautiful name for a beautiful creature and could be easily shortened to Kim."

Head slightly cocked, Toni gave Rusty an extended gaze, a smile creeping onto her face. "I like it," she finally said. "You're a genius!"

Kimana, who was called Kimmy from day one, was born with ivory skin and a downy tuft of red hair. The only hint of her mother's contribution would not become obvious until later, as she developed the graceful high cheekbones that Tekwoni, Haiwi, Thomas, and Po all had.

Haiwi had brought Kathy to Cody for the birth of the baby. At 92 years of age, Kathy was still of clear mind, though she was now walking with a cane for stability. Haiwi and Kathy shared a room with two beds in the cute, older home that Rusty and Toni had purchased in central

Cody. Haiwi was excited about the ongoing accomplishments of her Land Trust, but Thomas was retired and she had been spending more time with him, traveling and visiting friends across the country. The grandmother and great-grandmother showered Kimmy with love and baby gifts and assisted Toni and Rusty around the house as they settled into their new roles as the parents of an infant.

Tyler dropped in too, along with his wife Georgia. The two had met at a firefighter's picnic in Cody and had gotten married shortly after. Although they lived on a ranchette near Clark, they had come to town to share in the joy of the birth.

In keeping with the tradition passed on through the generations, Kimmy was exposed early to nature and the outdoors. At four years of age, Kimmy first accompanied Rusty on a hunting adventure, for rabbits with a bow and arrows. As it was and always had been with Rusty, the goal of the hunt was not the killing; it was the immersion in the sights, sounds, and smells of the field. Keeping it short so as not to discourage her with all of the walking, they shared a trove of sensory experiences. From the margin of the aspens next to them, they felt more than heard, the percussive drumming of a male ruffed grouse. On the breeze, they could discern the sweet, moist smell of the nearby creek. And they saw rabbits, many rabbits. Without ever lifting his bow, Rusty pointed out the locations of the motionless herbivores, hefting Kimmy onto his shoulders so she could see them in the tall grass. After numerous sightings, Rusty asked Kimmy to stay still as he raised his bow, steadied himself, and released the arrow. Looking down at his bemused daughter, his face became radiant. "We got one, Kim!"

Forgetting to remain quiet, Kimmy leaped for joy. "Yay!! Show me! Show me, Daddy!"

Taking the little girl by the hand, he led her to where the petite mountain cottontail lay, pierced by a single shaft. Kneeling with her, he invited her to stroke its soft fur, to run her fingers along its velvety ears, which she did reverently. Reaching into a pocket of his vest, he pulled out a worn leather pouch and extracted a single dry leaf of coyote tobacco. Gently opening the rabbit's mouth he placed the leaf on its tongue and just as gently closed its jaw. "This is what your people, the Shoshoni people, and other tribes, did to thank their prey for the gift of meat," he explained to the awestruck little girl.

After extracting the arrow and showing Kimmy the blood and the wound, Rusty asked her to place the rabbit in the back game pocket of his vest. Mesmerized by its beauty, but without a hint of sadness or remorse, Kimmy held the small creature for a long time before placing it in the vest. "It's so beautiful! Can we get another?" she asked hopefully.

"One is plenty for tonight's dinner, carrot top! No reason to take more than we need," Rusty answered.

"Okay, Daddy, but can we go again tomorrow?" the little girl asked excitedly.

"Soon baby, we'll go again soon," Rusty answered honestly, mussing her red hair.

On their way back to the pickup, they stopped suddenly in their tracks at the sound of a long, ascending tone floating on the breeze from a distant hilltop. Looking up at Rusty, Kimmy asked, "What is it, Daddy? What's making that sound?"

"It's a wolf, darling," Rusty answered with a gleam in his eye. "It's a beautiful sound, isn't it, baby?"

"Yes! It's beautiful!" Kimmy answered, emulating Rusty's faraway gaze. "Will it get us?" she asked with sudden concern.

"No, baby," Rusty replied softly. "Wolves are afraid of us. They don't want anything to do with us. They just want to be left alone to live, and have families and hunt, just like us."

"I like wolfs, Daddy. They sound nice."

"They are, sweetheart. I like 'em, too."

TO'-SĂ-WOO'-RAH

Tosa was as fat as she had ever been that autumn. Fat was a good thing. She would need it to sustain herself through nearly six months of torpor, a grizzly bear's version of hibernation. Even now as she began to excavate her den at the base of a massive, 800-year-old whitebark pine, she was burning calories that could help with the nursing of the two cubs she would give birth to in the cavity among the tree's roots.

Fortunately, the fall berry crop had been the best ever. At 23 years of age, Tosa could remember her early years when there were few berries to be had in the Lamar Valley. In those years the winters had been more difficult for her. Subsisting on roots and tubers, she had nowhere near the 40% body fat she enjoyed this winter. As a result of this early lack of high-energy fats, her first three litters of cubs were not nearly as robust as they should have been once they emerged from their winter dens, and she lost at least one cub from each litter based on this lack of vitality.

But this winter would be different. Everything she needed to attain her maximum weight had been abundant this past season. When she had emerged from last winter's den, after a series of particularly harsh storms, winter-killed bison and elk had been a readily available source of nutrition. In summer, when she had climbed to the park's highest slopes to escape the heat, the cutworm moths were in abundance, one of her highest protein food sources. And just before it was time for denning, she had been able to satiate herself on serviceberries and her favorite, chokecherries.

Once the den had been cleared of debris, Tosa settled into the four-foot diameter void among the roots. After two-and-a-half months of dozing, Tosa stirred only slightly as the cubs were born, moving just enough to allow them to crawl to her teats where she would suckle them with her nutrient-rich milk. In late April, after three months of nursing them in the den, Tosa led the cherubic cubs out into the light of Northern Yellowstone.

For the first couple of months outside of the den, Tosa was careful to avoid encounters with other large predators; wolves, mountain lions, and male grizzlies would all kill and eat a young cub if the opportunity presented itself. The well-nourished cubs grew quickly and soon accompanied their mom out into the open Lamar Valley.

It was late August and every species of berry was ripe. Buffaloberries and huckleberries were particularly abundant along the upper section of Soda Butte Creek, and Tosa, accompanied by her cubs, were stripping entire clusters into their mouths with their tongues. The tranquility of the moment was suddenly upset as a small group of elk splashed frantically across the creek just fifty yards from the bears, followed just seconds later by three gray wolves.

Grizzlies hate surprises, and a mother bear with two cubs even more so. Tosa stood up on her hind legs to get a better view of the chase, and the well-disciplined cubs huddled close to her. The big female bear watched as the lead wolf latched onto a cow elk's back leg, and then saw the other two wolves tackle the hobbled animal. Within moments they had the elk on the ground and were just beginning to tear into her.

Tosa's predatory instincts were now stimulated. She knew that the most fat-rich part of the elk was the organs, the first parts that would be gobbled up by the wolves. It was rare that she could get to a wolf-kill quickly enough to harvest the sweetbreads, more often arriving in time to claim some large pieces of haunch or neck meat. Time was of the essence, so she quickly weighed her options and considered the well-being of her cubs. Her mind made up, she roared at the cubs to follow as she took off at a gallop toward the unsuspecting wolves.

The first that the wolves were aware of the enraged bear was the flying leap she made onto the carcass. The surprised wolves tumbled away from her as she situated herself atop the body and started swinging her giant paws at them. The cubs had been right on her heels as she committed herself, and positioned themselves as close as they could be to her for protection from the wolves.

After their initial fright, the wolves' emotions turned to anger. The three, a small offshoot pack, had worked hard to get these elk right where they had wanted them, and they weren't giving up without a fight. They could see right away that the bear's weaknesses were the two cubs; she couldn't settle in to eat while needing to protect her young ones from the wolves. As wolves instinctively do, they focused their energy on her weak spot.

Each time Tosa turned to try to grab a mouthful of pancreas or kidney, the wolves leaped at the cubs. Each time the wolves rushed forward, Tosa spun with her stiletto-like claws, just missing the nimble wolves. It was clear that she was not going to get to enjoy her meal until she had eliminated the harassing wolves.

Leaping off of the carcass repeatedly, she gave a brief chase. Each time, one wolf would play the target, while a second wolf would try to tear off a chunk of elk flesh, and the third would rush the cubs. At 350 pounds, the bear, too, was amazingly quick and repeatedly turned to protect the cubs and reclaim the carcass.

At one point, a wolf got hold of one of the cubs, intent on dragging it away. Tosa was on it in a second, inflicting a quick, painful bite that caused the wolf to release the cub. With the cub safe for the moment, Tosa again mounted the carcass.

With one of their pack now injured, the cat-and-mouse game of three against one was looking less promising. Retreating a distance, the wolves took turns licking the wounds of their comrade. Though deep and painful, the punctures would heal in time. For now, though, their hopes of first dibs at the elk they had worked so hard for were dashed. They would bide their time until Tosa was done and hoped that there were some leftovers.

Leaving leftovers was not in Tosa's plans. Gorging herself first on the innards, then tearing off skin to expose muscle meat which she shared with the cubs, Tosa eventually lay down on top of the remaining carrion and went to sleep, her cubs snuggled tightly against her. There was not much left but bones to gnaw on when Tosa finally relinquished her prize to the wolves.

The cubs were fortunate to have been born and raised in a time of such plenty. Neither the berry feast nor the meat orgy would have been possible if they had been born when Tosa was.

TEPAIKKAPPEH

Tepa was one of those wolves who seemed to love travel. True to the definition of 'lone wolf', Tepa wandered from wolf territory to wolf territory both inside and outside of the park. Crossing territorial lines was risky business in the wolf world, and would often end up in a chase or an embrace. If a pack lacked a strong male leader, he might be welcomed as a needed hand to assist with hunting elk and fighting other packs. If strong leadership was already present in a pack, he might be considered a threat, in which case death would be the penalty for entering their domain. Fortunately, Tepa was charming when the pack was receptive and exceptionally fast when they weren't.

His encounters with other packs were not the cause of most of Tepa's problems, however. It was his repeated forays outside of the park, and his fondness for veal that most often got him into trouble. Although his ramblings had taken him out of the park into three states - Wyoming, Montana, and Idaho - it was the area between Gardiner, Montana, and Silver Gate, Montana that he most often crossed the boundary. The Absaroka Mountains formed a rugged knot here that held lots of wild game, few people, and the occasional cattle ranch on its borders. Another name that the area had just recently been given was Wolf Management Area #313, a hunting unit.

The Montana Department of Fish, Wildlife and Parks had for many years required that ranchers request an investigation by their staff if they suspected wolf depredation of their livestock. Tepa already had a 'rap sheet' as the probable offender in numerous calf deaths, but so far he hadn't been caught in the act. Although the first wolves relocated to Yellowstone had all been radio-collared, fourteen years and hundreds of wolves later a fair number of them had never had the tracking devices installed. Tepa had evaded all attempts to dart and collar him, so there was no tracking data to corroborate claims of his offenses.

At five years of age, Tepa had become quite smug in his ability to outrun or outwit any opponent, animal or human. He had been brazenly crossing borders since he was two; day or night, rain or shine, summer or winter. In his younger days, when a car would stop and a tourist would get out to snap his picture, he would run for the shelter of the trees. Nowadays he rarely even looked up, unless he was feeding on a kill, in which case he kept one eye out for competitors. Within his lifetime, humans had never meant anything other than curious observers, not to be feared other than an instinctive mistrust of them.

It was September 14, 2009. Tepa was up to his usual tricks, loping across the Buffalo Plateau northwest of Cooke City in Montana. He had seen hunters before, watched them, in fact, as they stalked the very game that he had been watching. But these hunters were different. They weren't watching the elk that were obvious on the next ridge, they were watching him. They had no bows or guns, not that he knew what guns were other than having heard them booming every fall. He slowed from a lope to a trot, his head turned to look at the humans. Their fixation on him was odd and was making him nervous. Picking up his pace he broke into a run, now glancing at them over his shoulder as he did so. Once he was directly downwind of them, he picked up the disgusting smell of body odor, cigarette smoke, and numerous other foul scents. Tepa had no way of knowing that the first Montana wolf hunting season in the state's history would open tomorrow morning, a half hour before sunrise.

The two hunters had driven over from Dillon, Montana to participate in the historic hunt. Vance and Dean considered themselves elk hunters, though they weren't particularly successful. Best friends, they had been hunting together for twenty-five years. Although they only harvested one elk between them every three or four years, and since wolf reintroduction they had actually improved their kill ratio slightly, they nevertheless blamed their lack of success on the wolves. The truth was, they were just poor hunters. They rarely woke up before sunrise, they were both overweight and the smell of cigarette smoke permeated everything they wore.

The pair had decided that it was their responsibility to be part of the solution to the wolf problem, just as the 15,601 other 2009 Montana wolf tag holders had. To scout out promising locations, and to beat the anticipated throng of hunters all hoping for a wolf pelt, they had made the three-hour drive from Dillon two days before the opener. Driving Dean's lumbering truck camper along miles of mountain roads, they had picked a site at the Timber Camp Campground. From the campground, the road eventually crossed the Buffalo Plateau, where they hoped to spy a wolf.

The hunters were elated to spot Tepa the day before the season started.

"Well, that's a damned good sign! I thought we were going to go days before seeing a wolf," an excited Vance gushed.

"Yeah, and he definitely didn't seem all that spooked," replied Dean. "He's gonna look good hangin' on the wall in my den!" he added confidently.

"Hah!" spouted Vance. "Not so fast there, buddy. You're gonna have to beat me to him."

"Twenty bucks says I take 'im down," challenged Dean with a wide smile.

"You're on, Hoss!" answered Vance, at which the two fist-bumped each other in anticipation of their imagined success.

Tepa meanwhile remained puzzled about the hunters. Why were they ignoring the elk so obviously grazing nearby? Why had they seemed fixated on watching him? This wasn't normal behavior. His curiosity getting the better of him, he decided to stick around the area until morning and get a better look at them.

Before the sun broke over Sugarloaf Mountain to the southeast of him, Tepa could hear the distant report of rifle shots. Growing up in the game-rich Rockies, the loner was no stranger to the sound of gunshots, although it seemed early to him. Normally, mid-September was the time when the less smelly and stealthier bow hunters were about in the woods. He associated the noisy gun hunters with the shorter cooler days of October. The shots he was hearing were directed at other Yellowstone wolves that had also picked a bad day to be outside of the park's borders. Unaware of this, Tepa crept forward to where he had seen the strange hunters the day before.

Vance and Dean had been so thrilled at their sighting the previous day that they had spent the evening toasting their anticipated opening-day harvest with a fifth of whiskey. Because of this, they had gotten their usual late start, so that by the time Tepa had arrived at the plateau's edge to watch for them, they were just chugging up in their pickup. This had given the bemused wolf an extended view of the men's preparations, as they parked and departed the vehicle. Cocking his head at the complicated sequence of rituals, he watched as they opened and closed the doors numerous times, pulling out one piece of equipment or clothing after another. After five minutes or so, they finally looked as though they were done at the truck and began to walk in the direction that Tepa was watching them from a quarter of a mile away.

This time he was upwind of them, but in his experience, humans lacked the ability to detect anything with their noses. As they ambled noisily in his direction, he became increasingly uncomfortable with their proximity. At 300 yards he stood up and stared at them, ready to depart if they came much closer. He could tell from the change in their body language and the quickening of their gestures that they had finally seen him. Still, he was perplexed about their intent and he recklessly ignored his intuition to flee.

"Holy shit!" Dean whispered forcefully, hurrying to get the gun strap off of his shoulder and raise his rifle. "Wolf! Right. Fuckin'. There!"

Vance had been quicker and already had his rifle against his cheek, trying to find the wolf in his scope. "I'm on him!" he hissed.

Vance's rifle spit fire as he launched his first shot. Without waiting to see if Vance's bullet connected, Dean got off his first volley. The recoil of the rifles made refinding their target in the scopes problematic, and without being certain whether they were still seeing the wolf standing or not they continued to jerk the triggers. The air was full of the reverberations of the shots and the smoky smell of the gunpowder. When finally they stopped shooting, Dean looked at Vance and asked, "Did you get him first or did I?"

Shivering with adrenalin, Vance answered crisply, "I definitely got the first shot off; you didn't even have your gun up yet."

"Yeah," said Dean sheepishly, "but I'm the better shot! Let's go see!"

The two crept slowly toward where the wolf had been standing; scanning the tall grass ahead of them for what would surely be a bullet-riddled carcass. Pacing off all of 300 yards, the pair spun around in circles searching for a body, blood, or any sign of their trophy.

Nearly a mile away, Tepa was still at a full run, not even bothering to look back. In their excited rush to get off as many shots as possible, the hunters' bullets had hit everywhere but their target. Unscathed by a single shot, Tepa had learned a valuable lesson: humans were no longer spectators, they were now predators. It was a lesson that four other Yellowstone wolves, 68 Montana wolves, and 260 Idaho wolves would die learning that season.

NAWA'A

"Oh my God, Mom, have you read this!?" Toni called out to Haiwi as she scanned the most recent online publication of the international journal *Biological Conservation*. Toni and Kimmy had come to visit Grandma for a few days while Rusty was on an extended guiding trip.

"No, I haven't yet, dear," Haiwi called back from the bathroom where she was just wrapping Kimmy in a towel from her bath. "Should I have? What's it about?" she asked, carrying the toddler into the family room where Toni was staring intently at her computer screen.

"It's a bombshell, Mom," said Toni without lifting her gaze from the screen. "It's about the wolves and how their reintroduction has cured many of the park's problems."

Helping Kimmy step into her pajamas, Haiwi asked, "Cure the park's problems? Which of the park's many problems would those be?" she asked curiously.

"You name it, wolves fixed it, according to this," Toni said distractedly, engrossed in the article. "Bison, beavers, aspens, willows, and cottonwoods, they are all making a huge comeback because the wolves are keeping the elk moving all of the time."

Now cradling a weary three-year-old on her lap, Haiwi momentarily looked at the ceiling as though searching her memory. "Didn't I just say how much more lush everything was looking the last time we drove through the park?" she asked.

"Yes, that's right, you did," Toni replied. "The authors are these two well-known professors from Oregon State, Bill Ripple and Bob Beschta. They're calling the phenomena a 'trophic cascade'. Apparently, the same phenomenon has been documented in other places, when predators or keystone species are restored to an ecosystem where they've been missing for a while."

Haiwi made a quiet "shush" to which Toni turned in the chair to see that Kimmy was nearly asleep in Haiwi's lap. Haiwi gave a subtle nod to Toni, indicating that she couldn't talk at the moment but Toni should continue her explanation.

"This is what many of us in the wolf business have been speculating about since '95!" Toni said in a projected whisper. Kimmy had nodded off to sleep and Haiwi gently laid her on the couch, propped a pillow next to her so she couldn't roll off, and came to read over Toni's shoulder.

After reading the abstract introducing the paper, Haiwi nodded her head vigorously. "Some of us had been expecting this back when we were advocating for reintroduction." She recalled, smiling, "There was an ecologist named Bob Paine, who was doing work with starfish and mussels in the 1960s, who eventually came up with the term 'trophic cascade'," she giggled. "We all thought the name sounded too 'sciencey'." She stopped and read more of the paper. "Yep, I remember talking to Grandma Kathy about this in the 1980s, referring to the degradation of the park since wolves had been removed in the 1920s as a 'bottom-up cascade'."

"Wow, Mom, you were really on top of it!" said Toni with a look of respect.

"Many voices pushed for the return of the wolf for exactly this reason, for decades before you and your generation made it happen." Haiwi stopped and looked for the phone. "We should call Kathy and read it to her; she'll be thrilled."

"I'll do that right now," laughed Toni, picking up the phone. Haiwi took the opportunity to take Kimmy to the bedroom.

"Hello, Grandma?" Toni asked lovingly as Kathy picked up the call on the fourth ring.

"Yes, dear, how nice to hear from you," the ever-cheerful Kathy replied.

"Grandma, I wanted to tell you about a paper that just came out about the wolves," said Toni, increasing the volume of her voice to assure that Kathy could hear her.

"The wolves! How I wish there had been wolves when I worked in the park," Kathy sighed.

"Well, Grandma, this paper says that the wolves have changed the park for the better." Toni began her succinct explanation. "It turns out the wolves keep the elk from eating the willows, aspens, and cottonwoods, and because of that the bison and beaver populations have rebounded. They're saying that the wolves are saving Yellowstone!"

"That's right, dear," Kathy said knowingly. "It's what we always thought would happen if wolves ever returned to the park. And now they have…oh my, how I wish Po was here to see it, and Robert, dear boy, he would have loved the wolves!"

"Robert?" Toni asked, "You mean your first husband who died in the war?"

"Yes, dear, I loved your grandfather dearly of course," Kathy answered wistfully, "but Robert was the one who taught me all about the wildlife. He was a lovely man."

"You've seen so much, Grandma! We should take a trip into the park again soon and see the wolves," offered Toni.

"I'd like that, dear; the infamous wolves are now the famous wolves, ha-ha!" Kathy laughed heartily.

And famous they had indeed become. Wolves had always been a great headline grabber. Whether it was 'Wolves Slaughter Sheep' or 'Hunters Slaughter Wolves', the media latched onto any wolf story they could drum up, and the public was always hungry for juicy news about their trials and triumphs. So when the scholarly thesis on wolves and the trophic cascade finally made it to the newspapers, then to broadcast media, the former villains of the valleys were recast as the heroes of the hills.

This heightened attention on changes brought on by the restoration of wolves also brought out a whole new cadre of scientists, eager to corroborate the findings of the Ripple and Beschta report. The park permitting desk was besieged with requests for research access. From botanists and ornithologists to the more esoteric fields of chiropterology (bats) and vulpinology (foxes), everyone it seemed wanted to find more trophic cascade evidence.

Over the ensuing four years, while sportsmen's groups focused on the wolves' impact on elk numbers, more studies were published highlighting the growing number of beneficiaries of the wolves' natural management of the once out-of-control elk population.

The greatly increased recruitment of young willows, cottonwoods, and aspen had been identified in the initial report as a contributing factor to an increase in the number of beavers in the park. A subsequent survey found that beaver numbers had increased from just one beaver in the park in 1995, to nineteen beavers in 2015.

A study of increases in songbird diversity and abundance in the newly resurgent riparian zone showed a positive correlation for a wide variety of avian species. Common Yellowthroat, Lincoln's Sparrow, Yellow Warbler, Warbling Vireo, Willow Flycatcher, Song Sparrow, and Wilson's Warbler all appeared to benefit from the changes in willow size and thicket composition.

The impacts that wolves had upon the park's over-large coyote population were readily observable to even non-scientists. Coyotes had been the park's top dog for nearly 70 years, and in some areas had not only decimated the prey base of mice, voles, and other small rodents, but had put a serious dent in the area's fox population. Once the wolves reclaimed their former hunting grounds, they were having nothing of the coyote's ascendancy. Wolf-watchers were often unwitting voyeurs to the spectacle of literal dog-eat-dog as the bigger, faster wolves would kill and sometimes even consume their canine cousins if the smaller predator ventured too close to a wolf-kill.

William Ripple and Robert Beschta themselves did not stop researching the trophic cascade with the publication of their seminal paper in 2011. To determine whether or not grizzly bears had benefitted from the return of the wolf, they analyzed grizzly scat from before, and nineteen years into wolf habitation. What they found was that the volume of buffaloberry, serviceberry and chokecherry seeds in the scat had increased dramatically since 1995. This correlated with the reduced elk population and the increased growth of berry-producing shrubs as over-browsing by elk was reduced.

In addition to an increase in plant-based foods, grizzlies and mountain lions also benefitted from the carrion created by the wolves. While mountain lions were unlikely to intentionally seek out confrontation with a wolf-pack, grizzlies had no such qualms. In areas of the park with a high density of grizzly bears, it was common for wolves to be driven off their kills more often than not. In other cases, bears and lions would come upon the leftovers of a wolf kill and easily drive off the coyotes, foxes, eagles, and ravens that were the usual clean-up crew.

While most of the research focused on plant and animal communities, the importance of the increase in ecotourism spending in Wyoming, Montana, and Idaho warranted an accounting of program expenses and income. A broad study of "Large Carnivore Viewing Opportunities" found that while the price tag for wolf reintroduction totaled approximately thirty million dollars, wolf tourism was bringing in thirty-five million dollars annually. For all of the acrimony from so many corners of the region, the wolves were gaining a powerful ally – the business community.

KATHY AND ALBERT

Ever since Kathy had rescued Albert from old Wid-dah', it seemed as though their lives were inexplicably linked. When Albert disappeared after the bear attack, Kathy had searched for him for months. When Toni first brought Rusty to a holiday dinner, Kathy never suspected that this handsome, intelligent red-headed young man was descended from the traumatized, freckled-face boy she had dragged from the woods more than seven decades before.

Their perspective on nature could not have been more different. Kathy was an avowed protector of wilderness and wild things – a product of her time with Robert and her many years as a park ranger. Albert was not a hunter so much as he was an exploiter, having been raised from a very young age to kill for profit and recreation.

Kathy, at 99, had lived a happy, fulfilling life. There had been times of sadness, as there must be in every life, but Kathy had always bounced right back, intent on the promises of better times ahead.

Albert, at 79, had spent most of his life dissatisfied, usually angry that others viewed the world differently than he did, complaining about the liberals and the environmentalists.

In just the last few years Kathy had finally given in and resorted to using a walker, as her legs had become progressively weaker. The walker allowed her to do more than she had been able to for a few years, and she would sometimes spend a full two hours wheeling it around her Bozeman neighborhood.

Albert had given in, too, but to an easy chair in front of the television. The 60 pounds he had gained made it harder for him to get around on his rebuilt foot.

One Saturday morning in 2015, Toni called to have Kimmy tell Grandma about winning her second-grade spelling bee. As Kimmy sat behind her repeatedly spelling out "s-p-a-g-h-e-t-t-i, s-p-a-g-h-e-t-t-i," Toni began to worry that Kathy wasn't picking up. Of course, Kathy might have been in the bathroom or speaking with her next-door neighbor, but something told Toni that things weren't right. Next, Toni called Haiwi but got her father, Thomas, instead. "Dad, can you run over and check on Grandma? She's not answering her phone and I have a bad feeling about it," she requested.

"Yeah sure, sweetheart, I'll call you when I get there," Thomas answered with concern in his voice.

Kathy had insisted on living independently and had a cozy little apartment just blocks from her daughter and son-in-law. After first knocking on the door and calling "Kathy? Kathy, it's Thomas. Kathy, are you ok?" Thomas went to the side window. Peering in he could see Kathy slumped on the couch with a book lying on her breast. "Kathy," he rapped on the window. "Kathy?" There was no movement. Fearing what he knew he would find, he used his copy of Kathy's key and let himself in.

Just as he had expected, Kathy had passed away, seemingly peaceful as she had been reading *The Singing Wilderness* by Sigurd Olson. Thomas, who had adored Kathy, sat down next to her and stroked her hand while whispering a line from the Cherokee Prayer Blessing, "May the rainbow always touch your shoulder…" his words trailed off as tears dampened his cheeks.

Before calling to report Kathy's death to the Sheriff's Department, Thomas called and reached Haiwi, who in turn called Toni in Cody. Haiwi joined Thomas at Kathy's and the two waited with Kathy's body for Toni and Kimmy to make the three-and-a-half-hour drive. Haiwi sat with her mom's body, brushed Kathy's hair with her fingers, and spoke soft words of love to her.

Before Toni arrived, Haiwi and Thomas were pleased to have Rusty show up. "I was in Livingston so I dropped everything and rushed over," he said. After laying Kathy out as naturally as possible, Haiwi went into the kitchen to start a meal, as Thomas and Rusty caught up with each other.

It wasn't long before Toni showed up at the door holding Kimmy's hand. Dropping to one knee before knocking, Toni explained again, "Remember, Kimana, Great-Grandmother's spirit has already gone to Tukumpeh. We are here to say goodbye to her body."

"I know, Mama," replied Kimmy. "We will only be able to talk with Great-Grandma Kathy in our prayers and dreams now."

"That's right, darling," affirmed Toni with a tear in her eye.

Haiwi opened the door and leaned to hug Kimmy, then while embracing Toni, asked, "Is she okay with this?"

Toni answered, "She understands that Kathy's spirit has gone to be with the creator."

As Thomas and Rusty watched, Haiwi stepped aside as Toni led Kimmy straight to where Kathy's body lay on the couch. In the same way that Haiwi and Thomas had done, Toni put her hand on Kathy's.

"Would you like to stroke her hand, Kim? When her spirit left it took her warmth with it, so her hand is a little cold."

"Yes, Mama," she said simply and stroked the hand next to where Toni held it. After a minute Kimmy became aware that others were watching, and turned and said, "Daddy, Grandpa, come here with us." Rusty, Thomas, and Haiwi all moved in close, and the group formed a chain of interlocking hands, beginning and ending with Kathy's.

Kathy's effervescent personality had made her friends wherever she went. Although she was not of native American ancestry, she had been widely loved as a champion of indigenous people and causes, primarily by way of her association with Po's coworkers at the Bureau of Indian Affairs, his peers at the University of Montana, and his friends and acquaintances within the Shoshoni tribe.

Within the National Park Service and specifically Yellowstone National Park, Kathy was legendary. Long after most of the park employees she had worked with were gone, she was still known among rangers as "Grizzly Kathy". A faded black-and-white photo of Kathy in her ranger outfit with a broken nose and bloodied face still graced a wall in the Museum of the National Park Ranger in the Norris area of the park.

The news of her death was met with sadness in Yellowstone and around the region. Although the Park Service was limited in its ability to pay any special tribute to her, the park's official non-profit partner, Eternal Yellowstone, saw an opportunity to bring attention to the good work of rangers by honoring one of their own. The group created the *Kathy Powell Award*, and every year hence invited the public to share stories of their positive experiences with park rangers. A committee selected the most compelling stories, then held a fundraising banquet and presented awards to those rangers who, like Kathy Powell, exhibited selfless devotion to caring for both park resources and park visitors.

In this way, Kathy's legacy lived on long after she departed.

Lillian, the El Salvadoran maid that Albert referred to as "The Mesican", sounded frantic on the other end of Rusty's phone.

"The hefe!" she nearly shouted in mixed English and Spanish. "Alberto, he is muerto! Dios mio! Lo siento mucho, que debo hacer, señor?"

"Slow down, Lillian, I can't understand you," Rusty replied, suspecting the meaning behind the distressed words.

"The boss, señor," began Lillian, more slowly this time as she sought the words in English. "Your papa, he is died, Señor Rusty. I am ... sorry, what shall I do, señor?"

Given Albert's poor diet, weight gain, and his sudden switch to a sedentary existence, Rusty had been dreading this news for some time. "Don't worry Lillian; I will head over there now. I will take care of everything; you can lock up and leave. I will make sure you get paid. Thank you." Rusty said concisely, planning what he would need to do next as he spoke.

Immediately after hanging up, Rusty called the Park County Sheriff's Department and arranged to meet an officer there that afternoon. Next, he called Toni, who was out grocery shopping while Kimmy was at school.

"Ohhh, I'm so sorry, love," reacted Toni to the news. "Shall I come with you? I can have Meredith pick up Kimmy after school."

"There's no reason that both of us should have to be there," said Rusty resignedly. "There's no telling what condition he'll be in, it may not be very pleasant." Then, as a new thought popped into his head, he added, "I'll see if Tyler can go with me, probably just spend the night there."

The good friend that he was, Tyler automatically said, "Of course, buddy, when are we leaving?" when Rusty called to give him the news. The two threw their overnight gear in the backseat of Rusty's Jeep and headed over to the Beartooth pass. Letting themselves into the cabin, their senses were immediately alerted to the fact that Albert had been dead for more than a day or two.

"It's been almost a week since I spoke to him," Rusty grimaced as they walked to where they could see Alberts's body slumped in his easy chair from behind, "and the maid only comes once a week."

Tyler, covering his nose with a bandana, said, "Shit dude, I'm so sorry."

"I knew it was coming. He pretty much just let himself go after my mom died," replied Rusty with his hand over his nose and mouth.

They heard a vehicle pull up and were happy to have an excuse to get some fresh air. "Hey, Marc," said Rusty putting his hand out. "This is my pal from Cody, Tyler Adams."

"Pleased to meetcha, Tyler, sorry it had to be this way," said the young, athletically built sheriff.

"Yeah, it stinks…ugh, I mean…sorry Rusty, I didn't mean it that way!"

Rusty chuckled, "That's okay, buddy, it does stink in there. Marc, you may want to wear a mask if you've got one."

"Actually, I think I've got three of 'em if you guys would like 'em too?" offered the sheriff. "Look like a natural death, Rust? No sign of foul play?" he asked delicately.

"No, he just ate and drank himself to death from the looks of it," said Rusty, shaking his head sadly. "For the last year I think he only left that chair to go the fridge or the toilet," he added.

"Alright then," began Marc as he snapped on some latex gloves. "I'm just gonna' check him out is all; you don't have to go in if you don't want. I've already contacted the county corner to have him send a van over."

"Thanks, Marc, have at it, I think we'll just wait out here," said Rusty, looking over at Tyler and nodding.

As they waited for the sheriff to complete his inspection, Tyler asked Rusty, "What are you going to have done with his body, Rust?"

"I've been thinkin' about that," Rusty replied, his eyes searching the sky. "I don't think they'll let me bury him here or in the forest. There's a pretty little cemetery just east of town near the Soda Butte campground where my mom is buried. I think that'll do."

"Sounds like a good spot for him. He sure did love yer' mom," said Tyler consolingly.

"Yep. For all his faults, he was a good husband and a good dad."

"Amen to that!" answered Tyler.

Just as Kathy had been revered by the local indigenous community and Park Service employees, Albert was something of a hero among gun groups and hunting clubs in the Big Sky State. Although he belonged to several local, state, and regional organizations, his home club was the Park County Hook and Bullet Club (PCHBC) in Livingston, Montana, a local affiliate of the National Gun Owners Association. For many years he had been a popular speaker at club meetings, sportsmen's shows, gun shows, and gun rights rallies. His imposing presence and fervent advocacy would surely be missed.

In honor of his contributions, PCHBC created a perpetual award and scholarship in his name. At their next fall "Sportsmen's Banquet", the club awarded a $1,000 scholarship to Jeremy Pershing, a promising young member of the Livingston High School Future Farmers of America. Jeremy had been accepted at BYU's Rexburg, Idaho Campus where he planned to major in Animal and Plant Science. What made Jeremy especially qualified for the award was his top ranking as a teen marksman in the Montana Handgun and Rifle Association's shooting competitions.

In this way, Kathy and Albert, who had been brought together by opposing beliefs in man's relationship with wildlife, would each leave a legacy that perpetuated those differences.

TSO-APE

The 34-mile, out-and-back hike from Yellowstone's Chittenden Bridge Picnic Area to Wapiti Lake is not one of the more popular hiking routes in the park; in fact, it is most often described as "swampy", "buggy" and "boring". Even for those hardy souls that decide to take it on, few stick it out all the way to the lake. The resultant dearth of humans is one of the main reasons that it had perennially supported a good-sized wolf pack, the Wapiti Lake Pack.

As young male wolves often do, Tso had found the large Wapiti Lake pack he had been born into wanting in unrelated females. Nature has provided wolves with a reluctance to breed with close relatives, spurring them to wander in search of new packs to mix their DNA with. Tso's wandering led him north, to the domain of the 8 Mile Pack near the park's northern gate. There he found three females who, coincidentally, were looking for an unrelated male. From this meeting, a brand new pack was formed – the Phantom Lake Pack.

The area that Tso and his new family chose to occupy was one of the most pack-dense areas of the park, with portions of six wolf clan territories converging very close to Yellowstone's northern boundary. With territories overlapping, border disputes were common. It was no wonder that the packs were so keen on protecting this turf; it also featured some of the park's largest concentrations of elk and bison. Unfortunately, the territories also overlapped a very human border, between Yellowstone and what had become Montana's most sought-after wolf-hunting zones, 313 and 316.

In 2021, Montana enacted an abrupt change in their hunting regulations, in part a result of the previous federal administration's removal of wolves from the Endangered Species List. The state's former "Wolf Management Plan" had attempted to balance the hunting and trapping harvest with the goal of sustainable expansion of the wolf population. A small but powerful segment of the economy viewed this policy as far too lax. Hunters and outfitters demanded that the legislature decrease wolf numbers immediately, citing a decline in the state's elk herd and a correspondingly lower success rate for elk hunters. Twenty-six thousand comments were received, the majority of which opposed more aggressive hunting techniques. Flaunting the will of the majority and the laws of his own state, anti-wolf Governor, Greg Gianforte, had recently received a warning for violating wolf-hunting regulations.

Among wolf advocates and even the disinterested general public, the resulting regulations for the 2021 season were seen as inhumane and shameful. Where previously trappers could use only leg traps, indiscriminate wire neck snares could now be used. Counter to the concept of "fair-chase", hunters could now employ various methods that had been outlawed for decades. Wolfers could put out an inviting, odoriferous carcass and wait nearby to shoot wolves that came to investigate it. Hunting and shooting wolves from aircraft was to be allowed, as was the night-hunting with spotlights. But the change that would have the greatest ramifications was the change in the 'bag-limit' or number of wolves any one individual could kill – from a maximum of two wolves in 2020 to twenty wolves per person in 2021, ten with a firearm and ten with a trap.

Even within the Montana Fish and Wildlife Commission, there was opposition to these allowances. "We are selling our souls and our fair chase in order to provide methods that are unnecessary and more likely to have repercussions," chastised Commissioner Pat Byorth.

Despite the competition surrounding the crowded territory in which Tso had established his pack, the family was thriving. Pups born in 2019 and 2020 brought the total number of wolves in the pack to fourteen. With this many mouths to feed, the pack needed to go wherever the elk went. Unfortunately, this meant outside of the protected boundaries of the park.

"Wolfer" was an old word that had originally referred to those who shot wolves to collect the government bounty offered in the early part of the 20th century. The title surfaced again once the Rocky Mountain states had begun allowing recreational wolf hunting. The new wolfers were not hunting for bounty, however. Their stated reasons ranged from "to save elk" to "to keep the wolf population in check". Their unspoken reason seemed to be retribution against the environmentalists. Whatever their reasons, they were committed to killing as many wolves as they could. For those that hunted areas 313 and 316 along the park's northern border, the new regulations gave them the ability to do just that.

Referred to as "boundary hunters", their method was antithetical to the rules of 'fair chase'. They would position themselves just outside of the unfenced northern border of the park and shoot wolves as soon as they crossed the boundary. The new regulations made this even easier, allowing hunters to place horse and elk carcasses just beyond the line, or use recorded wolf howls, to entice park wolves to head out of protection and into the hunt zone.

On an October day ostensibly like any other, Tso led his family in search of elk. The pack had been preying on a large herd of elk just outside of the village of Jardine, Montana, just north of Gardiner. The wolves had spent the night inside the park, but at first light they could hear an unknown wolf howling within their territory just north of the park border, between them and their prey.

Tso's hackles stood erect on his neck as he cocked his ears to try to pinpoint the location of the interloper. Throwing back his head, he returned a throaty howl, challenging the trespasser to flee or fight. Seemingly unconcerned, the intruder repeated the same howl many times, as Tso's whole pack now took up the challenge. Calling from a hillside somewhere above Bear Creek as it flowed down from Jardine, the cheeky encroacher was either very bold or incredibly ignorant.

After a half-hour of back-and-forth, the pack had enough. Tso, their bold leader, charged off in the direction of the offending wolf at a dead run, followed by adults, yearlings, and pups. Up ahead, their nemesis howled carelessly, goading the pack into a frenzy.

Just before a deafening new sound hit them, an adult female running near the front of the group jolted back and sideways, thrown onto the light layer of snow. Next, as the speed of sound lagged behind the ballistics, a shocking boom reverberated across the canyon. Tso stopped in his tracks and turned to look back at his pack. As he watched, another adult wolf, a male, was jerked off of his feet as a glob of blood erupted from his side, followed by another percussive explosion coming from right where the intruding wolf had been howling.

Tso headed back to the south at a gallop, the remainder of his pack right on his heels. As they fled, the explosions continued, though none of the wolves stopped to look back. None saw the last wolf in the line fall, a dark gray female. First, her rear legs had been knocked out from under her, then as she attempted to drag her useless rear limbs, her head was jolted sideways and she fell lifeless.

On the hill above them, the droning wolf recording stopped mid-howl as an index finger swiped closed an app on a smartphone.

Before the end of 2021, Tso and six more of his family would fall to the boundary hunters. Leaderless, and now composed of mostly yearlings and birth-year pups, the promising young Phantom Lake Pack was effectively eliminated. Family members scattered; some were absorbed into rival packs, and some disappeared and were never seen again.

The final 2021-2022 Montana harvest tally positively identified 25 wolves as having originated from Yellowstone, while some of another forty or more killed near the park's border may also have been park wolves. All told, 273 wolves were slain by hunters and trappers in the 2021-2022 Montana season. In neighboring Idaho, 486 wolves were either shot or killed in traps, while 30 wolves were destroyed in Wyoming.

SÜMÜTÜWA

The Wind River Reservation was composed of two tribes; about one-third of the population was Eastern Shoshoni, and nearly two-thirds were Northern Arapahoe. After the U.S. Government forced the two traditional enemies to share one reservation in 1878, there were years of animosity between the tribes. But by the twenty-first century, much of that ill-will had dissipated. Within the Shoshoni population, the largest portion had descended from the "Buffalo Eaters" clan, but the blood of the Mountain Shoshoni, or Tukudika, persisted in many.

Gus Daha, a member of the Eastern Shoshoni Tribal Council, was Pohogwe's grandnephew. Descended from the Tukudika, Gus possessed a reverence for the gray wolf, passed down from generations of oral history and tribal beliefs. As the tribe's representative to the Tribal Leaders Council of the Rockies (TLCR), Gus had a unique interest in the future of the wolves - Tekwoni Oketo, now Stewart, was Gus' second cousin, and those within the tribe who knew of her work on re-establishing the wolves were proud of her Eastern Shoshoni heritage. When he received the news that the TLCR was meeting to respond to the recent escalation in wolf killings, Gus made arrangements to attend.

The scenery along the nearly five-hour drive from Fort Washakie to the meeting in Billings, Montana never failed to capture Gus' imagination of what life must have been like for his ancestors in the Big Horn Valley. Arriving at the meeting site, Gus was impressed with the turnout and the energy as he sat down to listen to the presentation by the council president.

"Brothers and sisters," began Sam Proud Eagle, "we are here today to protect a family member. I refer, of course, to the gray wolf." As acting president of the Tribal Leaders Council, Sam was speaking to representatives of numerous tribes who shared the wolves' homeland, including the Blackfeet, Chippewa-Cree, Salish, Kootenai, Crow, Eastern Shoshoni, Little Shell Chippewa, Northern Arapaho, Northern Cheyenne, Shoshoni-Bannock, and others.

"The gray wolf is known by many names among tribal nations throughout this land," Proud Eagle continued, "and from time immemorial has held an esteemed place in the cultures and lifeways of our ancestors. Indeed, for some tribal nations, the gray wolf has guided and influenced their people in a foundational way, literally since the beginning of time - foundational to their place upon, and understanding of, the earth and stars." To this, Gus and many of his fellow members turned to one another, shaking their heads in affirmation.

"The U.S. Fish and Wildlife Service ignored our counsel with regards to the delisting of the gray wolf," he stated, his voice becoming harsher. "We have beaten them before, as we did in the lawsuit, 'Crow Tribe versus Zinke', when they tried to delist our brother the grizzly bear." This claim was greeted by whoops and shouts. "Since 2011, in the TLCR region of Montana, Idaho, and Wyoming, trophy hunters and trappers have killed some 3,500 gray wolves - that is over half of the existing population in those nine states. These gray wolves were killed in such large numbers due to federal protections being lifted.

There is no credible argument to remove Endangered Species protections from a keystone species that has not, by any measure, recovered. It is irrefutable that the gray wolf is functionally extinct in most of its historic range."

"For all of these reasons and many more, we join with the other tribal nations and representative tribal bodies in demanding the relisting of the gray wolf." Sam now made his request. "Shall we sign onto the treaty proposed by the Assembly of First Nations and the Global Indigenous Counsel requesting that the Secretary of the Interior stop the wolf culls?" The response of his fellow representatives was loud and clear. The tribes would challenge the federal government to act on their request. Gus was proud of the work of the council.

Indeed, tribes from all over the region, across the nation, and from around the world were speaking out critically on the U.S. government's failure to take into account the significance of gray wolves in their beliefs and culture. Just a few years prior, the International Indigenous Council (IIC) had presented official declarations on behalf of 130 tribes to the State of Wyoming, opposing its trophy hunt of the sacred grizzly bear. After the previous administration had stripped gray wolves of their endangered status, the tribes were now optimistic that the new administration that they had helped to get elected would restore the wolves to the list. Indigenous people everywhere were crushed when the new president failed to relist the wolves, and the Native American secretary of the interior declined to meet with them.

"It was like being injured by a good friend. It was suffering a loss of innocence," Tim Black Horse, of the

IIC, said of the president in a radio interview. When it came out that the new administration would adopt the same position on wolves as the previous, "That was such a horrible blow to our soul. To our innocence."

Meanwhile, a thousand miles to the east, six indigenous tribes filed a lawsuit against the State of Wisconsin in federal court claiming their treaty rights were violated. The six separate Chippewa bands cited that their treaties with the United States government had been violated by the state of Wisconsin when hunters had been allowed to kill 100 more gray wolves than the established state limit of 119. In their complaint, the tribes claimed that, "First, in setting the quota for the upcoming wolf hunt, defendants purposefully and knowingly discriminated against the Ojibwe Tribes by acting to nullify their share. Second, the defendants failed to use sound biological principles in establishing the quota for the upcoming hunt."

As a remedy, tribes asked a federal judge to rule that their rights had been violated when setting the harvest quota and bar the state from holding a hunt that fall. The six tribes said that the state had failed to put "adequate safeguards" in place to protect tribes' share of the wolf harvest quota, pointing to the February wolf hunt. The tribes pointed out that they would not have hunted the animals allotted to them but would have conserved them.

Indigenous people in all parts of the continent were moved by the slaughter of an animal brother and totem in a way that they had not been in many years. They would not stop fighting until wolves were again protected.

NATÜMENINNA

Judy Bosch managed the Vintner's Vault bottle store and wine bar in Livingston, Montana, an hour from Yellowstone's North Entrance. Livingston businesses had just experienced one of their busiest summer seasons ever in 2021, as tourists had descended on Yellowstone en masse after COVID-19 had kept millions from vacationing in 2020. The winter season was shaping up to be a record-breaker as well, thanks in part to northern Yellowstone's wolves. Wildlife watchers from around the world had discovered that the most exciting and arguably the best time of year to view the park's wolf packs was in winter, and they all had to come through Livingston to do so.

The demographics of wolf watchers matched up nicely to those of wine drinkers - primarily older, white, upper-income, college graduates - and Judy's shop was one of their go-to's when they were in the area. Elsewhere in Livingston, West Yellowstone, Gardiner, Cooke City, Silver City, and tiny villages throughout the region, many small businesses were beneficiaries of the magnetic attraction that wolves had on the public.

Sometime in the fall of 2021, Judy got the first inkling that there was an alarming threat to her business.

"The ranger told us that one of the most famous wolves in the park got shot," a distressed white-haired woman said to Judy as she poured her a $20 glass of Cabernet Sauvignon.

Judy had heard this complaint from time to time in years past, and tried to mollify her customers' concerns. "Ughh," she sighed, "I hate it when that happens. Every few years we lose a beloved park wolf on this side of the line and it tends to bring everyone down."

"Yes, but apparently this wasn't the only one, the ranger thought that two or three of them had been killed by hunters," the woman said loud enough for other patrons to take note.

Judy scanned the bar and could see that almost everyone was now paying attention. Biting her lip she replied carefully, "Oh no! I'm going to make some phone calls, this has got to stop!"

As those at the bar began to discuss this news among themselves, Judy slipped into the storeroom just long enough to say to her husband, "Crap, Peter! A woman at the bar said that a ranger's telling wolf watchers that a number of park wolves have been killed this winter. If it's true, that could put a serious dent in business. Can you check around and find out if that's correct?"

"Fuckin' wolfers!" replied Peter Bosch angrily. "Dammit! It's hard enough to make a living around here without giving those assholes a green light. I'll call around!"

"Thanks, Babe. I gotta get back in there and deal with it," Judy said as she backed out to the bar.

The crowd had become even more animated as two other patrons had also overheard the ranger that morning. "I've got my husband checking up on it," Judy announced, hoping to placate the customers. "If that's true, we're going to get some other businesses together and talk to the governor about it," she added.

While this didn't do much to calm the crowd, it did redirect the discussion toward Montana's state government and the recent removal of most wolf-hunting rules. When a similar over-kill took place in 2014, the government had backed down and reduced wolf limits in the two zones adjacent to the northern boundary to just 3 wolves total. But this year the state and the courts seemed committed to following through on their goal of slashing Montana's wolf population.

The very next day, Judy met with three other Livingston area business owners: a tour guide, an innkeeper, and a nature photographer.

"Is everyone getting the same intel that I am, that kill numbers of park wolves are way up over previous seasons?" asked Judy after the four sat down over coffee.

"I've seen it firsthand," said professional wildlife photographer, Rick Weiss. "The remnants of one of the packs staggered by me the other day looking lost," shaking his head slowly as he spoke. "There's no way they're gonna make it through the winter. It's only November!"

"Rick is spot on," followed up Janet Thompson, a biologist and tour leader for Wild About Wolves guiding service. "And that's not the only pack. We've observed three other packs that are suddenly without key members; it absolutely affects their hunting effectiveness."

"My guests are extremely disturbed," added Mary Beauchamps, owner of the Gateway Chalet Retreat. "One woman who comes out every year said that if this keeps up she won't be coming back – it's too depressing for her."

All four nodded in acknowledgment of the common sentiment they were feeling from their guests, patrons, and clients.

"We need to convene an emergency meeting of the larger group," offered Judy, to which all nodded their heads vigorously.

The Natural Pursuits Business Association (NPBA) was a diverse collection of businesses in the Yellowstone region whose livelihoods were largely based on the shared values of unspoiled wilderness, sustainable recreation, and functional wildlife populations. In recent years, the status of Yellowstone's wolves and their impact on business had become one of the group's primary focuses. What Judy had learned from some of her business peers was what the Association was already hearing from a number of their other members that the slaughter of park wolves was having a chilling effect on their livelihoods.

Some of the members had already taken it upon themselves to write a letter to the secretary of the interior seeking action. There was agreement among the entire group that the current wolf-hunting regulations were unacceptable.

A carefully-worded press release distributed to regional and national media outlets highlighted the following:

"The Natural Pursuits Business Association strongly recommends that Montana Fish Wildlife and Parks vacate their August 2021 ruling allowing for the excessive taking of wolves in Wildlife Management Units 313 and 316. The NPBA is not attempting to change other state or national regulations. We are intent on making changes to rules along the Yellowstone border. Prior to 2021, just two wolves were allowed to be harvested from the region immediately outside of the park's northern boundary, a sustainable harvest for the wolf packs as well as for large numbers of wildlife watchers. Under the newly enacted rules, as many as 82 or more wolves would be allowed to be killed in these two hunt zones, up to 20 per person in a combination of hunting and trapping."

"Whether you operate a convenience store, inn, dining establishment, or tour business, wolves are integral components of business success in the gateway communities surrounding the park. The media coverage regarding wolf killing on our side of the Yellowstone border will stem the flow of tourism in a significant way. For businesses, the large-scale killing of wolves equates to biting the hand that feeds us."

In recognition of the diversity of business types involved in the request, the following wording was included: *"NPBA is not an anti-hunting group. Many of our members are life-long hunters and fishermen and make their living in those industries. But given that the more than one million tourists visiting the region each year are typically what are known as 'non-consumptive users' (wildlife viewers and photographers), we must maintain a sustainable balance with consumptive (hunting, fishing, and trapping) uses."*

In conclusion, the press release cited the group's simple ask: that *Montana Fish Wildlife and Parks reinstate the previous harvest limits of just two wolves total per zone.*

Although the appeal by the NPBA helped to raise the public consciousness of the plight of the wolves, it did little to change the rules. In November of 2022, wolf advocates were optimistic that changes to the regulations for areas bordering the north side of the park would revert to 2020 levels. But on the last day of the month, a circuit court judge reversed his own initial ruling and allowed hunters and trappers another season of the liberal limits that had destroyed so many packs the previous year.

Yellowstone National Park hosted approximately 4.8 million visitors in the summer of 2021. Of those, a high percentage identified wolf-watching as their number one objective. Within the entire Greater Yellowstone Ecosystem, it was estimated the wolf-watchers brought in $82 million to local economies.

A Harris Poll telephone survey of 1,009 adults found that 87% considered gray wolves "a vital part of America's wilderness and natural heritage".

How much of that business might be lost if the vacationing public were to become angry and disenchanted with the region's aggressive wolf-killing policies? Could the federal and state governments be forced to change their regulations if enough economic pressure was brought to bear? How could such a campaign be organized and orchestrated? The nation's tribal people and many Montana businesses had started the snowball rolling.

KIMANA

The women of Kathy's line had developed a reputation for their outdoor ethos and activism. From Kathy's years with the Park Service, to Haiwi's work on preserving wilderness, to Tekwoni's wolf work. Now Kimmy had taken her place in the matriarchal order.

Where the women before her had been involved in grass-roots environmental advocacy, Kimmy had chosen a slightly different path. Attending the University of Colorado in Boulder, she had graduated two years earlier with a degree in the newly defined major of Sustainable Marketing. Most of her peers had taken advantage of the sudden demand for graduates in this new and growing field by signing on with major advertising agencies in New York, Chicago, and Los Angeles. But Kimmy's goal had never been a big income or an urban lifestyle; her objective was influencing policy change at the state and national levels. Kimmy was focused on forcing changes in wolf-hunting rules.

With the help of her parents, grandparents, and a sizable small business loan, Kimmy opened her own agency in 2031, which she named Preservation Promotions (PP). Occupying a modest-sized office space in downtown Bozeman, Kimmy furnished the unit with all of the requisite equipment: computers, electronic whiteboards, drafting equipment, video editing equipment, microphones, and more. She hired a graphic artist, a video editor, and a sound engineer. Believing that the name Kimmy was too youthful, she reverted to using her birth name, Kimana. Her indigenous name also inferred a relationship with nature that she sought to take advantage of.

Before the doors of PP were even opened, Kimana's family reputation had secured her three clients: Earth Equality, the law firm specializing in environmental litigation; Protectors of Wildlife, an organization that had developed the concept of compensating ranchers for livestock losses from endangered predators; and Eternal Yellowstone, the non-profit partner of Yellowstone National Park, founders of the Yellowstone Wolf Project. It was an auspicious beginning.

Not content to merely handle her clients' everyday needs of designing letterheads and creating Facebook posts, Kimana had a much bigger plan – to rally the world's wildlife lovers to evoke change. After just six months, Kimana began hinting at her scheme with her contacts at each organization.

"Did you know that boycotts have led to major social change throughout history?" she asked one client as they were discussing the 2018 defection of NRA sponsors after that organization's response to school shootings.

"What percentage of people considering a visit to Yellowstone would put off that trip if they thought it would save wolves?" she pondered aloud while analyzing the income attributed to wolf-watching.

"Would the business community just shit if someone suggested that visitors stay away from Yellowstone for a week?" she chuckled as though the question was ridiculous.

It didn't take long for her clients to call her on it. During a group lunch at Ted's Montana Grill in Bozeman, Steve Jones of Earth Equality asked, "So, Kimana, it's clear from your not-so-subtle questions and comments lately that you have something up your sleeve…want to tell us about it?"

Kimana's pale cheeks flushed as red as her hair. "Was I that obvious?" she asked sheepishly.

"Yes!" exclaimed all three of her lunch guests simultaneously.

"Well, since you asked…" she began, taking a deep breath in preparation for her big pitch. "For half a century a more, long before I was born, we have been begging and pleading on behalf of the wolves." The sober, nodding heads of her rapt listeners encouraged her to go on.

"We have continually chosen a somewhat defensive, rather than an offensive, approach with our adversaries. We have confronted conflicts from a position of weakness, rather than a position of strength. We have been reactive instead of proactive."

"Here, here!" offered Katherine Planter of Protectors of Wildlife.

"The ridiculous thing about it is," Kimana paused here for effect, "the numbers are overwhelmingly on our side!"

"Hell yes!" exclaimed an excited Wendy Otto, Eternal Yellowstone's Marketing Director.

In addition to her marketing chops, Kimana had a natural flair for salesmanship, and so far she had gotten the textbook "three yes's" in preparation for making the ask.

"The communities within Yellowstone's economic sphere of influence are earning in excess of 82 million dollars a year off of wildlife viewers and wolf-watchers. More than five million vacationers visited the park over the last year. In a recent poll of a representative sample of U.S. citizens, nine out of ten respondents said that wolves were an integral part of our natural landscape."

As she took a drink of water, Steve Jones said impatiently, "Kimana! You've got us! We get all this stuff…c'mon – what are you asking of us!"

"A one-week international boycott of Yellowstone National Park!" she blurted out.

There was a shocked silence as her three guests looked at each other. Finally, Wendy posed a question to all of her colleagues, "Could we even do that?"

To Kimana's way of thinking, it wasn't a hard 'no'.

NATEKWINAPPEH

"Wolves, take six," announced a young woman as she snapped a clapperboard shut.

"From 'the Big Bad Wolf' to 'The Wolf of Wall Street'," began Leonardo DiCaprio, ironically referring to his now 20-year-old blockbuster, "wolves have become one of the most maligned and persecuted animals in the world." Leonardo was just one of a handful of international celebrities who had readily signed on to lend their star power to a national advertising campaign.

Upon completion of his narration of what would first be aired as a four-minute-long "enviromercial", video was added, text was superimposed over the video and a copy of the final product was uploaded and sent to Kimana, who had been present during every step of the production. Immediately after the nationwide release of the full-length piece, a variety of :60-second, :30-second, and even :15-second television, radio, and social media advertisements would be aired. These would be accompanied by a billboard and print advertising campaign in national and regional magazines and newspapers.

Kimana was as nervous as she was excited as she sat in the compact viewing studio with her clients, the number of which had grown to six, plus her staff. Before queueing up the video, she stood before them to preface the piece.

"It's been hard to keep our campaign under wraps, but I think we've managed up to this point." Her clients were intrigued. "What you are about to watch is the first in a series of three videos that we'll be producing for the campaign. As I mentioned to you all earlier, we had chosen the three celebrities that we thought would not only be interested in helping us promote our cause, but a combination that we thought would have worldwide appeal. You are about to see one of the three. If you like the content, tone, and message, we will produce the other two. I am delighted to announce to you that our other two spokespeople are Greta Thunberg and Prince Harry!"

The response to this announcement was obvious in their comments.

"Oh my God!"

"You are frigging kidding!"

"That is off the charts!"

Kimana was beaming at their reaction to the news, and waited a few moments for the excitement to die down before saying, "And now, for our preview…"

The lights dim and native-American flute music plays softly, followed by the familiar face and calming tones of Leonardo Di Caprio.

"Wolves. They belong to all of us," DiCaprio states slowly, accompanied by a sound-bed of melodic wolf howls. DiCaprio's image dissolves into scenes of wolves throwing back their heads in song, as steam emanates from their muzzles, standing atop a hill of powdery snow as a full moon rises above them.

The narration continues. "From the beginning of time, the story of humans has been intertwined with that of wolves." The view pulls back to show that the howling wolves are on a bluff above a valley filled with teepees and campfires.

"It has been said," DiCaprio resumes, "that the indigenous people of North America modeled their family life and tribal society after the wolves, and highly valued their examples of loyalty and leadership." A split screen shows humans playing with their children on one side as wolves frolicked with their puppies on the other.

"They were the first wild animal domesticated by humans; their descendants are known as Man's Best Friend." An image of a single wolf walking across a field dissolves into that of a German shepherd being walked on a leash by a man.

The video returns briefly to Leonardo, as he asks, "When did our relationship go so sour?"

"From 'The Big Bad Wolf' to 'The Wolf of Wallstreet', wolves have become one of the most maligned and persecuted animals in the world." A worn clip of the animated film, The Big Bad Wolf, highlights the villainous antagonist.

"The belief in Manifest Destiny during the settling of North America erroneously taught us that man held dominion over the land and all other forms of life. Under that lie, wolves went from being our partners to being our competitors." The video displays vintage sepia-tone photos of hunters posing among thousands of bison carcasses and the bodies of indigenous people in front of destroyed teepees.

As the photos fade to pictures of rows of stiff, dead wolves displayed by sullen pioneers, the narration explains, "Farmers and hunters, seeking to preserve what they believed was theirs alone, sought to eradicate wolves. And did, as the last wolf was eliminated from the Rockies in the 1930s."

The video switches back, from black and white photos to a recent video of large groups of wolf-watchers oohing and aahing as they observe a pack with pups through their telescopes. "In the 1990s, the majority of Americans supported the reintroduction of wolves, and in the nearly forty years since, we have admired their wild spirits and family values."

"But hatred of the wolf has endured. In a country that considers itself civilized, the methods used to slaughter wolves are shockingly inhumane: clubbing, gassing, poisoning, strangling and worse have been and still are used, and many are still legal." A series of very short, disturbing images of modern-day hunters and trappers posing with dead wolves accompany the words.

Video of throngs of spectators at Old Faithful plays as Leonardo says, "Over 5 million people visit Yellowstone National Park each year to marvel at its wildlife, many to get a look at the park's famous wolves."

Newspaper headlines that read *Entire Pack Wiped Out* and *Yellowstone's Deadliest Season Yet* flash onto the screen as the narration explains, "And each fall a gory ritual repeats itself, as the same wolves that are loved and admired by visitors are slaughtered the moment they set foot outside of the park. Nothing has persuaded the state governments of Idaho, Montana, and Wyoming to stop this carnage. From scientific recommendations to the legal defense of the Endangered Species Act, the murders continue."

Here DiCaprio returns to the screen. "But there is one tool that has shown success in creating policy change when nothing else works – the power of the boycott." An image of Mahatma Gandhi leading his famous boycott of British goods appears.

DiCaprio continues, "Will we continue to allow a small minority of special interest ranching and hunting groups to deny us of our right to view the wildlife that we as Americans all share? Are we willing to make a small sacrifice ourselves to assure the survival of a species with such close ties to our history as humans?"

The scene switches from Leonardo to groups of sign-carrying pro-wolf protesters. "Concerned citizens all over the country and the world are joining together to send a message to the Rocky Mountain states: Wolves Belong To All Of Us!"

The dates *July 15 - July 21* are superimposed over a still shot of Old Faithful, with a red circle and slash through the dates. "Will you join us? To achieve our goal we are asking that this summer, from July 15th through July 21st, you boycott travel to Yellowstone National Park."

Leonardo returns to the screen, offering, "That could mean anything from scheduling your visit at some other time of the year to choosing another of America's beautiful National Parks."

"A large group of Wyoming businesses have signed onto this boycott." Images of popular Gardiner, Wyoming businesses are displayed. "They recognize not only the importance of stopping the extermination of wolves, but they understand the impact of wildlife watching on their livelihoods. They know that although the loss of business will be hard on them and their employees, the long-term survival of gray wolves and the sustainability of their businesses are worth the sacrifice.

Many will be closing their doors the week of the boycott as a show of solidarity."

A large group of business owners appear on screen in front of the Roosevelt Arch at Yellowstone's North Entrance, as Dr. James Stem speaks for the group. "We love Yellowstone National Park, and we realize that asking you not to visit is an extreme request. But we also believe that it is the only way that we can finally make lawmakers represent the will of the majority, not the special interest ranchers and hunters that have dictated anti-wolf policy for decades."

DiCaprio returns to the video for his final plea. "Please visit Yellowstone and patronize the businesses that support this boycott, but not from July 15th through 21st."

"Together we can show the world that 'wolves belong to all of us'."

As the lights come up, the group begins chatting among themselves. Looking from face to face, Kimana searches for a sign of acceptance. Impatient for a response she asks, "Thoughts? Criticisms? Accolades? I'm open to any of the above," she says cheerily, belying her fears.

Wendy speaks first. "My God, Kimana! It's moving, heart-wrenching, beautifully crafted and Leonardo is perfect!" She pauses, considering her next words carefully. "I'm trying to imagine the range of responses," she adds diplomatically.

Before Kimana can answer, Steve Jones raises his hand to speak. "If Sundance had a category for non-profit promotional videos, this would win it!" Unsure of what to say next, he looks to see who else is prepared to speak.

Having heard the others dodge the big question, Katherine addresses the elephant in the room. "What has your research suggested in terms of exposure Kimana? What can we expect in terms of legal action? I'm pretty sure someone's going to get sued over this, even death threats."

There. It was out on the table. Regardless of how accurate the assertions, how meticulously written and produced, and how compelling the images and video, what her clients were the most concerned about were the legal and personal ramifications. How much would they be sued for, what were their chances of losing, and would it ruin everything they had been working for?

"Funny you should ask." Kimana responded readily to the question she has planned for. "We've run the spot past our law firm. Boycotts are protected by the First Amendment. The claims we make can all be substantiated so there is no defamation, slander, or libel. As far as death threats, you've seen what these people do to wolves, it's reasonable to be concerned about intimidation."

"But the bigger answer," Kimana continued, dropping a bombshell, "is that we want to be sued."

Looks of shock and confusion were on every face, so Kimana hurried to placate the group.

"A lawsuit would multiply the reach of our campaign exponentially," she began, clearly excited by what she was saying. "We designed the piece to walk a very fine line, to state only true facts but to make an ask that we felt sure would spark a lawsuit." Smiles began creeping onto the faces of some of her clients as they started to understand.

"We front-load the ad budget to broadcast as many spots as we can at the beginning of the campaign," Kimana explained exuberantly. "We assume that someone, a business, an organization, or even a state government will ask for an injunction to stop the ads. By that time many will have already seen the spots. We expect that our social media ads will be shared millions of times, over which we, of course, have no control," she said with a sly smile.

NAKWEHE

As predicted, Preservation Promotions was slapped with an injunction on a Monday, within 24 hours of the airing of the video on Sunday.

The full-length, four-minute version only ran on networks capable of airing infomercials, generally at non-prime times. The :60 and :30-second versions were booked into every available Sunday night program on the major networks. The :15-second spots were wedged into any available slot, both nationally and regionally, airing thousands of times on the first day. On social media, Facebook and YouTube featured links to the full four-minute video.

By Tuesday, the injunction was on the front page of every major newspaper, followed by national radio and television news coverage. Interviews included the Attorney General of Montana, a spokesman for the Wyoming Beef Producers Association, and Jeremy Pershing, former scholarship recipient and current president of the Park County Hook and Bullet Club.

When contacted by the press regarding the injunction, Kimana stated simply, "Until we have our day in court, we agree to comply with the injunction against any further promotion of the July 15 through 21st boycott of Yellowstone."

Despite issuing an urgent order to "immediately cease airing any and all *Wolves Belong To All Of Us* advertisements", the video was nevertheless shared nearly 10 million times and viewed 330 million times on Facebook.

The attorney generals of all three states abutting Yellowstone did everything in their power to put a lid on talk of the boycott. Every press release they issued and the lawsuits they filed only served to expand the public's awareness of the dates.

Kimana's clients had incorporated prior to beginning the campaign and immediately dissolved the corporation before the first lawsuit, thereby protecting themselves against personal liability. The absence of anyone to hold accountable for the canceled advertising campaign frustrated the anti-wolf contingent. Knowing that the discussion of the boycott was alive and thriving on social media and in news reports had both business owners and government officials nervous.

One day, Kimana received a call from a man identifying himself as, "Ken Smith, I've been hired to try to resolve the boycott situation."

Kimana looked at her administrative assistant and silently mouthed "Oh...My...God!" before replying into the phone, "Hired by whom, Mr. Smith?"

"I'm not at liberty to say, Ms. Stewart," answered Smith politely, "but I am authorized to negotiate a resolution."

Not wanting to endanger any possible deal by probing too hard, Kimana agreed to meet with Smith.

The meeting arrangements felt very cloak-and-dagger. Kimana was not ordinarily given to paranoia, but having experienced the vitriol of some of her opponents, she made sure to let her assistant know the address. She met Smith in a small, dated restaurant on the edge of

Bozeman. The handsome 30-something Smith was already there when Kimana arrived, sitting in a booth against the wall. He stood up as she approached.

"Ken Smith," he said quietly, extending his hand.

"Kimana Stewart," she replied, shaking his hand firmly and taking a seat.

"Please pardon the question, Mr. Smith," she initiated the conversation, "but what assurances can you provide that you are authorized to broker any solutions?"

Smith reached into his coat pocket, pulled out a tri-folded letter, opened it, and showed it to her. The emblem at the top of the page featured a blue lake and green mountains encircled by the words Great Seal of The State of Montana. The text read, "To whom it may concern, Ken W. Smith is an authorized representative of the State of Montana", and was signed by the state's Natural Resources Policy Advisor.

"Will this suffice, Ms. Stewart?" Smith asked with sincerity.

"Thank you for that, Mr. Smith." Then getting right to business, Kimana asked, "What is it that you have to offer?"

"Yes, of course," Smith said, startled by her abruptness. "My clients are concerned that, even though the 'boycott campaign' was officially suspended, nothing is being done to stop the unofficial continuation of social media promotion and discussion of the event."

Kimana could not suppress a tiny smile. "So, if I may, Mr. Smith, it sounds like you're wondering if I could or would try to help assure that this boycott does not happen?"

"Quite right," answered Smith succinctly.

"Uh-huh," mused Kimana, mulling her response "and what do your clients wish to offer in exchange for this?"

Seeing that Kimana was very direct, he got right to the point. "Immediate changes to this fall's wolf harvest regulations."

"Only this coming season?" Kimana asked, the annoyance obvious in her tone. "You're offering a one-year change in the number of wolves that are shot in Montana?"

"That's correct," answered Smith. "That will give both sides time to negotiate future years while assuring that harvest numbers are rolled back for this year."

Kimana knew that the other side was scared of the potential consequences of a boycott, of which Ken Smith's presence was dramatic proof. Not only had she invested untold hours and her personal passion into this gamble, she knew that this was the one shot they had at obtaining lasting protection. The other side would never allow themselves to be put in this position again.

"You seem like a nice man, Ken," Kimana said, dramatizing her exasperation. "I don't want to waste your time or mine, so here's the deal. Anticipating this possibility, I have an 'anti-boycott' campaign already fully produced and in the can." Smith's eyes widened as she continued. "I am prepared to let the world know that the boycott is no longer necessary and that many Yellowstone area businesses are prepared to deeply discount their goods and services to fill July 15th through 21st to capacity and beyond."

Smith looked surprised, believing that he was on the verge of a quick resolution.

"But that campaign will remain in the can unless and until we get lasting and far-reaching concessions." Kimana became uncharacteristically serious. "Here are our requirements. All three states will..." Here Smith interrupted her.

"I'm sorry, Ms. Stewart; I am only representing the State of Montana."

"This is a package deal, Ken, it will be up to you to make it happen in Idaho and Wyoming, too," she stated firmly and continued. "All three states will impose a permanent 'No Wolf Hunting Zone' buffer of fifty miles from the park border..."

While his expression said 'no way', Smith just nodded that he understood the demand.

"Secondly," she resumed, "outside of the buffer zone, wolf hunting and trapping will revert to depredation hunting only. Farmers, ranchers, and wildlife managers can obtain permits to kill problem wolves. Those permits must be approved by wildlife biologists."

Smith tried but could not completely avoid rolling his eyes at what he believed was an impossible request.

"Thirdly. Methods of take shall be limited to rifles and leg-hold traps. Baiting, hunting with dogs, poisoning, spot-lighting, and any trap or snare other than leg-hold shall be forbidden," Kimana said with finality. "That's it, Mr. Smith, are you authorized to promise these changes?"

Smith looked shocked. "No, of course not, Ms. Stewart. With all due respect, these are not realistic demands, this is not good-faith bargaining. I will present these demands but I have little hope that any of them will fly."

"Mr. Smith," sounding now like a worn-out teacher, Kimana responded, "I'm certain that your clients have all of the economic data on tourism spending and tax dollar generation, but just so you know that we know, here it is. Visitors to Yellowstone spend over 500 million dollars annually in the businesses surrounding the park. Simple back-of-the-napkin math says that's just shy of 10 million dollars a week. But that doesn't take into account that mid-July is just about the busiest time of the year in the park, at least twice as busy as say, April. So figure maybe 20 million dollars for the week of July 15-21."

"Now that's for all three states, but far more visitors enter through Montana than any other state, so let's just say $15 million for that week for Montana. Most of those sales are for what are known as non-essential items, gifts, dining, and lodging. Non-essential items are taxed at 4% in Montana, so from that $15 million, the city governments make a combined $600,000."

His eyes were glazed over from trying to strategize while halfway listening to her statistics. Without addressing her economic data, he popped a compromise proposal. "If the state reverted to the old methods of take…"

"The states," corrected Kimana.

"If the states reverted to the original methods of take, leg-hold traps, and rifle hunting." Began Smith, rephrasing his offer. "And if the states set the harvest within twenty miles of the park boundary to just two wolves per zone. Aaaand…" he said, drawing out the word to emphasize the additional offering, "if we extended these changes to two years, would you assist in reversing the boycott?" he asked with a hopeful look in his eyes.

Kimana picked up her handbag, stood up, and said frankly, "Ken, please don't contact me again until your clients are serious about long-term solutions, and avoiding the boycott." She walked out without allowing Smith to respond.

Smith contacted Kimana numerous times over the next few months, but never with terms that satisfied what Kimana, her clients, or wildlife enthusiasts wanted.

PIANTI

Normally Pianti eyed the asphalt with suspicion before stepping onto it. At 1,800 pounds and nine years of age, he was still startled by the smoke-belching diesel trucks and honking cars that regularly sped by. Once he was on the roadway, however, he became fearless, sometimes tying up park traffic for hours in what are known in Yellowstone as "bison jams".

But today felt different, unlike any day since early springtime. Highway 191, where it passed the Upper Geyser Basin, better known as the location of Old Faithful, was nearly devoid of vehicles. Cars were passing so infrequently that Pianti simply laid down on the black surface to soak up the warmth. Soon 73 other buffalo were lying down with him. When a vehicle finally did roll up after twenty minutes, nothing could be done to compel the herd to move.

"I told'ja, Dad!" giggled seven-year-old Melissa from the back-seat. "Teacher said not to go to Yellowstone to save the wolves."

"Not that again, please!" grunted a frustrated Don Clark. "That's just a bunch of environmentalist hogwash!"

"Now, Don," intervened Melissa's mom, Marilyn, "please don't talk about Melissa's teacher that way."

Don Clark just scowled and went silent. He and his family were some of the few who defied the boycott and insisted on touring the park between July 15th through 21st. Don had bought into the 'anti-boycott' campaign that had been promoted vigorously on conservative news radio as a way to foil attempts by 'wolf-huggers' to interfere with states' rights to set their own wildlife policies.

What he and his family found were numerous shuttered businesses. Signs in windows of sandwich shops, gift stores, and even gas stations read "Closed For Wolves, Re-opening July 22nd." He couldn't believe what he was seeing. "The whole world has drunk the Kool-Aid!" he shouted when they couldn't find an open restroom for seven-year-old Melissa.

"I really gotta go, Daddy," she cried after ten minutes of searching.

Don pulled over where some trees came near the highway. "Marilyn, you'll have to take her out to the bushes," gesturing towards a nearby tree.

"No, Daddy, NO!" shouted Melissa. "I gotta go number two!"

Oh shit, Clark thought.

Fortunately, Marilyn intervened. "Melissa baby, come with me, you need to learn to poop in the woods!"

As the two went deep into the trees to find a place, Don tuned the car radio to the local talk radio station.

"*…and even some of the international airlines are attributing a decrease in passengers to the boycott, including Air France and Lufthansa…*"

Talking to himself, Don muttered, "Okay with me if it keeps the foreigners away."

"*…a spokesman for the fresh produce industry serving the mountain west reports that a sharp cut-back on orders has led to spoilage problems with some vegetables, primarily lettuce, spinach, and cabbage…*"

Don was fuming, shaking his head.

"...*was shot by a counter-protester during a pro-wolf demonstration in Gardiner, Montana. The governor has ordered state troopers to Gardiner...*"

Just then, Marilyn and Melissa got back in the car. "Success! Melissa is a real outdoorsy girl now."

"You can spare me the details," said Don, still angry at the news.

TESUAH

"Ken Smith on the line for you," said Kimana's assistant.

A wide smile blossomed on Kimana's face. "I'll take it in my office, thank you!" she said merrily.

Kimana was reveling in the accomplishments of day one of the boycotts. The last three months had been a grueling series of threats, lawsuits, dismissals, and doubts, but they had pulled it off. People who had been planning a trip to Yellowstone for many months had canceled by the thousands. Seventy-eight percent of the businesses that catered to Yellowstone in the gateway communities had supported the boycott by either reducing their hours or closing for the week. The boycott was underway; the thing that was missing was an agreement on wolf protection.

Now Ken Smith was calling and Kimana was hopeful for a breakthrough.

Picking up the line, Kimana said flatly, "Hello Ken," attempting to hide her excitement.

"Hello, Kimana," Smith replied, the two having spoken so often that they had dispensed with formalities.

"Do you have something for me?" she asked with anticipation.

"I do. You must be feeling good about day one," he said, making her wait for a substantive answer.

Kimmy said nothing. She could play his game, too.

After five seconds of stubborn silence, Ken said quietly, "The Game and Fish Commission is increasing the wolf harvest numbers for this fall, eliminating all buffer zones and allowing any methods of take. The state has decided to play chicken, Kimana."

It took every bit of self-discipline to suppress her rage as she responded without a hint of emotion. "Thank you, Ken. I guess we'll see who blinks. Goodbye for now."

The time was 4:30 p.m. Kimana spent the next seven hours online and in phone conversations, first with her clients, then with contacts she had made around the country. At midnight, the digital version of the New York Times was posted. The banner headline read simply: *Park Boycott Extended!*

The story cited that *Saturday evening at approximately 8 pm EST, Facebook, Twitter, and numerous other social media sites were inundated with reports that the Yellowstone National Park Boycott had been extended from one to two weeks. The reasons given were that despite overwhelming support for more protection of gray wolves, the Montana Fish and Wildlife Commission was instead proposing to allow an even greater number of wolves to be killed this fall.*

When contacted for confirmation, Kimana Stewart, owner of the agency that produced the original boycott campaign, said, "I can neither confirm nor deny these claims. My agency relinquished any ownership of this campaign based on a court injunction. The people own this campaign. It is the people, after all, who share in the proprietorship of the lands, waters, and wildlife of this country. Over 90% of the people in this country want wolves protected. A state agency thinks that it can ignore the will of the people. It appears as though the people are exercising their First Amendment rights by rising up and extending their boycott of the park. It wouldn't surprise me if the boycott grows to include visitation to any of the states surrounding the park.

As soon as the New York Times story was published, content creators on the social media sites had a new link to post. In this way news of the boycott extension was spread worldwide in mere minutes.

Having spent nearly all night working, Kimana was sleeping hard when she finally realized her cell phone was ringing. The phone was set to ring only for a select few people and she recognized the ringtone. "Ken, what an unexpected surprise," she said in a scratchy but sarcastic voice.

"Bravo, Kimana." She could hear Smith clapping his hands as he spoke. "You knocked that one out of the park!"

"Hooray for me," Kimana responded wearily. "What does that even mean, Ken?"

"You woke up three different governors in the middle of the night, Ms. Stewart," Smith announced, still chuckling. "That's pretty impressive!"

Getting down to business, he said, "The governors are willing to intervene with their game commissions. They will limit take methods to rifles and leg traps on a depredation permit-only basis. They agree to the fifty-mile no-kill zone. And, they will make the agreement for five years, with a review of the policy and regulations every five years thereafter."

Kimana jumped in. "And they will announce this in a press conference when?" she asked curtly.

"Did anyone ever tell you that you're good at this?" Smith said in a flattering tone. "Press conference at three p.m. Mountain Standard Time if all of the terms are acceptable."

"I'll get back to you soon," she said, giving away her excitement, "and Ken?" she asked.

"Oh no! What else?" he asked only half-jokingly.

"I actually think you're a good guy!"

There was a pregnant pause, then Smith said, "Then I must be bad at my job!"

At three o'clock that afternoon, the Governor of Montana gave a long, painful-to-listen-to speech. The majority of his address was spent explaining how his override of the game commission's wolf-hunting regulations had everything to do with science and data and nothing at all to do with radical activists or their subversive boycott.

By 3:10 p.m., Kimana was back online and on the phone.

By 3:20 p.m., the internet was full of messages and memes, the substance of which were, *We Won!* and *Wolves Win!*

By 3:30 p.m., phones were ringing at every RV park, bed and breakfast, inn, and motel within an hour of Yellowstone.

By 3:40 p.m., waiters, bartenders, cooks, dishwashers, gas station attendants, and motel maids were called back to work.

At midnight, the online editions of the east coast newspapers ran headlines such as, *Yellowstone Open for Business* and *States Cave to Boycotters.*

At 6 a.m. the following morning, visitors began arriving at the Northwest, West, East, and South Gates.

By 10 a.m., the usual line of cars were waiting to pay their entry fees or flash their park passes.

GOONIPE

A born organizer, Tekwoni was thrilled to have received so many affirmative RSVPs to her "Family and Friends Reunion" invitation. There were just 16 campsites in Yellowstone's Slough Creek Campground, but Toni "knew a guy" and had pulled some strings, reserving half of them.

Rusty and Toni were the first to arrive, erecting a large communal dining canopy on their campsite. Next Haiwi, now 84, and Thomas, 85, arrived pulling a tiny fiberglass travel trailer behind their SUV. The four were thrilled to be joined by Po's grand-nephew, Gus Daha, who had made the trip up from Fort Washakie to visit. The surprise of the weekend was provided by Kimana, who showed up with her new man – Ken Smith.

Rusty and Toni rushed out to greet their old friend Tyler, his wife Georgia, their son Jack and his wife Chloe, and their two grandchildren ages 4 and 6. Kimana was elated to see two of her clients, Steve Jones and Wendy Otto along with their partners, pull in to join the group.

Early afternoon was spent looking through Kathy's photo albums and telling stories about bygone days in the park. As the day waned, Haiwi and Toni prepared a rice dish using traditional Shoshoni ingredients – pine nuts, berries, and seeds. Rusty and Tyler started a fire to cook elk ribs and backstraps.

Evening fell, and in a ritual as old as time, the clan gathered around the roasting meat. All at once, they fell quiet as a primordial harmony pierced the cool evening.

From the hillside above them, the Isa, creator gods of Shoshoni mythology, began singing their approval. One, two, three, then nearly twenty took up the song. First low and sonorous, then joined by a lilting soprano voice, some notes long and drawn out, some short and abrupt. The Isa, the gray wolves, were near; it is a promising sign for the future of the species.

Toni's agenda for the next day included an afternoon hike to upper Slough Creek, a picturesque valley just a mile and a half from the campground. Haiwi, Thomas, and Gus remained in camp as the others made the mildly challenging uphill trek. Dropping into the open plain, the group found an elevated vantage point from which to quietly observe the pastoral setting.

It was early summer and the elk had just emerged from a willow thicket they had foraged in briefly. The herd began feeding on the sedges, bromes, and clovers of the valley floor, moving up into the aspens on the flanks of the surrounding hills.

Where once beavers had been absent from the landscape, beaver dams now flooded portions of the open valley, which had regenerated the dense thickets of willow shrubs and berry patches that the elk browsed through. The herd shared this copse with many other creatures. Bright yellow warblers and warbling vireos sang in the vegetation all around them, being carefully watched by the hungry sharp-shinned hawks in the adjacent lodgepole pines. In the small brooks and ponds connecting the willow patches, young cutthroat trout dined on flies and nymphs, helping the fish grow big and strong enough to migrate to the Lamar River. The nearby berry patches were a favorite dining spot for both black bears and grizzly bears, the latter of which would also seek out elk calves hidden among the willows in the late spring.

The reunion group watched patiently, soaking in the bucolic scene. The adults pointed out the creatures and taught their stories to the two children. Binoculars and spotting scopes were set up to provide long-distance views.

As the sun began to dip behind the western peaks, Kimana pointed to the opposite hillside and whispered loudly, "Wolves!" The entire group trained their optics to the area, one by one obtaining a view of the pack as it loped down a sage-covered slope towards the valley floor.

The elk suddenly stood upright, ears erect, their noses pointed towards the gray and black forms moving in their direction. Wolves and elk began the dance that they were designed for, surrounded by the complete menagerie of the plants, animals, and humans that had always coexisted there - all of the threads and stitches of the region's tapestry, the building blocks and strands of Yellowstone's DNA.

GLOSSARY

Glossary of Native American Words and Names Used in this Book.

My intent in using indigenous words and names throughout the novel is to honor the indigenous peoples and their relationship to the natural world in the regions they lived. Please note that within tribal nations there are often numerous regional variations. For the most part I have attempted to use the form of the word from tribal populations closest to the area that a chapter is set in. My apologies for any incorrect forms used herein.

Aashi: A Crow word meaning "antler"
Aisen: A Shoshoni word meaning "gray"
Apisoyiinat: A Blackfoot word meaning "to be rusty"
Apoyi: A Blackfoot word meaning "to be brown"
Atisow: A Plains Cree word meaning "she is tan"
Bahaitee': A Shoshoni word for the number "3".
Baingwi: A Shoshoni word meaning "trout"
Begapi: A Shoshoni word meaning "tan buckskin"
Bia: A Shoshoni word meaning "mother"
Daha'a: A Shoshoni word meaning "Nephew, brother's child"
Disua: A Shoshoni word meaning "brave"
Dosabi: A Fort Hall Shoshoni word meaning "white"
Doyaduku: A Duckwater Shoshoni word meaning "mountain lion"
Dukubichi: A Shoshoni word meaning "cat"
Duyupe: A Shoshoni word meaning "boy"
Goonipe: A Shoshoni word meaning "cycled; gone around in a circle"
Gotoope: A Fort Hall Shoshoni word meaning "fire"

Ha'nii': A Fort Hall Shoshoni word meaning "beaver"

Haiwi: A Fort Hall Shoshoni word meaning "mourning dove"

Hoa: A Shoshoni word meaning "bow"

Hoawoppih: A Shoshoni word meaning "warrior"

Ichíilikaashe: A Crow word meaning "elk"

Idaho: A word falsely attributed to the Shoshoni, alleged to mean "gem of the mountains"

Inak: A Blackfoot word meaning "small"

Iinii: A Blackfoot word meaning "elk"

Isa: A Shoshoni word meaning "wolf"

Isskoo: A Blackfoot word meaning "return"

Izhape: A Fort Hall Shoshoni word meaning "coyote"

Kimana: A Shoshoni word meaning "butterfly"

Kwi'na: a Shoshoni word meaning "hawk"

Kuttaa: A Shoshoni word meaning "hard, tough, strong"

Mahihkam: A Cree word meaning "gray wolf"

Manteca: A Spanish word meaning "butter"

Matsi: A Blackfoot word meaning "pretty"

Nakwehe: A Shoshoni word meaning "wrestle"

Nasuyekwi": A Shoshoni word meaning "to be arrogant"

Natekwinappeh" A Shoshoni word meaning "famous, well-known"

Natümeninna: A Shoshoni word meaning "store"

Nawa'a: A Shoshoni word meaning "join, connect"

Niimiapii: A Blackfoot word meaning "dirt"

Nuki: A Shoshoni word meaning "run"

Oha: A Shoshoni word meaning "yellow or golden"

Oksina: A Blackfoot word meaning "mean, grouchy"

Ómahkapi'si: A Blackfoot word meaning "wolf"

Pahaitte: A Shoshoni word meaning "three"

Paikkah: A Shoshoni word meaning "to kill"

Pianti: A Shoshoni word meaning "big, large, tall"

Pohogwe: A Shoshoni word meaning "Eastern Shoshoni"

Pühüppüh: A Panamint Shoshoni word meaning "hair, fur, skin, hide, pelt"

Reinita: a Spanish word meaning "warbler"

Senkapin: A Shoshoni word meaning "aspen"

Siikapi: A Blackfoot word meaning "gray"

Sikimi: A Blackfoot word meaning "to be black"

Sikotahko: A Blackfoot word meaning "brown"

Sümütüwa: A Panamint Shoshoni word meaning "have a meeting, have a council"

Sspii: A Blackfoot word meaning "tall"

Tekai: A Shoshoni word meaning "hunt"

Tepaikkappeh: A Shoshoni word meaning "game someone has killed"

Tekwoni: A Yurok word meaning "northern spotted owl"

Tesuah: A Shoshoni word meaning "to be brave or skillful at fighting"

Tia: A Maori word meaning "elk or deer"

To'-să-woo'-rah: A Ruby Valley Shoshoni word meaning "grizzly bear"

Toyatukkupittsi: A Shoshoni word meaning "mountain lion"

Tso-ape: A Fort Hall Shoshoni word meaning "ghost"

Tukumpeh: A Shoshoni word meaning "heaven or sky"

Waahni': A Fort Hall Shoshoni word meaning "fox"

Wahatehwe: A Fort Hall Shoshoni word meaning "two"

Wid-dah': A Shoshoni word Meaning "grizzly bear"

Sources:

Shoshoni Dictionary
Shoshoni Language Project
The University of Utah
https://shoshoniproject.utah.edu/

Plains Cree Dictionary
Algonquian Dictionaries Project
https://dictionary.plainscree.atlas-ling.ca/#/help

Crow Dictionary Online
Crow Language Consortium

https://dictionary.crowlanguage.org/

Blackfoot Dictionary
Algonquian Dictionaries Project
https://dictionary.blackfoot.atlas-ling.ca/#!/help

ABOUT THE AUTHOR

Scott Huber has worked as a park ranger, an outdoor educator, and a wildlife tour guide in Yellowstone and the Grand Tetons. In addition to being an avid birder, he is a lifelong hiker, fisherman and hunter.

Scott was first enchanted by the beautiful songs of gray wolves near Wyoming's Sunlight Basin. In Yellowstone's Lamar Valley, Scott was privileged to experience close encounters with wolves and their pups.

The author and his wife have a cabin located between the Absaroka Mountains and the Wind River Range in northwestern Wyoming. They winter in bio-diverse Portal, Arizona.